By James Odell

A novel in the Empire of Gaul series

Text Copyright © 2020 James Odell

All Rights Reserved

Published by James A Odell

ISBN 978-1-9998296-1-2 Paperback

ISBN 978-1-9998296-2-9 e-book

Cover artwork by More Visual Ltd

Contents

Chapter 1: The Flight South

Gaul, Early June, 451 AD

The gates of Trier, with its richly elaborate stonework, had been constructed in the glorious days when the city had been the capital of the empire. Most of the carved decorations had been damaged over the years, but the gateway still performed its duty of protecting the city.

Magnus rode through the street of the city toward the north gate, leading his spare horse. He cursed the pedestrians and commanded them to get out of his way. The garrison commander had given his permission for all non-combatants to leave the city, and the street was clogged with stragglers making their way to the gate, taking this last chance to leave.

The guards posted at the gate had orders to arrest any man of military age who tried to leave. As Magnus approached, the sergeant clutched his spear and stepped forward. "Your mission, sir?"

Magnus gestured to his leather dispatch case. "I'm on an official mission, sergeant. The garrison commander has ordered me to deliver a dispatch to the messenger station. I can show you my orders if you wish."

The gate-sergeant peered up at him from under the rim of his helmet. "No need for that, sir. You watch out for yourself. Those messengers are an odd lot. Almost as dangerous as the Huns."

"Yes, I know, but I have my orders."

The sergeant jerked a thumb at his men, who stepped aside to let Magnus past. "Good luck, sir, and Godspeed."

"Thanks." Magnus rode out under the stone arch, leading his spare horse. For the first mile he had to force his way past the refugees. Once the road cleared, he urged his horses to move faster. But he set an easy pace. They had a long way to go.

The sky was clear, except for a few harmless white clouds scudding before a strengthening westerly wind. He was grateful that the wind was at his back.

He changed his horses frequently, trying not to exhaust either one too early. The land sloped upwards now, away from the river, through a forest. If he kept up this pace too long it would kill his horses, but the news he bore was important enough to risk a couple of horses. He paused to look behind him, but Trier was hidden by the intervening hills.

The path came clear of the trees at last. He descended through a vineyard. Ahead of him he could see the river once again. The path turned to the right, parallel to the river. One of the mountains up ahead must be the Mehring Berg.

The mountain was long and low, with deep gullies running down the mountain's flanks. The slopes were covered with dark forests.

The north side of the mountain was in shadow. There was something vaguely sinister about the mountain. Magnus could not define it exactly, but he knew that he would never have gone there by choice.

These mountains to the west of the Rhine were said to be full of dragons, fierce and unpredictable, attacking one man but befriending the next. According to rumour, the mountain men of the courier service were almost as bad.

Magnus had been riding for two hours now and had covered perhaps twelve miles, most of it uphill. The horses were tiring now. Magnus changed horses once again, brushed aside his misgivings, and continued along the gravel path that led towards the peak.

The hillside was getting steeper. To his left, through a gap in the trees, he caught a glimpse of the river far below. To his right the sides of the mountain towered above him, indicating that he still had a long way to go.

The horses were too tired to carry him now. He dismounted and continued on his way, leading his horses, until he reached a meadow.

He had reached the messenger post at last. Compared to the dark of the forest he had escaped from, the grass of the meadow was a lush green.

The wind at his back was cold. In front of him was a row of single storey buildings, workshops or bunkhouses. The walls were stone, their eaves of thatch reaching almost to the ground.

Two flying machines, with flimsy wings set above a long central keel, were positioned outside the huts. Each machine had a single seat in front of the strut that held up the wings. One of the machines was canted over, the lower wingtip weighted down to prevent it from being blown away.

Magnus realised that the men clustered round the other machine were dismantling it. As he watched, one of the wings was carried into one of the long huts.

The horses whinnied and snorted, and the men turned to face the newcomer. One of them shouted a greeting but his words were lost. Attracted by the sound of horses, the remainder of the staff poured out of their low huts.

Most of them wore tunics of unbleached wool, decorated with a vertical stripe of blue. A few women and children followed after the men.

An old man stroked the nose of the lead horse. "That's a terrible way to treat horses, boy," he said.

"I know. But I had no choice. Can anyone here care for them?"

The old man sniffed. "Where are you from, stranger?"

"I've come from Trier. I'm an officer of the British unit stationed there. The rest of the troop is trapped, now."

The old man had stopped listening, his attention concentrated on the horses. Magnus turned as a shorter man made his way through the crowd.

Magnus tried to be polite. "Good evening, captain."

The man's blond hair was brushed painfully back, his beard neatly trimmed. The aviator grinned impudently. "I'm not an officer, my lord. I'm only a lowly sergeant."

Magnus recognised the type. The sergeant came from the lower ranks of society, was intelligent, had acquired a valuable skill, and resented the patrician class who prevented him from rising further. And Magnus's accent betrayed him as a product of the patrician class. "Your name, sergeant?"

"Sergeant Dumnorix, my lord. In command of this humble messenger station. What can we do for you?"

Magnus started again. "Trier's under siege by the Huns. Or if it isn't yet, it will be by noon tomorrow. I have a message for the Magister Militum in Lyon. It must reach him by the fastest possible means."

"The Huns? Are you sure, sir? We heard they were marching on Mainz, but -."

"Of course I am, damn it! Their scouts nearly caught me. They boast they burnt Mainz." He turned to look down the valley. "I'm surprised you haven't seen any burning farmsteads. You must get our message to Lyon." Magnus realised that the crowd had gathered to listen.

"I see. Will they come here, sir?" The sergeant's mocking tone had vanished.

"It's quite possible. Foragers will come looking for supplies."

"Well, we can get you to Argentorate before nightfall, sir. There's a station in the hills, a day's march west of the city, still functioning. The Huns ignored it."

Magnus was shocked. "No, no, I can't pilot those things. Give my message to your best pilot."

The sergeant was stubborn. "It'd look better if you delivered the message in person. If one of us tells the boss the Huns have crossed the border, he won't believe us. But you've got the right accent, he'll believe you."

The sergeant was grinning at Magnus's dismay. The trouble was, the man was right, damn him. "But ..."

"Besides, sir, if we wait until morning, we might have Hun foragers poking around."

He had not thought of that. "Very well. I'll go."

"Good. We have a two-seater machine here. We can get you and your message to Lyon, never fear." He shouted instructions and half a dozen men raced off to one of the long sheds.

The rest of the crowd gathered closer. "Ask him," one of the women said.

The sergeant's humour vanished. "Sir, if the Huns do come – will the high command expect us to stay here? Fight?" he asked. "Should we defend the signal station?"

Magnus looked around. The place was defenceless. "No. There's no point. Abandon it. Save everything of value. Can you fly the machines to somewhere safer?"

"Well, yes -."

"But what about the ground crew?" the woman asked. She was taller than the sergeant.

"Excuse me, sir. This is my wife," the sergeant said. "What should the fitters do? The women?"

Magnus was irritated. Why was the sergeant asking him? "They'll have to walk out. But you're right. They can't stay. Abandon everything you can't carry."

"Would you - would you put that in writing, sir?"

He wanted to say that he had no authority to give such an order, but the look of desperation on the man's face stopped him. "Very well. Get me something to write on and I'll put my name to it."

The sergeant rushed off to one of the huts and came back with a wax tablet. That forced Magnus to be concise. He wrote, erased, and wrote again.

'Sergeant Dumnorix: you are hereby ordered to save your trained personnel and abandon your signal station. You are also ordered to return to the station as soon as it is safe to do so. By my order, Magnus Vitalinus, troop commander.'

Magnus made it as pompous as possible. There was almost no room for his name at the bottom. His rank was almost unreadable. If the worst happened, that might be useful.

The sergeant read through the message. "Thank you, sir."

Magnus looked again at the flying machines. They looked far more flimsy, somehow, now that he knew he was going to be riding in one. "What are they made of, sergeant?"

"Our machines? Linen stretched over a wooden frame. Very light, but very strong as well."

"What holds them together? I hope the nails are well crafted."

"Nails, sir? No, nails would be too heavy. Mostly we use glue. Don't worry, we test everything before each flight." The man's ready grin had returned.

"Sergeant, how do you get the machine into the air? Is it true that you throw the machine and its pilot off a cliff?"

"Oh, no. We only do that when the wind is *really* strong. When the wind's moderate, we have to use more sophisticated methods."

Dumnorix bent down, plucked up some straw and cast it into the air. The breeze swept the stalks up over his head. The sergeant – and everyone else - turned to watch the stalks blown eastward. "It's getting stronger. It won't last, though. We'd better get everything into the air in the next hour."

Everybody rushed about, full of enthusiasm. Magnus thought they enjoyed the idea of throwing a patrician off a cliff.

Half a dozen men carried the fuselage of a flying machine, larger than the others, out of one of the sheds. Other teams emerged, carrying long, fabric-covered structures - the wings.

"This is our two-seater," Sergeant Dumnorix said proudly.

Magnus was not impressed. The wicker seats were attached directly to the landing skid. The seats were in line, not side by side. The bodywork was flimsy, fabric over a wicker frame. The doped linen was painted white.

With a lot of shouting and laughter, the wings were held horizontal, at right angles to the fuselage. "Port wing up a bit … higher … forward, forward … Starboard wing down a little. Hold it there … done!" Dumnorix pushed a bronze bolt through a hole in the wing-stubs to fasten the wings together.

The machine was then canted over, one wingtip resting on the ground. The linen stretched over the wings was so thin it appeared translucent. Magnus could make out the delicate wooden spars that gave the wing its shape.

Another man, wearing a heavy sheepskin jacket over a woolen tunic and trousers, leaned into the cockpit and began pulling and pushing at the controls of the machine.

"Oh, this is your pilot, Acco," the sergeant said. "He's got plenty of experience."

Magnus judged that Acco was approaching middle age, careworn. He was taller than either Magnus or the sergeant. His hair was blond, with the same swept back style as Dumnorix. He walked with a slight stoop and avoided looking directly at anyone. "The lad doesn't look like much," he remarked.

"He's a patrician, so mind your manners," the sergeant scolded.

"Ha!" The pilot walked around the machine, examining it critically. He grasped the wingtip, moving it up and down, forcing the entire thing to flex.

Magnus winced. "Does he have to do that?"

Dumnorix was serious for once. "We've got to check that the wing isn't broken. If it bends instead of flexing, we know something's wrong."

Acco completed his inspection. "It'll do." He pulled on a tight-fitting leather hat, then climbed into the front seat, and began pulling and pushing the control yoke.

"You take the back seat," Dumnorix said. "Your cloak – bring it with you. Roll it up and stuff it in the wing root. You'll need it."

"For sleeping in?"

"It's an officer's cloak. It shows your rank."

"Oh. Right." Reluctantly, Magnus climbed in. He shoved his dispatch case in the stowage space alongside his cloak.

The ground crew carried a long coil of rope out of a shed and carefully laid it out straight. It formed a Y shape, with the shortest length pointing towards the flying machine.

"So, it's a catapult powered by twenty people?" Magnus did not regard the notion of being catapulted into the air as an improvement.

"Exactly." The sergeant grinned.

The men split into two teams, picked up the ends of the long ropes and set off down the hill. They moved with the efficiency that came of long practice. Magnus found the thought reassuring. The sergeant bent down and picked up the end of the short rope. It had a steel ring attached to it. "Ready, Acco?"

"As ready as I'll ever be," the pilot said. He sounded bored.

Dumnorix knelt down and attached the steel ring to a hook under the machine.

Magnus told himself that he must not scream. He did not want Sergeant Dumnorix to laugh at him.

The sergeant backed off and held up the wingtip. "Are you ready down there? Take the strain…" the ropes stretched taut. Magnus braced himself.

"On my mark, three, two, one – go!"

The flying machine bumped once on the coarse grass and then they were airborne, floating smoothly. But they were pointed down towards the bottom of the hill. Were they going to float gently down there? The ride was smoother than he had expected. The pilot turned his machine left, parallel to the hill.

The wind rushed past him. Magnus realised that he had never moved so fast in his life before. He had heard stories of flying machines covering fifty miles in an hour and now, with the wind roaring past him, the stories seemed plausible.

After a few minutes, the pilot did a neat U-turn and headed back towards the messenger station. Magnus could see the roofs of the buildings, ahead and to the right, and realised that they had been climbing steadily. The ground crew were already pulling the second flying machine into position. He looked north and could even make out the dot that must be Trier, ten or eleven miles away.

Minute after minute went by. They were far higher now, but they were still flying back and forth along the line of the hill. Magnus realised that his feeling of unease was actually boredom. "Pilot, we're not going anywhere. I can still see the station. They're launching more machines." Acco ignored him so he shouted louder.

The pilot turned and shouted over his shoulder. "We have to gain height first. Lots of flat land between us and Argentorate. When we cross that we'll lose altitude. If we start out too low, we'll never reach the far side."

"I see." A few minutes later they turned south. They followed the hills on the east bank of the Saar river. The pilot kept parallel to the crest of the hillside, giving a running commentary as they went. Magnus could not hear most of it. Once, Magnus glimpsed two shepherds far below on the hillside, turned towards the imperial messenger.

"Some pilots think you have to stay level with the hilltop," Acco shouted over his shoulder. "But it's best to stay two or three hundred feet higher. More, if the wind's strong enough. That's where the strongest lift is, you see."

Acco seemed to be expecting an answer. "Yes, I see."

"Do you have any servants, boy? If you're a patrician, you must have. All patricians have servants."

Magnus felt compelled to answer. "I have a groom to look after my horses. He had to leave London in a hurry. Actually, one of those horses was his."

"You took his horse?" Acco sounded accusing.

"I bought it for him. And if I left it behind in Trier, they would have eaten it when the food ran out."

"True, I suppose."

A few minutes later, the pilot shouted again. "That's the Saar Forest. Our halfway point. There's a relay station there, in case messengers are forced down by the weather. The others will be landing there."

"Fifty miles? We've come fifty miles?" He had not believed it when the aviators had talked of fifty miles an hour.

Acco ignored this. "The dragons don't like the forest. These weak hills don't give them enough lift. They say they prefer the mountains further south."

Magnus wondered whether he was trapped in a machine with a madman. He tried to think of a tactful reply. "Do the dragons talk to you often, pilot Acco?"

"Only if I ask them politely ... and then listen very carefully. Or if they think it's important. But they think such strange things are important ... It's difficult to understand them. The dragons are very wise."

Magnus was at a loss for words. "I see." To his relief, the pilot changed the subject.

"We can't head straight south. We'll have to turn south east for a bit. Stay in the mountains ..."

"Yes." The mountains ahead were bigger than anything Magnus had seen so far. He was feeling the chill, but he decided it was worth it. Very few men had experienced a journey like this. He noticed that the sun was moving round towards the south west.

A few minutes later the pilot turned his machine again. "This is the northern tip of the Vosago Mountains. I'd planned to land here, spend the night at the Argentorate messenger station. Captain Brennos at Argentorate is all right. But, do you know, I think I'll press on. If these conditions hold, we could get all the way to Lyon before dark."

Magnus was cold, he was suffering from cramp, but the lives of his colleagues might depend upon him getting his message to Lord Aetius as fast as possible. "Whatever you think best, aviator."

"We turn south west now. Conditions from here on improve. Higher mountains, and a continuous ridge… It'll be a close-run thing. We'll try it."

Five hours later, they were still travelling south. Magnus, despite his discomfort, had fallen into a doze. Acco disturbed him. "That's Lyon in sight now. I told you we could get here before dark. See? That fancy stone building on the top of the hill, that's the governor's palace. But they say it's about to slide down the hill, so it's been abandoned. The old forum's there too, although you can't see it. We don't land there, of course, we land on a meadow about a mile upstream."

The sun, a bright orange disk, was touching the horizon. The flight had taken longer than he had realised.

Acco flew over the cliff top and performed a neat half-circle. The machine descended steeply, then leveled out, facing directly into wind. They touched down, skidded forward, and came to a stop only twenty yards away from the other machines.

Magnus's limbs were so stiff, he had to be helped out of the cockpit. Crippling pain stole over him as the blood returned to his numbed hands and feet.

The messenger station at Lyon was busier than Trier. Half a dozen flying machines were lined up along one side of the meadow. One machine was being dismantled. Acco insisted that his own machine should be dragged to the edge of the field in case another late arrival needed to land there.

Finally, Magnus was able to pick up his cloak and the all-important dispatch case. The messenger station consisted of several long, low storage sheds and workshops, similar to the ones he had seen at Trier.

The administration building, long and low, with a thatched roof, was similar to the storage sheds. Acco led the way inside. A team of men and women were setting up trestle tables. Judging by the smell, venison was on the menu this evening.

Magnus introduced himself to the captain in charge of the station, Commius. The captain was a southerner, taller than Magnus. His eyes were large and tended to water. He wore his black hair in the fashionable style, longer than usual, with a carefully arranged bulk over his ears. Magnus could smell the spikenard in the hair oil he used.

When Magnus explained that he had brought dispatches from Trier, the captain was impressed. "This is most important. We must go at once. I'll escort you to military headquarters in person, sir."

"I think you probably outrank me, captain," Magnus said.

Commius blinked. "I'm sure you'll soon win promotion, sir!"

"Thank you, captain." Magnus was too tired to argue.

Commius told his men to attach two horses to a two-wheeled messenger cart. "It would be quicker to walk, but that would be undignified, of course."

Magnus would have preferred to walk off the symptoms of cramp. But Commius was very concerned about his dignity.

"It's not far, won't take long. It's unfortunate that the general has made his headquarters here ..."

"The general?"

"Lord Aetius, I mean. Magister Militum of the Field Army in Gaul. His arrival created a lot of extra work for us. Dispatches arrive here from the four quarters of the empire, almost every day. Our workshops can't cope. I'll be glad when the general moves somewhere else and we can return to normal," he said. "On the other hand, I get to meet the great man almost every day. It's an honour."

Magnus was most impressed by his first sight of Lyon.

"Three major roads met here," Commius said. "One from Aquitaine, one from the Rhine, and one from the south. The Romans built the old city on top of the hill – a good defensive position. The new city was built on the islands where the Saone joined the Rhone."

"I see."

"It's nice to have a man of culture and intelligence to talk to, sir. The new cathedral's at the foot of the hill. Of course, you can't see it from here."

"Of course," Magnus said. The dark was closing in. Flambeaus were being lit outside the houses of prosperous citizens. The captain drove through the winding streets of upper Lyon to Aetius's residence. This was built halfway up the hill, overlooking the lower city on the bank of the Saone.

"The general is very wealthy, you understand, sir. Very cultured. So gracious! Although I must admit he can be a difficult customer. If you weren't accompanied by somebody he knows, it could take days for you to see him. And this news is too important for that."

"Yes, indeed, captain."

"Lord Aetius prefers to keep most people at a distance. He's the Master of the Army, appointed by the emperor, so he looks down on anyone lower down the social scale -."

"You make him sound like a snob."

Commius was shocked. "No, no! He's surrounded by fortune seekers, adventurers of the worst kind. He doesn't want them wasting his time. And he's brilliant, quite brilliant! Although I admit, if he meets anyone who's his social equal, but slow on the uptake, he shows them that he's brighter than they are. He *growls* at people. I hope you don't mind me telling you this. You'll see the truth of it soon enough, and a word of warning might save you a bit of trouble."

"Thank you. Is he really that clever? I've heard stories …"

"Oh, yes. He was accused of treason in Italy, did you know? But somehow, he persuaded the emperor's mother into sending him to Gaul instead of executing him. He arrived here without friends, and persuaded the old emperor Vindex to appoint him as Master of the Army. Now he's made himself the most powerful man in Gaul. He's the only person who can keep the Gallic Empire together."

"I see." The captain's gushing praise was tiresome. Magnus decided that he preferred Sergeant Dumnorix's cynicism.

The captain smiled. "May I ask - are you a patrician, like Aetius?"

"My grandfather is. But I'm the younger son of a younger son -."

"It's always a pleasure to meet a member of a noble family, sir. And so unusual for a nobleman to demean himself by travelling in one of our machines!"

Magnus was embarrassed and felt he needed to justify himself. "It was a military emergency."

"Of course, of course, sir. And have you got a proper education?"

"Well – I learned enough to bluff my way through."

"I'm sure you're being modest, sir. That's good enough for Aetius. And here we are, sir."

Magnus decided that the general must have taken over the grandest house in the city. Full dark had descended by now and a pair of flambeaus had been lit each side of the wide double doorway. The captain drew up and explained his mission once again to the sentry.

The sergeant recognised the captain, waved them through the archway to the inner courtyard and promised to summon a groom for the horses. Magnus saw that this house was built on a similar pattern to the great houses he had seen in London: servants on the ground floor, public rooms such as dining rooms on the floor above, the family's private rooms above that. A wide stone staircase led up to the first floor.

One of Aetius's secretaries intercepted them at the top of the staircase to ask them their business. "A message from Trier, you say, captain? Come this way."

Magnus suddenly realised that the secretary was wearing a white military cloak over his tunic. "Excuse me a moment." He stopped to unroll his own cloak, shake it out, and pull it round his shoulders.

"Very elegant, sir. It suits you," Commius said. "Lord Aetius comes from a very wealthy family, you know. They have estates here in Gaul, very wealthy. That enabled Lord

Aetius to hire a bodyguard, almost a private army ... Some of them are Huns, you know."

The secretary led them round the balcony to the commander's room. They found Aetius, commander of the Imperial Field Army, in what must have been the house's dining room. The only furniture was a large table and a few elegant chairs, but the tapestries and hangings covering the walls, showing hunting scenes in red and green, were magnificent.

"The person who owns this pile must be worth a fortune," Magnus said.

"Hush," the captain said, shocked.

The desk was covered with a pile of writing-tablets, a wine-jar, and several empty silver cups. Two candles had been lit at each end of the desk. Aetius was lounging in an elaborately carved chair, toying with an empty wine cup. He was tall, but sleek and lean. His carefully trimmed greying hair was worn in the same fashionable style that Commius favoured. His face was lined and sombre. His tunic was white, richly decorated at shoulder and hem with a geometrical pattern in black, red and green. Magnus remembered that the general was old enough to have sons of his own serving in the army.

The general ignored the servants who were clearing the table. The servants, in their turn, took care not to disturb him. Standing behind Aetius's chair, doing nothing, were a couple of men who were clearly not servants. Over woollen tunics and breeches each man wore a leather caftan. Both had a long cavalry sword hanging from a baldric. They watched the newcomers with suspicion.

Both warriors had craggy, weather-beaten faces. It was difficult to guess their age but at least thirty years of hard living lay behind the older man. They wore felt caps, but the older man had pushed his back to show that his hair was cut very short at the front.

Magnus spoke in an undertone. "Captain, who are those men standing behind Lord Aetius's chair?"

"They're part of his bodyguard," Commius murmured. "They're Huns. The older man is called Optila. Some sort of officer, I believe."

The secretary coughed. "Captain Commius of the Messenger Corps with urgent dispatches for you, my lord."

Magnus was suddenly nervous. Aetius was an experienced general, appointed by the emperor. Aetius had plenty of experience of the Huns: he spent some time as a hostage of the Huns as a youth.

Aetius, bored, raised his eyebrows. Commius? You're from the messenger station, aren't you? What bad news have you brought this time? I hope this won't take long, captain. The servants are preparing the table for dinner." The question was voiced in a growl.

"Yes, my lord." The closer that Commius got to the general, the more nervous he seemed to become. He drew himself up and saluted. "My companion here is from the British expeditionary force. They were stationed in Trier." He pushed Magnus forward.

Magnus bowed, as he had been taught. "My lord, I was sent by the commander in Trier. The Huns are advancing on the city. He asks that you come to his aid."

Aetius straightened up and put his cup down on the table with a sharp click. Suddenly, his boredom was gone. "You have definite news of the Huns, boy? I've been expecting this, ever since they sacked Argentorate again! Some people said they would be satisfied with one city - but I knew better. You say they have reached Trier?"

Military routine overcame Magnus's nervousness. "Yes, my lord. Our scouts encountered their foraging parties."

Aetius scowled. "Then they probably sacked the border town of Mainz."

"Their foragers boasted of it, sir."

"You *talked* to them, boy?" This question was voiced in a growl.

Everyone in the room seemed to be staring at him. Magnus struggled to explain. "Well - we shouted insults across a stream, sir. Their Latin was poor."

Aetius relaxed. "Ah, yes. By your manners, you come from a noble family."

Commius seized the opportunity. "Ah – may I introduce Magnus Vitalinus. He commands a troop of light cavalry."

"Vitalinus? The richest landowner in Britain, I believe. It's always a pleasure to meet a member of his family," Aetius said with practised courtesy.

Magnus was not sure how to take that. "Thank you, my lord."

"Do you have a written report? From the commander of the garrison? Let's see it!"

Magnus handed over the sealed packet then stepped back a respectful distance to allow Aetius to read the report.

Commius tapped Magnus on the shoulder. "You're doing all right, sir. I'll make my way home."

Aetius looked up. "Commander Magnus, you're invited to stay to dinner in my house this evening." The words were courteous enough, but Aetius's habitual growl made the polite invitation sound menacing.

"Thank you, my lord."

Commius saw his opportunity and made his escape.

Aetius read through the report a second time and folded it up. "I assume you are a grandson of the great Vortigern Vitalinus?"

"Vortigern was my great-uncle, sir," Magnus admitted.

"Good, good." Aetius seemed to be pleased. "It's useful to have powerful relatives. The Vitalinus family is the most powerful in Britain, so they say."

Magnus was embarrassed. His grandfather had several estates in Gaul, certainly. His father owned a single farm, but Magnus had nothing.

Aetius turned to his secretary. "Magnus will be dining with us. See that he is cleaned up before he rejoins us this evening."

Magnus returned to the dining room an hour later to find it already full. He learned from Aetius's secretary that the owner of the house was absent but his wife, Lady Sulpicia, acted as the general's hostess.

"Magnus, your place is at the high table, amongst Aetius's officers and their ladies."

"Oh. An honour I had not expected," he said. His military cloak was crumpled past repair, and he devoutly hoped that no one would comment upon its condition. He took his place in a straight-backed chair, silently thanking his grandfather for those painful lessons in table manners.

These guests were the same sort of political people who visited his uncle's house: sophisticated, clever, and eager to show just how clever they were. The ladies wore very little jewellery, but their silk dresses, dyed red or blue, were expensive and their makeup was in the latest fashion. Their hairstyles also followed the latest fashion, with lots of curls piled up on top of the head.

All of the guests indulged in a mild but unending game of sneering at each other. Magnus, who had spent the last year among soldiers, knew he could not compete.

The wine was excellent, and Aetius drank several glasses of it. Magnus decided it would be unwise to over-indulge this evening. As one course followed another, he noticed that the guests flattered Aetius, never making him the butt of their snide remarks.

"At one time, Lyon was the capital of the Roman province of Lugdunensis, covering a quarter of Gaul," a thin man said to Magnus. "But those glory days are long gone. Before the empire had split into three."

Aetius overheard this. "Not at all, sir. These days the city's the home of the archbishop of Gaul."

The thin man was surprised at this intervention but responded promptly. "True, my lord. What higher honour could a city wish for?"

"And now the city makes an excellent military headquarters for me," Aetius said.

The thin man fell silent and the other diners tittered.

Magnus decided that Captain Commius had been right: most of the people here were snobs, but the general was the worst of them.

As the meal drew to a close the general told his hostess that he would soon have to leave her charming household. "We have a new threat, and I have decided to lead my army north to face it."

Lady Sulpicia was thin and used heavy makeup to hide the lines on her face. She was wearing a silk dress, dyed an expensive red. Her hairstyle was the most elaborate in the room. "How dreadful! Spending a whole month among those uncouth soldiers! And you said the imperial troops were second-rate."

"Thank you, my dear. Your sympathy will console me on the march north. The imperial troops are of poor quality, I admit, but I won't have to depend upon them. I hope for reinforcements from Italy. And I'll take my Burgundian allies with me. I promised I'd give them their kingdom back if I could. And they have reason enough to hate Attila." He gestured to a servant, who refilled his wine glass again.

"We shall be sorry to see you go, my dear Aetius," another lady said. But, of course, your strategy must be kept secret!"

Lord Aetius must have thought this question impertinent, for he responded with a low growl. "Hardly, madam. I am outnumbered. Attila must guess my secret easily enough. Don't you think, Magnus?"

He was startled at being singled out but managed to recover. "Yes, sir. Keep to the high ground and tempt the Huns to attack us."

A man wearing a green wool cloak over a matching tunic leaned forward. "And if you cannot tempt the Huns to attack your army?"

Aetius gulped at his wine. "If I cannot arrange a battle on ground of my own choosing, I shall not offer battle. On level ground, against superior numbers, I would lose. I don't mind sacrificing soldiers to win a battle, but throwing them away to no good purpose is wasteful."

"Yes, indeed," Lady Sulpicia said.

"We can expect to lose at least a thousand men. But it's better to lose your allies than your own men," Aetius said.

Magnus, alone amongst strangers, cut off from his companions, and ignorant of the topics of conversation that were considered fashionable in Lyon, felt that he was out of touch and at a loose end.

These melancholy thoughts were interrupted by Aetius. "Magnus – your journey south must have been grim. Almost three hundred miles! It's an exhausting ride."

"Well – I must admit that I travelled in a flying machine, sir."

This revelation set off a round of exclamations. Aetius cut through them. "One of those death traps! Weren't you afraid, Magnus?"

"Terrified, sir." There was a ripple of laughter.

"Tell us about it," Aetius demanded. Magnus described the cold and the cramp he had suffered to the general and his companions, which amused his listeners. He mentioned some of the things he had seen during the flight. The only thing he left out was Acco's strange conversation.

"But at least it was over in a single day. A week in the saddle would have been just as bad." This drew a laugh from the lords and ladies.

"Ah, yes." The general was fascinated. "You did it in a day. And you passed Argentorate on your way south?"

"Yes, sir. They tell me the messenger station is in the hills to the west of the city. But the winds were favourable, so my pilot decided to press on."

"Yes, I'm glad you made that decision. Every day is going to count. Magnus, you seem to understand these messengers. Perhaps you can help. You're not like that low-born fool Commius."

Lady Sulpicia sniffed. "Such a vulgar man. And such a repulsive toady. He looks like a sheep."

Magnus was caught out. "Ah – yes, sir."

"You belong to the patrician order," Aetius growled. "You understand, Magnus. I have been appointed as Magister Militum, charged with the sacred duty of keeping the empire safe. You share that burden as well. The lower orders may be repugnant, but they are an essential part of society. Where would we be without them, eh? So, if we want to maintain ourselves, we are obliged to protect them."

"Yes, sir," Magnus said, not sure that he understood, and not sure that he agreed. "My father says something like that. But he says it's our duty to protect society."

"What a curious expression," the man in green said. "Our duty, indeed!"

"My father is considered to be a bit strange," Magnus said.

Aetius ignored this. "The lower orders have a duty to serve us, Magnus. They expect us to make their decisions for them. I want those messengers to earn their keep for once. I want you to go up to that messenger station and tell them to find out all they can for me, Magnus!"

*   *   *

Trier, early June

Midnight was approaching. Conwyn of London was pacing the walls of Trier, acting as a sentry.

He had arrived in Trier as Magnus's servant. When the siege had begun, they had given him a spear and a helmet that was too large and too heavy and told him he was vital to the defence of the city.

The sky was free of cloud and the Milky Way was clearly visible. The night was far from quiet. There were foxes out there, with their almost human cry.

The night was getting cold and he walked back and forth to keep himself warm. Until a few days ago he had been

28

Magnus's groom, a personal servant, not in the army and not subject to military discipline. Life had been dull but safe. Then the Huns had crossed the Rhine and Magnus had been sent on his forlorn hope. In this crisis, Conwyn knew he could not refuse to take part in the defence. Besides, Magnus had taken both the horses. There was nothing else for him to do.

In the distance, he could see the fires of the barbarian camp. In the still night he could hear them singing - a boisterous drinking song. The barbarians were confident. A few days before they had offered to spare the city if it handed over all its gold. The commander had replied that he knew what barbarian promises were worth.

The barbarians had no siege equipment, but there was always the risk of a surprise attack. In a siege the advantage was always with the defenders, but before long the barbarians' patience would run out and they would risk a direct assault.

The fox cried again. Startled, Conwyn glanced round, but of course there was nothing to see. He told himself that, in a way, the sound was reassuring. If the Huns were out there, the creatures would be silent. His feet were getting cold, so he continued his pacing. Would the barbarians attack? And when? Had Magnus got through?

Conwyn was fond of his boss. The spendthrift young patrician was defensive about his short stature and tended to make up for it with a show of being tough, but underneath that he was friendly. He was certainly less harsh than Conwyn's puritanical father had been. Had Magnus reached Lyon? Had he persuaded the emperor or his generals to send help? To Conwyn, alone in the dark, it seemed unlikely.

Chapter 2: The March North

Signal station at Argentorate, June

The pilots and ground crew - and the women - of the Argentorate messenger station squeezed into the mess hall to hear what Magnus had to say. The room was lit with a few smoky oil lamps and was badly ventilated. It had not been built to hold so many people at once and it was already getting stuffy.

The wind outside was building up to a storm. Magnus could hear the patter of rain. No one had suggested holding the meeting outside.

The captain at Argentorate was a Gaul called Brennos. He was of average height, although still taller than Magnus, and dour. He was broad-shouldered, looking more like a blacksmith than an aviator. He had a neat moustache and, like many of the aviators, he bleached his hair. He stood at Magnus's right hand, but a couple of paces to one side, as if to distance himself from the message that Magnus bore.

The captain raised his voice. "Gentlemen! Quiet, if you please. I would like to introduce Magnus Vitalinus, sent to us by the people at army headquarters."

Magnus, looking round at the pilots who had crowded into the room, could tell that these Argentorate pilots resented him.

The Argentorate messenger station was positioned eighteen miles west of the city, where the old military road crossed the northern limit of the Vosges Mountains. Brennos had explained that the station had been positioned here, on the western face of the mountains, so as to catch the prevailing winds.

When the Huns had sacked the city, that distance has saved the couriers. Now the station had been chosen as a base for the new campaign.

Some of the pilots based at Trier had managed to escape and had joined the garrison. Magnus recognised Acco, the senior pilot from Trier, standing in the front row.

"Good evening, gentlemen." Magnus spoke in Gallic. He had learned that everyone resented his clipped patrician accent. It was easier to improve his Gallic than to change his Latin. "You may have heard why I'm here. The general is leading his men north from Lyon. He wants me to gather together all the information you have on the Huns." He attempted a small joke. "I know you can do this without any help from me, but I was the one the general pointed his finger at. Do you want to question his judgement?" This question was met with stony silence. "Right."

"So, you're going to take our reports to the general?" Acco asked. "They say the general chews Commius' head off, every time he delivers bad news."

"Yes, that's what Captain Commius told me," Magnus said.

"Rather you than me, then," Acco said, and the room relaxed slightly.

Brennos silenced the assembly with a glance. "We've received news, brought by refugees from Mainz, that Attila has divided his forces. He led the main army north towards Kolonia. Less than half his total force had marched west to lay siege to Trier."

Magnus nodded. "The general will want confirmation of that … Do you know whether Trier has fallen to the Huns?" This question was met with an uncomfortable silence.

31

Acco spoke up. "The messenger station was abandoned. The news we have is several days old."

"Yes, I know." When Magnus first arrived, he had asked whether the irreverent Sergeant Dumnorix had made it to Argentorate. Captain Brennos, at his most dour, had told him that some of the ground crew and their families from Trier had reached safety, but Sergeant Dumnorix was missing.

"But is it possible to fly over the city, Acco, to see if it's still intact? The general is marching north. He's worried about being ambushed by the Huns. I want to give him some answers when he arrives."

"Have you gained official approval for, for scouting missions, sir?" Captain Brennos asked. "We're usually restricted to delivering the mail."

"Oh, yes, certainly. The general needs to know about the Huns. If it's possible to scout out the city, I want it done."

Brennos nodded. "Very well. It's worth trying."

"That sounds more fun than delivering the mail," someone at the back said.

*

Magnus was standing on the edge of the landing field of the signal station. It was on a desolate windswept mountaintop, poking up above the forest cover. The sky had cleared, and the sun had slowly warmed the hillside. At dawn everyone had grumbled at the lack of wind, but now it was strong enough to raise swirls of dust.

Magnus stood alongside the fragile single-seat flying machine. This design was very basic, with no bodywork to protect the pilot from the elements. The wicker seat was attached directly to the landing skid. At the moment the machine was tipped over, with the right wingtip resting on the ground. He could make out the delicate wooden spars that gave the wing its shape.

He had realised that these aviators would not respect any man who had not learned to fly. Their respect was vital if his mission was to succeed. Looking at the fragile machine, he wondered whether their cooperation was worth the risk.

A few men with nothing better to do had gathered to watch. Magnus recognised Acco's careworn features among the crowd.

Captain Brennos had offered to teach him in person. "Get in, boy, get in! We need some ballast to weigh it down."

The men of the ground handling team grinned. Reluctantly, Magnus seated himself and fastened the waist strap. Because the machine was canted over, the starboard wingtip resting on the ground, he slid to the right side of the seat.

The ground handling team turned the flying machine round to face the wind. Brennos squatted down, facing Magnus. His bantering manner vanished, and he was a matter-of-fact instructor. "The purpose of this exercise is for you to use the controls to keep the wings level. That and nothing else. You won't be flying today – the wind isn't strong enough. Do the best you can, lad."

Acco stepped forward and picked up the starboard wingtip so the wings were level, then let go. The starboard wingtip began to fall. Magnus wriggled so he was sitting upright.

"Push the yoke to the left," the captain said.

Magnus did so, the starboard wingtip rose, but then the port wingtip crashed into the ground. He winced. "Sorry."

"No harm done, lad. Good reflexes, but too decisive. You need a delicate touch. Try again."

Another member of the ground crew raised the port wingtip, made sure the wings were balanced, and let go. That wingtip continued to rise, so Magnus pushed the yoke gently to the left. To his surprise, the wings levelled again. After a minute of constant effort, the wings had still not touched the ground, but Magnus was sweating with the strain.

"You're doing very well – for a spoilt aristocrat," Brennos told him.

"But what if the machine takes off?" Magnus demanded.

"I told you, the wind's too light for that."

"Push the yoke forward, lad, that'll get the nose down," one of the ground crew shouted. His fellows grinned.

Magnus concentrated on keeping the wings level. He did not want the captain to sneer at him. "I'm a younger son of a younger son. I hardly count as a member of the patrician order."

"Keep your mind on your lesson, young man," Brennos said.

Then a gust of wind hit the glider. The wings creaked with the strain. Brennos yelped in surprise and jumped clear. Magnus was suddenly twenty feet in the air. Below him, men were shouting, but he could not make it out. What had that man said? Desperately, he shoved the yoke forward. The nose of the machine dropped; he could see the ground below. Men were staring up, appalled.

But the ground was rushing closer. He was going to crash. He pulled the yoke back and the machine levelled off. For a moment he thought he was going to land safely and impress his critics. But to his dismay the machine rose in the air again.

What had he done wrong? How could he get this wretched machine down without killing himself? He pushed the yoke forward again savagely, then waited until the last possible moment before pulling the yoke back. The wings were not level, but he no longer cared about that.

The main skid hit the ground hard. The port wingtip hit the ground and the wing crumpled.

Captain Brennos and the ground crew ran up. "Are you all right, lad?"

He undid his strap and stood up, shaking with fear and anger. "Did you do that on purpose, captain?" he demanded in his most haughty tones.

The captain did not seem to mind. "No, no. Apart from all else, the master carpenter is going to be very angry with me."

Magnus glanced at the wreckage of the port wing. "I'm terribly sorry."

"No, no, the instructor is responsible for the mistakes made by his pupil. I underestimated the strength of the wind. I'll apologise to the master carpenter. But are you all right? No pain? With heavy landings, it's usually the backbone that gets damaged ..."

"No, I'm fine."

Everyone was staring at him.

"Are you all right, lad? You sound too quiet to me. It isn't natural."

Magnus let his anger show. "What I'd like to do, captain, is kick you from here to Argentorate."

Brennos grinned. "Ah. *That's* all right. I knew one fellow once, had an accident, acted as if nothing was wrong, but collapsed hours later at the dinner-table. We guessed his heart just stopped."

"It's my patrician upbringing. I was told never to show any feelings."

"Yes, some aviators take the same view. But students will progress faster if they don't hide their problems."

"He's a solo pilot now," Acco said. "First solo flight and first crash."

Magnus was appalled. "No, no."

Captain Brennos agreed. "It was an accident. How far did he get? Five yards?"

"A flight is a flight," someone at the back of the crowd said. "He flew alone, and he lived to tell the tale."

Magnus thought it best to ignore them. "Captain, what did I do wrong? Why did it jump back into the air like that?"

"Well … when you pushed the yoke forward, you put the machine into a dive. But that built up speed. That gave the wings more lift – so you gained height. We've all done it."

"I want to learn what I should have done. Show me."

Magnus, riding a borrowed horse along the narrow country road, came within sight of the walls of Metz at last. The air was sultry. Magnus hoped it would not lead to a thunderstorm.

The military road north had taken the army to Metz, four days' march south of Trier. The town, on the east bank of the River Moselle, was small, much declined from its days of prosperity. When the walls had been built, during the troubles a century ago, most of the outlying parts of the city had been excluded.

The country road from the messenger station took Magnus through the abandoned suburbs and up to the east gate.

The gate-guard was made up of Aetius's troopers. "Your business?" the sergeant asked.

"I'm from the messenger station. I have dispatches for Lord Aetius." His accent, of course, proclaimed his rank.

"Oh, right." The sentry pointed. "The general 'as grabbed the largest 'ouse in the city for 'is 'eadquarters. It's on the main road, big doorway. You can't miss it."

"Thank you."

The house was big enough to have a stable attached. Magnus left his horse in the care of Aetius's grooms and found the general in the courtyard, sitting on a stone bench, with his advisors standing around him. Behind him stood two men from his bodyguard of Huns. Perhaps the general had decided that the airless rooms made it impossible for men to stay indoors.

The wind had blown some leaves into a corner and no-one had bothered to sweep them up.

Aetius looked up at his approach. "Good evening, Magnus. What's your report?"

Magnus felt uncomfortable looking down at the general. "The aviators have moved their base of operations north, to the Saar. The messenger station there is very basic, but it's closer to your headquarters. Last time the aviators looked, two days ago, the barbarians are still laying siege to Trier."

Aetius glanced at a writing tablet on his lap. "Trier is holding out? That's good to know. Magnus, I'm worried about the road north. We could be ambushed by Huns riding south. They're better fighters than the rabble under my command. If they took us by surprise, even a small force could wipe us out. It would be safer to take the mountain road, but that would take twice as long."

"Oh, the road north is empty, sir."

"Damn your eyes, how can you possibly know that?" Aetius growled. His anger was rising. His staff and his Hun bodyguard eyed Magnus coldly.

Magnus wondered how much he ought to explain. "The aviators travelling up to Trier fly parallel to the military road, sir. They can see the road, and they can tell whether it's empty or not. A lone horseman would be invisible, but an army would be plain to see." He thought of a detail that a soldier would understand. "A marching army raises dust. And there isn't any on that road, sir."

"Really …" Aetius considered this. His anger had vanished. "And the messengers say the road north of Metz is clear?"

"Yes, sir." Magnus wondered whether he had said too much.

Aetius leapt to his feet. "This is excellent! I can know where the enemy force is, yet they are ignorant of my whereabouts. Magnus, I want your aviators to do it again. Tell them to fly the length of the road and check for ambushes. Ride back to the messenger station tonight and kick those lazy bastards into action. I'll keep the army here until you confirm the road is clear."

Magnus was saddle sore, suffering from lack of sleep, yet there was only one answer he could give. "Yes, sir."

He glanced up at the clouds. They were white, rounded like pillows, and slow-moving. He had learned enough about flying and the weather to know that conditions tomorrow probably would be favourable.

Magnus was cold. He had chosen the front seat of the flying machine. He knew by now just how chilly the upper air could get, so he was wearing a borrowed leather jacket, helmet and mittens. All were black, stiff and creased from long use.

He had been ordered to lean on the aviators, to ensure that a reconnaissance was carried out and to report back to the general.

Instead, he had decided to go on one of the scouting missions himself. He and Captain Brennos were flying north, following the line of the hills towards Trier.

It was strange to think that if conditions were favourable he could be delivering his report to Aetius tomorrow evening.

They followed the crest of the hills, always trying to stay in the strongest updraft. Magnus, in the front seat, was aware that down below were barbarians, waiting to kill him if he fell into their hands.

Finally, the captain banked the flying machine. "There it is, lad."

Magnus looked down at the wingtip. Far below, the walled city looked tiny. Magnus could make out the individual streets, but not whether the houses were intact. At least there was no smoke. The camp of the besiegers was almost as large as the city. He turned and shouted over his shoulder. "Can't you get any lower?"

"If I did, lad, we'd never regain the height – and we'd never make it back to the mountains."

"Right." Getting back with the information they had gleaned – however meagre it might be – was their main priority. "Can we fly over the city? Show them we know of their plight?"

"We've instructions never to fly over cities. The townsfolk think our shadow is unlucky."

He had never heard that superstition in Britain. "Then can we fly over the Hun encampment? Try to frighten them? I hear they're superstitious."

"Ha! It's worth a try, sir."

They flew across the enemy encampment and turned south towards the hills. Their course took them over the Trier messenger station.

Magnus noticed a mark on the ground, white against black. "See that, captain? What does it mean?"

"Where?" The captain banked the machine for a better look. "Oh. It means the airfield is *not* suitable for landing. The ground crew probably forgot to remove it when they ran."

"But Sergeant Dumnorix never turned up. Is it possible he's still here?"

"Well – he's the sort who takes his duty seriously. You could be right. But we can't land. It would bring the Huns down on us. But it's worth watching."

*   *   *

As Rua led his little troop of Huns down the long eastern slope of the mountains, an enormous wall of cloud reared up in the western skies.

The men approached the great encampment, and the black storm-cloud caught up with them. A few big raindrops splashed down, and thunder rolled out of the west.

Uldis and the other riders hunkered down in their saddles and urged their horses on, reluctant to return in such a storm, with bad news. Their leader, Zabergan, would take it as a portent, just as they did. A cloud this black could only be a sign. Evil in the west. Maybe Attila's plan to conquer the Gauls and the Franks would have to be abandoned.

Smoke rose up from the vast camp's cooking fires, looking like a great sacrifice, the smells of goat, sheep and rabbit familiar even at this distance. At the gate, the Hun sentries told them where their kin were camped.

Rua looked at the men around him. "Join your kin and make camp." He thought things over. "Uldis. Come with me."

Uldis swallowed and nodded. He was not courageous but had the stoic manner of Attila's oldest veterans.

The two men rode by the outer sentries and through the camp to Zabergan's tent. To the west and north lightning bolts tormented the black clouds. Bleda could feel the hairs on his forearms standing up.

The two men reached Zabergan's tent, dismounted, and stood waiting. Guards came out of the tent, drawing aside the flaps of the doorway and standing to attention, ready with drawn bows.

Zabergan appeared in the doorway, his face pale, his skin sweating, the whites of his eyes visible all the way round. He stared down at Rua. "Did you kill the dragons?"

"No, my lord."

"Then why are you back?"

"The dragons do not live in these hills. My companion Uldis will confirm this. These hills are too low. They only roost in the high mountains, so high the trees can't grow there."

Zabergan eyed his unloved scout commander. "Why are you back?"

"I could not take my men so far south without first asking your permission." Rua's voice was steady, and he met Zabergan's fierce gaze without fear. But Zabergan was not pleased. Uldis swallowed.

"These Germans only follow us because they're afraid of us. If they see us fail, they'll no longer fear us. Don't you understand?" To his guards he said in a calmer voice, "Take this man and kill him. And his horse. Make a bonfire and burn everything."

Uldis watched, appalled. Two of the guards pushed his hearth-companion to his knees. A third swung a sword and removed Rua's head with a single stroke. A fourth heaved what was left of Rua's body over his horse and led the beast away.

Zabergan turned his gaze on Uldis, who tried not to flinch.

"Take your men out of this camp, now, before the storm breaks. Before they've had time to blab their failure. Take them south to those mountains. And don't return until you've killed a dragon, as I ordered."

"Yes, my lord."

*   *   *

Tolosa, June, 451 AD

Avitus, patrician, friend of Aetius, companion of the emperor, and now ambassador to the court of King Theodoric, did his best to ignore the smells of horses, men and compost as he led his horse through the streets of Tolosa. The city had been built by the Romans, after all, and the monumental buildings still looked splendid. Up close, the truth was more squalid.

He walked beside the royal official, Euric, while his companions followed behind, grumbling about mud and filth on the streets. The sky was overcast. That seemed fitting, somehow. There had been rain recently. All of the vacant lots had been reduced to mud.

Ten miles to the east, the hills of Mons and its messenger station marked the western frontier of the empire. A generation before, ambitious kings had burnt the station and pushed their frontier up into the hills. Then Aetius had defeated the Goths and forced them back inside the old

42

frontier. Avitus knew that bit of history was going to make his embassy more difficult.

The king's henchman, Euric, had met them outside the city gate, accompanied by a dozen warriors. That was a compliment of sorts, but Euric had been surly and showed little respect for Avitus's rank. He spoke with a harsh accent, but his Latin was clear. Now the carpenters who blocked the street were shouting obscenities as they struggled with their timbers and the mud. It was all so demeaning.

"Houses of wood and brick." His nephew sniffed his disapproval.

Avitus sighed. "At least they're building something. Most Roman cities are just fading away. The best we can do is carry out repairs."

The city was built on the east bank of the River Garonne. In more prosperous times the river had carried some trade, down to the western ocean, but those days were long gone. Tolosa was now a frontier city.

The royal official halted outside an inn. "Shelter has been arranged here for the king's guest, his retinue, and his horses."

"Please thank the king on my behalf," Avitus said.

"Certainly. Tonight, my lord, the king has invited you to dine with us at his high table. And your companions, of course."

Avitus hid his relief. This invitation to dine was an important step. "Thank you, sir."

The official bowed, then went on his way.

The innkeeper was unenthusiastic until Avitus handed over a fistful of coins. "The king's messenger said you had stables for the horses?"

The innkeeper, a Gaul, was suddenly all smiles. "Of course, sir, of course. That has been arranged. We have everything a traveller needs. My boy will take care of your horses for you." The man led them upstairs and apologetically showed them their rooms.

Avitus's young son-in-law, Sidonius, looked round distastefully. "This is no fit place for a patrician."

The boy was still full of his dignity. "No. But it must be borne, for one night, at least. Perhaps, tomorrow, King Theodoric will give us rooms in his palace."

On the other side of the street, the voices of two women rose in argument. They were speaking in a harsh Germanic dialect, too fast for Avitus to follow.

Sidonius grimaced. "Who are those ill-bred harridans? And why doesn't someone make them shut up?"

He smiled faintly. "They'll probably tell you that they're the daughters and sisters of warriors, and your equals in rank."

After a chilly sponge bath, Avitus put on a heavy silk lavender-grey embroidered tunic, and thick dark purple wool trousers. He swung the satisfying weight of a white courtier's cloak over it and fastened the cloak with a fashionable brooch. A heavy gold signet ring completed his appearance. He collected his companions, who had also refurbished themselves, and led the way through the narrow, squalid streets to Theodoric's palace.

Avitus's appearance and bearing brought him before the officer of the day. "Lord Avitus? If you'll wait a moment, I'll send a messenger for the king's own secretary."

The secretary was lean, middle-aged, and harried. He was also, of course, a citizen of the empire, and a gentleman, rather than a Goth.

Avitus did not blame him for accepting Theodoric's service. This land had been given to the Visigoths by the emperor a generation ago, leaving the local nobility to survive as best they could. Avitus favoured the man with a half bow, equal to equal.

"My name is Eparchius Avitus, and I come from Vienne on a diplomatic mission of great urgency." He displayed the seals on his letters, but folded them back to his chest when the secretary reached for them.

"We were advised that you were on your way, my lord," the secretary said. "You have been invited to dine at his majesty's high table ..."

"Yes. I bear letters of introduction to the king of the Visigoths from the Magister Militum of Gaul." That probably carried more weight than the emperor's recommendation, these days. "I have been ordered to seek an audition."

The secretary tilted his head judiciously. "I'll see what I can do for you, my lord. But you've come too late in the day."

"I understand. I'm well acquainted with the king's routine."

The secretary's brows went up. "You have been introduced to the king?"

"Oh, yes. I was introduced to the king fourteen years ago." Avitus knew Theodoric's court well. He had helped to negotiate a peace treaty and had kept on good terms with the king ever since. That was one of the reasons that the Magister Militum had chosen him for this embassy.

"Ah. You understand, of course, that the king only listens to petitions in the afternoon, after he returns from the hunt. He's preparing for dinner now."

"Yes, I quite understand."

"Very well, sir. I will advise the king of your arrival. If you return with your letters tomorrow, I'll see that you can present your petition to his highness."

"Thank you, sir." Avitus bowed again, satisfied.

"I will introduce you to the steward. After the meal - you must be tired from your journey," the secretary said. "I suggest that you retire early to your lodgings and refresh yourself for tomorrow."

Was that a hint to get out of the secretary's hair? Avitus bowed again and withdrew.

"Will they see us, sir?" Sidonius asked. "To have ridden all this way, only to be kept waiting on the doorstep like some supplicant . . ."

"Oh, yes, they'll see us. Although we are supplicants, in a way. Not for ourselves, but for the empire." Avitus smiled faintly. "They'll see us, and then they'll keep us waiting.

"Now, during the meal, you must not show any disdain for your host's manners. And you must not, whatever you do, be so gauche as to attempt to discuss business."

"Of course not, sir."

He knew they were about to be confined by the king's routine. Tonight, there would be supper accompanied by storytelling or music. At least the king's musicians were bearable. Neither side would mention the ambassador's mission.

The king of the Visigoths, Theodoric, spent his days in prayer, gaming, hunting, hearing petitions and business, then closing with a supper party accompanied by soothing music. Avitus knew that he did not deviate from this routine for anything less than a major disaster.

Tomorrow the king would hear more petitions. The king's generals would debate the news that Avitus had brought, endlessly. Avitus would be invited to participate in the hunting and gaming. And meanwhile, time would be running out.

The following day, just after noon, Avitus and his companions returned to the palace. Theodoric always listened to petitions in the afternoon. He considered it was late enough for everyone to be fully awake, but too early for anyone to be drunk. Unfortunately, Avitus's sleep had been ruined the night before by two gothic women arguing ceaselessly.

In the great hall the ambassador and his companions were met by the king's secretary who, of course, told them to wait. It seemed that everyone in this large room was waiting to see the king. Young Sidonius fretted anxiously, but Avitus advised him to remain calm.

Eventually, the king's secretary returned. "Come this way, if it please you, my lord."

Avitus swallowed and followed the secretary across the great hall of the palace. A lot of people were milling about, but one glance told Avitus that the king was not among them. The secretary led them to a doorway, blocked only by a heavy curtain, and flanked by a couple of bored guards.

The secretary bowed Avitus and his companions inside, and in a loud clear voice announced their names and ranks.

It was not a throne room, but a less formal chamber. It was quite small, and half-filled by a broad table. Half a dozen men were present, but Avitus had no trouble picking out Theodoric.

The king was stringy and balding, and many years hard campaigning lay behind him. But he remained vigorous; his campaigning days were not over yet. He sat, relaxed and alert, in a cushioned chair. On either side of him stood his advisers, warriors like himself.

Avitus stepped forward and bowed. "My lord, I bring urgent letters from Lord Aetius, the Magister Militum, at Lyon."

The king smiled. "Welcome to Tolosa, my friend Avitus," he said. "What brings you to my court? I don't think it is a courtesy visit this time."

"No, your majesty. Attila, king of the Huns, has led his army west of the Rhine." That got their attention. Good. "We expect him to ravage all of Gaul in the months ahead. Lord Aetius, commander of the army in Gaul, asks you to come to his aid."

"And why should the Visigoths do that?" one of the noblemen rumbled. "Aetius has attacked us in the past. Yes, and he's used Hun mercenaries to do it."

Avitus swallowed. Had this warrior fought against Aetius? "Attila is not the sort of man to respect frontiers. He threatens the kingdom of the Visigoths as well as the Imperial lands. Unless he is stopped, he'll march all the way to Tolosa and strip it bare."

The noblemen turned to their king.

"Yes," Theodoric said. "From what I hear of him, Attila's quite capable of challenging us. Friend Avitus, this is not a question that can be answered in a moment. I will have to think on this. I ask you to wait."

"Yes, of course, your majesty."

"But enough of formality, Avitus. Tonight, you will dine with us. And your companions, of course."

Avitus hid his relief. This renewed invitation to dine was another important step. "Thank you, your majesty. You are most generous." Once again, he bowed himself out.

*   *   *

Vosges Mountains, June, 451 AD

The squad of Hun warriors trudged up the mountain track. They resented the necessity that had forced them to leave their horses behind. But these steep slopes would lame a horse and the Huns cared more for their horses than they did for men. The climbers were awkward on these mountains and more than once a man fell. But no bones were broken and each time Uldis, given command for this mission, kicked the warrior to his feet and hastened the men on their way.

They laboriously made their way up the mountain to the crag. The climbers wore loosely woven woollen tunics and breeches, designed to keep out the cold. In addition, they all wore leather caftans, which they were reluctant to remove, so they were sweating profusely. Their tall leather boots were totally unsuitable for scrambling over rocks. All of the warriors carried powerful composite bows, while the more experienced carried swords as well.

"The beasts are here," the swordsman said. "The dragons are watching us. I can feel it."

He had won his sword as loot after the battle of Mainz. His companions regarded him as a fool because he carried the blade everywhere, although he had never learned how to use it.

"Shut up and climb," Uldis said. He had not wanted to be given command of this raid. He knew the men were nervous. They came from the plains, thousands of miles to the east. They had experience of killing animals bigger than themselves, but this was new.

The warriors were afraid, although none would admit it. They had never encountered dragons before. They knew how to bring down wolves, but how did you attack beasts that could fly?

The great king had divided his forces after the sack of Mainz and had taken the main army north. The secondary force had been ordered to sack Trier and then continue west. The army commander, angry at the defiance of the city and the vigilance of the flying machines, had decided to express his anger in a way that would make everyone listen.

Uldis thought they had been sent on a fool's errand. But you did not tell the boss he was wrong, not if you wanted to keep your head. But what was he going to say if he returned empty-handed? Reporting failure was dangerous too. He decided he would say the dragons had fled as he approached. The dragons could fly, so why not?

The prisoner had told them that the dragons were real and that they roosted in the mountains, but explained that only men suffering from altitude sickness could see them. Uldis had dismissed this as nonsense. Dragons did not exist and only a man suffering from delirium could see them.

But what if the prisoner had meant something different? What if the dragons were invisible and only revealed themselves to men in a delirium? And how high did you have to climb before the altitude sickness got you?

He called a halt to let the men get their breath back. This mountain air seemed to drain away your energy. Even your thoughts moved more slowly.

"There's no such thing as dragons," the archer said. "What's the boss going to do when we report back and tell him we couldn't find his dragons?" The archer had won his name because he was regarded as the best archer in the regiment.

Uldis had a simple answer. "Break's over. Get moving again." He thought the archer might be useful against beasts that could fly. Although if the dragons were as big as the legends said, arrowheads might not be much use. He kept that thought to himself. The men were frightened enough already.

"The beasts are here all right. They're watching us. I can feel it," the swordsman said.

"Shut up, you fool," Uldis said. "Save your breath for the climb." He was sweating, and not from the exertion alone. The bare rock was a strange colour here, in several hues, almost like scales.

They were negotiating a difficult patch, with a sheer drop on their left. Then the swordsman shouted. "It's on that rock! Can't you see it? It's the same colour as the rock!"

Uldis saw the dragon - its bright scales glinted in the sunlight, but their metallic sheen resembled the rocks it was lying on. Uldis thought the swordsman was babbling. But then an eye opened, watching the climbers with interest. The Beast was huge, bigger than a horse, its mouth full of pointed teeth.

One man screamed and ran. Uldis was not surprised. He was scared too. Could they pretend, afterwards, that the man had not run? No. Two men could keep a secret if one was dead. If the king learned that his warriors had lied to him, they would all lose their heads. But first they must finish the matter in hand.

An archer, behind the swordsmen, let loose an arrow. But it bounced off the Beast's metallic scales.

The Beast opened its mouth and lunged forward. It missed Uldis. Its jaws closed on air. The swordsman took a step back, then another. In his fear he did not attempt to draw his sword. "It's watching me! I'm a dead man!"

He took another step back, lost his footing, and fell. He slid to the edge of the precipice. He scrambled for a handhold, failed, and fell. The warrior's scream ceased abruptly when he hit the ground below.

The remaining men backed away. The dragon turned its back on them.

But the attack had shown how clumsy the big beasts were on the ground. Swords would be useless; perhaps arrows and long spears could do the trick.

Uldis grimaced. Two men lost already. This would take a lot of explaining. Perhaps it would be better not to report back at all.

*   *   *

Trier, Late June.

The sun shone down out of a clear blue sky. Conwyn was on sentry duty once again, in the full glare of the sun, sweating inside his leather jerkin. His stomach was growling. The garrison was now on half rations. All the fresh food was gone. Now they were reduced to salt meat and dry biscuits.

Conwyn was on the roof of the eastern gate tower, watching the enemy camp. Would the barbarians attack? He asked himself, as he did every day, whether Magnus had got through to the aviators and sent a message to the Magister Militum. Was hope of rescue a delusion?

He had a second reason for worry. What if the city was saved but Magnus was killed in the fighting? What would happen to him, a landless man in a strange country?

He heard footsteps on the stone stairs, and he turned to see the commander of the British troops come into view.

The commander was an English speaker, his barbaric name Latinized as Fullofaudes. He was tall and broad-shouldered, with long, blond hair and a bristling moustache, looking very much the barbarian leader.

He glanced at the barbarian encampment, with the smoke from its cooking fires, then turned away. He was followed by his British subordinate, Alban, taller and leaner.

"Good morning, boy." Fullofaudes said. He spoke in slow, careful Latin. "Conwyn, is it?"

"Yes, sir."

"I've heard good things of you, Conwyn. You're sharp and conscientious in your duties."

"Thank you, sir." When officers and landowners started talking like that, Conwyn became suspicious.

"We need good men in the troop. When this is over, I suggest you consider enlisting."

So that was it. "Sorry, sir, but I serve Captain Magnus, sir."

"You think he's still alive? Your loyalty does you credit." The commander glanced at the encampment again. He was impatient.

"I hate this waiting, Alban. I wish the bastards would attack and get it over with. They must know that the garrison is losing heart. Local levies." His tone implied that the British troops under his command were as determined as ever.

"Yes, sir," Alban said.

Then a shadow passed over them. Conwyn glanced up, squinting, and guessed what it was. He raised a hand to block out the sun. The object, no more than a dot, had turned towards the barbarian encampment. "Look! A flying machine!"

The two officers were looking up too. "Hell's teeth, the lad's right," the Englishman said.

"Perhaps Magnus got through after all," Conwyn said. He found this cheering. He was fond of his boss.

The commander was doubtful. "The Huns would have overrun the messenger station as soon as they got here."

Alban was more urbane. "Then the machine must have come from another site, sir. Argentorate, perhaps. Or even Lyon. They say those machines can cover tremendous distances."

The commander thought this through. "Then Aetius must know of our plight. Perhaps he sent the machine to check up on us."

Alban glanced up at the machine and grinned. "If he did that, then he's probably on his way here."

The Englishman nodded. "Yes. I hear he doesn't hang about. They say he drives his men hard. It'll be awkward for the likes of us when he gets here."

"Permission to tell the men, sir?" Alban sounded eager.

The commander was doubtful. "I don't want to raise false hopes. On the other hand … some of them may have seen it too. Very well, Alban."

*   *   *

Aviator Bolgios was aware that he was losing height. He had gone too far from the mountain, hoping to get a close look at the road to Trier, but his gamble had failed. There was nothing to be seen.

He should have turned for home at once, but instead he had flown parallel to the road, hoping to see something of value. By the time he had admitted defeat and turned for home he was dangerously low.

The saying was that if you had 1000 feet in height you could travel 10,000 feet over the ground. And if he reached the ridge, the updraft would give him the height he needed to get home. Alas, the ridge was more than 10,000 feet away. The wind was in his favour, pushing him eastwards, but it was not enough.

Desperately, he kept trying. Some experts could find rising air over ploughed fields. No, it was futile. That bastard Acco had told him he often found rising air over pig pens. Today, Bolgios was desperate enough to try it. But all he could see were forests and ploughed fields and sheep grazing. No. He was going to have to land.

But he had given up too late; he had not spent any time looking for suitable landing sites. There were no big fields within reach.

The nearest big field had recently been ploughed. If he attempted to land there, the plough ridges would wreck his machine. It would be as if he had been thrown from a galloping horse. The neighbouring field was a meadow, smoother but small. It would have to do.

He headed downwind, then turned and began his approach. He realised at once that he was too high. When his machine touched down, he was almost halfway into the field. He thought for a moment that he was going to pull it off and walk away from the landing. Then he saw the low stone wall rushing towards him. He tried to turn the machine, but he was too late. The machine hit the wall and crumpled. He was thrown forward.

Stone wall. Pain. Through the pain, Bolgios was aware of broken bones protruding through the skin. He tried to make sense of that and through the pain he realised that he would never fly again. Suddenly the realisation came to him that unless help came he was likely to bleed to death.

He tried to move, to free himself from the wreckage. But the pain was too great.

Would nobody come to help him? Where were those wretched peasants? They had no brains at all.

He had come from a peasant family. When he reached his eighth year, he had realised that he faced a life of unending toil. Their labour fed the community, they fed the empire, their rents enriched the patrician. But instead of receiving praise they were sneered at by everyone. If they weren't born stupid, their simple lifestyle slowly destroyed their wits. He had hated that thought, he hated the patricians, so he had run off and found a life with the aviators. The messenger service needed men with quick wits. Many aviators died young, but at least it was quick. Most of the time.

He thought through his landing again. Why had he made such a basic mistake? Never allow yourself to get low; never get too far from the hills that gave you lift. But the general needed that information, and the Huns had killed dragons.

Then Bolgios heard horses. Not peasants, certainly. He turned, as far as the pain would let him, and watched them as they rode towards him. Was it the general's cavalry? These horses were tough, rough-coated mounts with short legs. What general would accept such disreputable mounts? The riders were as scruffy as their horses.

Then Bolgios recognised the riders as Huns. They had long dark hair running untidily down their backs. No imperial officer would permit that. Some of the riders had shaved, revealing ritual scars on their cheeks. They were jabbering to one another in no language he recognised. When they dismounted, he realised that they were grinning. No. He would never fly again.

*   *   *

Magnus flew on another reconnaissance mission, piloted by Acco this time. His own skill as a pilot was improving but he did not trust his abilities over enemy territory.

The General had led the imperial troops and his Burgundian allies north along the old military road. He was now fifty miles north of Argentorate, a day's ride south of Trier. He was now demanding daily reports from the aviators. Magnus hoped that today he could find something new to tell the general.

The aviators were operating from the messenger station on the hills of the Saar forest that Acco had called the Halfway Point. They were flying every day that the weather allowed, observing Trier and looking for their enemy. Magnus was flying almost daily.

"There's Trier," Acco said. "It looks the same as it did the last time I was here."

"Yes." Magnus hoped this was a case of 'no news is good news'. "Right, Acco, we can turn back."

"And not before time."

As usual, Magnus flew over the signal station to the east of Trier. On the hilltop he spotted the signal, huge letters marked out with whitewash on the grass. "What's that, Acco? Go lower, I want to see."

"How will we get back up again?" Acco asked.

"The messenger station is on a hill, isn't it? And we've got a good breeze. Won't that provide the updraft we need?"

"Yes, but it'll take us an hour to regain the height we've lost." Acco said. "I want to get back home in time for dinner." But even as he grumbled, he obediently took his machine lower.

Finally, Magnus was able to read the message, marked out with sheets. 'Huns gone – remove digit'.

"This looks like the work of Sergeant Dumnorix," Acco said.

Magnus grinned. "Right, Acco, let's get back to the Halfway Point. I'll have to report this to Aetius in person."

*   *   *

The massive stone gate-houses of Trier were richly ornamented, monuments to power as much as a defence, built in the days when the empire was wealthy enough to build extravagant civil defences.

Aetius rode toward the gate, accompanied by his staff officers and his bodyguard. Magnus had included himself amongst them. His British companions formed part of the garrison and he was eager to find out how they had survived during the siege.

The gates of the city were thrown open as the cavalcade approached and a delegation marched out to greet Aetius. The leaders of the delegation were the bishop of the city and the garrison commander, Maximus. Aetius was tactful enough to dismount. "Good afternoon, commander, your grace."

The bishop delivered a well-rehearsed speech, welcoming the general and praising him as the savior of the city. Aetius listened, unmoved. Everyone in the army knew that the general disliked displays of enthusiasm of any kind. The bishop reached the end of his speech at last and the general thanked him gravely.

Then Maximus took over and, in a laconic speech, thanked the city's savior for his timely arrival. Once again, the general listened with a show of gravity, although his answering comments were abrupt.

Maximus gestured to the soldier standing at his right hand. "My lord, may I introduce you to Fullofaudes, the commander of the British troop. His men have made a great contribution to the defence of the city."

Fullofaudes was tall, with long, blond hair. This afternoon his expressive face was lined with worry. "It's wonderful to meet such a great general, my lord. I am certain your prompt action has saved the city."

Aetius was bored at this praise. Magnus was afraid that he would say something offensive.

Fullofaudes was intelligent enough to keep his speech as short as possible. He concluded with a little bow and stepped back behind Maximus.

Maximus, shorter and leaner, possessed an aristocratic confidence. "We had one stroke of luck, sir. Attila divided his forces and led the main army north towards Kolonia. The force he left behind, to lay siege to Trier, made up less than half his total force. So, when you arrived, the barbarians found themselves facing a relieving force of unexpected size."

"Yes, commander? How did you respond?" Aetius prompted. His patience was wearing thin.

"I sent out scouts as soon as the barbarians abandoned the siege. They've moved west, along the road to Reims."

Aetius nodded. "Yes, my own scouts tell a similar story. I shall want to move on as early as possible tomorrow."

"Of course, sir …" Maximus smiled. "My lord, the magistrates have prepared quarters for their illustrious guest. If you would care to -."

Aetius cut him off. "Food? Lodging? Excellent, commander. Lead the way, if you please."

Magnus lingered behind. He watched the garrison commander and Aetius walk away, then turned to Fullofaudes. "Hello, sir."

The Englishman looked puzzled for a moment. Then recognition came and his face creased into a smile. "Magnus! So you delivered my message!"

He grinned back. "Yes, sir."

"You've changed. I didn't recognise you for a moment."

"Well – a lot has happened to me in the last few days."

"You can say that again! First the Huns and then the general. And I don't know which was worse … I'll find you a beer and then you can tell me about it."

"Yes, sir."

Back in his quarters, Fullofaudes poured out some beer. "Magnus, if we have to deal with the general, I want you to do all the talking. I know nothing of generals, you understand."

"Surely, sir …"

"I've been talking to citizens here. They say that Aetius is an evil character, and quite mad. He sees plots everywhere, and suspects everyone." Fullofaudes was literate but his handwriting was poor. He had been eager to dump his correspondence on Magnus in the past. "There'll be less trouble if you do the talking."

"Very well, sir."

"You'll have to hunt down that groom of yours. I put him on sentry duty during the siege, but now you're back you'll want him to tend your horses for you."

All of the garrison officers, including Magnus and his commander, were invited to the celebratory banquet. Fullofaudes was uncomfortable about being in such high-born company.

Maximus intelligently kept his welcoming speech short. Aetius took the opportunity to question the garrison officers, tactfully and skillfully.

"And where's Attila?" Aetius asked.

"All of the refugees we've questioned tell us that Attila took the main part of his force north, towards Kolonia," Maximus said. "They're consistent about that."

"Good, good," Aetius said. "That would explain why the barbarians abandoned the siege without a fight. If we have only half of Attila's army to deal with, we might be able to achieve a modest victory." He looked round. "Magnus, tell your aviators I want them to keep track of Attila for me."

"But I have to rejoin my troop, sir. They're stationed here in Trier." Magnus looked round at his commander, but Fullofaudes made a hushing gesture.

"Never mind that. They've coped without you up till now," Aetius said. "Your task of liaison with these aviators is too important. Magnus, I want to know everything possible about the movements of the Huns."

"Yes, sir."

Aetius turned to Maximus. "I want to lead the army north to save Kolonia, if I can."

Maximus frowned. "My lord, I predict that the Franks will refuse to allow imperial troops on their territory."

"Even if it means their towns being looted by the Huns?"

"Yes, my lord. They've just gained their independence from the empire. They don't want to lose that."

"Hell and damnation," Aetius growled. "But I can't fight two enemies at once. If your prediction is correct, I'll have to sacrifice Kolonia to the Huns."

A week later, Magnus delivered his report on the activities of Attila's troops. Aetius had taken over the garrison commander's residence as his headquarters. The general was sitting in the shade of a colonnaded courtyard. Half a dozen members of Aetius's bodyguard of Huns kept away curious onlookers.

Aetius noticed Magnus approaching and leaned back in his comfortable wicker chair. "Yes, Magnus?"

"My lord, the barbarians' southern army has responded to our surveillance by moving west. The aviators are flying in difficult conditions, and it's a struggle to keep the southern barbarian army under surveillance."

"I don't give a damn about their problems, Magnus. Make your report."

"Yes, sir. The aviators are able to confirm that the Huns have abandoned the road that leads west to Reims and instead have turned south towards Metz." Magnus was nervous about bringing this unpleasant news to Aetius.

The general frowned. "You're confident that this information is reliable, Magnus? My strategy depends upon that."

"Yes, my lord." He did not add that he had seen the barbarian army himself. The general was not interested in such details.

"Good," Aetius said. "Because I intend to abandon Trier. I'll leave only Commander Maximus and the regular garrison. I'll take everyone else, including the British cavalry, and march on Metz. So, are you confident your intelligence is reliable, Magnus?" Aetius's staff officers – and everyone else – stared at Magnus.

Magnus felt a moment's panic. The fate of Trier depended upon his judgement. "Yes, my lord. Although the aviators will have to continue flying their missions."

"Yes, of course. Every day, you hear me? As long as I know where the Huns are, when I march south, they can't entrap me."

Chapter 3: An Interlude in London

August, 451 AD

In August, Claudia Aurelianus arrived in London with her family, her parents, and her nurse. The annual visit to London was a tradition. The head of the Aurelianus family had the right to attend the meetings of the governor's council and her father was careful to never miss a session.

Claudia accompanied her parents to the capital every autumn, although last year's visit had not gone well.

Her father grumbled about the city, as he did on every visit. "The smell is dreadful. But what can you expect in August? We really should have waited until October."

"Yes, dear," mother said.

"Look at those abandoned houses! This is shocking. Every time I come here, another house has fallen down or been turned into a midden. London's dying, I tell you."

But father was always grumbling. She could not imagine anything more alive than this: the bustling crowds, the shop fronts, the street hawkers selling everything from woven baskets to fresh fish.

Their carriage stopped outside the town house of her uncle. Although it was one of the largest houses in London, close to the forum, it was a lot smaller than the family villa in the Limestone Edge. It was built round a courtyard, but instead of a garden in the middle there were just a few bushes in tubs. There was only one gateway to the street. Father said the heavy wooden door was in case of riots. You could never trust townsmen, he said. They had no respect for their betters.

With the whole family staying there, it was very crowded. This year, Aunt Enid told her she would have to share a room with her cousin Morwenna, who was eleven. The room was tiny, but Claudia did not mind. She had three brothers and two older sisters, Morwenna had a brother and a very young sister. She wanted to talk with someone her own age.

Claudia was a brunette, while Morwenna's hair was black. Claudia gravelly agreed to her cousin's suggestion that they complemented each other perfectly.

"That's lucky," Morwenna said.

"Hush, you mustn't say things like that."

"Why not? But we'd better not be late for dinner."

Claudia liked uncle's dining room. The walls were decorated with the picture of an imaginary garden, all deep reds and browns. When the family sat down for dinner, she found that her father was feeling quarrelsome. "Gaius, you must not allow any army officers into this house."

Uncle raised his eyebrows. "Most of them come from good families. Do you want to offend every powerful family in Britain?"

"You know what I mean," father said. "I don't want any debauched young reprobates wandering here and chatting with my daughter."

"Are you referring to that young man last year? His behaviour was impeccable while he was in this house. I wouldn't have allowed him in if it wasn't. He was courteous to us all. That's more than I can say about some members of our family."

Claudia wondered whether uncle was referring to her brothers. She smiled, then hastily lowered her head so that no-one could see.

"It's not his behavior in this house that I'm complaining about. His conduct in Southwark -."

Uncle's anger was beginning to show. "Are you asking me to exclude every gentleman who's ever visited Southwark, brother? We'll be short of company if I do that."

That was when Aunt Enid spoiled things by leading the ladies off to the sewing room. Claudia could hear her father's voice, but it was too muffled by the intervening walls for her to make out what was being said.

Her cousin Morwenna was much younger than herself, but somehow she seemed terribly mature and sophisticated. She could speak casually of 'the palace', 'the governor', 'the count' and 'army officers' as if she saw them every day. Well, perhaps she did.

That evening, together in their bedroom, Morwenna was suddenly shy. "Claudia, have – have they told you anything about the marriage?"

"Yes, a little." She knew from the start that this year would be different. Old Ambrosius, a key member of father's clique, had died that spring. Father wanted to assure the younger Ambrosius's loyalty with a dynastic marriage. The marriage negotiations had been going on for months, but father felt that an agreement was in sight. "Father says my marriage will probably take place this winter."

"But – do you even know what Ambrosius looks like?"

"Oh, yes. I saw him last autumn, although I wasn't allowed to speak to him. All I remember is that I thought he was plump and indolent."

Morwenna did not look happy at these revelations. "What does your mother say?"

"Oh, Mother tells me that the match is a suitable one. Now that he's inherited, you see, he's one of the richest men in Britain. He now feels he's prosperous enough to support a wife. Although I thought that didn't sound very encouraging."

"No, indeed," Morwenna said.

"Mother was annoyed at me. She said I should be more enthusiastic. I would be a leader of society, with my own household to run. And – she said I would have my children to console me."

"But - what did you say to that, Claudia?"

"I couldn't think of anything polite, so I thought it best if I didn't say anything at all. Mother doesn't seem to enjoy managing *her* household. She's always grumbling about the amount of time it takes up." And did she want a string of brats in Ambrosius's image? Or like her odious brother, come to that.

Morwenna changed the subject. "I'm allowed to read all of the books in Daddy's library. Except the ones in Greek, of course."

"I think you're terribly lucky. Out library at home's a lot bigger. But the only books I'm allowed to read are the saint's lives. Grandfather used to say that everything else was unsuitable for a delicately reared maiden of high birth."

"What's wrong with other books?"

The unsuitable books were about men. Claudia realised it would be unwise to talk about that to a girl of her cousin's age. Embarrassed, unable to think of anything to say, she remained silent.

Morwenna did not seem to mind. "I like the stories you tell," she said. "The traditional tales. The ones your grandmother told you."

Her grandmother, mama's mother, had told her that British traditions were just as important as Roman ones. "The British tales?"

"Yes. The ones about dragons and ogres."

She smiled. "The ones about the battles men fight, and the women they betray."

"Yes." Morwenna's eyes shone. "Could you tell me them again?"

Claudia was flattered. "Some of them, if you like."

"How did you memorise them all?"

She shook her head. "I don't. Grandmother says the stories shouldn't be written down. Each tale should be told differently each time. That keeps them alive, she says. Only the heart of the story remains unchanged."

The next morning Morwenna asked Uncle Gaius for permission to take Claudia for a walk. This was something they did every year. "Of course, dear," uncle said.

But for some reason father was reluctant. "Take a couple of servants with you, girl. Don't go near the docks, don't go near the fort. And don't go into the forum unless your mother or aunt accompanies you."

So, after the midday meal, they walked west along the via Decumana, with two of the servants following carefully behind. They turned north towards the Aldersgate, but the servant objected, because it would take them too near to the fort. Morwenna made a face and led them to the Newgate instead, as if she had intended that from the start. Then, on the way back, she turned aside and led them up to the old amphitheatre.

Claudia decided this was a disappointment: just a shallow oval, surrounded by a raised earthen bank. The servants waited patiently while Morwenna explained that the stone gateway had been taken away to repair the city wall. "The place is mainly used as a horse-market these days. Although the soldiers sometimes put on exhibitions here."

Morwenna's real reason for the diversion was that the amphitheatre was close to the fort. Claudia hoped to see some officers and was terribly excited when two marched by.

"I wouldn't have dared do this by myself," Morwenna confessed in a whisper.

The officers gave appraising glances at Claudia. She was getting used to that. She liked it. It meant she was growing up. The soldiers looked warlike with their fierce moustaches and leather riding trousers.

Father disapproved of her meeting soldiers, even officers. He said they were all barbarians, either Saxon immigrants or English settlers. They had no land, were very poor, and had no influence in politics.

They returned to Uncle's house an hour before sunset, very pleased with themselves. Morwenna asked her mother when they could go to the forum. Claudia thought she was pushing her luck. She was not surprised when Aunt Enid said they would have to wait until the day after tomorrow. They accepted this and retired to their room to change for dinner and discuss the day's expedition.

Her father did not hesitate to discuss politics in front of his womenfolk. Claudia had discovered that if she concentrated on her embroidery and listened, she could learn a great deal. As a result, the complexity of her embroidery patterns was interlinked in her mind with affairs of state.

Father was worried about the news from Gaul. He had a contract to supply the army there, but if the position worsened his profits might vanish. Claudia had learned that while Gaul was unstable it made sense for army contractors to place their orders in Britain.

"Stability in Britain is our greatest achievement, Gaius, and our greatest asset. But that's only worthwhile if the army can pay its debts."

For once, Uncle Gaius agreed with father. "Every ship arriving from the continent seems to bring worse news. Each new city that's looted by the Huns is a disaster. Argentorate, Mainz, Kolonia, Turnacum, then Camaracum, Samarobriva, Caesaromagus. And now Lutetia. What city will they pillage next?"

"Kolonia was handed over to the Burgundians. Turnacum was taken over by the Franks. And so was Camaracum. Who cares about them?" Father said.

Claudia sat still. The expeditionary force had been sent to Trier, and the city was said to be holding out. She wondered where Magnus was. Perhaps he was dead already. At least if she married a middle-aged patrician she would not have to live in dread of news from the continent.

Over the next few days, lots of people came to pay their respects to father, who would receive them in the dining room. Most of the visitors merely ignored Claudia, but a few were more polite. Morwenna suggested that some of them came to see her because they had heard she was so beautiful, but she told her that was silly. Most of them were quite old and just came to talk politics with father and uncle. Some of the younger visitors did talk to her, though. A few made an effort to say something courteous, which obliged her to say something polite in return. They were the sons of visiting councillors. But most were so haughty they reminded her of her brother Justin.

Some of the visitors were guardsmen from the Governor's palace. They usually came to talk politics too. Affairs of state, they called it. Claudia and Morwenna agreed they were far more interesting than the councillors. They always wore their military cloaks over their tunics. Some of them were British, rather than foreign mercenaries. That made them more interesting, somehow. A few of them were relatives of the councillors. They could talk to her about things she understood. Father seemed annoyed that these interesting men wanted to talk to her. But he could not forbid it. They came from her own social class, after all.

She looked out for the Vitalinus boy, the one who had caused the trouble last year, but of course he had been sent to Gaul to fight the Huns. She wondered how he was getting on.

Justin, her brother, paid a visit too. He was in the governor's bodyguard, with a white military cloak to show off, but that wasn't enough for him.

"I want promotion, and a posting to the heart of the empire. I want to transfer to the emperor's bodyguard, father. That's a steppingstone to the appointments that really matter, duke or count."

Father shook his head. "Family influence isn't enough. If you want promotion, my boy, you'll have to earn it."

Justin was not happy about that, but he found time for a few words with her as well. "I don't like this marriage that father has cooked up for you. Ambrosius is totally unsuitable. Why are you marrying someone twice your age?"

"I must marry into a patrician family, of course. Someone wealthy enough to support me in a suitable style. Mother says now he's inherited, he feels he's prosperous enough to support a wife."

Julian sniffed in disdain. "He hasn't been short of silver before. Until now he's been spending prodigious amounts on debauchery in Southwark."

71

She was stung. "Jealous, brother?" she asked sweetly.

"You'd better watch that tongue of yours when you're married."

Claudia looked away. The weather was fine, the sky was clear. On the continent they were fighting a war, but people in Britain could ignore it and go about their normal lives.

Chapter 4: The Wanderers

Gaul, August, 451 AD

Magnus had decided to accompany Acco on another reconnaissance flight, trying to locate the enemy.

After Aetius had reached Metz, the weather had closed in. For two days rain and low cloud made flying impossible. The aviators had resumed their missions as soon as conditions improved, but the barbarians were nowhere to be seen.

A series of flights had established that the barbarian army was not east or west of Metz. That left only the north, but no one knew where they had gone. Aetius demanded, loudly and repeatedly, to know where they were. But the aviators were flying at the limit of their endurance. They reported to Magnus that the barbarians must be at least twenty miles away from the city; all they could see were trees and fields.

Now Magnus could see that for himself. He had chosen to fly with Acco, who despite his eccentricities was an excellent aviator. Yes, the reports had been accurate. All he could see were woods and empty fields. He noted that the crops had benefited from the recent rain. But where were the farmers, the peasants?

"This is useless. Let's try further east, Acco."

"The upcurrent just died!" Acco shouted.

"What's that?"

"We're losing height. We must turn back!" the aviator shouted.

"We must carry on – we haven't found the Huns."

"To hell with you, boy. I'm turning back." He pushed his machine into a steep turn.

As soon as they turned and Magnus could see the mountains once more, he realised that they were a long way from home. His unease grew when he realised how much height they were losing.

"We're not going to make it!"

"I could have told you that, boy." A few minutes later he muttered to himself. "Below a thousand feet. Time to choose a place to land …"

Magnus wanted to tell Acco to keep trying, but held his peace. The aviator was the expert. Acco selected a flat meadow and began his approach. Magnus decided it was a lot more exciting when you had to find your landing site.

They touched down, skidded forward, and came to a stop. Magnus undid his straps and climbed out. "Congratulations on your landing, aviator."

Acco grunted in reply. "There's no point in staying where we are. We'll have to abandon our machine."

Magnus knew by now just how valuable flying machines were. "The hills are to the south and east," he said. "We're less than twenty miles from the Saar station."

"Trier is closer," Acco said. "It's a lot further when you have to walk." The pilot was helpless and insecure on the ground.

"But Trier is to the north of us. And the Huns were heading north," Magnus said. "We must get moving. I'm worried there may be Huns about."

"You said there weren't any Huns."

"I said I couldn't see any."

They started walking. They had no food and no water. The farm tracks leading through the woods were muddy.

They also twisted and turned, leaving them blind to what lay ahead.

That evening, they sought shelter. Magnus guessed that the dwelling, set back from the road, had originally been a small villa but had now dwindled to a simple farmstead.

If this was a working farm, where were the workers? The cattle in the field were short, stocky creatures. There were no horses of any kind. Had Attila's men stolen them?

"I'm worried," Acco said. "What if ..."

"If the Huns had come this way, they'd have taken the cattle. And probably burned the farmhouse too."

"We could keep going, find an abandoned barn or something," Acco said.

"I want something to eat," Magnus said.

"But what if they're waiting for us?"

"They might make an effort to ambush a troop of cavalry, Acco, but not us two."

"They want to get their hands on aviators. If they knew we were aviators ..."

Magnus knew this was absurd. "If they knew where we landed, and if they knew the road we would take, they might go looking for us. But an ambush? No."

He and Acco walked into the shadowy farmyard. Despite the heat, all of the doors were closed – most unusual. The only living things were the pigeons which coed at their presence. It was a working farmyard – the person in charge had made sure that everything was stored neatly.

But where was everyone? Magnus wished he had a sword ready at his hip. There were buildings on three sides. The pigeons, surprised, took flight, making Acco to yelp in surprise.

A door burst open. The man was brandishing something. Magnus had his dagger out of its scabbard before he realised that the man running towards him was a peasant, the sort who didn't realise how stupid it was to run towards nervous men with edged weapons.

The man stopped and lowered his pitchfork. "You're not barbarians, come to rob us? Or soldiers?"

"Devil fry you! Do we look like soldiers, blockhead?" Acco asked.

Other men were coming out of hiding now and, behind them, a few women. Magnus found that reassuring. If the women thought it safe, it probably was.

"Can we spend the night here?"

The farmers were suspicious and reluctant to help strangers. Magnus let Acco do all the talking. Unfortunately, the aviator came from the Central Mountains, which gave him an accent that made these northerners look at him askance. His outlandish appearance made the farmers suspicious.

"What are they saying, Acco?" Magnus asked.

"I asked them whether the Huns had passed this way. They say they haven't, but I don't believe them."

The eldest farmer ignored Acco and spoke to Magnus in slow careful Latin. "I ask whether we are safe from the Huns, lord."

"Yes. Attila has led his men north, away from the mountains," Magnus assured them. He asked about the roads east to the Saar.

The farmer explained that there were no military roads, only secondary roads and farm tracks. "You can spend the night in the hayloft. It's warm and dry."

As soon as they were alone, Acco started grumbling. "You shouldn't give them false hope."

"And you shouldn't frighten them for no good reason," Magnus said.

That night, their sleep was disturbed by the sound of a steady fall of rain. Although the rain had stopped before they left the farm, the country lanes were reduced to muddy trails and their boots were soon waterlogged.

By afternoon, they were faced with the problem of finding shelter for the night again. The narrow lane they were following had entered a dense wood.

"Getting dark," Acco said. "If we can't find a farmhouse, we'd better find a barn. That might be best. Half-witted peasants are almost as dangerous as the Huns.'

"Shut up. I want to listen," Magnus said irritably. Acco fell silent. Apart from the noise of their footsteps, everything was quiet.

An hour later, Acco said he could hear horses approaching from the east.

The road led down to a stream. Up ahead, they could see that the road turned to the right. The trees on each side concealed what lay ahead.

"Nonsense," Magnus said. "I know what horses sound like."

"Well, it isn't cattle, is it?"

Magnus decided to humour Acco's fears. They turned off the road, forced their way through a set of bushes and waited. Somebody was coming down the path.

Only one horse, Magnus thought. Why were they riding so slowly?

After an intolerable delay, they saw a woodcutter lead a pair of donkeys round the bend in the track. Acco hissed with annoyance.

Magnus was embarrassed. He knew that he ought to be able to tell the difference between a horse and a donkey.

He raised a hand. "Don't startle the man," he whispered. Together, they watched the woodcutter continue on his way.

Magnus led Acco back onto the road. He thought it best not to say anything. They continued on their way.

Magnus found that he had to bully Acco to get moving each morning. The aviator still believed that the Huns were hunting for him. The farmers they spoke to talked of barbarian foraging parties, in the next village or the next valley, but fortunately Magnus and Acco missed them.

The march through the mud took Magnus and Acco three days. All that time, Magnus was fretting that he was out of touch. Where was the army? But the farmers could not tell him that either.

On the morning of the fourth day their farm track reached a major road cutting through the forest. The metalled road was free of mud.

"Thank God for that," Acco said. "We turn left here. I've seen this road often enough, but I've never used it."

"What do you mean by that?"

"There's a landing site up ahead. I've flown over the road many a time. Come on." The road began to descend into a valley. Then, below them, through a gap in the trees, the river came into view, with the hills on the far bank towering above them. Somewhere up there must be the hill to the messenger station.

"But how are we going to get across the river, Acco?"

"There's a ford, sir. Quite shallow at this time of year." With their destination in sight, Acco was suddenly a lot more cheerful. "I never thought we'd make it. It's your doing, sir."

"There's no need to call me sir, aviator."

"I would have given up if it hadn't been for you, sir."

Magnus, embarrassed, did not attempt to reply. Let Acco think he was short of breath from the walk.

Together, they walked down to the ford. Suddenly, Magnus had a new set of problems to worry about. What had been happening while he was lost in the woods? Where was the enemy? And where was Aetius now?

When they reached the messenger station, Magnus demanded to be told the news. He learned that Aetius was still in Metz and the Huns had withdrawn northwards or, some said, the north west. So, he and Acco had never been any danger. Magnus wished he had known that at the time.

Which city would the Huns single out next?

Chapter 5: Cenabum

August, 451 AD

The field army was camped in the rolling hills north-west of Autun, on the road from Lutetia to Lyon. This was a land of wooded hills and a poor soil. With pastures that were good for only a few cattle, villages and farms were few and far between.

The aviators told Magnus that the Huns had moved west, forcing Aetius to lead his army south to the crossroads at Autun to keep watch on his enemy. Regular flights from the hilltop messenger station allowed Aetius to keep in touch with the heart of the empire.

Magnus hitched a flight to the messenger station in the hills above Autun. The sergeant told him that Aetius had taken over a grand villa halfway between the city and the messenger station.

He walked the two miles down the hill. He was wearing a sleeveless leather jerkin over undyed white tunic and leggings.

He asked the sentries at the gate about the whereabouts of Aetius. They directed him to the dining room.

Aetius was reclining in a battered wicker armchair. He was wearing an informal woollen tunic, but his had been bleached white. Magnus found that Aetius was in no mood to be hospitable.

"Take more care in future, Magnus. You must not risk your life in these stunts. Leave the dangerous tasks to these peasant fliers. They're expendable."

"Yes, sir."

"The local pilots are useless, Magnus. I want you to chivvy them up. Tell them to find Attila for me."

"I'm sure they're doing all they can, sir." Magnus had already spoken to the local pilots and had a good opinion of them.

"That isn't good enough," Aetius said. "I want to know where the Huns have gone, Magnus. I need to know where they're going to attack next."

"I'm sorry, my lord. The Huns have retreated north. The aviators can't follow them there. They can only ride the mountain-side up-drafts." Magnus was embarrassed and nervous. Telling a general the limit of his power was dangerous.

Aetius took this calmly. "So, the flying machines need a line of hills?"

"Yes, my lord."

"I suppose that explains the borders of the Gallic Empire." He smiled at his little joke.

Magnus smiled politely. "Yes, sir. All the aviators can be certain of, my lord, is that the barbarians haven't turned south or east, towards the mountains."

"There's no chance of your people finding him, you say?"

"No, sir. He's avoiding us."

Aetius showed more interest. "You think so? Your aviators have forced him to change his strategy?" He did not give Magnus the opportunity to answer. "Well, if you're right, he won't come south. He knows I'll be waiting for him. So, he'll continue to move west. Cenabum, perhaps. That's a tempting target for him."

"Well – yes, my lord."

Aetius was not listening. He stood up and spread the map across the table. "There are mountains to the south and east. If he wants to avoid your aviators, I predict he'll cross the

Seine, somewhere *here*, and head west to Cenabum." He placed his palm over the section of map that represented the northern plains, then clenched his hand into a fist.

"Yes. We can gamble on that. If he turns south, your aviators will spot him and bring me warning. If you can't find him, then Cenabum is the place to head for." He stepped back.

"If I'm to take on Atilla's combined force, I'll need allies. The Visigoths, the Franks, anyone. The emperor has written to his opposite number in Rome, asking for aid. We're that desperate."

"But – will they come, sir?"

"Some of them, at least. We received a message yesterday from my colleague Avitus. He tells me that the king of the Visigoths has already left Tolosa with his army."

Aetius seemed to be in a genial mood. "The Huns' greatest advantage is to move fast and take us by surprise. But your aviators give us advanced warning. We can be there to meet them. But only, it seems, if the terrain is suitable."

"I'm sorry about that, my lord."

"I can't blame you for the limitations of your machines ... But it means Attila could march all the way to Aquitaine, destroying every city in his path, without you spotting them!"

"Well, yes, sir."

Aetius came to a decision and beckoned his secretary forward. "Draft letters to all of my allied commanders. Say that Attila is headed for Cenabum and ask them to join me there. Be careful to get the mode of address exactly right. These barbarian warlords are very touchy about that."

"Yes, my lord. But if I may be permitted to say so, is it wise to say where Attila is going? If he chooses some other road ..."

"It may not be wise, but it's necessary. These barbarians will ignore my request if I admit any doubt." Aetius turned to Magnus. "In the morning, take these letters to your aviators."

*   *   *

Lord Julius Valerius Majorian listened, bored, to the junior officers gossiping on the far side of the room. When was Aetius going to arrive? Majorian was sitting on a cold marble bench in the atrium of the Magister Militum's headquarters. Aetius had, as usual, commandeered the best available villa for this purpose.

Aetius's staff officers were busy organising the next day's march. The general wanted another early start, damn him. Majorian was the highest-ranking man in the room but everyone was ignoring him. The bustle went on around him. He was inclined to sulk.

Majorian was broad-shouldered, taller than the average. His clothes were carefully tailored to avoid emphasising these features. He had decided not to grow a beard, although that was now fashionable. He was graced with a strong chin and wanted everyone to know it.

He had been sent west by Emperor Valentinian as commander of the Roman expeditionary force, to protect the ungrateful West from the Huns. He commanded the largest contingent of the allied force. Yet no-one showed him the respect due to his status as a patrician and a senator. The militia soldiers regarded themselves as the equal of any man in the professional army. To them, he was an aristocratic amateur.

"I hate this country," Majorian told the young British officer, Magnus.

"Yes, my lord," the young patrician said politely.

Majorian ignored him. "This pathetic western empire is dirt poor and is getting poorer." All except the richest preferred their own barbaric language and were proud of the fact that it had equal status with Latin.

"The climate's terrible and the soil is waterlogged. Is it surprising that decent harvests are impossible here?" The wine was second rate and the empire's most valuable crop, olives, would not grow at all. The richest landowners might be increasing their power, but their material wealth was dwindling. The fact that Aetius could establish his headquarters in an abandoned villa every night emphasised the west's poverty.

He would like to resign and go home, but that would be inconvenient. He was treasurer of the army and was making a tidy profit from the post. If he returned to Italy, he would have to abandon half his winnings.

He looked round. There was still no sign of Aetius. He reached a decision. "This is a waste of my time. I'm going back to my quarters. I can discuss my problems with Lord Aetius at dinner. He never misses that."

He turned to his sergeant. "Come on." He stood and strode towards the doorway.

Two men of his escort stepped forward to clear the way, but they were a moment too late. A messenger, full of self-importance, pushed past the startled guards and jostled him in the doorway.

"Sorry," the man mumbled. "I have a message for Lord Aetius -."

"Oaf. Apologise at once!" Majorian roared.

The man glared. "I apologise, sir." His reluctance was apparent, and the man's heavy accent betrayed his provincial origins. He was dressed in home-spuns. A low-born peasant.

Majorian was insulted. His honour, and that of his family, had been diminished. He struck the man across the face. "Show better respect to your betters! The correct form of address is 'my lord', not 'sir', and well you know it!"

His anger grew. "I'll have you scourged! The skin will be flayed from your back. But if you survive, you'll learn to show proper respect to your betters!"

Majorian's gestured to his sergeant, who grabbed the messenger and twisted his arms behind his back. The atrium went quiet. Everyone turned to gape at the scene in the doorway.

Majorian realised that he was shouting and stopped. A patrician should remain calm and dignified at all times. A lack of self-restraint diminished his class.

The prisoner was defiant. "I'm a soldier! Three hundred years ago my ancestors were warriors! They fought against you Romans -."

Majorian backhanded him. "You lost, fool! Your ancestors lost their land. They became tenants of Roman citizens. Field hands."

The prisoner disregarded this. "But now Gaul needs us. So now we provide military service. We have farms on government land. Next -."

Majorian backhanded the fool again. "Silence! You're still a tenant, to be dismissed at will. And I'll ensure that all of your family are kicked out and left to starve."

This threat to his family gave the man pause, but he still had a trace of defiance left. "It's government land. And while we protect Gaul, we can't be dismissed. If the government breaks that promise, we'll all mutiny."

Majorian noticed he had said mutiny and not revolt. This peasant was thinking in military terms. What had happened to this country? What monster had this Western empire created? He slapped the man again. "Apologise!"

The man flinched back, truly frightened now. "Yes, my lord, I apologise. I meant no disrespect. Please forgive me. I ..." he trailed off into a mumble.

For a moment, Majorian hesitated. Should he let the matter drop? No. This fellow would provide a useful example. Besides, he wanted his revenge for being on this wretched campaign.

A second peasant soldier appeared in the doorway. He stopped, gaping open-mouthed at the drama in front of him.

Majorian gestured to his bodyguard, not trusting himself to speak. He swallowed. "Shackle the prisoner until it is time for his punishment."

"Yes, my lord." The mercenary avoided his stare. That was gratifying.

The peasant leader, restrained by two of Majorian's mercenaries, managed to turn to his companion, still dithering in the doorway. "Go! Get help. Run!" The man dashed off.

Majorian looked round to see that everyone was staring at him. Even that British boy, who came from a good patrician family, looked appalled, almost as if he sympathised with the peasant who had assaulted him.

"Have you no work to do?" he demanded.

The British subaltern hesitated. "My lord, Bercucnos is an officer in a militia unit. He's a popular commander."

"An officer? Nonsense. He's lowborn trash, and he'll suffer the fate he deserves."

The mercenary completed the task of binding the prisoner. "What do we do now, my lord?"

"We take him to my quarters." Majorian was contemptuous of the militiamen outside. "That rabble wouldn't dare obstruct a senator."

"They wouldn't stop you, my lord," the subaltern said. "But if there's an – unpleasantness - your dignity might be impaired. Best to send a messenger to summon more of your bodyguards. Ten should be enough."

The mercenary frowned. "Twenty would be better, my lord."

For the first time, Majorian realised he might be in danger. "Do it."

*   *   *

Magnus, sitting with the other junior officers, listened to the militiamen outside the villa, grumbling about the detention of their commander.

Magnus and the rest of Aetius's staff had been stuck here since Majorian went crazy and arrested that militia officer. The man's unit had – understandably – been annoyed. Majorian, equally stubborn, refused to give way. The Italian had taken Magnus's intervention as a personal insult.

If this dragged on, Magnus intended to leave by the back window, but Majorian would never do that. Magnus hoped that Aetius would be here soon. Perhaps the general could sort this out.

The sound of shouting outside made Magnus look up. The militia unit was showing how angry it was.

The sentries at the door tensed. The shouting outside grew louder and then died down. Someone was addressing the crowd, although Magnus could not make out what was being said, but the crowd responded with a cheer.

Majorian, was sitting on an ornamental chair in his corner, his military cloak wrapped around him. Magnus assumed that his air of patrician indifference was feigned.

Somebody outside barked an order. The sentries stepped back. Two men of the Magister's Hun bodyguard pushed through the doorway and glared round.

"Room, atten-shun!" the senior one shouted. They stood aside and Aetius walked in. As usual, he was wearing his white military cloak. He was looking surly. Magnus and his companions leapt to their feet.

Majorian hesitated a moment, to emphasise his patrician rank, then stood to greet Aetius. "Good evening, Lord Aetius! How the hell did you get past those mutineers?" Magnus, and the other junior officers, hardly dared to breathe.

"They aren't mutineers yet, Majorian," Aetius growled. "Not until they ignore *my* orders. And I do not intend to push them that far."

"They threatened me!"

Aetius's expression was unreadable. "I was polite to them, Majorian. I suggest that you try it sometime. Although … I had to promise that I would see that justice is done. You have caused me great embarrassment. My lord."

Majorian gestured to his prisoner. "This fellow insulted my rank and my senatorial status! An insult to one senator demeans all senators – would you have ignored such an insult?"

Magnus guessed that Majorian was outraged that Aetius – a fellow patrician - showed no sympathy for his plight.

Aetius ignored the question. "Bah. The fellow's an officer. He owns enough land to qualify for the equestrian order. He commands a hundred men. We can't treat him as if he's a peasant. Is this him?"

Majorian's anger grew. "Over there." The wretched man was in a corner, as far from the door as possible, flanked by two of Majorian's troopers.

Aetius walked over to the man. "Good afternoon, Bercucnos. The loyalty of your men is commendable. Now, how did you offend Lord Majorian? In your own words, captain, if you please." He spoke in his usual abrupt manner.

Majorian was outraged. He interrupted Bernucnos's stammered reply. "Lord Aetius! Are you going to prefer this man's word to mine?"

Aetius glared. "I merely want a second view of events, my lord Majorian. Now let me finish this." He turned back to the prisoner. "You apologised, you say?"

"Yes, my lord."

Majorian was annoyed. "This peasant insulted me past pardon!"

Aetius turned on him. "Do I have to explain, Majorian? The man is an officer, technically a member of the equestrian order. I cannot afford to offend the largest contingent of soldiers in the army."

"A militia officer barely deserves the title." Majorian was surly.

Magnus was surprised at just how angry Aetius was. "That militia company is more useful to me than the thousand rag-tag mercenaries you brought with you."

"The fellow cannot escape unpunished! He struck a patrician. I refuse to back down. I cannot be *seen* to back down. Don't you understand? That would humiliate me, my family and the patrician order."

Aetius accepted this, after a fashion. "Yes. It would be bad for discipline too." He glanced down at the gaping prisoner. "But we can't flog an officer."

Magnus hesitated a moment, then stepped forward. "My lord, you could strip him of his rank. Break him to infantryman."

"Yes. I could do that," Aetius said.

"You're too soft," Majorian said. Perhaps he was thinking of the angry militia regiment outside.

"There's going to be a battle soon. And casualties are going to be heavy. We're going to need every man we can find."

Majorian tried to restrain his temper. "Very well."

And I could hint that after the next battle I'll reward his bravery with a commission."

Majorian was diverted. "If there is a battle. Do you trust this militia rabble to take part?"

"Oh, yes, there's going to be a battle. If you cannot accept my judgement, Majorian, it might be best if you resigned your position and returned to Italy."

The room was deathly still. Majorian looked appalled. He was treasurer of the army. Magnus wondered whether the slanderous rumours of peculation were in fact true. How much did the Italian general stand to lose if he resigned?

"No, no. I'm happy to stay," Majorian said. "I'll accept any compromise you think is suitable."

"Just so we're clear on that point," Aetius said.

*   *   *

Britain, August

The day of Claudia's marriage had arrived. She was unhappy but resigned. Her mother had supported her father's decision for this marriage, and she knew there was no way out. She would have to make the best of it. At least she would manage her own household at last. Ambrosius was rich, with servants to make her life one of ease.

The morning was cold, but the sky was clear. There would be no rain to spoil the ceremony. Her cousin Morwenna and her other friends and relatives clustered around her, giggling. They congratulated her on netting such a wealthy, powerful, high-ranking husband. A few of her friends had told her, privately, they felt he was too old. One had even said she hoped the stress of marriage would kill the old scoundrel off. But today they kept their silence, so as not to spoil the mood.

Claudia, in turn, forced herself to be calm. A patrician lady was not supposed to indulge in hysterics.

They fastened the floral wreath on her head, then pulled a fold of her mantle over it. Giggling, they led her out to the courtyard.

She was surprised to find that the man waiting for her in the courtyard, wearing a snowy white cloak over a fawn tunic, was her younger brother, Justin.

Claudia's friends hushed. "Where's Geraint?" she demanded.

"You know what Geraint is like, sister. He will shirk any unpleasant task." He was slim, elegant, and moved like a dancer. His carefully modulated voice lacked any hint of sympathy.

"And do you consider this task unpleasant?"

"Oh, yes. Ambrosius isn't a good match, whether you regard him as a political ally or as a husband. But father has made his decision." He made a little gesture of apology, holding out his right hand, palm up, to show it was empty. "I am here to ensure you won't shame the family by running away."

She took a calming breath, stepped closer and lowered her voice. "It's a bit late for that. I'd have run weeks ago if I could. If there was anywhere to go."

"But there isn't. You're trapped, and so am I."

"Yes, I understand that."

"Good. You will not disgrace the family today by any display of defiance, sister."

"No. I won't do that."

"I'll be leaving Britain, two days from now. The governor's sending another fifty men to Gaul, to fight the Huns. Father pulled some strings and I was given command. With a bit of luck, I'll get there before the fighting's over."

She was shocked. "But why, brother?"

"You wouldn't understand. I want promotion, and combat experience will give me that. I want to escape, too. And I'll do anything to achieve it."

A servant opened the outer door and the wedding party moved out into the street. Justin escorted her to her new household. The weather was fine, the sky was clear. On the continent they were fighting a war, but people in Britain could ignore it and go about their normal lives.

*   *   *

Magnus had, for weeks, been hoping to rejoin his British comrades. Now that the army was moving across the flat northern plain, the aviators could not help. He hinted that his task of liaison with the aviators was no longer necessary. Aetius finally let him have his way.

Was it a coincidence, or malice on Aetius's part, that he had been appointed to picket duty?

The men under his command, a squadron of light cavalry, were quite capable of carrying out this task without his supervision. He was only needed if things went wrong.

Each man wore chain-mail armour and carried a long sword at his side. An oval shield was looped over every horse's pommel. Some of the men carried javelins in a quiver, while others carried bows in protective cases.

Between Avaricum and Cenabum, the country was damp, flat, and featureless. The old Roman road, leading arrow straight, was the only safe route through the forests and marshes of central Gaul. In the old days, the forest would have been kept well clear of the road, but in these troubled times the undergrowth had been allowed to sprout unchecked.

Magnus knew that the major city of Cenabum was situated on the north bank of the river Loire, where the river changed direction and started to flow south-west. Five days after leaving Avaricum, the British light cavalry advanced cautiously along the military road towards the south bank of the river.

All that morning, Magnus and his men had been passing farmhouses and country homes. The owners had all gone, but the farmhands said that the Huns were just a few miles to the north.

The sky was overcast, with low clouds moving steadily east. Magnus judged that dusk would come early this evening. He was supposed to be on the lookout for ambushes, but he had learned that wild boar and deer roamed these forests. Giving a false alarm would be almost as embarrassing as being ambushed.

The road led them out of the forest, and they came within sight of the river at last. It was dark and turbulent. A couple of the troopers whooped.

Magnus judged the river to be five hundred yards wide. A score of herons were wading in the shallows. On the far side of the river was the city. Its long low walls of grey limestone ran right down to the waterfront. The wooden bridge had collapsed long ago. The city walls, from this distance, looked carefully maintained, giving them an impressive air of permanence. He looked for the besiegers and their camp, but there was nothing.

Magnus sent a courier back to his commander with the news that they had reached the river. He ordered five men to keep watch of the riverbank and told the remainder to rest their horses.

Soon the men of the troop were sitting around open fires. As Magnus watched his men at their roadside encampment, his servant Conwyn brought him some mint tea. "Are you sure you wouldn't prefer wine, sir?"

"I need something hot." Magnus cradled the cup in his hands. "Thank you, it smells wonderful … I've decided that this has to be the most dismal spot in central Gaul: damp, flat, boring, and foggy."

"Oh, I don't know, sir. Sometimes these forests and ponds and marshes are magical – when the heather's in bloom and the ponds are full of water lilies. And the woods must be great for mushrooms in the autumn."

"I pray we're not here that long." Magnus took a sip at his tea.

Magnus and his men were still admiring the view across the river when Fullofaudes, the commander of the Numerus Britannica, rode up with his men.

"What 'ave you found for me, Magnus?" Fullofaudes was an experienced mercenary commander, broad-shouldered and tough. In his youth, he had emigrated from north Germany to Britain to join the province's army. He had then risen up through the ranks. Although he could read Latin, he found writing an effort. He was pleased to be appointed as commander of the expeditionary force. He had told his officers that if this campaign went well, he hoped to be promoted to Count of the Irish Shore on his return to Britain.

Magnus put his cup aside and stood up. He gestured to the riverbank. "There, sir. Cenabum."

"Ah. Yes, walled city, north of a river. That must be Cenabum. The place is bigger than I thought."

"It looks intact," Magnus said.

"But where are the Huns? The general said we could ambush the Huns while they were still in camp. But that sounded like a wild 'ope to me."

"My guess is that the Huns have gone, sir. I think they heard we were coming and decided to retreat eastwards."

Fullofaudes glanced across at the city. "You may be right. We'll 'ave to ask the bishop."

"So the allies have saved the city, at least."

Fullofaudes ignored that. "We can't go any further, not without a boat. The general will want to know where the barbarians 'ave gone. You've done enough for today, Magnus. I'll find Alban, send him east, to try and locate the barbarians. Oh – while I'm doing that, send a courier to inform the general we've reached the river unopposed."

"Yes, sir."

The men of the Numerus were soon preparing a meal. One good thing about this waterlogged wasteland was that there were plenty of ducks, geese, quails and pheasants. The local patrician probably had hunting rights over these forests, but the army ignored such technicalities.

They watched as a flat-bottomed boat, big enough to accommodate horses, made its way across the river. Its crew, when they landed, told Fullofaudes that they had been sent by the city magistrates and the bishop.

They were interrupted when Aetius and his senior officers rode up. Aetius recognised Fullofaudes. "Good afternoon, commander. Thank you for your dispatch." He ignored Fullofaudes's stammered reply.

Aetius glanced at the city walls on the far side of the river. "So, you think that Attila, rather than force the issue, has abandoned the siege?"

"Yes, my lord," Fullofaudes said.

"Are you certain there's no sign of the Huns?"

Fullofaudes hesitated and Magnus intervened on his behalf. "Not on this side of the river, my lord."

"I see. You may make camp here, commander. I'm not taking the army any further today."

Fullofaudes wilted with relief. "Thank you, my lord. Ah – the city magistrates 'ave sent a ferry across the river, sir."

Aetius glanced at the waiting flat-bottomed boat and its loitering crew. He grimaced. "Another batch of merchants, I suppose?"

"I don't know, sir. But I think the bishop'll be expecting you as well."

"Then I'd better go and greet them. It would be rude to ignore them." The general and his staff led their horses onto the boat. The crew picked up their oars.

Magnus watched their progress across the water. "They'll receive a triumphal welcome in the city." As a mere squadron commander, he was glad to be excluded.

"The boss seems to 'ate merchants," Fullofaudes said.

"He hates flattery more," Magnus said.

At sunset, eight days later, Magnus led his weary men back to the army's overnight camp. For the last week, day after day, they had scouted ahead of the main force, checking for ambushes. The allied army moved faster than the Huns, encumbered with their loot and baggage train, and now they had finally caught up with them on the Seine.

Magnus reported back and found that Aetius had established his headquarters in another abandoned farmhouse. The barbarian sentries of the general's bodyguard recognised him and let him through.

Aetius was taking off his chain mail, assisted by two members of his Hun bodyguard. His secretary dithered in the background.

The tail of the mail shirt was pulled clear of Aetius's head and he straightened up with a sigh. His servant carried the chain mail out of the room, staggering under the weight of the metal. Under the chain mail, Aetius was wearing a brown leather jerkin. He shrugged his shoulders, glad to be free of the burden. He looked up and smiled. "Ah, Magnus. What news?"

"The Huns have turned to face us, sir. They have the high ground. I think they intend to fight tomorrow." He was nervous. He knew that a battle would be fought tomorrow, and it would decide the fate of Gaul.

Aetius smiled. "At last! I've been dreading this battle, you know, Magnus. Actually, knowing when it'll happen is a relief." He found a glass and poured himself some wine. "I shall have to summon my . . . allies. We shall have to choose our ground carefully." He paused. "Magnus, go and take your own armour off. You and your men had better get some rest ... And thank you. You and your men have done well."

"Thank you, sir. I'll tell them."

That evening, Aetius summoned the allied commanders, including Fullofaudes. Magnus and the other British officers saw to their horses, checked up on their men, then lit a campfire and began preparing their dinner. The stew was bubbling nicely when Fullofaudes returned to the British camp.

Nectaridius looked up. "Well, boss? What did the man say?"

Fullofaudes sat down and stretched out his legs. "I kept my mouth shut and listened to Aetius. The man can talk, I'll allow him that. He persuaded the allied kings to accept a defensive policy. Some of 'em thought a cavalry charge would win the day, but he reminded 'em the Huns 'ave never been defeated. He told 'em that merely surviving an attack by the Huns would be victory enough."

"And how did they react to that?"

"Oh, they agreed readily enough. But they argued about the line of battle. The Visigoths' king Theodoric demanded the place of honour for 'is men on the right wing. Typical barbarian warrior. All 'e thought about was 'is honour. No idea of tactics at all."

"Who got the centre of the line?" Nectaridius asked.

"The Alans. Another load of undisciplined barbarians. Personally, I think Aetius put 'em there so they can't run away." Fullofaudes turned to Magnus. "So, the imperial troops get the left wing. Aetius wants all 'is light cavalry on the end of the left wing. He 'opes you can attack the Huns on the flank."

Magnus swallowed. The thought of outdoing the Huns was absurd. "Yes, sir. I'll do the best I can."

Fullofaudes' tone softened. "You've already done your part, to my way of thinking. Your men found the Huns for us." He sniffed. "What's for dinner?"

"Rabbit stew," Nectaridius told him.

"What, again?"

"Just be thankful it isn't gruel, boss. That's all that most of the men are eating tonight."

"Oh, all right."

Nectaridius ladled some more stew into his bowl and turned to face Magnus. "Why did you join the army, lad?" he asked lazily. "It's been bothering me for weeks."

Fullofaudes grinned. "Most of those aristocratic boys join up because some girl has turned 'em down. So they join the army to forget about 'er."

"It wasn't like that at all," Magnus said hotly. "I got into trouble. After I'd been in front of the magistrate a second time, my uncle told my father that I'd be less of an embarrassment in the army."

"Was your uncle in the army too?" Nectaridius asked.

"Yes. He was an embarrassment to the family as well, my father says." He hesitated. "I admit, though, that I volunteered for duty in Gaul to get away from a woman."

"You get 'er into trouble?" Fullofaudes asked casually, not really expecting an answer.

"No. I wanted to marry her." He had met Claudia Aurelianus when she had visited London with her father. She had been attracted to the young palace guardsman. He had hoped to marry her, but her parents had decided otherwise. "I came from the Vitalinus family, with no land and no prospects, her father's the head of the Aurelianus family, so the old man rejected my offer."

"I never believed those stories about aristocratic feuding," Fullofaudes said.

"Oh. Well." He shrugged. "If I'd come from the wealthy side of the family, her parents might have been more eager. But they thought I was too wild, or not wealthy enough. The last I heard, her parents were considering a marriage offer from a wealthy landowner twice her age."

There was an uncomfortable silence. Then Fullofaudes slapped him on the shoulder. "Never mind, Magnus! Next year, you can go home with your pay, covered in glory, and you can pick any girl you choose!"

Chapter 6: The Battle

The horns sounding at dawn woke Conwyn from a troubled sleep. A bout of rain had swept over the ridge in the middle of the night, making life miserable for everyone. Although the rain had passed on, the cloud remained, cloaking the camp in damp gloom. Now shouts rang around the camp, driving warriors from their blankets.

Conwyn lit a fire and warmed up some thin vegetable soup. He tried to eat, although his stomach protested. The horses had to be fed too, of course, so he was kept busy. Working was better than thinking about what was going to happen next.

Magnus was up early too, and was soon kicking his men awake. "Up! Get up! D'you want the Huns to be ready before us?"

He walked over to Conwyn's fire. "Have you got any of that soup for me? Thank you." He lowered his voice. "The horses?"

"Already fed and watered, sir."

"Good man." Magnus bullied his men into getting ready. Conwyn realised that he was trying to sound like a veteran of a dozen campaigns. The men hurried through their morning stirabout, then helped each other into their chain mail. The noise of the army coming to order was building up, a wave breaking around him, harsh under the low dark cloud.

Magnus thanked him for the soup, and Conwyn helped him into his armour. Finally, Magnus fastened his baldric over his right shoulder. "Thank you, Conwyn."

"Your cloak, sir?"

"It would just get in the way. I won't need it - going to be warm work today."

Fullofaudes strode through the British camp, adding his voice to the tumult. "Alban, why aren't you mounted yet!" he bellowed. "Where's my marching order? Nectaridius, your men are slacking this morning. It's a lovely day for a fight! And why is my armour the only one that shines? Did you all run out of polish last night? Let's be 'aving you! Archers, keep those bows stowed. Move it, move it! I want those Hun bastards pissing down their legs at our very advance!"

The horses, sensing the anxiety and tension in the air, stamped and snorted. Conwyn brought Magnus's horse to him. Magnus thanked him and stowed his bow in the quiver behind the saddle before mounting the horse.

"Magnus!" Fullofaudes bellowed. "Are your men ready yet?"

"Yes, sir," Magnus said with quiet confidence.

"Are they? Good. That's more than Alban can say. Carry on." He strode away.

Magnus grinned. "Thank you, Conwyn."

Conwyn grinned back, too nervous to speak. The soldiers walked their horses to the hilltop and took their places in the battle line facing the direction of the enemy camp.

Magnus was at the left of the line, so Conwyn's place was there too, behind Alban's troop of British heavy cavalry. He and another groom had been given the task of holding the spare horses of Magnus's troop, with orders to keep them ready in case of need. There was no sign of the enemy.

"Perhaps they aren't going to fight," a balding Gaul said.

Opposite the allied line was another gently rounded hill, covered by a wood. Conwyn guessed that the ridge was over a mile long. The low ground between the two ridges contained a few trees and farm buildings, but nothing moved. Then Conwyn saw movement on the hill, half a mile to his right.

A wave of horsemen came out of the wood, rode forward a few yards and stopped, facing the centre of the allied line. The barbarians made no attempt to draw up in a straight line. Instead, small groups of riders swirled about, like boiling water in a cauldron. The Huns. The best cavalry in the world, it was said.

"Look," Conwyn said.

"We outnumber them two to one," the Gaul said. Then another group appeared over the hill and came to a stop, opposite Conwyn.

"They must be the Huns' vassals, the Ostrogoths," the Gaul said.

Conwyn was shocked to see just how many barbarians there were. Everyone said the Huns had never lost a battle. Although, as Magnus had told him last night, Attila had abandoned his siege rather than risk a battle. This day, he knew, was something he would boast about for the rest of his life. Unless, of course, the Huns won the day and slaughtered their enemies.

In the allied ranks, more and more fighting men came forward and joined the line. Soon, Conwyn's view of the enemy was hidden. He decided he preferred it that way. He could imagine that wave of horsemen, riding towards him.

There was a pause. Neither side wanted to attack first. He heard shouting. The Gaul pursed his lips, trying to look wise. "They're insulting us. Trying to make us chase them."

* * *

The morning sun burnt its way through a thin layer of cloud. Aetius had a perfect view of the pagan forces. They advanced in their battle line, over a width in excess of a thousand yards, making an imposing spectacle. In the centre was the infantry, moving briskly across the plain, flowing around isolated trees or farm buildings, the stamping of their feet sounding the rhythm for their songs.

The enemy cavalry rode wide on both flanks, their order impressive even from a distance of half a mile. Aetius watched units of his horse archers in the field ahead, doing their best to prevent the Huns from launching an attack on his flank. So far, they had succeeded; his horse archers were less skilled than the Huns, but they had faster, fresher horses.

He signalled the right wheel and his regulars began to deploy into their battle line. Everybody knew what to do and the manoeuvre was carried out in exemplary order. In an hour, his troops were formed up and the allied line was complete. The Huns continued to close, increasing their pace, while further pagan forces arrived.

The enemy was not yet within range, so Aetius rode down the front of his line, to steady his men. This was not the time for grand speeches; this was the time to be seen and to bring courage to those in the front line. The novices would be impressed and encouraged at the sight of their commander out in front of the army.

"Strength!" he called. "You are Soldiers of Gaul. Fight hard, never take a backward step."

He repeated his words along the line, shouting over the taunts of the advancing enemy. Further to the right, the ageing King Theodoric was doing much the same thing. The gap between the imperial and Visigothic troops was not quite closed. Aetius rode round the right wing of the imperial forces and galloped back to his central viewing position.

The contingent of Alans marched forward to fill the gap. The Alans were brave fighters, but Aetius thought that their king, Sangiban, was not loyal to any cause except his own. He wanted to keep the fellow under his eye. Placed in the centre of the line, any sort of evasion was impossible.

A battering noise swept across the plain. The enemy foot soldiers clashed their weapons against their shields, shouted their battle cries and moved to attack. So, there was going to be no squaring up at short distance, no baiting, no prolonged exchange of arrows.

Aetius felt his heart quicken as the thrill coursed through him.

The pagan infantry increased their pace. Their light cavalry rode at a slow trot each side of them, champing to be set free to gallop. Individual riders did just that, breaking free, then wheeling round and cantering back to protect the infantry. Aetius would have preferred it if they lost all discipline and charged, but fear of their leader kept them to their duty.

Behind the four ranks of Imperial infantry with their shields and spears, archers stood with arrows thrust point-down into the grass, bows strung and ready. On came the barbarians, into arrow range, meaning to hit the Allied army hard and fast.

Orders rang out. A volley of arrows shot through the air, hammering into the pagan ranks. At close range, the arrows had a devastating effect.

* * *

The Gaul standing next to Conwyn was still calmly analysing the battle. "They're still shouting insults. Stupid pagans. It's all bluff, so far."

A few arrows, at maximum range and lacking force, added bite to the insults. Conwyn murmured to the horses, soothing them.

The Allied line stood firm, but the pagan infantry kept up their steady advance. Attila sent his skirmishers to try the usual stratagem of attack and pretended retreat, hoping to draw the allied troops from their line of battle.

Magnus had told everyone in his troop about that. Conwyn was afraid that the undisciplined irregulars would fall for it, but the local men were too cautious, and every pagan attempt failed.

"They'll try brute force next," the Gaul said wisely. "Charges at key points along the line."

*   *   *

Aetius saw men in the pagan ranks stumble and fall, but their comrades did not falter.

Then the barbarian cavalry lost patience and charged – about half of it as far as Aetius could see. It was an extraordinary sight, three thousand horses and riders thundering on. They drove hard around the flanks of their infantry, undaunted by the arrows directed against them.

All along the allied line, commanders shouted their orders. The front rank locked their shields while those behind lowered their spears. If the pagan cavalry had expected the Gauls to flee, they were disappointed.

The infantry line held firm, their spears held at the level of the horses' eyes. Instead, the charging cavalry broke, like a wave hitting the shore. Riders turned aside or were thrown when their mounts flinched. A few riders, exploiting a gap in the Allied line, hacked and slashed, but they were isolated and were soon brought down.

Aetius had experienced many battles, but he was shocked by the intensity of the violence. He knew that it could not be kept up for long.

The barbarian infantry reached the allied line at last. The initial collision was signified by a rippling back of the allied forces, followed by an immediate steadying. His soldiers used their large oval shields as battering tools, thumping them forward, never allowing an opening for enemy swords or spears.

Aetius watched anxiously. Neither side had broken; neither could be said to be winning. It was now that the master general could make the moves to win the day. He turned to the messengers standing behind him. "Tell my captains. Keep them holding, wear them down."

On his left, the Imperial heavy cavalry deployed at an angle to the Allied line, waiting for their orders.

*   *   *

Alban, leading his troop of British heavy cavalry, watched his commander impatiently. The day was getting warm and his heavy armour was uncomfortable. More important, his horse was beginning to tire. Fullofaudes, a mercenary of eighteen years' experience, lacked imagination and would not understand how this delay was eating at his troop's morale.

Alban noted that the shallow valley between the two armies had a stream running through it. That obstacle could cause problems later.

Fullofaudes made a decision at last. He drew his sword, raised it above his head, and turned in the saddle. "Forward! For the Empire!"

The words were absurd, but Alban was so relieved to be moving at last that he found himself cheering.

Fullofaudes pointed his sword forwards and spurred his horse into a gallop. The Imperial force crashed into the troop of lightly equipped Huns, who scattered. There was a confusion of horses, shields, shouting men and steel.

A pagan rider appeared at Alban's left, his buckler raised. Alban swung left, his sword biting into the rider's arm. The man blocked his next thrust but a lance from Alban's companion pierced his shoulder and took him from his horse.

Alban carried on deeper into the melee, his troop behind him. The Huns were withdrawing, abandoning their wounded, leaving him with a clearer view. Arrows from the British cavalry carved through the sky, falling ahead. The Huns responded in kind, before wheeling around and charging their tormentors.

Alban's opponent was straight ahead. He turned his horse left and struck out right, his sword catching his enemy a glancing blow across his metal helmet.

The man's sword swung wide. Alban stabbed straight, taking the man under the arm. Imperial horsemen appeared on his left and right. His opponent tried to turn, but his horse reared and threw him.

One of the British riders was driven from his saddle, a spear in his chest. Ahead, the wall of Hun cavalry was deep and dense. Both sides slowed.

Further along the line, Fullofaudes was busy. "Horse archers, forward! Keep them back."

Alban turned his horse sharply, leaving room for the archers. He heard Fullofaudes shouting his order again. The squad of archers spread in front of him, firing from the saddle, guiding their mounts at the canter with thigh and heel. Alban's men reformed their line, then rode through the line of archers and urged their mounts into a charge.

The Huns refused to face them. Instead, they turned their horses and ran for it. They ignored the ford and continued north, scattering. Was this a genuine retreat, or some sort of trap? The lightly armed Huns were best at skirmishing, running rings around heavier but less nimble armoured warriors. This narrow battlefield, restricted by the river, had robbed them of their advantage and they had suffered heavy casualties.

The dead and dying were an obstacle to both sides. Alban looked round for his commander.

Retreat or ruse, either way Fullofaudes was too experienced to take the risk. "Hold!" he bellowed, with a theatrical sweep of his sword that caught every man's attention.

"Horse archers, guard against them! Everyone else, make for the ford. Cut off the reinforcements. Leave the rest to the infantry."

Not very heroic, Alban thought, but very professional. Exactly the right choice.

*   *   *

Euric, commander of the right wing of the Visigoths and trusted companion to the king Theodoric, recognised the attacking infantry as Gepids, vassals of the Huns.

They charged up the hill towards the allied line. Their formation had started out as a solid block, twenty-five men wide and sixteen deep. This neat alignment had soon been lost; the men in the centre, feeling more secure, had surged forward while those to the flanks had hung back. The block had become a wedge, pointing straight at Euric.

Fifty paces from the allied line, the Gepids paused, to shout insults at their foes and to dress their line. The waiting Visigoths stood firm and responded with their own battle cry, starting on a low note and swelling to a loud roar. A few archers, standing behind Euric, loosed a few shots, more to discourage the attackers than expecting to inflict serious casualties.

The Gepids realised that shouting alone would not be enough. They surged forward, determined to cover the last stretch of ground as quickly as possible.

"Archers!" Euric snapped.

The archers forming the seventh rank of the allied line let loose a volley. Euric noted with satisfaction that a lot of the attacking front line fell as the arrows showered down. "Good shooting. Keep it up."

The men in the front two ranks crouched, locked their shields and fixed their spears firmly into the ground, holding them inclined forward. They were ready to resist any pressure from the enemy, their shoulders pressed against their shields.

As the Gepids drew closer, the men of the fifth and sixth ranks let loose a volley of javelins, bringing down more of the enemy. The archers continued to shoot at high trajectory, dropping arrows onto the rear of the enemy formation.

The charging men stopped. "Shields!" Euric shouted.

Euric brought up his own shield to cover his body and the lower part of his face. The Gepids threw their javelins and Euric ducked. A shaft thumped hard into his shield, the tip piercing through and grazing his forearm.

The Gepids had merely paused; they continued their charge, closing rapidly with the allied line.

The two front lines met with a crash. Now it was a shoving match, a trial of stamina. As long as Euric's men kept their footing and did not slip, they were unlikely to receive serious injury. In a tight press such as this, there was little room for either side to use their weapons effectively.

Euric remembered what Aetius had said the night before. This battle would be won by infantry, because cavalry were useless at charging a defensive line. Soldiers might be brave enough and stupid enough to charge a line of spears, but horses were not. Cavalry were only good for skirmishing, attacking the enemy flank, and chasing down a fleeing enemy.

The Gepids had a great advantage: they belonged to an army that had never been beaten. One man on the allied front line lost his footing. The men on each side tried to close the gap but the Gepids exploited the weakness and inched forward.

Euric checked that his sword was loose in its scabbard. If the line crumbled enough for the fighting to reach him, a sword would not make much difference, but at least he could take a few of the bastards with him.

*   *   *

Magnus led his men along the front of the allied line towards the Gepids. He had hoped to take the pagans by surprise but, as he drew near, the nearest barbarians turned to face him. They formed a shield wall and presented an array of javelins that his horses would not approach.

All Magnus's men could do was to shout insults and throw a few javelins. It was not much, but the Gepids' attack on the Visigoths faltered as more of the attackers realised they were being threatened on two sides. Magnus encouraged his men to dash in close and throw another volley of javelins. It was a gesture, but his men performed with enthusiasm, taunting the enemy with their insults. As he hoped, the Gepids broke off their attack on the Visigoths to face this new threat. Sullenly, the Gepids abandoned their charge and began a careful withdrawal back down the hill.

Magnus led his troop forward, hoping to find a weak spot in their defence. If the enemy force broke and ran, he could ensure that most of them would not reach their own line.

But the Gepids were too experienced for that. They kept a shield wall facing towards him, no matter where he tried to attack.

Eventually, Magnus called his men off. They were getting too close to the enemy line and risked getting ambushed in their turn. Magnus was frustrated. He had not achieved anything. The enemy had escaped.

*   *   *

Euric, standing in the fifth rank with his sword drawn, hid his relief by bellowing at his men to straighten their line. The imperial cavalry, appearing behind the attackers, had diverted the Gepids, made them feel uncertain. That had been enough.

The sight of the Gepids pulling back, retreating back down the hill, leaving their dead and wounded behind them, cheered his men.

"Hold, there! Steady, boys."

The Gepids would be back, of course, and fear of Attila would make them try harder next time. Until then, the only thing that he and his men could do was wait. He lowered his shield and sheathed his sword.

"Relax, lads, while you can. More arrows for the archers. And get the wounded to the rear." Absently, he rubbed the scratch on his forearm.

*　　*　　*

The sun was dropping towards the horizon now. Conwyn, watching the battle, felt helpless.

The fighting that day was long and hard. Neither the Huns nor their German confederates were able to drive the allies out of their defensive position.

Conwyn thought that the Visigoths, to the right of the line, suffered the heaviest attacks but King Theodoric and his men stood firm. A steady trickle of wounded were brought back to the rear.

Conwyn, who knew little about wounds and had his hands full, could only help with the most basic chores. His stomach curdled at the sight of wounds pumping blood. He felt bile sting the back of his throat and he swallowed desperately. The blood unsettled the horses, so he had to soothe them too.

Then Magnus brought his troops behind the line to water their horses and grab a moment's rest. Conwyn realised they were a man short. He did not ask why.

Magnus dismounted. Conwyn noted that his chain mail had a new scratch on it. There would be a massive bruise under that, he knew. "Your spare horse is ready, sir."

"Thanks, Conwyn. I must try harder," he mumbled. "We're not achieving very much."

Conwyn checked the saddle girth on Magnus's fresh horse. "We're at the extreme end of the left wing, sir," he said consolingly.

"And we're lightly-armoured skirmishers. I know. We can't take on the heavily-protected barbarians."

Conwyn handed him a water bottle. Magnus took a mouthful of water and spat it out again, then took a cautious sip. "Thanks."

Magnus glanced round at his men and swung himself into the saddle. With an air of determination, he led his men forward again.

Conwyn began the task of rubbing down the tired horses. That kept his mind busy but gave him plenty of opportunity to watch the battle.

The barbarian skirmishers would advance to maximum bowshot range, let off a volley or two, and then retire. Conwyn realised that one of those arrows might get him, but he refused to move back. His duty today was to keep Magnus's horse ready.

Again and again, Magnus would retaliate to these attacks by trying to cut the Hun skirmishers off from their main force, but the barbarians were too wily for that. Conwyn knew that for Magnus and his men to charge after the Huns would be suicidal.

"The sun's getting low," the other horse-holder said. "We may survive this yet."

* * *

At the end of the day, despite heavy losses, the allies still held their line. When Magnus led his men back to join the rest of the British contingent, he expected them to boast of their triumphs. Instead, they were grimly discussing the

114

casualties: those who had died and who was not expected to last until the morning.

Everyone in the army agreed that holding the line was achievement enough: the all-conquering Huns had been brought to a halt at last. But it was a draw rather than a victory, and everyone knew it. The army of the Huns was still intact. They would probably attack again on the following day.

Both sides had lost thousands. Word spread through the camp that king Theodoric of the Visigoths, defending the right wing, was amongst those killed.

The British camp was bustling with activity. Horses were being unsaddled and rubbed down.

"So, you're safe, Magnus," Nectaridius said. "We heard you saw a lot of action."

"Nothing but skirmishing, though." He had taken one blow on his armour. It hurt like hell, but he didn't want these seasoned campaigners to think he was boasting. "I lost three men. I'll have to report to the commander."

"Haven't you heard? We've lost two of our officers. One of them was Fullofaudes."

"Oh. I see." Magnus could not think of anything else to say. He began to realise that he and his light cavalry had got off lightly. Well, his men's horses had to be tended to, whatever the casualty list. He assumed that Nectaridius, the senior squadron commander, would assume overall command.

That evening, round the campfire, the British officers discussed the battle. Magnus's bruise was spectacular, and Conwyn had applied a cold compress to it.

But Nectaridius, although a German mercenary officer, was nothing like Fullofaudes. He was barely literate and had been eager to dump his paperwork on Magnus in the past.

He distrusted the civilisation that he had spent all his life defending.

"This is a terrible burden. The commander has to report to Aetius, explain how mistakes happened. I know nothing of generals. I've been talking to officers in the regular army. They say that Aetius is impossible to work with. He despises provincials and anyone who isn't a scholar. He sees plots everywhere, and suspects everyone."

Alban, commander of a troop of British heavy cavalry, nodded. "He's a dangerous man to deal with. Anyone who gives him advice that he doesn't like becomes his instant enemy."

A murmur of agreement went round the other squadron commanders. Magnus sympathised. None of them wanted the task of reporting to the Magister Militum.

"I want to go home a hero, and win a promotion on the base of it," Alban said. "But if Aetius puts a black mark in my record, my career's finished."

"True enough," Nectaridius said.

"He and Majorian are feuding all the time," Alban said. "And Majorian has the ear of the emperor in Rome. Be polite to one and you offend the other. Either way, your career's finished."

"It's not my record I'm worried about," Nectaridius said. "They say that the Magister Militum assassinates anyone he thinks is his enemy."

Magnus hid a smile. "Come now, sir. Aetius isn't as bad as all that."

Nectaridius scowled. "The only one of us who has any experience of Counts and Dukes is Magnus here."

The others cheered up. Magnus, with dismay, realised what they had in mind. "No, no. I'm far too junior for command! This is my first year as squadron commander. And this is my only experience of combat."

"The right sort of experience is what matters," Nectaridius said. "You've done your staff work with the governor in Britain." He looked round. "Shall we vote on it, lads?"

Magnus was not in the least flattered. He felt that he had been singled out for all the wrong reasons. He wanted promotion for successful leadership in battle, not for his skill as a courtier.

Chapter 7: Aftermath of victory

Northern Gaul, August, 451 AD

Two days later, just after nightfall, Magnus hurriedly washed and shaved. He dressed in his best white tunic and cloak, then reported back to Aetius's farmhouse headquarters. This farmhouse lacked all of the luxuries that Aetius took for granted, but nothing better was available. The main room was shabby, but at least the roof did not leak.

The Magister Militum had taken the opportunity to shave and put on his richest blue silk tunic. He had an air of composure that Magnus could only envy.

Majorian the Italian was there too, looking sour. He was wearing a military cloak, plain except for the purple tablion that indicated his rank, over a green tunic, but had not found the time to freshen himself up. The Italian officer was broad-shouldered, much taller than Magnus, with a strong chin. His cloak was freshly cleaned and free of creases.

Magnus gave Majorian the bow appropriate to a patrician.

Sitting at Majorian's left hand was Ricimer, the barbarian general who commanded a detachment from the Mobile Army. Aetius had spoken of him as a brave commander who had served him well. Judging by his name he was a German. He was wiry, with the musculature of one who exercised daily.

All of the allied commanders were sitting at the long table, including the king of the Burgundians and Euric, war leader of the Visigoths. Further down the table were the junior army officers. The wine jug moved from one person to another.

Magnus took his place at the foot of the table and listened while the allied commanders exchanged stories of the casualties their armies had suffered.

Aetius put down his cup. "Gentlemen, if you please." He did not raise his voice, but the room hushed. "Magnus. I wish to congratulate you on your scouting expedition today."

Magnus stood up. "Thank you, sir."

"Magnus, please explain what you saw this morning." Everyone turned to stare at Magnus.

"We all know what the boy saw," the king of the Burgundians said. "I don't need to hear it again."

Magnus glanced at Aetius, who gave a little gesture of encouragement.

"Yes, sir. The Huns have abandoned their camp and have begun to retreat eastwards -."

"You followed them throughout the day?" Aetius growled.

"Yes, sir. A strong rearguard prevented me from getting too close, but it was clear what decision Attila has made."

"They've abandoned the battlefield? Left us in possession?" the Burgundian said. "I don't believe it."

"It could be a trap," Euric, the Visigoth, said.

"We shall certainly have to be wary of traps," Aetius said. "Thank you, Magnus. That will be all."

"Yes, my lord." Magnus sat down again, relieved.

Aetius turned to his allies. "Gentlemen, I want to take all our cavalry after the Huns - and destroy them."

"I agree," Euric said. "My warriors are eager to revenge our dead king. We demand a place in this new battle."

The Burgundian was more reluctant. "We've turned back the Huns. But the cost has been high. Chase after the Huns, yes. Drive them out of Gaul, and my lands, yes. Why does the Magister Militum want to risk everything by attempting more?"

Euric sneered. "My men are prepared to take part in this campaign. If there's a battle, we'll take the position of greatest danger on the right wing."

The Burgundian sneered back. "If you lead us into a trap, there'll be no time to form a line of battle."

"The Huns still outnumber us, don't forget," Majorian said. "We cannot afford to take more casualties."

Euric grinned. "But Attila doesn't trust his confederates any more. And they know he isn't invincible."

Ricimer, the German mercenary, stirred himself. He spoke Latin with a strong German accent. "We seem to have the strategic advantage," he said.

"What's that you say?" the Burgundian commander said.

"Attila is now reacting to our moves, rather than the other way round," Majorian said.

"Ah, yes. I see."

Aetius had been enjoying this squabble but now he intervened. "I intend to use my light cavalry to scout ahead. God willing, they will scent out any traps," he said.

The Burgundian king accepted this. "Very well. Lord Aetius, I promise that I will accompany you with my very best men."

Aetius turned to each leader in turn. All of them agreed to accompany Aetius east. Aetius raised his cup. "Thank you, gentlemen. To our success!"

The kings and warlords drank one toast after another. Finally, they said their farewells and departed back to their own camps. Aetius, without raising his voice, told his imperial officers to stay behind. Majorian, with a show of reluctance, sank back into his seat.

The assembled officers looked weary rather than exuberant. They all knew there would be more fighting ahead.

Aetius, a trained orator, began. "Gentlemen, I congratulate you all on your achievements over the last few days. It is now clear that we have rescued the empire – and your homes - from the gravest danger it has ever faced. But we must now plan for the future. I want to make sure that the Huns do not threaten the empire again."

"Attila has suffered an embarrassing failure," Ricimer said. "But his army is as dangerous as ever. If we attempted to destroy them, they would inflict heavy casualties upon us."

"The price would be worth paying, sir, if our homes were made safe from the Huns," a cavalry officer said.

One after another, all the other officers agreed. Magnus judged that there was nothing sycophantic about this. They genuinely wanted to exploit their success and destroy a dangerous menace.

"Thank you, gentlemen. Lord Majorian, do you agree?" Aetius said.

"In my opinion, the risk is too great. We need to keep our army intact for the next crisis."

"And what crisis might that be?" Aetius asked.

"The Visigoths are growing more arrogant. Their leaders insult me! With Attila humiliated, the Visigoths are now the greatest threat to the empire. It would be better to let the Huns go."

"No," Aetius said. "We must concentrate on today's enemy, not dream about imaginary problems in the future."

"If we try to destroy the Huns, our casualties will be high," Majorian said. "Of course, mercenaries are expendable. But we'll have to move cautiously."

Aetius smiled. "Move cautiously? Yes, I agree." He looked round at the assembled officers. "Thank you for your support, gentlemen."

The meeting began to break up. Majorian pushed back his chair and stalked out. Ricimer said something about muster rolls and left. Other officers gave similar excuses and drifted away. Magnus was among the last to leave.

"Ah, Magnus," Aetius said. "I hear that I should congratulate you on your promotion, commander."

How did he know? "Thank you, sir. But I believe that my brother-officers chose me for all the wrong reasons."

Aetius smiled. "You're a trifle young for the post, perhaps. But I'm sure that you'll do well enough."

"Thank you, sir."

"Magnus, we must ensure that Attila does not surprise us. You told me once that your aviators could only help if the enemy moved east or south."

"Yes, my lord. That territory is suitable for flyers."

"I think that Attila knows that. So he'll take his men north-east towards Mainz. I want your fly boys to find out if I'm right."

"Very well, sir. I'll send them a request to start searching."

Aetius smiled. "Of course, Attila could try to outguess us and take his men due south. Towards the capital."

"Yes, sir. But if he tries that, I promise the aviators will give us fair warning."

Aetius seemed to tire of the subject. "There's no need to be so formal. Sit down, man! Here, have a drink with me."

"Thank you, sir."

While a servant hurried to pour out the wine, Aetius asked about the political position in Britain. Magnus decided that Aetius was drinking too much.

"Magnus, the allied army could probably destroy the Huns. But is Lord Majorian right? Should we let them go?"

"But why, sir?"

Aetius looked down at his wine cup. "I'll tell you, Magnus. You're a gentleman, I can confide in you. I really wonder whether I ought to keep the Huns intact in case I want to recruit them against the Visigoths later."

"No, sir." For Magnus, the answer was brutally simple. "The Huns are the greater threat."

Aetius gestured, and the servant refilled his wine cup. Aetius half-emptied it in one gulp. "Yes … It's a pity they can't both lose."

Aetius took another gulp. "Yes … The next battle could destroy the Imperial army. Safer to let the Huns escape."

Magnus took a sip of his own wine for the sake of appearances. He understood Aetius's dilemma. If there was another battle, with heavy losses, the whole balance of power in Gaul could change.

Aetius drained his cup. "If I decide to move against the Huns, should I take my professional soldiers? Or should I take the militia? What if the Franks decided to attack our cities while I'm away?"

Magnus felt completely out of his depth. Aetius had probably been considering this issue for months. How could a junior officer come up with an answer in an instant? How could he provide an intelligent answer to a man who could see every side of a problem?

"Might I suggest, sir, that you should take contingents from as many sources as possible? Ensure that the Visigoths send their best men. And the Italian expeditionary force."

Aetius considered this. "An interesting compromise."

"Britain can spare these troops for a year or two, but your Gaulish auxiliaries are needed on the frontier."

"Keeping an eye on the Franks?" Aetius stared at his empty wine cup. "Yes. And, and, take as many barbarians as I can. That way, whoever lost, the empire would lose an enemy."

Then Majorian returned, his long military cloak flowing around him. "Lord Aetius? I would like a word with you. Concerning your strategy."

"You mean the march against the Huns? Certainly."

Majorian glared at Magnus. "In private, Lord Aetius, if you please."

"Of course, my lord," Magnus said. He escaped from the farmhouse, wondering whether anything would come of the conversation. Of course, in the morning, Aetius might not even remember the conversation.

Chapter 8: Reinforcements

Northern Gaul, September

The farmhouse contained a small inner courtyard that provided shelter from the harsh winds. Magnus dragged a chair out from the kitchen, sat on it with one boot up on the table and rocked it onto its rear legs. From there, he could see through the doorway to the farmyard. For the time being he was free of duties.

The sun shone pleasantly through the branches of the aromatic cedar, casting a dappled shade on to the ground beneath. A gentle breeze fluttered through the courtyard and the birds twittered in the branches of the trees. The old buildings were coated with ivy, which rustled in the wind. Alas, the courtyard had been neglected. A dusting of moss had crept up the legs of the chairs, the surface of the table had acquired a crust of bird droppings and the grass had not been mown for weeks.

He heard horses on the farm track, not one or two but a whole troop. They stopped and Magnus wondered what would happen next. Trouble for someone.

The officer's patrician tones reached Magnus clearly. "You! Where can I find the Numerus Britannica?"

"What's that, sir?" the sentry asked, startled. He was from the western tribes.

The officer raised his voice. "I have brought fifty cavalrymen to join the Numerus Britannica. I have to report to my commander. Now where do I find him, you fool?"

"Over there, sir." Magnus could imagine the sentry pointing. Magnus sighed and swung his feet to the ground.

A moment later the young officer strode into the inner courtyard.

Magnus stood and stepped forward. "I'm Magnus Vitalinus, commander of the Numerus. And you are?"

The officer turned to face him. He was a thin, wiry, self-assured young man. Younger, indeed, than Magnus. For a moment, he glared at this interruption. Then he straightened to attention. "Julian Aurelianus reporting to the Numerus Britannica, sir. The people at the gate told me I should report to you."

"Aurelianus?" Magnus suddenly recognised the newcomer. He had known Julian from his days on the Governor's bodyguard. He was the third son of the wealthiest man in Britain, and the younger brother of Claudia Aurelianus.

"I've brought fifty light cavalry with me, sir," Aurelianus reported.

"Welcome to Gaul, Julian," he said, uncomfortable. He wondered why the well-connected Julian had volunteered for overseas service. A comfortable role on the Governor's bodyguard had suited him perfectly. "You'd better see to your men first of all. There's plenty of room, after all. You can use those stables east of the main courtyard. And your men can use the building beyond it as their barracks. After that, report back here. I'll introduce you to the camp commander after you've had a bath."

"There's no need to wait, surely? My second-in-command can cope with the chores." Julian turned. "Cynon!"

The man jogged into the courtyard. "Sir?"

"You heard the commander. See that the horses are properly cared for, then take the men to that building beyond the stables."

"Yes, sir."

Magnus was irritated by Julian's high-handed attitude, but there was nothing he could do. He led his new subordinate to the officers' quarters on the far side of the farmyard. The place was stuffy and badly lit.

"Take a seat, Julian. Would you like some wine? But I warn you. Cheap Gaulish wine is just as bad as British wine."

Julian sat in a wicker chair. "Thank you, Magnus. I hear that you're to be congratulated on your promotion." He sounded resentful.

He grimaced. "Dead men's shoes. I survived and Fullofaudes didn't." He paused. "Here, take a glass."

"Ah – thank you. You were never so modest back home, Magnus. Is the responsibility of command getting you down? You achieved great success in leading the Numerus Britannica in battle."

"The men know what to do, and so do the squadron commanders. My main problem is dealing with the Magister Militum. That's why the other commanders were so eager to step aside."

Julian was suddenly very serious. "And what's Aetius like? Is he as clever and sophisticated as they say?"

"Oh, yes. He could convince himself that a dice had eight sides."

Julian considered this. "And how do you cope with him?"

"Well enough," he admitted. "Aetius puts great store in my aristocratic background. My grandfather had almost as much land as him. And it helps that my father made me go to school, so I can look knowledgeable when Aetius quotes the classics. But what's been happening back in Britain?"

"Oh, the frontiers are quiet. Your great-uncle is ailing. Irish pirates are raiding the west coast." He hesitated. "In my family, I have very bad news for you, I'm afraid. My sister Claudia was married to Ambrosius last month."

"I know about that," Magnus growled.

Magnus had first met Claudia Aurelianus when she had visited London with her father. He had hoped to marry her, but her parents had decided otherwise. Despite his aristocratic relatives, her parents and the rest of her family had not been impressed. Her parents had arranged a marriage into the Ambrosius family instead, to a landowner much older than herself.

"Julian, did I make the wrong decision? If I had gone back home, with my prize money, would the Aurelianus family have accepted me?"

Julian shook his head. "I'm afraid not. The marriage negotiations were already under way a year ago. Nothing you could have done would have stopped that."

"No, I suppose not." He poured more wine into their glasses.

Julian sat back in his wicker chair. "Thank you. Aetius' call for reinforcements has changed things among the auxiliary troops. All the warriors in the tribal lands are eager to qualify for overseas service and earn the emperor's gold. That's made them easier to handle for the time being."

"The emperor can't afford to hire more than five hundred British troops. I expect we'll need, oh, fifty replacements a year."

Julian shrugged. "They know that. It just makes the competition more fierce." He drank some wine. "But enough talk of me and Britain, Magnus. What's happening at the heart of the empire?"

Magnus hesitated. What was the best way to say this? "One thing, Julian. When we're on duty, you will address me as 'sir' or 'commander'."

Julian glowered his resentment.

Magnus smiled thinly. "D'you remember what we were told when we joined up? We salute the officer's uniform, not the fool who's wearing it. Off duty, we're messmates. On duty, I'm the commander. Anything else would imperil discipline."

"Very well. I'll remember. Sir."

"Right. I'll show you the way to the bath-house."

That evening, at dinner, Magnus introduced Aurelianus to the other British officers. The English-speaking officers were impressed by his aristocratic connections, but the British Alban was not.

Julian was younger than Magnus, but far more ambitious. After his third cup of wine, he told them that he wanted to win promotion to the emperor's bodyguard. "I expect my family connections to win me promotion, just as soon as I've completed my term with the expeditionary force."

Alban, farther down the table, watched this and sneered. He leaned closer to Magnus. "He's a cocky young bastard," he said. "And not half as tough as he thinks he is." It was clear that he detested the new arrival.

"Oh, dear," Magnus said. "Am I as bad as he is?"

Alban was surprised. "Good heavens no, sir. Your men like you. You never said you were going to use your father's influence to gain promotion."

"No, I'm afraid my father doesn't have that sort of influence. And even if he did, he'd tell me I'd have to earn it."

*   *   *

Three days later, Magnus and his troop were riding along a farm track through gently rolling countryside. The sky had clouded over again, a threat of rain later. As they made their way east, the trees closed in on both sides. The track was narrow and twisted and turned among the trees, so it was impossible to see far ahead. The undergrowth made an ambush all too possible.

Over the last few days, Magnus and his troopers had been constantly in action. They were doing their best to harass and disrupt the barbarian foraging parties. The Huns, who had been used to leisurely pauses while they looted everything they found, were instead forced to remain on the defensive.

According to reports from other scouting parties the Huns were supposed to be taking a parallel road, farther south, but nobody in the British troop trusted that.

The role of point man was deeply unpopular, so Magnus changed the men round every few minutes. Leaders were not supposed to risk themselves in the advance guard, but he ignored that and took his turn with the rest of his men.

Then an excited scout brought back news. "Careful, sir, the sergeant sent me to say there's open farmland just ahead. Not just a village, a proper farm."

Magnus grimaced. "Let's take a look."

They made their way to the edge of the cleared ground and joined up with sergeant Madog. All of them kept within the cover of the trees. A quarter of a mile away was a cluster of farm buildings. They had square walls and tiled roofs, marks of prosperity. It all looked harmless enough.

"Look!" Madog said. Approaching the farm from the right were a dozen barbarian horsemen. Each rider was leading a spare horse. Scouts or foragers, Magnus guessed, looking for meat on the hoof and any portable valuables.

The riders and their horses looked tired. All of the men were wearing knee-length caftans. Two, perhaps leaders, were wearing scale armour. Four men were wearing iron helmets instead of fur caps.

"Huns. Twelve of them," Madog said. "Twenty of us - and they haven't noticed us yet. Should be easy."

"Yes, but are there only twelve of them?" Magnus asked irritably. "What if there are a dozen more in the barn?"

His men grumbled at this caution. Against his better judgement, he ordered his men to advance. As soon as they were clear of the trees, Magnus knew that any hope of surprise was lost.

"Spread out, spread out! Come on, move it!"

As they advanced across the field, one of the Huns shouted a warning. The barbarians were suddenly wide awake.

Magnus expected the Huns to run for it. After all, their most famous tactic was a pretended retreat followed by a counter-charge.

But they decided to make a stand. Perhaps they were contemptuous of this troop of light cavalry. Magnus, feeling he had no other option, pulled his sword from its scabbard.

"Charge!" He urged his horse into a gallop. The results surprised everyone.

Magnus was worried about his horse's footing and anxious about staying in the saddle. He rode straight at a warrior wearing scale armour and attempted to cut him down.

He felt the shock up his arm as the blow landed. Then he saw another barbarian coming at him. He managed to parry the man's blow, but then the force of the charge carried him right through the melee.

He reined in and turned back, but found that all the Huns were cut down. Three horses bolted, riderless.

Everything slowed down. He became aware that his sword arm was strained. That the sweat down his back was cooling.

Magnus's men dismounted and began checking. One of the Huns tried to get to his feet. A sword sliced down, and he was still. One of Magnus's men was already rounding up the spare horses.

"Check the farm buildings," Magnus said.

"I don't believe it!" Madog said. "Two dozen Hun ponies! Two sets of mail armour. And for no loss!"

"Two wounded," Magnus growled. Pyll had taken a cut in his sword-arm, above the elbow, and Ieuan had a deep cut in his thigh.

"A small price to pay, sir."

The farm hands were frightened but unharmed and eager to show their gratitude for their rescue. Magnus's troopers stripped the dead, arranged for Ieuan to be tended at the farmhouse, and brought their loot back to camp.

The next day, Magnus inspected his troop's horses. Although the men of his troop were staying in the camp today there was lots to do. According to rumours, Aetius intended to cross the river when the infantry caught up. Until then, the British cavalry had the task of guarding the army's left flank.

Magnus had not quite completed his task when Aurelianus' second-in-command, a man from the western tribes named Cynon, led his men towards the picket lines. Magnus turned to watch them ride up. He thought it was typical of Aurelianus to delegate chores like this to a subordinate.

Cynon recognised him, dismounted, and led his horse over to him. His face was drawn. "Sir, I have to report that we've lost Aurelianus. He was cut down at a ford across a river."

"Good God. How did it happen?"

"We were scouting ahead, sir. The usual thing, but he led us a bit further than usual. Hoping to find some news that would please the general."

"I see, yes, go on."

"It was open ground, farmland. Then we encountered a Hun foraging party. Looters, scavengers. Less than fifty. But Aurelianus told us he wanted the exact number, so he could report to Aetius. But we went too close and the Huns charged at us." He stopped, clearly nervous.

"Yes, and then?" Magnus said.

"Aurelianus told us to get the news back. He told us to run for it. I got the archers across the river, to give the rest of us covering." He paused and rubbed his face.

"You know what the rivers here are like, sir. Rocks and boulders underfoot. Aurelianus should have led his horse across. But he tried to ride, too proud to get his boots dirty, and his horse went down, and he fell heavily. Aurelianus was all right, but instead of running for it he tried to get his horse on its feet."

Magnus nodded. Aurelianus had spent most of his savings on that horse.

"Then the Huns caught up with us. My archers kept them at a distance, but Aurelianus was within range, closer, a perfect target. By the time he realised he was in danger, it was too late. They filled him with arrows."

Magnus tried to think. What should a commander say? "You got your men back, then."

Cynon nodded. "The Huns soon tired of the sport."

"I see. How many of them were there?"

"Fifty-three when we first saw them. Forty-eight after the skirmish at the river. Besides Aurelianus, we had two wounded."

He made a note. "Right. I'll tell Aetius." He hesitated. "You did well to get your men back."

Cynon looked relieved. "Thank you, sir."

Aurelianus's death was the talk of the Numerus Britannica that evening. He had not been a popular officer and very few mourned him.

"Good riddance," Alban said, just loud enough for Magnus to hear. "Pity about the horse, though."

Later that evening Conwyn, his groom, brought Magnus a different problem. "Excuse me, sir. I've come about Aurelianus. His servant, I mean."

"His groom had better stay with Cynon. He'll need those horses now."

"Yes, sir. But Aurelianus's body servant begged me to help him out. He wants me to ask you to take him on. He's terrified of being cast adrift in a strange land."

"Why didn't he ask me himself?"

"He's too scared, sir."

"What makes you think I need a body servant, Conwyn?" But Conwyn merely grinned.

"I can't afford it," Magnus said. "I can barely afford your wages. You know that."

Conwyn did not give up. "The fellow's prepared to work for nothing. Or so he says."

"As bad as that? Is there nobody in the army who can afford to take him on?"

"No-one he can get an introduction to. Perhaps he's hoping that if he works for you, he'll meet someone."

"Can he cook?"

"Better than me, sir."

"Well, in that case . . . we can feed him, I suppose."

Conwyn grinned. "Yes, sir."

*   *   *

Ambrosius family villa, Britain

Claudia Ambrosius was sitting on a couch in the villa's morning room, staring out over the orchard. The day was warm and airless. She would have preferred to be doing something energetic, but her husband disapproved of what he termed unseemly behaviour.

She remembered her mother saying that no matter how unhappy her marriage might be, she would have her house to run and her children to console her. She had found that running the household was an interesting challenge. Her husband gave her an inadequate budget and very little authority.

Claudia returned to her task of preparing a list of the things to buy on her next visit to London. She looked up as Ambrosius walked slowly into the room. Some men aged well, but he did not. He preferred beer to wine, and drank far too much of it.

He stopped and peered down at her. "A messenger called. He had a letter, addressed to you, sent by someone called Magnus. He says your brother Julian is dead."

"God rest his soul," she said automatically. "But –you opened it?"

"Of course," he said casually.

She suppressed her anger. "May I read it, my lord?"

He hesitated. "Very well."

The letter was concise.

Magnus Vitalinus, Commander of the Numerus Britannicus, writing from Gaul, to Lady Claudia Ambrosius, greetings.

My lady, it is with great regret that I must inform you of the death of your brother Julian. I assure you that Julian fought well in the campaign to save Gaul from the Huns and that he died honourably in battle.

When the Huns abandoned Cenabium and turned against us, we fought a great battle. The Huns suffered a defeat and retreated eastwards. The Magister Militum led the army after them, to ensure that the barbarians did not attack another city.

Your brother's noble sacrifice, scouting ahead of the army, allowed the Magister Militum to locate the barbarians. By the time you receive this, a battle may have been fought.

I would be grateful if you could inform my father that I am in good health.

Your obedient servant, Magnus V.

Claudia read the brief note with a pang of regret. She and Julian had never been fond of each other.

Ambrosius was suspicious and jealous. "Who is this Magnus fellow? Did you know him?"

She tried to concentrate on a suitable answer. "He was on the governor's bodyguard. A great-nephew of Vitalinus, but quite penniless. He and Julian served together. He left for Gaul before I was married."

She hesitated. "We ought to send a copy of this to my father. And your other allies. They'll want to know."

"Why?"

She suppressed her impatience. "This battle affects the whole empire. Yes, Constantinople as well as Rome and Vienne. My father heads an important political faction. He'll want to be aware of these changes."

"You exaggerate, surely? Why should I send a courier across the province? Read that to me again."

Patiently, she did so. Ambrosius thought this over. "Yes, you're right. Send the letter to my father-in-law."

She was reluctant to lose the letter. Instead of sending it, she copied it out. She would not have attempted that small defiance a year ago.

She was right about the letter's importance. A week later, her father rode over with a couple of his cronies, cousins of hers. Her husband was feeling a bit better and received his guests sitting in a cushioned chair in the villa's morning room.

Her father was a bit slimmer than her husband and a lot smarter. He was dressed for travelling, in a grey tunic and brigga. He shrugged off his heavy blue riding cloak as he strode into the room.

Her husband was abrupt with his guests, forgetting the usual formal greetings. Claudia remembered her duty as lady of the house, and courteously asked her guests whether they wanted any refreshments.

"Yes, of course, but not just yet, my girl," her father said irritably. He waved the copy of Magnus's letter at Ambrosius. "This is terrible. A battle against the Huns. And another expected. Why didn't that fool Aetius let them escape across the Rhine?"

"Any surprises could wreck our efforts at the Council meeting this autumn, uncle," one of her young cousins said.

"Yes, I know," her father said. "You say the letter was delivered by the messenger service? How the hell did he manage that?"

She broke the silence. "You and Ambrosius are both senators, and the governor's advisers. You regularly receive official dispatches. Magnus could have told the messengers that it contained vital military information."

Her father snorted. "So it does, but not in the way you mean. It's about the war, and it's vital to my strategy."

"But why did this fellow Magnus write to you?" her husband asked.

"Well - I think he wants his father to know he is well. But his father isn't on the list of official recipients. You are."

"Then why not write to his great-uncle Vitalinus, ask him to forward the letter?"

Her father intervened. "Because old man Vitalinus is as stingy as he is sour. Young Magnus obviously thought you were a soft touch, eh, girl?"

"Yes, father." She repressed the thought that Magnus might have written to her for her own sake.

"Daughter, I want this fellow Magnus to write to us again. Tell us what's happening now. The new governor refuses to tell me anything, afraid of being accused of favouritism. Folly."

Her husband glanced at her. "This Magnus fellow won't do that for us," he said sourly.

Father grunted. He unfolded the letter and read it again. "He says that Cenabium is saved. I wish he'd written more."

He turned to her. "Girl, I want you to write to this fellow. Thank him for his letter. Say anything you like. Ask him to write again. Ask him to tell us what's going on."

"Yes, father."

"And let me see it before you send it." He turned to her husband. "When are you going to London, Ambrosius? We need your vote at the meetings of the Council."

"I'm not sure that I can make it, Aurelianus."

Father did not like that at all. "If we're going to be a man short, it's even more important that we're forewarned of any surprises."

Chapter 9: Correspondence

Northern Gaul

Magnus watched as the cavalry trooper hammered in a couple of tent pegs. The half dozen British cavalrymen were standing just out of bowshot range of the enemy camp.

The sound of the mallet striking the wooden pegs sounded like thunder in the quiet evening. Another trooper, holding the reins of their horses, watched with interest. The man with the mallet was satisfied at last and began the task of stretching a picket line between the pegs. The line, not by coincidence, pointed to the gate of the Huns' camp.

"This is folly," Alban said. "Any closer and we'll be within effective range." Stress had driven away any hint of deference.

Magnus did not blame him. This whole approach to the enemy camp had been nerve-racking. Every hundred paces, or every time the path turned, they had hammered in a couple of pegs. The watching Huns must have thought they were crazy.

Over the past week there had been no pitched battles, but the British light cavalry had found constant action. Magnus and his troopers continued to harass the enemy foraging parties.

What had started as a careful withdrawal by the Huns began to look like a retreat. Aetius was careful not to take any risks, but in a series of clever moves he forced the Huns back to Metz.

The Huns were getting more cautious. Magnus had reported to Aetius that their foraging parties were now larger, they avoided ambushes and, as a result, their foragers were a lot less efficient.

Aetius had been delighted at the news. The Huns could only rob ten farms instead of a hundred. But Magnus was not happy at all.

The wounded trooper Ieuan had sent word that his thigh wound was healing. The surgeon said he would be able to ride again soon. But Pyll's cut in his sword-arm, apparently so minor, had turned gangrenous. The only thing that would save his life was amputation, but he refused.

Aetius was not satisfied at the army's progress. He had ordered this crazy stunt.

Magnus turned back to watch the Huns setting up camp for the night. Fires were being lit and they had set up a crude barricade. Magnus was close enough to see curious faces turned towards them. Most of them wore felt caps and leather caftans fastened at the collar. None bothered with armour.

"Which is the strongest part of their perimeter?" he asked. "Remember to point. We've got to look like a normal scouting party."

Alban pointed theatrically. "The brush is piled highest there."

"And the weakest?"

"The gate. But they'll guard that." He pointed again. "The fence is lowest there."

"Good. We'll try and get closer to that stretch."

"This isn't going to work. Only fools would set out picket lines here. The bastards have got to guess why we're planting them."

"Never mind that. Can you find your way back here in the dark?"

"Well – probably."

"Good. That's all that matters."

"Sir!" The trooper with the mallet shouted. "The devils are coming to get us!"

Magnus looked around. The brushwood that had been blocking the gateway had been pulled aside and a troop of wild Hun cavalry streamed out.

Magnus grabbed the reins of his horse. "Right. Run for it, lads!"

In a well-practised scramble, they jumped on their horses and galloped off. The picket lines, of course, were abandoned. The British troopers were riding light and their horses had been rested, but it was a close run. The Huns kept up the chase all the way back to the allied camp.

Magnus turned in his saddle to watch the Huns ride away. Grinning, he slid to the ground and patted his horse's neck to soothe it. "Have you got the rest of the tent pegs? Good. Rest the horses, then we'll do the same for the camp of the Ostrogoths. Let's hope they'll be less fiery."

*   *   *

The barbarian camp was a sea of confusion. One campfire had been doused with water, sending smoke billowing. Women ran screaming. Horses pulled free of their picket lines and bolted.

Euric, war leader of the Visigoths, took a moment to glance around. The planning, at least, had gone perfectly, he thought. They had decided upon a night attack and had managed to achieve complete surprise. They had broken into the Huns' main encampment and for a few precious minutes had managed to slaughter the Huns while they still slept. But that golden moment was over. Now the Huns were awake, armed, and fighting back.

Euric had demanded the place of honour for his men, the attack on the Huns themselves. They wanted to avenge their dead king. Aetius had agreed readily. Perhaps too readily, Euric thought. Everyone knew that Aetius was devious and suspicious of the Visigoths. Had that trickster planned some treachery?

Euric glared under the rim of his helmet. They had to break through! One more thrust and the desperate resistance of the Huns would crumble, he and his men would break through to the hostages and free them. Attila would lose a whole year's profits and, more important, the respect of his followers.

But if the barbarians held their line . . . if they held, he knew that in a few more minutes the Ostrogoths would realise that the assaults on their perimeter were no more than a diversion by the Romans, that the real attack was here, and they would come to the aid of their masters.

And then it would be the Visigoths who were caught. The whole future of the war had now narrowed down to this yelling, clanging tumult, maybe one hundred men on each side, as the champions of the Allied army and the last hard core of Attila's personal forces fought it out. He and his men struggled to break into the central square of Attila's tents, their opponents standing poised and confident among the tangle of their guy-ropes, bracing themselves to hold out for five minutes more after the unimaginable shock of the Visigothic assault.

And the pagans were doing it too. Euric's hand tensed on the bloody sword-hilt and he swayed as if to move forward. Instantly the brawny shadows on either side of him, the captains of his bodyguard, edged slightly forward, blocking him in with their shields and bodies. They would not let him throw himself into the melee. As soon as the initial slaughter of sleeping men had stopped and the fight had begun, they had been in front of him.

"Easy, my lord," muttered the captain. "We'll get through these bastards yet."

As he spoke the battle surged in front of them, first a few feet forward as a Hun went down and the Visigoths rushed at the momentary gap, then a step back. Above the helmets and the raised shields, a long cavalry sword whirled, to a crash of steel on mail. In the dark, Euric saw a figure jump up on some platform and twirl the sword in one hand like a toy, daring the Visigoths to come on. They did, fiercely, and all Euric could see was straining backs.

"We must have killed a thousand of the bastards already," the bodyguard on his other hand muttered. In a moment, Euric knew, one or the other of them would say "Time to get out of here, my lord," and he would be hustled away. If they could get away.

One break, Euric prayed. Almighty God eternal, one break in this line and we will be through and attacking them from all sides. The war will be over, and the pagans destroyed. Attila, even if he escapes, will be broken. No more hostages taken, no more cities pillaged and burnt to the ground. The Visigoths would recover their position as the most powerful nation in Gaul, his own power would be assured, and Aetius would be his grateful servant. But if they stood another minute, long enough for a mower to whet a scythe . . . then it is we who will break, and it will be me whose career will be broken. If he could get away.

*   *   *

144

Magnus strained to see into the darkness and listened to the clamour in the enemy camp. What was going on in there? He felt very vulnerable in the dark, despite his men around him. Earlier this evening he had reconnoitered the approaches to the camp, then after nightfall he had led the main army here. He and his men had taken part in the initial mad rush, the grim slaughter of sleeping men, then Aetius had told him to withdraw to the perimeter, to guard his line of retreat. But if the Ostrogoths attacked, what could his three hundred men do against ten times that number?

He started. Some figures were running out of the dark towards them. From the direction of the enemy camp.

His men saw them too. "To arms! To arms! They're attacking!" the voice held a twinge of panic.

"Steady, boys, steady," Alban said.

"We outnumber them," Magnus said. He switched to Latin to make the traditional challenge. "Halt! Who goes there? Halt! Don't any of you speak Latin?"

The running figures stopped, no more than shadows in the dark, vague and threatening. Then a man stepped forward. His clothes were filthy but had been made from good broadcloth. "Yes, I do. We all do." He held up his wrists to show his manacles. "We escaped from the Huns."

Magnus realized the attack had achieved one of its objectives at least. These slaves made up almost half of Attila's captured wealth. "So Euric reached you, then. How is his attack going?"

The man shook his head. "All I know is that our guards vanished. So we took the chance to break free."

More and more figures were appearing out of the darkness. Magnus turned to Alban. "Get these people away from here. Escort them back to our camp. Let them set up their own camp for the night, downstream of ours. We can decide what to do with them in the morning."

Alban nodded. "Yes, sir. Do you want me to strike off their shackles?"

"If you can find a blacksmith in this confusion, yes. If not – that, too, can wait 'til morning." He thrust aside the thought that some of these wretches might have been the slaves of patrician masters before the Huns captured them. They deserved their freedom after this.

The last of the hostages vanished in the direction of the allied camp and Magnus turned back to the clamour of the unseen battle. What was going on in there?

* * *

Neither side broke. Instead, the Huns gave way, step by step, as if luring their opponents into a trap. Step by step, the Visigoths followed. They fought their way through to the slave-pens, to find them empty.

Had they had seized the opportunity to make a break for freedom? Euric prayed they had run for the edge of the camp and not towards the centre. Well, in this chaos, there was no way to find out.

The Huns sullenly gave way, never allowing their shield-wall to break. Surely now his captain would say, "Time to go, my lord." But he did not. Euric realised that if Attila's lackeys the Ostrogoths arrived now, he and his men would be trapped. Attila's disaster would be turned into a modest victory. Where were the Ostrogoths? Why were they so late arriving? They must have heard the clamour of his attack. They weren't incompetent.

Euric and his men fought their way forward to a large tent. One side of the tent had collapsed, and it made hazardous footing. More than one pagan who tripped as he withdrew never got up again. The remainder of the tent collapsed, and the fighting flowed around it. Euric could make out silk cushions and rich woollen carpets. Someone must have smashed a scent bottle, for a rich honeyed perfume hung over everything.

Euric had heard enough lurid tales about Attila's tent to be able to recognise it, even in the dark. But the place seemed empty. No hostages to rescue, then.

What to do now?

Euric came to a decision. "Time to get out of here. Give the signal to withdraw."

His captain was shocked. "My lord! We have a chance to kill that demon Attila himself!"

Euric tried to force himself to think. "Captain, I've already achieved more than I dared hope for. If we withdraw now, Attila will know that we can attack him again, any time we choose. Fear of him will be gone. That fear's been worth more than a thousand men to him. But if we linger too long and are trapped, we lose all that." And Attila's barbarian allies would not dare challenge their master. But he kept that thought to himself.

The captain stared at him in the uncertain light. He looked unconvinced.

Euric tried again. "Captain, we must escape from this cleanly or we lose everything. I want all of Christendom to remember that Attila ran from us in his shift, not that he cut us down to the last man."

The captain grinned behind his beard. "Very well, my lord." He turned to the trumpeter. "Sound the signal."

The horn brayed its message. Euric prayed that his men would recognise the signal - and obey it.

The withdrawal went smoothly, or as smoothly as things went in a night battle. Nobody stayed to linger or broke and ran. These were good men, Euric thought, the best in the army.

The Huns pressed forward as the Visigoths withdrew, of course, but they were cautious about it. None of them wanted to be the last man killed in this battle. And the Ostrogoths had still not arrived to help their master. Perhaps Aetius and his Romans had fought like men after all.

Once clear of the enemy camp, he found young Magnus and his British cavalry waiting to cover their withdrawal. They, too, had followed their orders. And their leader kept a clear head. A good man, that, Euric thought.

*   *   *

Magnus was very surprised when he received a message from the lady Claudia. The boy's father had not bothered to reply at all. He read the letter with interest.

Claudia Ambrosius to Magnus Vitalinus, commander of the Numerus Britannica, greetings. I thank you for your letter. It was very kind of you to write to me. The Aurelianus family shares your grief at my brother's death, but it is a comfort to know that he died honourably in the emperor's service. Please write to me about the situation in Gaul. Has there been a battle? Did the cities suffer terribly from the Huns?

Your father and the rest of his household are well. Farewell, commander. I hope you prosper, and I salute you. Claudia A.

The main part of the letter was written in an elegant script, presumably by her husband's secretary. She had probably added that last line herself.

He wondered how she had managed it. Why had her husband permitted it? Did he know whom she was writing to? Did he care? Perhaps she had not told him. Or perhaps he was the one interested in the situation in Gaul.

He was disappointed by how short the letter was. Then he reminded himself that sending a letter across the empire would cost a fortune. She would have to keep it short. He read it again. Claudia had managed to say a lot in a few words. He noted that she had asked him to describe the political situation, but he could not afford long letters either. He decided to send a reply, even if he had to borrow the money to pay for it. An interesting challenge.

He drafted a cautious reply, explaining the political situation, carefully phrased on the assumption that her husband would read it too.

*   *   *

Britain, Mid-September

Claudia had to wear a mantle over her dress for her walks around the garden now. The days were drawing in. The autumn equinox would soon be upon them, and her husband wanted to go to London to attend the council meetings. He could have hired a house, or some rooms at an inn, but that would have cost him money, so they were going to stay at her Uncle Gaius's town house. No doubt her parents would be there too.

She sighed. She had thought that one advantage of marriage was that she would run her own household, but she was returning to her mother's tutelage once again. It would have been simpler for her to stay here on the farm, but Ambrosius did not trust her out of his sight.

These unhappy thoughts were interrupted when Ambrosius walked into the garden. "A courier brought this from Corinium. Another letter from that fellow Magnus. Read it, woman."

"Very well, my lord." She broke the seal.

Magnus Vitalinus, Commander of the Numerus Britannicus, writing from the messenger station at Argentorate in Gaul, to Lady Claudia, greetings.

My lady, you asked me to let you know of any developments here in Gaul. We have fought a great battle and defeated the Huns. In the days that followed the battle, the Huns withdrew eastwards. The Magister Militum and his allies followed them up. However, the Huns have now retreated across the Rhine and the allied forces are reluctant to advance any further. They have saved their farms and feel that no further sacrifice is necessary.

The Magister Militum has reluctantly accepted this. We expect to go to winter quarters shortly. I would be grateful if you could inform my father that I am in good health.

Your obedient servant, Magnus V.

Claudia glanced up. "Do – do you want me to write back?" That would be the biggest challenge in her boring routine.

"No, why? He says the Huns are in retreat. The war's over. Why waste money on sending another letter across the continent?"

Claudia believed that her father would think differently, but there was no point in saying so. "My father would like to see it, though, my lord."

He thought this over. "Yes. Send it on."

*   *   *

Lyon, Mid-September

The two-seater flying machine circled the city of Lyon, gently losing height. Magnus, in the front seat, was most impressed by the sight. The old part of the city was built on the steep sides of a hill overlooking the low-lying islands where the Saone joined the Rhone. At the foot of the hill, on the river bank, was the bishop's new cathedral. The city, though hundreds of miles from the sea, was actually a port, with the noisy dock area, as large as the upper city, occupying the islands between the two rivers.

The city lay halfway between the Visigoths to the south-west and the Franks to the north-east. Once, it had been the capital of the province of Lugdunensis, covering a quarter of Gaul. But those glory days were long gone.

Three major roads met here, one from Aquitaine, one from the Rhine, and one from Vienne to the south. The city was bigger than any in Britain, yet he knew that there were several other cities in Gaul of similar size.

The pilot took his machine north to the messenger station, turned into wind and began his final approach. He made a perfect touchdown and skidded to a standstill. The pilot kept his machine balanced on its central skid for a few moments before allowing the starboard wingtip to settle onto the grass.

Magnus climbed out onto the windswept hilltop and stretched his cramped muscles. "Showoff," he growled, but the pilot merely grinned.

The retrieval crew who came running across the field refused to let a guest share in the task of dragging the machine clear of the landing field.

"Thanks for the lift, aviator," Magnus said. "I've got to find Captain Commius." Magnus had a problem and he hoped that Captain Commius had the answer.

In the grandly-named administration building, Magnus asked for the captain. Lyon had been the senior base in the messenger corps during this campaign and Commius had worked miracles to keep network operating effectively.

But a new problem had arisen. Magnus thought Commius was the best man for the task, but Aetius despised the captain as a low-born commoner. The captain also lacked the self-confidence to stand up to Aetius. That made his job impossible.

Magnus found the mess hall was badly lit. The pilots and the ground crew were assembling for the evening meal and the room was filled with cheerful banter. Magnus detected rosemary and mutton. Commius was a southerner, tall, with black hair, intelligent, with a good education. The captain was usually a dapper man, but today the wind was cold, and he was dressed in a disreputable sheepskin jacket, muddy trousers, and a bright red scarf tucked into the collar of his tunic.

He recognised Magnus at once. "Welcome to Lyon, sir! Are the Huns still running?"

"Well - Captain Brennos at Argentorate says they're moving south-east past the Black Mountains." Magnus had flown a mission with Sergeant Brennos, determined to see for himself.

"That's good to hear," Commius said.

Magnus lowered his voice. "But Lord Aetius wants to take the army across the Rhine. The plan is that the Burgundians will occupy their old territory around Heidelberg and Aetius will take the territory between the Burgundians and the Alps. All of the old imperial territory."

Commius looked shocked. "That's crazy! We can't defend that territory. If the Huns turn back the army'll be crushed."

Magnus thought this was all too likely. "Perhaps. But Aetius thinks his men can hold the passes if reinforcements can reach them in time. And that's the reason I'm here. Aetius wants us to set up a series of messenger stations to back up the new garrisons."

Commius gaped at him. "We can't talk here. Come this way." He led the way to the captain's cramped quarters.

The captain paused to remove his scarf. "Take the chair, sir." He leaned against the wall. "Aetius must be crazy. If the Huns decide to invade again, we can't possibly stop them."

"I agree it's risky, captain, but Aetius seems determined to try. He thinks he's been given an opportunity and he's going to grab it with both hands. He wants everything north of the Alps and west of Lake Brigantinus. He's asked me whether the messengers could maintain contact with garrisons in the mountains. After all, Trier held out long enough for the army to reach them."

"Well ...if the Magister Militum thinks it's possible, I'm sure he has his reasons for it."

"You think so?" Most of the people at headquarters thought Aetius's policy was reckless, but few dared to say so.

"Well … if these new forts are built strongly enough, and if the messenger service can give warning, perhaps the new frontier can hold. That's a lot of maybes, sir."

"Yes, captain."

"Although the technical problems are basic enough. The mountains provide ideal conditions." Commius displayed a moment's enthusiasm. "But – the risk is too great. And the advantage is too small. You realise, sir, that territory is claimed by Rome?"

Magnus raised his eyebrows. "That territory has changed hands once a generation for the last two hundred years. If our two little empires hadn't wasted so much energy fighting over it, we might have kept the Huns out. But now Aetius sees an opportunity to seize it for Gaul once again."

The captain sat on a wooden storage chest. "I see. Well, we used to have stations in that area, until the Huns pushed us out. Our old hands will know."

"It's a relief to know that. Can you gather them here? We need to re-open those stations."

"But - no new posts have been set up for decades! Nobody knows how"

"Then we'll have to find out how to do it, captain."

The captain hesitated, wondering how to phrase a question. Magnus helped him out. "Lord Aetius wants me to supervise this change. He says that I'm an experienced commander, so he thinks I'll have no trouble organising these new posts."

He paused to see how Commius took this. "I don't agree, of course, captain. The messenger service is far more complicated than any cavalry troop."

The captain was scowling. "So, you're being put in authority over me? I serve the messenger service for eighteen years and as a reward I'm put under the command of a puppy who knows nothing about flying?"

Magnus decided to try flattery. "I know this is your task, Commius. You'll be doing all the work, you're good at it, and you should get the credit for it. But I'm not going to argue with Aetius."

The Captain's frown was replaced by a smile. "I can understand that, sir."

"So, we must recreate a whole messenger route."

Commius shrugged helplessly. "I admit that I don't know where to start, sir. I think it would be best to be cautious, check every detail. If I make any mistakes, Aetius would be unforgiving."

"No, no." Magnus knew that the captain was wrong. "I'm certain that Aetius would criticise inaction far more than an initiative that went wrong. I know damn well he will."

"I trust your judgement in that," Commius said. "But how are you going to organise this? How will you find the men?"

Magnus had already asked himself this question. How did you set up a messenger station? A whole chain of them?

If he did not know how a messenger station operated, he would have to find somebody who did. He would need to find experienced captains and skilled ground crew. But who would volunteer for such a task?

"There's Sergeant Dumnorix at Trier. He's competent. We could promote him, put him in command of a major base."

Commius was shocked. "Dumnorix is happy where he is, sir. He commands a tiny station at the far end of a messenger route. He's good, but he's too rough for a bigger station. He'll offend too many people. I'll be forced to take away his rank before six months have passed."

155

"I don't think I have any choice, captain. Lord Aetius said he wanted the garrisons in place – and the messenger service operating – before the snows blocked the high passes. That only gives me a couple of months."

"But - in the mountains, the first snows have already fallen. Didn't you know? Winter comes early in the mountains. Yes, and spring comes late."

"No, I didn't know that." Magnus realised he had only a few weeks. "Captain – don't you know any men ready for promotion? Vacancies must be rare. Surely you know someone waiting his turn. Or – men who have been turned down because they're not quite good enough."

"You can't be serious! We have plenty of men like that, sulking because they feel overlooked for promotion. Experienced aviators who think they can do anything. But they've no tact and no administrative skills. If a man like that was put in command of a post, his men would murder him before the year was out. And then I would get the blame. Every messenger station across Gaul has a troublemaker who thinks like that."

"Really, captain? I've decided that's what I'll have to do. I'll recruit those men."

The captain jerked upright. "That's crazy. Most of those troublemakers have a grudge against their superiors. They have no leadership skills at all. Give them authority and you'll have disaster."

"We must do something, captain. The Magister Militum expects it of us." He hesitated, then took the plunge. "I accept full responsibility for this. I'll make it clear that I'm acting against your advice."

The captain looked unhappy. "Very well, yes, sir. I'll give you their names."

"Thank you, captain. That leaves the problem of finding suitable sites for new stations. A survey could take months."

"Oh, that's the easy part, sir," Commius said. "There used to be a string of messenger stations along the northern edge of the Alps. They had to be abandoned, two decades ago, when the Huns first appeared. They were designed to link up the frontier garrisons." He bit his lip.

"Acco might know where they are. He was supposed to leave for the north this morning, but his machine needed some work on it. He'll be in the mess."

"Very well. Let's go to dinner. Then we can talk to Acco."

After the dinner plates had been cleared away, they sat down, one each side of Acco. The aviator was scrawny, his hair bleached. "Easy with the wine, Acco," Commius said. "You're going to need your wits about you."

"I can drink you under the table," Acco said.

Magnus intervened and explained the problem to him. Acco was interested. "Those old stations? I can draw you a map. But it'll be cold up in the peaks."

"It's perfect flying territory. You can't have everything," Commius told him.

As the discussion continued, the other aviators gathered round. "That brings back memories. They say the run to Oenipons was excellent," Acco said.

"Perhaps we can try it again," a young pilot suggested. He was tall and extremely thin.

Magnus interrupted. "Aetius says his infantry must not cross over into Italian territory. And he says the aviators must not either. The Romans claim the Danube as theirs."

"Not even to find out where the Huns are?" the young pilot asked.

"No," Magnus said. "Aetius doesn't want a war with Emperor Valentinian as well as Attila."

Chapter 10: Disputed Territory

Vitudurum, Autumn 451 AD

Aetius and the infantry commander Maxentius rode side by side through the narrow streets of the town of Curia, with Magnus and an escort of ten cavalrymen following just behind. Today the sky was overcast, with the hint of snow in the air.

The town of Curia was built on the right bank of the River Plessur, about a mile above its junction with the Rhine. It was overshadowed to the east by the Mittenberg and to the south by the Pizokel.

The old forts along the northern edge of the Alps had been abandoned fifteen years before when the Huns first raided west. Now, as the Huns retreated, each fort was repaired in turn and put back into use. No one believed these garrisons could hold out for long without reinforcements, so as each fort was opened up, the neighbouring messenger station was brought back into service.

Magnus glanced up. Both peaks were hidden by the low cloud. Today it was easy to believe the local stories that each peak was inhabited by a dragon. But he knew that he would have to set up a messenger station on one of those hilltops.

The townsfolk lining the street were mainly dressed in undyed grey woollen tunics. They seemed to be as gloomy as their climate and watched in silence as they rode past. The riders stopped outside the gateway of the old fort.

At one time the town had been the capital of a Roman province and their legions had built a fort on one of the foothills of the Mittenberg. Now the town was the heart of a diocese and the bishop had built his cathedral in one corner of the fort.

The town was small, but it lay on the major road that went from the Rhine, through the Julier Pass, to Italy. A branch of that road went to the Danube and the east. That was what had brought Aetius here today.

The riders dismounted. Then, in a theatrical gesture, each of the three officers in turn pulled his baldric over his head, wrapped it round his sword, and handed both to Aetius's servant.

Aetius ignored the crowd with patrician disdain. "I hate having to be polite to this back-country hick."

Magnus could only respond with something Aetius already knew. "The bishop's backing is vital to your plans, sir."

"I'd like to squeeze some taxes out of these people."

"These mountains are impoverished, sir. If you try to impose a tax on them, they'll rise in revolt."

"I know, I know," Aetius said. A servant opened the heavy outer door. Aetius turned his back on the crowd and walked under the archway to the bishop's residence.

Magnus and Maxentius followed Aetius. This steeply-sloping courtyard had once formed part of the old Roman fortress. The builders had chosen a strong defensive position overlooking the river below.

"Magnus ..." Commander Maxentius spoke in an undertone. "Could the bishop really defy Lord Aetius?"

"He could tell his people that this province belongs to Rome, and that they should resist us. It would be a futile gesture, and his people would suffer for it. But ..."

"It would ruin our chances of stopping the Huns. Yes, I see."

The bishop's receiving room was built of squared stone taken from the old fort. The room had a high ceiling, but it was cold and gloomy. The shutters had been closed to keep out the cold, casting the room into gloomy shadow.

Bishop Asinio was sitting in a hard wooden chair, his heavy undyed grey woollen robes pulled around him. The arms of the chair were carved into the shape of dragons' heads. His subordinates stood on each side of him. He was middle-aged and lean, his grey hair covered by a cap. Magnus knew that the bishop was a local man. He might come from a landowning family, but he was a mountain-man for all that.

"Welcome to my residence, Lord Aetius."

"Thank you, your grace," Aetius said, suddenly courteous. "Your grace, I intend to protect your people from the Huns."

"That's good to hear, my lord. But why have you come to Curia?"

"I need to establish a garrison, to guard the Julier pass," Aetius said.

"That's absurd. If the Huns advance west, they'll surely take an easier route, west of Lake Brigantinus."

If Aetius was annoyed at being lectured in strategy by a priest, he did not let it show. "Yes, your grace. But if Attila hears that the western route is blocked and this one is not, he'll decide this is easier after all."

Asinio considered this. "Perhaps. How what burden do you intend to impose on us?"

"We plan to rebuild the old messenger station, on the mountain. I must ask you to arrange for the garrison to be provisioned."

"Those aviators are godless reprobates, with no respect for authority," Asinio said.

Magnus hid a smile. "There is much in what you say, sir."

"Your grace, may I introduce Magnus Vitalinus? He's an officer in the army, of patrician birth." He subjected Magnus to a glower, then turned to the bishop with a smile. "Your grace, my men will not impose upon you. The garrison will pay for the food they need."

Aetius was serious about that, although Magnus did not know where his commander was going to find the silver.

Asinio was not impressed. "And how many soldiers will you impose on us, to confiscate our food and leave us to starve?"

"No more than a hundred men, your grace." Aetius was conciliatory.

The bishop raised his eyebrows. "Absurd! In the old days we had five hundred soldiers here, a heavy burden. How can you hold off the Huns with less?"

"If the Huns come this way, the messengers will send me word and I'll lead the army to relieve the fort," Aetius said. A ripple of dismay spread among the listeners.

Asinio clutched the arms of his chair. His knuckles were white. "If the Huns do choose this route, a hundred men wouldn't be enough to protect my people. You'd need a thousand to stop those Godless monsters."

Aetius shrugged. "I don't have enough men to guard every pass. The government can't afford to recruit that many. And, as you say, this land can't support that many soldiers."

Asinio acknowledged the truth of this. "But - my people..."

Magnus recognised his cue. "There is an alternative, your grace. The Rhine frontier is defended by a volunteer militia.

That could work here. The walls of the old fort are still standing."

"What of it, young man?"

If your people were attacked, your Grace, they could take refuge here. They could help the garrison defend it."

"But it's illegal for peasants to bear arms," the bishop said. "Would you truthfully permit this? Volunteer soldiers?"

Aetius took over. "Yes. This crisis justifies it. Of course, the Italian emperor might object."

"I see … But if the Huns do attack the empire, they're unlikely to use the Julier route. They're more likely to use the Fluela Pass, further north," Asinio said. He put his hands in his lap, more confident now.

"Yes, your grace, that is possible. We plan to set up a new fort at Davos, to guard that Pass."

Magnus was unhappy about that too. He knew would have to find a site for a messenger station there.

Asinio tensed. "Is there no limit to your ambition? How much further will you move?"

"No more than that, your Grace. Moving further would take us into Roman territory. We don't want to offend Valentinian."

The bishop snorted. The Italian emperor was incapable of protesting at anything. "No, indeed. But what will you do if the emperor's army commander leads his men into these mountains?"

"The orders I have given my men are clear, your Grace," Aetius said. "If the Romans march north, we must withdraw."

The bishop relaxed slightly. "In that case … I welcome you, sir, and will support your efforts to protect my people from the pagans."

Aetius bowed. "Thank you, sir."

Magnus flew into Vitudurum for the third time since it had been re-established. The fort was three valleys south of Lake Brigantinus. In this country, distances were counted in valleys and passes over the mountains.

Aetius had made sure all the forts had a garrison, told his subordinates he had absolute trust in their abilities, then returned to the comfort of Lyon. Magnus was left with the task of keeping the messenger service operating. He knew the garrisons were now dependent upon the aviators he had selected.

In the past, Vitudurum had been a central link in east-west routes. Magnus had decided that the place would regain its old key role. Sergeant Dumnorix from Trier, with his long experience and proven competence, had been promoted to captain and put in charge.

Dumnorix, short, blond, with a neatly trimmed beard, was enthusiastic about his posting. "I've got a good team here, sir. The aviators are enthusiastic. They've got what it takes."

"That's good to hear, captain."

At sunset, he dragged Magnus from the comfort of the dining hall. "Look at that view, sir!" He waved his arm in a grand gesture.

"Look! One mountain range after another. The most spectacular view in the world. The forests around Trier have nothing to match this. And the wind on those ridges gives us fantastic flights."

Magnus had to admit that the view was spectacular. The early snows had already fallen and the high peaks were capped in white. Here in the valley the sun had already set, but the peaks were still in sunlight. Up there, winter had arrived, but in the lower valleys it was still autumn.

Magnus tried to avoid being carried away by the captain's enthusiasm. "Yes, captain. But you can't maintain this route without supplies."

"I know what you mean, sir. Everything the ground crew need has to be brought up, by pack mules." He shrugged. "But I promise you I'll cope. The local people are supplying most of our basic needs."

Magnus hesitated. Had he made a mistake in appointing Dumnorix to this post? But what, after all, could he do?

"I'm glad to hear that you've found answers, captain."

"Yes, sir. But sometimes, I think this isn't going to work. I warn you, you're taking a tremendous risk. It isn't just a single station, it's a whole network! Each man has to play his part, and some of the men in the smaller stations aren't up to the task. You were too hasty in selecting them."

Magnus tried to hide his dismay. If the ever-confident Dumnorix had his doubts … Some of the new captains seemed far too young for the task. Others had grown old and bitter hoping for this opportunity. "Privately, captain, I agree with you. But I had no choice."

Magnus's strategy had been to appoint an ambitious man as captain, then give the captain a batch of skilled craftsmen as his ground crew. On a couple of occasions, the team members had never met before. Magnus would tell them he had every confidence in them, and then move on to the next station, hoping that nothing went wrong.

Magnus knew that his approach was high handed. It was a patrician approach, and he was almost ashamed to use it. But nothing better was available. He told himself that if any of the men he had chosen turned out to be duds, he could demote them again.

Dumnorix lowered his voice. "Some of the boys distrust Aetius – he's got too much power. That fool Commius at Lyon is too subservient. He grovels too easily. The general's got his own private army. What if he tried to make himself emperor? We'd have a civil war."

Magnus was uncomfortable. "We need Aetius to save the empire. Nobody else is up to it."

"Perhaps," Dumnorix said.

Magnus drew a breath. "Captain, I want you to arrange regular flights to each garrison in the mountains, every week if possible, whether the aviators have messages to carry or not."

The captain grinned. "The chancellor's office won't like that, sir. We're supposed to keep flights to essential journeys only."

"Yes, I know. But I'm going to insist on this one. I'll take this to Aetius if I have to. I want to assure the garrisons they're not forgotten. Captain, I want you to tell the pilots to carry mail to the soldiers. Letters from their families. Non-official messages."

Dumnorix was shocked. "That's one of the oldest rules of the service. No personal messages. You can't tell the boys to break it."

"I'm not breaking the rule, captain. I'm re-writing it. I want the soldiers in those mountains to know that the empire appreciates them. That's just as important as the promise of reinforcements."

Dumnorix was impressed. "I've been accused of being a dangerous radical. But I'm nothing compared to you."

Magnus grinned back. "Nonsense, captain. It's simply a matter of morale."

"Come on, sir, it's time for dinner. You're our guest for the evening, of course."

"Thank you."

Back in the dining hall, the aviators and ground crew had gathered for their meal. The year was closing in and charcoal braziers glowed cheerfully at each end of the hut. The tempting smell of fried onions overlaid that of mushrooms. As Magnus was not in the official line of command it was easier for him to be accepted informally.

Dumnorix's self-confidence had returned. "Commander Magnus, may I introduce you to our Chief Artificer, Paul, and his wife, Cartimandua. Until my wife joins me here, she's the senior married woman here." She was wearing a gown of pale blue wool.

"Good evening, madam," Magnus said politely. He might outrank her socially, but she was his hostess this evening. "But isn't it dangerous to move up here? The Huns may return in the spring."

"Our womenfolk weave the linen for our machines," Dumnorix said. "And a lot of other tasks we don't mention in the records."

Magnus made a mental note of that comment and thanked his hosts for their hospitality. "Your beer is better than anything we get in Lyon. Home-made and freshly brewed. Just the way I like it."

After the meal was over, the women left the hall and the drinking began. Dumnorix called forward a junior pilot. "Sir, I'd like to introduce Orgetorix. He's one of our best aviators. He's only been at Vitudurum for a couple of weeks, but he's made himself an expert in all the mountain routes."

"Good evening," Magnus said. The aviator, who looked scarcely old enough to grow a beard, was accompanied by a couple of his pals. "I've been hearing a lot about you."

"Yes, sir?" The boy was blond, blue eyed, painfully thin, and tall, so Magnus had to look up at him. He wore brightly coloured red and green trousers, blue tunic and a self-assured manner. Magnus decided that Dumnorix would be unable to keep this buck in line.

He smiled. "I can fly, but I'm out of practice. I know better than to fly through these mountains alone, Orgetorix. I have to get to Davos tomorrow. I need a skilled aviator to handle the machine for me. Can you get me there?" Davos was a grim frontier fortress just west of the watershed, the furthest east of Aetius's new garrisons.

"In a single day? That would make things interesting, sir."

"Do you think you can do it?"

"Of course? Why not? It's an interesting challenge." Orgetorix seemed delighted to be asked to fly the route. "The men of the garrison'll be gratified for your visit."

"That's nice to hear."

"Sir, may I say something?"

Magnus leaned back in his chair. "Of course. What is it, Orgetorix?"

"Sir, we've pushed the frontier to the upper Rhine valley. Why not go farther? In the old days, the empire used to hold Bavaria, everything south of the Danube."

One of the aviator's cronies leaned forward. "Sir, we'd like your permission to scout farther east. Across the watershed."

"You know your orders on that," Magnus said. "The Magister Militum has forbidden any flights over Roman territory."

The young pilot refused to accept this answer. "We have to keep a watch for Attila, sir, to see that he doesn't try to invade, but you say we can't watch the eastern passes! That's absurd. He could take that route to invade Italy!"

This man was no older than Magnus himself. Magnus asked himself why he had to act the role of the fusty general while Orgetorix could act as a carefree adolescent. What had happened to him over the last six months?

"This isn't a joking matter, pilot. Valentinian has written to Aetius, reminding him that the Danube is Roman territory."

"Valentinian's too weak to intervene, sir."

"Perhaps. But Aetius doesn't want any misunderstandings between us and Rome."

"But we're all fighting the Huns. Surely Valentinian isn't that stupid?"

Magnus decided to ignore that question. He became aware that several men had gathered round, waiting for his answer. "Lord Aetius was quite specific on this point, aviator. Do you want to accompany me to Lyon and ask him in person?"

To his relief, the boy backed down. "No! I mean, no, thank you, sir."

Chapter 11: The High Pass

Upper Rhine Valley, 10th April 452 AD

Spring had come at last and the new campaigning season was about to begin. The veterans of last year's campaign hoped nothing would come of it.

Orgetorix had volunteered to deliver dispatches to Davos, a frontier fortress, high up in the mountains. This was the farthest east of Aetius's new garrisons, responsible for guarding the Pass del Fluela. It was an unpopular route for the pilots, and the captain had been surprised when he had volunteered, but Orgetorix had an ulterior motive.

The snow had melted in the valleys, but in the higher reaches it was still winter. The highest peaks remained covered all year. Most of his journey would be at that altitude. The air was cold, but the scenery was breathtaking.

The landing field was on top of the mountain opposite the fort. The mountain ridge was like a serrated sawblade, with steep sides and a summit that was barely wide enough for a man to walk along. But at one point the ridge top widened into a stony meadow that was just big enough for a flying machine to land on. It was a difficult approach, but the meadow had been clearly marked. If you fluffed your approach you could always go round and try again, but Orgetorix was pleased that he got it right first time.

The ground crew invited him to spend the night, but he knew the soldiers in the fort would never forgive him if he flew home without meeting them. Besides, the conditions at the site were primitive.

There were several hours of daylight left so, accompanied by a couple of guides, he trudged down the narrow mountain track to the fort in the valley below. The fort, built to accommodate five hundred men, was very basic, with earthen embankments and timber gatehouses.

The men of the garrison, cut off from the outside world, were bored. As Orgetorix had expected, the men were gratified for his visit and the mail he brought. He was welcomed as the guest of honour at dinner that evening.

He told them the latest gossip of Vienne and Vitudurum. "Aetius wants us to find the Huns for him, but they've withdrawn somewhere to the north east, out of range of our new bases."

"Bohemia?" the commander asked. Maxentius was a German mercenary who had taken a new name for himself when he joined the army. He was a dependable officer who had risen through the ranks. Orgetorix suspected he had been chosen for this posting mainly because he was unlikely to complain about being sent so far from civilisation.

"Yes. Have you heard anything?"

"Nothing at all. We're wasting our time here," Maxentius said. "If the Huns do attack this summer, it'll be round the edge of Lake Brigantium. They'd be crazy to attempt these passes."

"If that happens, you'll be sent to reinforce the garrison at Vitudurum," Orgetorix said.

Maxentius waved this aside. "Nothing's going to happen during the summer either. My main problem is boredom among the men. They're counting the days to the end of their spell of duty."

The soldiers entertained him by describing the dragons that haunted the mountains around the fort. "According to local farmers and hunters, each mountain peak is inhabited by a different creature. They say each one's different."

"I've never *seen* any dragons, myself," Orgetorix said cheerfully. "But the older pilots tell me that they're gentle creatures. They say it's bad luck to harm them, though."

The next morning, the skies were clear, and the wind patterns were ideal. Orgetorix asked a few cautious questions. The weather-wise among the garrison told him that conditions were unlikely to change for five days at least.

That was the news that Orgetorix had been waiting for. The hot pilots were daring each other to fly further and further - and get home again safely. No-one had suffered the humiliation of walking home yet, but he knew it was only a matter of time. He was confident it wouldn't be him. Another problem with this unofficial contest was that Captain Dumnorix at Vitudurum regularly asked you why your flight had taken longer than expected. But the younger pilots agreed the captain was an old woman and would accept any story you gave him.

Kai had started the contest by boasting that he had reached the Pass dal Fuorn, east of Davos, marking the watershed between the tributaries of the Danube and those of the Padus. Then Britomaris had gone one further and reached the Pass dal Reschen, on the old route from Verona to the Oenus River.

Orgetorix wanted to outdo both his rivals and reach the Bavaria Pass between Verona and Oenipons. He had asked the old timers back in Vitudurum about the routes. These men had flown the routes before the Huns arrived. Three had shaken their heads and said the route was dangerous without any intermediated landing sites. But one aviator had winked and described the route in detail and said that even today he was a better pilot than Orgetorix would ever be.

Orgetorix had flattered the old man and listened carefully. He knew that conditions would have to be perfect if his attempt was going to succeed. All morning, he studied the weather patterns. He realised that all of the conditions he needed were in his favour. West in the morning, veering to north or north east later.

That afternoon, he said his farewell to the commander of the fort and collected the sealed packet that contained their mail. Maxentius and his men were disappointed to see him go so soon but, glad of the break in their routine, turned out to wave him off. Twelve of the men, desperate to relieve their boredom, volunteered to accompany him up the mountain and haul on the ropes for him.

The climb back up the narrow track to the landing field took him most of the day. This time he gratefully accepted the ground crew's offer of a night in their bunkhouse.

At first light the next morning, Orgetorix got up and checked the weather. But dawn showed the skies to be clear. He asked the sergeant of the station.

"There's no rush, lad. The wind is going to improve all day. If you wait until noon, you'll have a perfect wind to take you home."

"I don't want to tempt fate. I want to start now." The temptation to sample such excellent flying territory was irresistible.

So, an hour after sunrise, he asked the men of the ground crew to launch him. They knew the importance of seizing every opportunity and complied without suspicion.

They launched him into a strong updraft. Perfect. He gave the ground crew a farewell wave and turned north. After a few minutes he was able to turn east. The winds were less helpful now, but a little patient climbing took him across the watershed into the valley of the Oenus.

Flying conditions were superb. It should be possible to fly hundreds of miles in a single day. The sky was perfectly clear, and he could see one range of snow-covered peaks after another. No aviator had seen these eastern mountains since the arrival of the Huns. No one need know he had flown so far east – and back again.

He was flying higher and higher, not because he needed to, but because these mountain conditions made it so easy. If you climbed high enough, you could trade height for speed. He would have to do that later, but not yet.

He was following the cliff as closely as he dared, to get the strongest lift. Then he realised that a dragon had appeared alongside him. He gaped in surprise. It was a magnificent beast, covered in green metallic scales. Was it going to talk to him? Some pilots said the dragons talked to them. It was probably going to tell him to turn back. He had ventured too far already.

You are too high. This altitude is dangerous for you. You must lose height.

Had the dragon spoken? Had he imagined it? Was he going to turn out like Acco?

But - he realised that the beast was right. He was too high, dangerously high. And there was no need for it. He could lose height and still continue on his way. And the noble beast had not said he must turn back.

When he had descended to a safer height, he waved his thanks for the warning. But the dragon was gone.

A few minutes later he realised that he was not going to make it. He was running short of time. Unless he turned back soon, he would not reach Vitudurum before sunset. He had already outdone Britomaris but, tempted, he decided to press on a little farther. Conditions this good might not recur for a month or more.

He reached the village of Oenipons a few minutes later. Down there somewhere must be the bridge, or what was left of it. This was the mouth of the pass. If he turned south, he would reach the pass to Italy. He had hoped to reach the pass, but there was no time.

He began to think of the route back to Vitudurum if he could not reach it by nightfall, what alternatives did he have? What intermediate stations could he land in?

He should turn west, now, and start trading his height for speed. But then he spotted the bridge far below and turned for a better look. Men were gathered on the north bank, waiting for their turn to cross. Were they farmers looking for fresh grazing? Or were they traders, hoping for a profit despite the war?

But there had to be hundreds of them. They were so eager to cross that they were using rafts to ferry their livestock across. They covered the road for miles. No, thousands of them. Tens of thousands. A closer look confirmed that the animals were horses. It must be the Huns, on their way to invade Italy. They weren't interested in the Gallic Empire after all; they were heading for a richer target.

He had to get back to Vitudurum. And he had to do it today. He had to tell what he had found. He was faced with a dilemma: should he admit he had disobeyed orders?

Orgetorix arrived back at Vitudurum, an hour before sunset, exhausted by the long flight, still absorbed by his dilemma. Despite his fatigue, he got his machine down safely. He found his buddies Kai and Britomaris waiting on the field for him. As they pulled his machine to the hangar, he tried to tell them where he had gone and what he had seen.

"Never mind boasting," Kai interrupted. "You'd better get changed for dinner. Magnus the patrician has arrived on another inspection."

His main feeling was relief. There would be no need to bluff his way to headquarters in Lyon. He felt a twinge of guilt. "What's he checking up on? Is it us?"

Kai grinned. Gotcha! "No, no. Go and clean up."

It seemed that Magnus had arrived on a social visit, to thank everyone at the signal station for the work they had done. During the evening meal, Dumnorix treated Magnus as a guest and an equal, not a senior officer.

"I thank you again for your hospitality," Magnus told the Chief Artificer's wife. "Although the real reason I came north is because I like your beer." That got a laugh and Orgetorix felt guilty that his news was going to ruin Magnus's visit.

As the evening drew on, Orgetorix began to worry that Magnus would be too drunk to understand what he had to say. He summoned up his courage and edged forward. He managed to corner the little patrician, trying to hide how worried he felt. "Excuse me, sir …"

Magnus looked annoyed. "What intractable domestic problem have you brought me? I don't have the authority to deal with them. You'll have to speak with the captain."

"It's not like that at all, sir." Clumsily, stammering in his haste, Orgetorix explained the problem. "It's the Huns. I've seen them. But I don't want to – to go to the people in Lyon to tell what I've seen, sir." He was terrified of Aetius and his headquarters staff.

He boyishly described the updrafts, then realised his mistake. Stick to his discovery. Orgetorix decided he must not mention the dragon. Instead he explained how he had calculated the number of men at the river crossing. He realised that he was not doing very well and stumbled to a halt. He watched Magnus for his reaction.

*   *   *

Magnus listened patiently as the pilot stammered his tale. The messenger service was running smoothly. Captain Commius, who had been so reluctant to take the responsibility for setting up the new route, was perfectly capable of keeping it running.

Then he realised just what Orgetorix was confessing to. His first reaction was jealousy. This tall man was a better pilot than he would ever be. Why couldn't he escape from his responsibilities and do things like that? Instead, he had to sit here and play the role of the moralising grandfather.

"They covered the riverbank?"

"Yes, sir - my lord. A whole mile downstream, waiting their turn."

"And the whole length of the pass?"

"I – didn't look. I assumed so, but ..."

"Yes, we have to assume the worst. You did the right thing to come here. I'll speak to Aetius. I'll try to keep your name out of it."

The man's relief was genuine. "Thank you, sir."

Dumnorix, who had listened in silence, was outraged. "They could be heading up the valley of the Oenus, across the pass, to invade Gaul."

Orgetorix was stubborn. "They were heading south."

"We'll have to guard against that," Magnus said. "But I think the lad's right. Italy's a much more tempting target. And it's defenseless."

Lyon, 14th April

Magnus arrived back in Lyon late in the afternoon. He was now faced with the task of taking the story to Aetius. The men of the garrison told him that Aetius was dining at home. With important guests, they said.

That was a disappointment. He had hoped to catch Aetius alone in his study. He walked down to the city and reached Aetius's luxurious town house just after sunset.

Aetius's secretary stopped Magnus in the doorway. "The General is hosting a formal dinner. Can it wait?"

"No." Magnus did not hesitate. "If I bring this news to Lord Aetius in the morning, he'll want to know why the news was kept from him."

The secretary subjected him to a searching look. "Very well. I'll show you the way."

The room was very large. The table had been moved to one end and took up less than a quarter of the space. Magnus found that the meal was over and the general and his guests from Italy, ladies as well as gentlemen, were watching some dancers. Their red dresses had extravagant hanging sleeves and tightly fitting waists. At the far side of the room, a group of musicians were playing an accompaniment.

A few of the watchers looked round as he approached. But all they saw was a messenger, tired and bedraggled, and turned their attention back to the dancers.

Two men of the generals' Hun bodyguard stood behind their commander, ignoring the entertainment and eyeing the Italians with disdain.

Aetius was sitting back in his padded chair, toying with a silver wine cup on the table in front of him. A lady in a green silk dress was sitting in the chair to his left, but the chair to his right was empty. The general looked up as he approached. He was wearing a white woolen tunic and hair oil scented with spikenard. "Business, Magnus?"

"I'm afraid so, sir."

"I hope this is important. Can't it wait until the morning? Does the fate of the empire depend upon hearing this now?"

"It just might, sir."

Aetius raised an eyebrow. He gestured to the empty chair to his right. "You think so? Sit down."

The fine lady at his left pouted but said nothing.

Magnus began to explain in a low murmur. To Magnus's relief, the general recognised the value of the news. The twirling dancers were forgotten.

"Do you believe this man's story?"

"Yes, sir."

The General was amused. "Fine the boy ten silver pieces for disobeying orders but reward him eleven pieces for his initiative."

"Yes, sir."

Aetius stared across the dining room, oblivious to the dancers. "You must find out where the Huns are going."

Magnus thought of the problems involved in such a simple order. "Yes, sir."

"I want daily reports ... Or whenever the weather is favourable."

"Yes, sir." Magnus had already ordered that on his own initiative, but he was relieved to have his order confirmed.

The dance came to an end and the aristocratic audience applauded. Aetius made a pretence of joining in. "That fool Valentinian can't defend his empire. I'll have to do something ... you're dismissed. Find my secretary and send him here."

"Yes, sir," Magnus said, glad to make his escape.

*   *   *

Lyon, 21st April

Orgetorix arrived in Lyon with urgent dispatches. He had flown a difficult mission the day before, today's flight had been wearying and he was strained. He made his landing with exaggerated care.

He hated visiting the city. It was a place of dangerous intrigues, the general's supporters feuding with the emperor's representatives in the chancellery. Whenever Orgetorix visited the city, his pockets empty, the townsmen sneered at him as a back-country hick. The worst of it was that they were probably right. The messenger station was a mile outside the city walls, but that too was tainted with the political maneuvering.

He hoped to spend a couple of nights in the messenger station and to be ordered north again, without ever having to leave the field, but that prig Commius spotted him. "You have news of the Huns?"

"Yes, captain. I've got a written summary for you."

The aviators at Vitudurum, flying ever-longer missions, were trying to keep track of the barbarians. They were using Davos as a staging post for the long flights east. You couldn't wait for perfect conditions, you just had to hope that the weather didn't deteriorate after you took off.

They barbarians had been heading south to Verona. But for a couple of days bad weather had made flying impossible. When conditions improved, the aviators had discovered that they had lost track of their quarry.

"Then what are you waiting for?" Commius said. "Take your dispatches to Lord Magnus in person. He's in the barracks, in the heart of the city."

Orgetorix hid a sigh and made his way through the crowded streets of the upper city to the barracks. He found Magnus sitting out of doors, slumped on a bench in a courtyard overshadowed by trees. He looked exhausted. It was a surprisingly quiet spot in this bustling city.

Magnus looked up. "Orgetorix? D'you have good news for me?" he growled.

"Well … it depends upon what you mean by good news, sir. We've found the Huns, but they've turned east, towards Trieste."

Magnus sat up. "Any news is better than none. I'll have to tell Aetius of this at once."

"Rather you than me, sir," he said airily.

Magnus grinned. "Right, you can come too," he said. "It'll do you good. I hate the thought of taking that sort of message to the general."

Orgetorix had to lengthen his stride to keep up as Magnus led the way through the city to Aetius's headquarters. The general's bodyguards – Huns – recognised Magnus and waved them through. Magnus seemed to know his way around this sprawling house. They found Aetius in his study, reading reports. To Orgetorix's surprise, they found the Magister Militum in a good mood.

Magnus commended the aviator to Aetius. To Orgetorix's relief, the Magister Militum merely looked bored. He realised that Aetius must receive an endless supply of adventurers seeking praise or reward. Once again, he stammered out his report.

"Slow down, pilot. Take your time."

"Sorry, sir. We – we found the Huns on the road to Trieste, sir."

"They've turned east, you say? I'll have to tell Valentinian about that. I doubt if he knows."

"Yes, my lord," Magnus said.

Aetius was inclined to grumble. "I've sent reports of developments by horse courier, at my own expense you understand, to the Pope and to Emperor Valentinian in Ravenna. It's costing me a fortune."

"Perhaps lord Valentinian has already heard of this development," Magnus said.

"I doubt it. That boy hasn't a clue." For once, Aetius seemed eager to gossip. "Although he's aware of Attila's advance. Didn't you know? A courier reached Vienne yesterday with news from Italy. Apparently, he nearly killed his horse getting there. The chancellor was kind enough to forward the message to me."

"I hope it's good news, sir."

"Good and bad. The Emperor Valentinian has appealed to the Eastern Emperor in Constantinople for aid. But he's also sent an appeal to Emperor Vindex in Vienne. So, before long, Vindex is going to ask me whether I can send an expeditionary force. Valentinian made a point of reminding us that Italy had sent an expeditionary force to Gaul last year, when the Huns were threatening us."

Orgetorix was terrified of this casual talk of affairs of state. Magnus seemed to have similar doubts.

"Is this confidential, sir?" Magnus asked.

Aetius shook his head. "Not at all. Quite the opposite. We can turn this to advantage, Magnus. I want to advertise this. I've drafted a proclamation, explaining the emperor's request. I want the messenger service to carry copies of it to every city in the Gallic Empire ..."

Orgetorix wondered whether perhaps the general was preparing for his next step – an invasion? He was relieved when the Magister Militum dismissed them and they were able to escape. They made their way back to the street.

"That went better than I expected," Magnus said. "You can tell everyone that you've been introduced to the Magister Militum."

"It's an honour I'd rather have done without," he retorted, and Magnus laughed.

Chapter 12: The Italian Campaign

Limestone Edge, Britain, 24 April AD

Claudia had persuaded her husband to permit her a day's outing to the messengers' airfield. He had complained that he was too ill to accompany her, but eventually had let her go, on condition that she was accompanied by the steward's wife, Branwen.

Claudia travelled in her two-wheeled chaise, which was dainty but capable of good speed, and which could accommodate both ladies. She was wearing a fine woollen dress, green, but sadly faded. Over it she wore a hooded cape of grey wool, unfashionable but modest and warm. They were followed by six unsmiling men of her husband's bodyguard, on horseback.

They reached the messenger station at last. In one corner of the hilltop meadow a few scrawny sheep were diligently cropping the grass short. With steep inclines to both east and west, the landing field looked very small indeed. Claudia decided that the messenger station, at the eastern end of the meadow, was a curious place. Its long low wooden huts had a ramshackle, temporary air.

To the west, they could see the River Severn. Beyond that was another range of hills. The wind coming in from the estuary was bracing.

Two men strolled across the grass to meet them. The young man held the horses' heads. The other, a middle-aged man with blond hair, wearing a faded blue tunic, smiled up at them. "Good morning, ladies. I'm Captain Rhys. Welcome to Edge. We shall try to make your visit a pleasant one."

"Good morning, Captain," Claudia said. Rhys was a commoner - it was clear from his accent that his first language was Brittonic.

"Captain - do you ever see dragons here?" Branwen asked.

Claudia was embarrassed, but Rhys did not seem to mind. "The Limestone Edge is not the place for dragons, lady. Not high enough."

He pointed west, across the Severn. "See that line on the horizon? The Black Mountains, that's the place for dragons. Pilots carrying dispatches to Chester fly parallel to the Black Mountains. They see dragons regularly."

Branwen's mouth had fallen open. "And do they talk to you, Captain?"

"Silence, Branwen," Claudia said. "Captain, I apologise for my companion's forwardness."

Rhys smiled. "That's all right, my lady. A few aviators are able to hear when the dragons speak. But I'm not one of them."

Claudia wanted to ask what the dragons looked like, but she did not want to sound like Branwen. "Thank you, Captain."

The captain and his wife offered them refreshment, answered their questions about how the messenger station was run and fulfilled their role as hosts. Claudia could well understand the aviators' reputation for having a girl in every city they visited. But, under the eye of his wife, Rhys' manners were impeccable.

The day turned out to be boring. Two machines had been launched, before Claudia arrived, but that was all. She had hoped for some sort of flying display, but apparently the empire's machines were too valuable to be risked in such frivolous activity. Watching craftsmen painstakingly glue the struts of a wing together was not very exciting.

Despite being bored, she was sad to leave. She was discussing the return journey with the commander of her escort, a veteran warrior from Denmark, when a shout made her turn. The warrior's eyes widened. "Look!"

Claudia looked up to see a machine fly past the meadow. "Isn't the meadow rather small for him to land in?" she asked Rhys.

"Well, yes, but if he overshoots, he just flies over the edge and back into the updraft."

The pilot flew east for a hundred yards, then turned his machine to face directly into wind. He touched down right at the threshold and skidded towards the storage buildings. He came to a halt fifty yards from where they were standing.

"Show off," Rhys said. The two ladies accompanied him as he strolled over to greet the messenger. The pilot was protected by a nacelle, but as they approached, he unfastened it and lifted it off. He unfastened a waist-strap and climbed out.

"I've got urgent dispatches, Captain. One to be relayed to Chester. One for the bishop, and letters for every council member within twenty miles."

"What is it, aviator?" Rhys asked.

"Haven't you heard? The packet-boat reached Dover two days ago. The Huns have invaded Italy. The Roman Emperor, Valentinian, has fled from Ravenna and taken up residence in Rome. It's said Aetius wants to go and help."

Claudia and Branwen exchanged a look. "Lord Ambrosius must be told of this at once," Claudia said.

"And your father too, surely, my lady?" Branwen asked.

"Yes, but he's at his estate in the Midlands; a hundred miles from the nearest messenger station."

*   *   *

Lyon, 26 April

Magnus climbed the hill to the messenger station behind Lyon. The day was warm but windless. No one would be flying today. He could have ridden to the station, but he wanted to postpone the forthcoming interview for as long as possible. He found the captain in his quarters. Commius was taller than Magnus, blond, dressed in a neat blue tunic.

Commius smiled. "Good afternoon, sir. Sit down, sit down. Something tells me you're bringing bad news."

"I'm afraid so, Captain. The Pope has written to Lord Aetius, asking him to save Rome from the pagans." At least, that was what Aetius was saying. Magnus did not know whether it was true or not, but it made excellent propaganda.

"I'm sure Lord Aetius has an answer, sir." Captain Commius was fascinated, as always, by the activities of Aetius and his inner circle.

"Well - Lord Aetius has told me that he's taking an expeditionary force to Italy. So he wants your aviators to keep him in touch with his headquarters in Gaul. And the emperor in Vienne, of course."

"Oh God, not again ... Ah, yes. Of course, sir."

"Aetius wants us to ensure that he's never more than fifty miles from a messenger station. Unfortunately, he gave me the task of creating the courier stations he needs."

187

Commius looked just as dismayed as Magnus felt. "It can't be done, sir. It'll take at least a year to sort out the mess you caused last year! We still haven't sorted out all the problems from going into the upper Rhine."

"We have to try, Captain. The cities of Italy depend upon Lord Aetius to deliver them from the Huns. And he'll be most displeased with us if we ignore a direct order."

Commius swallowed. "Yes, sir."

"Aetius hopes to reach Milan ten days after leaving here and he wants us ready by then."

"Ten days?"

Magnus tried to be upbeat. "At least we know what to do, Captain. A lot of the work will fall on your shoulders, I'm afraid. And neither of us can expect any credit. If everything goes perfectly, we'll be taken for granted."

Commius was amused. "We're used to that, sir."

"Our first task will be to set up a messenger station as close to Milan as possible."

"But how will we find the extra men, sir? We scraped the barrel last year."

"We can transfer some from the upper Rhine. This isn't a permanent set-up, remember. In a few weeks, the campaign will be over, and the men can return to their regular stations."

"Yes, but still … I remember we rejected a couple of men because they were too old," Commius said. "We could promote them, make it clear it's temporary, then pension them off in the autumn."

Magnus was glad that Commius was being positive. "Yes. Put their names down. Then there's Sergeant Dumnorix - Captain now. He was resourceful last year. Now that the Huns are in Italy, he's wasted there. I'll have to find a task for him."

"He's totally unsuitable for command, sir. Unless he improves, I'll be forced to take away his rank before he's had it six months."

"This campaign isn't going to last six months, Captain." He thought for a moment. "I'll see to Dumnorix myself."

"We can't possibly find enough men. The messenger service is so small."

Magnus had to admit that the man was right. "We'll just have to recruit Italians when we get there."

*   *   *

Vitudurum, 28th April

Magnus persuaded Orgetorix to fly him to Vitudurum, at the foot of the mountains. His first task was to speak to Dumnorix.

He found the captain in his quarters, slouching in a wicker chair, his feet on his bed. He sat up and placed his feet on the ground as Magnus entered. Dumnorix's jaunty irreverence was gone. The thought saddened Magnus.

Magnus leaned on the doorframe and looked down at the captain. "I'm disappointed in you. But this is so boring, isn't it? Trier was a nice comfortable backwater. Then the Huns arrived. That made things interesting. Your performance was excellent. But since you got here your record is ..."

Dumnorix looked glum. "Yes, sir."

"You even missed the pranks that Orgetorix and his cronies got up to. Although I'm glad you did. We wouldn't have heard about the Huns otherwise."

Dumnorix refused to apologise. "It was interesting at first, setting everything up. But the boys can cope without any help from me, they make the interesting decisions. I only get the awkward questions. Yes, this place is boring … the only thing I'm supposed to do is carry out inspections. What're you going to do, sir?"

"Now, technically, I haven't the authority to do anything. The general asked me to set up these messenger stations, but he didn't give me the rank to go with the job."

Dumnorix's smile was bleak. "Nobody's going to question your authority here. And nobody's going to question Aetius either."

"No, I suppose not. Well, I recommend that you resign. Then I can appoint somebody else here. The sort of person who enjoys bookwork. And I can find a suitable task for you."

"Yes, sir?" Dumnorix straightened up.

"You've heard that the general's going to invade Italy, to stop the Huns? He needs you aviators to find the barbarians for him."

"What?"

"We'll have to move fast, though. Aetius intends to march out of Lyon at first light tomorrow."

Dumnorix stood up. "Why didn't you say so before, damn you? Of course I'll go! And I can find half a dozen others who'll say the same."

Magnus kept his face impassive. "Commius says I can only take troublemakers. He can't afford to lose dependable types."

"Damn Commius. He's a crawler. But the boys I have in mind are hellraisers, all right."

*   *   *

Ambrosius family villa, Britain, May, 452 AD

Claudia had found that running the household was an interesting challenge. Her husband gave her an inadequate budget and very little authority. This could have led to endless disputes with the steward, for the man had all the experience she lacked.

But the poor man suffered from similar problems. His authority was regularly undermined by her husband. So, instead of quarrelling, she and the steward had developed an unspoken agreement to cooperate on any issue that came up. It worked quite well, although on one occasion her husband had spotted what they were doing and accused them of collusion.

She remembered her mother saying that no matter how unhappy her marriage might be, she would have her house to run and her children to console her. At the thought, she put a hand on her flat stomach. No children had arrived yet. Her husband blamed her for that too, of course. Although, on one occasion, the steward's wife had commented that in twenty years of debauchery, Ambrosius had not produced a single bastard. His own father had mocked him for it.

Her boredom was disturbed when a servant told her that her father had arrived. She hurried to the villa's reception room. Her husband was unwell and received his guests sitting in a cushioned chair.

Father was dressed for travelling, in grey tunic and brigga. He was accompanied by a couple of his cronies, cousins of hers. As Claudia walked in, he shrugged off his heavy blue riding cloak. "Good morning, daughter."

Claudia knew her duty as lady of the house. "Do you want any refreshments, father? Wine? A tisane? Bread?"

"Oh, wine. But that can wait, girl. Have you heard the news from Italy? Another invasion! I need to know what's happening."

"How can we do that?" Ambrosius asked.

"That fellow Magnus, remember? I want you to write to him, Claudia. Apologise for not replying last year. Ask him for information. I need to know what's going on."

Ambrosius, by his expression, was not happy at this abrupt command. Claudia hid her annoyance. She wanted to know what was happening in Italy just as much as her father did. "Yes, father, as you wish."

*   *   *

Milan, 11th May 452 AD

Magnus made his way to the reception room in the old imperial palace in Milan. The sentries recognized him and let him pass, but one of Aetius's secretaries stopped him at the door. "Your business, sir?"

"My name's Vitalinus, commander of cavalry. I've been summoned to Aetius's staff conference."

He was wearing his military cloak, pure white except for a large purple rectangle set against the edge. It was draped so that it covered his left shoulder and left his right shoulder free. Its only decoration was the circular brooch, bronze with silver trim, that held it in place.

Aetius had reached the city two days ago, with his advance guard.

"Vitalinus? His grace has been asking for you," the secretary said. "And it's nothing to do with cavalry." He did not explain further.

Magnus had discovered that Milan was bigger than Lyon. It was more crowded, bustling, and wealthy. This was not just a provincial capital, after all. Milan had been the headquarters of the Roman Field Army for over a century. Before Emperor Honorius had moved to Ravenna, it had served as the capital of the empire.

"Is it true that the Field Army hasn't been given any orders to march against the Huns?" Magnus failed to keep the disgust out of his voice.

The secretary kept his tone neutral. "I can't say, sir."

The room was one of the finest in the palace, with a mosaic floor and painted panels on the walls. The long far wall was pierced with a row of doors, giving onto a balcony that in turn overlooked the grey city walls and the distant snow-capped mountains.

Aetius was already there, standing against the far wall, flanked by a contingent of Huns from his personal bodyguard. He too was wearing a military cloak, although the rectangle on his was decorated with elaborate embroidery in purple thread. It was fastened with the crossbow brooch that only imperial courtiers were allowed to wear.

Aetius looked up as Magnus approached. "Magnus! You've been busy, I hope?"

"Yes, sir. I've been in Como, sir, setting up a messenger station -."

"We'll speak of this later."

"Yes, sir." Magnus moved aside so Aetius could greet the next arrival.

Then Senator Majorian arrived, accompanied by his retinue. Magnus had been disturbed to learn that the Roman Emperor Valentinian had given Majorian the title of Master of Horse and put him in command of the Roman Field Army.

The senator was dressed in his court robes, a mantle decorated with an elaborate pattern of stylised flowers in purple thread. Instead of using a brooch, the senator used the heavy folds of the cloth to hold it in place.

Magnus knew that court robes were only worn by emperors and consuls. He appreciated that by choosing it, Majorian was claiming equality in rank with Aetius.

The senator was accompanied by Ricimer, the mercenary commander. He was wearing a military cloak over a tunic embroidered with roundels at the shoulders. He came from the Suevi, one of those German tribes that had fled from Attila. He looked very much the mercenary general. Around his neck he was wearing a gold torque, a gift from the Roman Emperor Valentinian. He was accompanied by a couple of his own subordinates. They looked the part of barbarian mercenaries, with long blond hair and warrior moustaches.

Aetius took a step forward and the room fell silent. "It seems everyone's arrived," he said. "Gentlemen, my latest news is that the Huns have advanced on the city of Aquileia, at the head of the Adriatic, and laid siege to it. I intend to leave at first light tomorrow and march east to break the siege."

"Out of the question," Majorian said. "That would leave the road to Rome open. We must keep the army here and protect the capital."

"And what of Aquileia?" Aetius demanded.

Majorian shrugged. "We shall have to sacrifice a minor city in order to protect a major one."

Aetius frowned. "I wish to make it clear that, as Magister Militum, I outrank everyone else. I'm assuming overall command of the forces here in Milan."

Magnus was appalled at this blunt statement. Aetius was rarely so offensive to members of his own patrician class. There was a stir amongst Majorian's German subordinates. None of them liked this.

Majorian scowled. "You were given that title by your emperor in Vienne. We're on Roman soil here. So naturally I must assume the burden of command."

"I see. You can stay here if you wish." Aetius glanced round at the assembled officers. "Gentlemen, my intention is to march on Aquileia and break the siege. Although the most I hope for is to drive the Huns away from the city."

"But you defeated the Huns last year - sir," Ricimer said. "Can't you do it again?"

"Last year, I had the assistance of the Visigoths and the Burgundians. Their forces were equal in size to my own."

"Can't you ask them to help you again?"

"They were fighting to defend their homes and their farms. They won't fight the Huns in Italy unless we pay them."

"And we can't do that," Majorian said. The two patricians exchanged a look.

Now it was Aetius's turn to scowl. "I ask again - how will you deploy your forces against the Huns, lord Majorian?"

Magnus held his breath.

Majorian's voice was carefully neutral. "I will stay here with half my men, to guard the road south, and send the remainder with you to break the siege."

"If you stay here with half of your men, then the force I brought with me will be the largest component of the expeditionary force. Naturally, I shall assume command." Once again, Aetius glanced around the room. Suddenly, he had the full attention of every man there. "I will lead the warriors east while the cowards remain here."

Majorian kept an aloof patrician silence, but Ricimer hissed in anger. "How dare you accuse us of cowardice, you perfumed fop?"

Suddenly his barbarian subordinates were on edge, balanced, ready for a command. Aetius's bodyguard of Huns barely moved, but Magnus realised they too were on guard, ready to defend Aetius or kill his enemies at a word. The rest of the assembly barely dared to breathe, caught in the middle.

Aetius and Majorian acted as if they were the only two men in the room.

Majorian spoke smoothly, as if conferring a favour. "Very well. I shall lead the entire Roman Field Army against the barbarian invaders."

"Thank you," Aetius said. "Gentlemen, I want you to tell your men to prepare for a march. We must reach Aquileia as soon as possible. We don't have much time."

Everyone nodded his understanding. Magnus breathed easily again.

Majorian stalked out, followed by Ricimer. The Roman officers shuffled out after him. Soon only Magnus, Aetius, and the general's bodyguard of Huns remained.

Aetius seated himself in a cushioned chair and called for wine. "Sit down, Magnus."

"Thank you, sir."

"You're in good health? Your family is well?" The general asked. "Good, good. Let's get down to business. I'd like to think I can take Attila by surprise, but it's most likely he'll get wind of my advance and turn to face me. I'm worried about ambushes. I want your aviators to scout out the enemy for me."

Magnus had been expecting this. "Yes, sir. I plan to set up a chain of stations along the southern flanks of the mountains."

Aetius glanced out over the balcony at the distant mountains. "That's too far north. I want the messenger stations in the Padus valley, as close to my headquarters as possible."

Magnus was wary. "The flying machines can only operate in hilly country, sir. The valley of the Padus is too flat. The aviators would have to land in the mountains and then send the news to you by courier."

"Fifty miles or more. A day's ride," Aetius said.

"Yes, sir. If you want the aviators to warn you of ambushes, you'll have to take the northern road, close to the mountains."

Aetius was not happy. "Let's look at a map." He jumped up and strode over to the table. "The northern road … Milan, Bergamo, Brescia, Verona, and then Vicenza. You say this would allow your aviators to scout out any barbarian ambushes?"

"Yes, sir. It would also allow you to receive messages from Lyon."

Aetius sat back in his chair. "Your plan has one flaw, Magnus. What if the Huns don't co-operate? What if they take the main road, south of the Padus, to Piacenza?"

Magnus, deeply embarrassed, said nothing. Aetius laughed.

*   *   *

Julian Alps, 18th May

Just after noon, six two-seater flying machines circled a barren alpine meadow in the Julian Alps, in the hills above Udine. Riding as second pilot in one of the two-seaters was Sergeant Dumnorix. "This is the best we've seen so far, aviator. Take us in to land."

"Right you are."

Nobody had done this before. Nobody had tried anything remotely like this. Pilots would discuss this exploit round winter hearths for decades to come. But would it be a triumph or a heroic failure? The little patrician had suggested it, as a way of speeding things up. And a way of dodging the Huns on the plain. Why tag meekly behind the army when you could fly past them? Then that fool Orgetorix had said it would be fun, and here they were.

Dumnorix's machine touched down, skidded forward, and came to a stop. He scrambled out. He and the pilot pushed the machine to the edge of the meadow. One at a time, the other machines came in to land. Five of them touched down and skidded to a stop without incident. Two of the heavy machines carried, instead of a second pilot, the heavy cable necessary to get flying machines back into the air.

The last pilot touched down successfully but then let his left wing-tip drop too early. The tip hit a boulder and the machine spun round in a half circle. The pilot scrambled out unscathed, but the wing was crumpled. "Sorry, Captain."

"We're lucky yours was the only one, pilot." Dumnorix had been broken to sergeant, then given a 'temporary commission' for this one task. The little patrician had told him that a man of his abilities was wasted at a backwater station. He'd been right, damn him.

Dumnorix still thought the idea was crazy, but he had to admit that the flying among these mountains was superb. At least he wasn't going to get bored with *this* command.

As the army had advanced eastwards, young Magnus had set up a series of five signal stations. Now he had asked Dumnorix to organise another, the farthest, here in the Julian Alps.

This one was due to be the last in the chain, due north of Aquileia. Rumour had it that the city was still holding out. The general, leading his army across Italy, was desperate for up-to-date information.

Dumnorix looked round the meadow. In mountains such as this the climate changed, not by the season, but by the altitude. This high up, it was still spring, although in the valley below summer had arrived.

Two of his men were already pulling the lengths of cable out of the flying machines. His little force consisted of six pilots, himself, and three craftsmen to keep the machines operational. There was no shelter for his men, not even tents.

The rigger was already examining the crumpled wing. "Can you repair it?" Dumnorix asked gently.

The rigger climbed to his feet. His joints creaked. "No. It'd take a week in a fully equipped repair shop. The most I can do is use it for spare parts when you mess up my other machines."

This was an old argument, one that Dumnorix knew he could not win.

Sunlight lay on the meadow and on all the northern crags that watched over it. Higher up, on the crags and on the ridges above them, everything was dazzling white. It might

199

look pretty, but it would be cold. Dumnorix was glad he wouldn't be flying up there. He turned to look south. Somewhere down there, across the plain, the Huns were laying siege to Aquileia. When he had enough men – and if the weather remained favourable - he would send his best aviators to look at the city.

The countryside looked empty and desolate, but within an hour twenty local tribesmen had turned up. They were wearing rough grey homespun capes over their tunics. Perhaps they expected the weather to take a turn for the worse.

They were not hostile, and asked questions eagerly, in an archaic Latin dialect, but they were suspicious of the aviators until Dumnorix explained his mission.

"You are from Gaul? We hear that the men who fly the machines live free. You do not have to call any man your master."

Dumnorix, who had been expecting a question about dragons, was taken aback. "There is some truth in that, yes."

The grey farmers were suddenly helpful. "We have shelter and food, further down the mountain, with our flocks. But we can make an overnight shelter for you here."

"Thank you." Dumnorix knew how significant the offer of food was to these tribesmen. He began the delicate task of persuading the farmers to act as ground crew, hauling on the ropes to get one of the flying machines back into the air. The other aviators clustered around, listening gravely, careful not to interfere.

The grey farmers seemed to regard the request as an honour and were enthusiastic. Dumnorix wondered how long that would last.

Now that they had enough men to get the machines airborne, the aviators clamoured to be first to get into the air again. But who should he choose, and where should he send them?

"Acco, I want you to take a report back to the new airfield at Brescia. I've got a message for the young patrician. You can probably cover the whole distance back there in a single day."

Aetius and Magnus were with the army, half a day's ride south of the city. "Tell the lad that we've set up camp at a useful spot."

Acco was inclined to sulk. "It would look better in writing, Sarge."

He sighed. "Right. I've got a message tablet somewhere. Tomorrow I'll try a flight over the city."

Acco did not approve. "Now, Sarge, the young patrician said you weren't to take any risks. You'd better wait until I get back."

"Shut up and do what you're told."

*   *   *

A few days later, Magnus persuaded Acco to fly him to the improvised station in the Julian Alps in a two-seater. Acco was getting on towards middle age, experienced, careworn. He had the same casual lack of respect towards authority that Magnus remembered.

Magnus, sitting behind Acco, took one look at the landing field – and the wreck in one corner - and let Acco cope with the landing. The new landing site was a hillside meadow, not very wide and had a steep drop on either side.

After they had skidded to a stop, he congratulated Acco on his landing. He climbed out and looked around. A few grey-clad farmers were standing at the edge of the meadow gazing at the wreck. The air was refreshingly cool up here, unlike the plain below. The wind was fresh, ideal for flying, and the flying machines were tied down with ropes and tent pegs to prevent the breeze from blowing them over.

Summer had reached these high pastures at last and the flowers were in bloom.

Dumnorix walked over to greet him. "Welcome to Easternmost Field, sir. I've contacted the local people. In a few days, the farmers will be bringing their cattle up here for the summer grazing."

"I see." The men were living in tents and crude huts made of stone and turf. The pilots and fitters who clustered around to greet him seemed glad to see him. Magnus couldn't get used to that. Bashfully, he accepted the greetings of the pilots.

"Captain Dumnorix, I congratulate you on your achievements so far. You've done wonders in very difficult conditions." He sounded pompous to his own ears, but the captain did not seem to mind.

"Thank you, sir." He seemed to relish this frontier existence. The strain of command was another matter.

"Captain, I would like to speak to you in private."

"Right you are, sir." Dumnorix led the way along the perimeter of the airfield. "Our first mission reached the city easily enough, sir. We could see that the place was still intact. But the Huns started hunting for us immediately after our first flight -."

"As soon as that?"

"Yes, sir. You'd think we offended them. They've sent scouting parties into the foothills. The local tribesmen have been telling us everything the Huns get up to. But the barbarians didn't know where to start looking."

"Captain, I want more information about Aquileia."

Dumnorix did not argue. "Very well. As soon as the weather is favourable. It was no good today. We could fly west to the Dolomites and Brescia but not south."

Two days after Magnus arrived, an hour after sunrise, Acco pronounced that the wind conditions were suitable. No-one queried his judgement. They prepared the flying machine for another mission to the city.

Captain Dumnorix agreed that Acco was their best pilot for such a demanding mission. Magnus decided that if he wanted to get a look at the beleaguered city, he would have to pull rank and accompany Acco.

"You're crazy," Dumnorix told him. "But I can see your mind's made up."

"You'd better dress up against the cold, lad," Acco said.

The ground crew – most of them local farmers - dragged the two-seater to the brow of the hill. Magnus and Acco took their places. With great enthusiasm the farmers ran down the meadow, dragging the ropes behind them. The ropes stretched tight. The men holding down the machine let go and the machine sprang forward, off the hill and into the updrafts.

As usual, Acco spent the first hour patiently gaining height. This painstaking struggle to gain height was the part that Magnus was least good at. Eventually Acco was satisfied and they turned south.

The aviator was more talkative than usual. "You see, lad, the wind pours down the mountainside like water. And when it reaches the bottom, it bounces up again."

"Yes." This was the man who said that dragons talked to him. This description sounded crazy, too. Except that Magnus could see that they were gaining height, steadily, minute after minute, and there was no cliff to force the air up.

"The wave forms parallel to the mountains, sir. Always."

Magnus glanced round. Yes, their course was parallel with the nearest mountain ridge. And they were going up. But how did Acco know where to find this rising air? He was afraid to ask.

"That cloud looks pretty." Magnus had assumed that the long narrow cloud was stationary, but as they drew closer, he could see that it was writhing in constant movement.

"That marks the cap of the wave, sir. We must be very careful not to fly through it. It's made of ice, you see. If we fly through it, all the water droplets on the wings will freeze. Yess, and the water on our clothes, too."

"Ice?" Magnus was reminded just how cold his fingers were. He should have worn heavier gloves.

They turned south once more, and lost height steadily, until Acco found the next wave pattern. Magnus, looking up, could see that this wave had a wispy cap cloud too.

Acco repeated this procedure, patiently, until they could just make out the city, far below.

"There's Aquileia for you, sir."

"Well done, Acco." Magnus could make out the city walls and the streets, narrow straight lines. The walls seemed to be intact, but he could not make out more. The smoke came from the barbarian encampment. Cooking fires, nothing more.

Magnus was reminded of Trier. This southern city was larger, and the barbarian encampment was bigger too. "Could we get any closer, to let the townsmen see us? We're too high to see anything."

"Sorry, lad, but this wave pattern doesn't work below two thousand feet. If we drop below that, we'll never get back home. Yess, and wave patterns can collapse, just like that. All it takes is a shift in the wind direction."

Magnus realised that he possessed important military information. He knew exactly where the barbarian army was, while the Huns could only guess where Aetius was. And the general needed that information.

He decided that getting back with their inadequate information was better than taking further risks and not getting back at all. "Very well, Acco. Let's go back home."

"Right you are, sir."

Back at the messenger station, Magnus gave a terse report to Dumnorix. "We reached the city. It looks all right ... Captain, Acco found 'wave' for us. How often does that happen?"

"About one day in three, sir." The captain smiled. "But you could have three good days in a row, then nothing for a month."

"That's what I thought. I want you to make the attempt, every day that looks remotely hopeful. But -."

"Don't risk the men. Right, sir."

Magnus wrote a brief note to Aetius, while the captain peered over his shoulder. "Short and concise. Captain, I want you to ask your most reliable aviator to take it to Brescia."

"Yes, sir," Captain Dumnorix said. "But I warn you, expect trouble. If the Huns saw you, they'll be mad as fire."

The townsmen may not have spotted the flying machine, but the Huns must have done, for in the days that followed they responded energetically. They sent scouting parties deeper into the mountains.

The grey farmers reported to Magnus that the barbarian search parties were aggressive, but few in number and spread thin. The local mountain men tried to ambush the Huns and often succeeded.

Over the next few days, a vicious guerilla war developed. The wind conditions rarely created wave patterns, so most days long flights to the city were impossible. Most of the aviators' missions were restricted to spotting Hun scouting parties. Not once did the mountain tribes ask the aviators to leave.

Magnus, sitting in the sunshine outside his shelter with a wooden board across his lap, was trying to draft a report of less than sixty words. He decided not to mention that they were short of trained pilots and he had flown several missions himself.

'I estimate the hunt for the five aviators here at the camp - and the ground crew and the tribesmen who are supporting them - has drawn in a fifth of the Huns. They are getting closer but scouting flights continue. M. V.'

He sealed the message. "Captain, tomorrow I want you to find a courier to take this west."

"Yes, sir. Do you think the general will believe your estimate?" Dumnorix asked.

"Well, he knows how much Attila hates you aviators."

Magnus realised that in this strange campaign the Huns had lost their usual advantages. They usually depended upon moving fast, taking their enemy by surprise and hitting hard. In this mountain war they could do none of that. The siege forced them to stay in one place. The mountains were unfamiliar territory for them. The mountaineers could predict their approach, arranged ambushes and frequently inflicted heavy casualties.

Magnus was the first to notice the grey-clad farmer walking up the hill at a brisk pace. The hillmen could cover immense distances but rarely seemed to hurry. This urgency was unusual.

The messenger spoke to his fellow hillmen in his own dialect, then translated for the aviators. "The Huns are coming. Never been this close before. Can you help?"

Everyone turned to Magnus, not because he was a leader, but because he was a warrior. He tried to adjust his thinking. "How many of them are there?"

"Eight. But there's only fifteen of us. Those barbarians are trained for war, but we are not. We have weapons for you …"

Magnus hesitated only a moment. He was a soldier and these men had been risking their lives to help him. "I'll help, if you can find a weapon for me."

The tribesmen at the camp ran for their weapons, ready to leave at once. Captain Dumnorix and several others volunteered too, including one of the fitters. "Better to fight than to be cut down running."

"We're ready, let's go," Magnus told the tribesmen.

The messenger thanked them and led them down the hill. "We must hurry, hurry!"

Just above the tree line, they joined up with the main body of tribesmen. Magnus and his companions were panting. The tribal leader produced a strange batch of weapons. Six bows in cases, probably taken from the Huns. One sword. One helmet.

The bows were composite in structure, but Magnus knew how to string them. "The trouble is, if you want to be accurate with these, you have to practise daily - and I haven't picked one up since the campaign started."

Captain Dumnorix tested the draw of one of the bows. "I've used a longbow to put meat on the table, but I've never used one of these things."

"We'll have to wait until they get really close," Magnus said.

One fitter admitted he knew how to use a composite bow. Magnus wondered whether he was a deserter from the emperor's army, then dismissed the thought. It was of no consequence. He took the sword, excellent Gallic manufacture – had the Huns looted it from a soldier? At Mainz, perhaps? But he rejected the helmet, as it was heavy and would slow him down.

One of the tribesmen said he could hear the horsemen climbing through the woods. In a panic, they spread out and concealed themselves in a dried-up watercourse.

Magnus, lying prone, peering around a tuft of coarse grass, counted the horsemen as they appeared from the trees. Six, seven – no, eight of them. The Huns should have been leading their horses up this slope, but for some reason they chose to ride. They halted and exclaimed, perhaps at the barren landscape.

Each rider had a strung bow in a bow-case and a full quiver. One of the horsemen, perhaps the leader, was wearing chain mail armour. The horses were exhausted, probably from the climb. The men, too, were unwilling to go farther.

As the horsemen argued, Magnus's anxiety grew. The longer the delay, the more likely the ambushers would be spotted. And, at long range, the Hun archers would have a tremendous advantage.

The Hun leader shouted at his men and pointed upwards. It was clear they were looking for the messenger station. The horsemen grumbled but urged their horses to resume their climb.

Magnus waited until the riders were within range. "Now!"

One advantage of a composite bow was that you could shoot from a kneeling position. For his first shot he aimed for the leader's horse. But instead the arrow hit the leader's mail. It probably only inflicted a flesh wound.

His second shot took down the horse of the man at the rear. He didn't want the man fetching reinforcements.

Everyone was shooting now. Most of the arrows went wide. Three other riders were struck down, but the leader survived. He shouted and charged at Magnus.

A shot from a tribesman hit his horse and the creature stumbled. The leader, screaming with rage, leapt from his horse. He pulled a long cavalry sword from its scabbard and advanced on Magnus.

Magnus threw down his bow and drew his sword. He was shorter than his enemy, out of practice and without protection. Dismayed, he parried desperately. The man made another attempt, which told Magnus that his opponent was inexperienced. He had probably not owned a sword until this campaign started.

Magnus parried a second time, feinted right, then slipped under the man's guard and struck at his ribcage. The sword crashed against the Hun's mail. It did not cut but had probably cracked his ribs. The man screamed but did not drop his sword. He was still dangerous. Magnus's second stroke was at the man's head. Desperate, he put all his force behind the blow. That struck home, sending a shock up his arm, and the man crumpled.

Magnus was unharmed but panting. When he looked up, he saw that all of the Huns were dead. One of the farmers had a flesh wound from an arrow.

"That's one scouting party that won't report what it's found," Dumnorix said with satisfaction. "We'd better keep the bows, though."

The hillmen, in their gratitude, wanted Magnus to keep the sword. He declined, telling them he could not fly home with it because it was too heavy. He promised to keep the bow and practice with it daily.

Captain Dumnorix was panting as they made their way back up the hill. "The Huns are going to try again, sir. We can't be that lucky every time ..."

"Yes, I agree," Magnus said, although he knew what that meant. "You'll have to assume the worst. You'll have to retreat. Can you move further into the mountains? Further from the plain?" They turned to look at the mountains to the north.

"Yes, sir, but that'll take us farther from Aquileia. With the greater distance to travel, reaching the city will be almost impossible."

"Perhaps, but we can't afford to lose the entire messenger station. The men come first."

"Very well, sir." the captain sounded relieved. "I'll tell the lads tonight, get things moving in the morning."

Magnus decided to stay to participate in the transfer. The local farmers offered to carry their heavy gear. At least there wasn't much to carry. They salvaged every hinge and control cable from the wrecked machine and burned what was left.

That evening the leader of the grey farmers remarked that summer in the high meadows was drawing to a close. In a few days they would have to begin the task of driving their herds back down to the valleys.

But, before they could make the transfer, a messenger arrived with a note from Aetius. Magnus was sternly ordered to report to headquarters. The aviator carried a verbal message to back up the note. "His nibs says, sir, he wants you leading your cavalry the way you're supposed to."

Magnus knew that he had run out of excuses. He would have to return to the army.

*

Valley of the Padus, Early June 452 AD

East of Grappa, the army had to leave the mountains behind and venture over the flat plain. The aviators could not fly over them, unless the weather was perfect, and Aetius was now dependent upon the cavalry to warn him of the enemy. Aetius fretted at the army's slow progress and that made him short tempered. He knew that Aquileia could still fall to the barbarians and that a single day could be decisive.

South and east of Treviso, the land was flat and boring. The hills to the north were patched with tantalising vineyards. Further north were the foothills of the mountains. The sky was clear, with very little wind. Many of the northerners were suffering from painful sunburn.

The army reached the old military coastal road, the Via Annia, and the speed of their advance increased. The road and its bridges were solidly constructed. The next river, the Tagliamento, was the last major obstacle in their path. The river, meandering across the plain, was almost three miles wide, with a multitude of islands.

Magnus and his men reached the old posting station at Latisana. They could see that the buildings on the far bank had been abandoned. A barge was rotting on its moorings. The stone bridge, although in a poor state of repair, was still serviceable. Magnus guessed that here the river was no more than two hundred yards wide. At this time of year, the watercourse was quite shallow. Both banks were heavily wooded. It all seemed so peaceful.

"At least we reached it before they did," sergeant Madog said.

"The bridge is too narrow," Magnus said. "It'll take the army a couple of days to get across." He dismounted and began drafting a dispatch for Aetius.

Magnus was too busy to look up. A minute later the sergeant shook him by the arm.

"Look, sir, look," Madog said.

Magnus glanced up. "Hell." The horsemen on the far bank, tiny at this distance, were unmistakably Huns.

"Foragers, sir. We'll soon chase them off." But even as he spoke another troop of riders appeared.

There was no time for a proper written report. "Trooper! Tell Aetius we've reached the bridge, but we've got a score of Huns on the far bank. Tell him I expect more to arrive and I need reinforcements. Got that?"

He sent the trooper racing back to the general. Then he turned to face the enemy.

His archers managed to block the far end of the bridge. They were confident they could hold off the enemy until reinforcements arrived. But if the Huns found a ford upstream, he would be cut off.

Then an advance guard of imperial heavy cavalry arrived. More and more men were arriving from both directions. Each army was deploying, trying to form a battle line.

A galloper brought news from Aetius. "You're to dismount, sir. The rest of the army's to do the same, soon as they reach the river ... He's put his regulars, you know who I mean, sir, to in the centre, guarding the bridge. The light cavalry are on the left. Majorian's lot are on the right, because the general doesn't know how well they fight."

"Right. I understand." He led his men a hundred yards north. They dismounted and Magnus told his groom to lead the horses to the rear.

The main force of Huns gathered around the eastern end of the bridge. Things were moving fast. The men of the enemy advance guard were outnumbered, but they did not hesitate. After screaming insults at their enemies, they rode across the river, sending up huge amounts of spray.

Magnus tensed, his shield in one hand and his long cavalry sword in the other, but the riverbank made an excellent defensive line. The gravelly bed that formed the floor of the river was shallow for the most part, but treacherous. Three deep channels meandered across it, forcing the attackers to swim their horses. One horseman after another lost his grip and disappeared from view.

By the time the Huns reached the west bank, they were reduced to a few groups of riders. All the violence was concentrated fifty yards upstream of the bridge. Magnus and the men about him, further upstream, did not have to lift their weapons. After a few minutes of vicious fighting, the remainder of the Huns gave up. The imperial army tended to its wounded and waited.

This is only the beginning," Magnus told his men. "They won't stop now."

More and more Huns were reaching the far bank of the river. They formed a line and attempted to charge across, but the result was the same. Once again, the charge lost its impetus. The imperial troops, encouraged by the previous success, knew what to expect.

As more Huns forced their way across, the fighting spread along the riverbank. Then the enemy reached Magnus, and he had no time to observe the rest of the battle.

A barbarian, swinging a longsword, urged his horse to climb the riverbank. Magnus parried, acquiring a notch in his shield and a couple of bruises. The barbarian was unharmed. But his horse slipped on the wet grass and slid back into the river. Its rider screamed curses and scrambled free. He tried climb the riverbank, while still holding his sword.

Magnus, ready now, landed a blow on the man's shoulder. The barbarian lost his footing. He slid down the bank and vanished from sight. No-one attempted to take his place. Magnus realised that he had survived, and the second skirmish had been won.

Everybody expected the Huns to try again, but they seemed dispirited. They had lost too many men and too many horses. For the rest of that day, the armies merely glared at each other.

Chapter 13: A fickle wind

Valley of the Padus, June 452 AD

Magnus was summoned to Aetius's quarters, a prosperous farmhouse. The pilot Orgetorix was in the atrium, dressed for riding. He was standing to attention and looked scared. Lord Majorian was there too, lounging in a chair.

"Ah, Magnus. Come in." Aetius turned to the pilot. "Tell Magnus what you told me."

"Yes, sir. Conditions were good, sir, so I flew south, over the plain. I saw a large party of Huns moving west, sir. A quarter of their force. At least, the ground they covered was a quarter the size of their camp."

Aetius turned to Magnus. "Do you trust this man's judgement?"

Magnus was puzzled. "Yes, my lord."

"Because, you see, Attila wouldn't split up his force like that. If Attila sent his allies west, they might double-cross him - surrender. If he led his own men west, his allies might do a deal with the citizens of Aquileia. So, if he *is* moving west, his entire force is moving against us. Do you believe this man, Magnus?"

The room was quiet. Magnus glanced at the wretched aviator, terrified of decisions of this magnitude. "Yes, sir, I do. I'm certain Orgetorix spotted a large force of men. So, their entire force must be moving against us."

Aetius nodded. "In that case, I can't afford to be trapped here. We'll have to withdraw."

"But what about Aquileia?" Majorian demanded. "You made such a fuss about the city. Are you going to abandon it?"

"Don't you see it, Lord Majorian? Our task was to force our enemy to break off the siege. If they're marching west, then I've saved the city without having to fight a battle."

"There'll be a battle when they reach here," Majorian said.

"Yes, and that is why we must withdraw. Back to the mountains."

Magnus was very surprised, a week later, when Orgetorix brought him a personal letter. "It travelled by normal courier to Lyon, sir. Then Commius spotted it and sent it on." He winked. "The letter's perfumed."

Magnus subjected Orgetorix to a glare. "Thank you, aviator. And I'll have to thank Commius too."

Claudia Ambrosius to Magnus Vitalinus, commander of the Numerus Britannica, greetings. I trust you are in good health. I apologise for not replying to your letter, after your kindness in writing to me. Your parents are in good health. Your great-uncle, Lord Vitalinus, is said to be ailing. Here in Britain we are greatly concerned about the events in Italy. I would be most grateful if you could write to me about the situation there. Has there been a battle? Did the cities suffer terribly from the Huns?

Farewell, commander. I hope you prosper, and I salute you. Claudia A.

*   *   *

Britain, July 452 AD

Claudia tried to keep any emotion out of her voice as she read the letter to her father and his companions.

Magnus Vitalinus, Commander of the Numerus Britannicus, writing from Asolo, Italy, to Lady Claudia, greetings.

My lady, you asked about the events here in Italy. The Huns have been forced to abandon their attack on Aquileia. When they turned against us, we withdrew in good order, towards the mountains. We expect the Huns to follow us. By the time you receive this, a battle may have been fought.

Lord Aetius has to be cautious. The imperial forces are outnumbered by the barbarians. Although Lord Majorian has added his men to ours, the Roman Emperor Valentinian fled to Rome and has taken no part in the campaign. We trust that good generalship and discipline will save the day ...

Claudia's father and her husband listened in silence. "The city was saved," she said.

"Who cares about that?" Her father was grim. "Another battle. And that fool Valentinian is totally discredited ..."

"If this fellow Magnus is right," Ambrosius said.

"Oh, I'm sure he can be trusted in this, at least. This victory strengthens the hand of Vindex in Gaul."

So, her father had spotted that too. Claudia did not interrupt.

"Yes, I saw that," her husband said.

"Is there anything else?" her father asked.

"Only a footnote, father." She cleared her throat.

My duties place me in regular contact with the
messengers. I am earning their respect by learning to fly.
Your obedient servant, Magnus V.

Her father snorted. "Flying? Every member of the
Vitalinus family is crazy."

"But what are we to do?" Claudia held her breath.

Her father scowled. "Claudia, write back. Ask him what's
going on."

She tried to hide her eagerness. "Yes, father."

*   *   *

Today it was Magnus's turn to go looking for the enemy.
The sky was cloudless, without any wind. The air was
humid, which made the heat seem twice as bad. Magnus
knew that the aviators would be unable to fly any scouting
missions.

Magnus led his men out of the camp and down the dusty
road. They were looking for the Huns.

Over the past week, the allied army had carefully
withdrawn in the face of superior numbers, until they were
west of the River Piave. This put them no more than an
hour's ride from the messenger station in the mountains.

Each army was trying to gain the advantage. Until now,
the aviators had prevented the barbarians from ambushing
the allied troops.

But, the day before, the wind had died, and the aviators
had been unable to get off the ground. Magnus knew that
today would be just as bad. The only source of information
remaining to Aetius was the cavalry.

Magnus led his troop south to patrol the roads and tracks along the bank of the river, looking for signs of the enemy. They knew they could be in combat at any moment, so they were always on edge.

Aetius needed to know whether the Huns were advancing north towards his position or west towards another vulnerable city. Magnus and Nectaridius, as commanders of the light cavalry, had agreed to take it in turns to carry out this task. Yesterday, Nectaridius had taken his men on a patrol but had been unable to find anything.

He admitted that he had got most of his information about the movement of the Huns from refugees fleeing north. The Huns were busy to the south-east, sure enough. But they kept themselves out of reach of the scouting missions.

Magnus and his companions heard grim stories that the Huns had sent foraging parties across the north Italian plain. Lord Majorian, caught between his roles as general and senator, grumbled that the Huns would head for Ravenna and the road down the east coast. Aetius thought it more likely that Attila would attempt to advance west towards Milan.

For a couple of hours, the British troops found nothing. The peasants they questioned had seen nothing. Yet the troopers never let down their guard. If they encountered the enemy, it was Magnus's task to ensure that at least one of his men escaped to take the news to Aetius.

He and his troopers advanced towards a modest farmhouse, surrounded by a circle of trees, providing shade to the buildings. That dark patch of ground looked tempting. He just make out the occupants of the farmyard who had, quite understandably, chosen to work in the shade.

As they drew closer, Magnus realised they were barbarians, looting the farmhouse with the thoroughness of long practice. Magnus guessed there were no more than twenty of them. He was angry for himself for not identifying the horsemen for what they were. He heard a shout. They had been spotted.

For Magnus, it was almost a relief. At least they knew where the enemy was. He wheeled his horse around. "You know the drill! Back to the rearguard!"

Everyone knew exactly what to do. They exchanged arrow shots with the Huns at maximum range, then turned and ran for it. Their main task now was to bring back news of their discovery. To his relief, no-one had been injured in the exchange.

Magnus expected the lightly armed Huns to chase after them and had prepared an elaborate ambush. At close quarters, his troopers' chain mail and long cavalry swords would give them an advantage.

But, when he reached sergeant Madog and the reserves and turned to face his attackers, he realised no-one was following them.

"You all right, sir?" Madog asked.

"Yes." He saw that the Huns had abandoned their loot and were riding south.

"They'll turn back in a minute and put some more arrows into us. That's their usual trick," sergeant Madog said.

But the Huns kept on riding south. After a tense wait, Magnus realised that today nothing was going to happen. The barbarians were becoming cautious.

"We outnumber them," Madog said. "Perhaps we should give chase."

"No," Magnus said, more abruptly than he intended. "The Huns could be planning an ambush of their own. Don't forget, our task is to bring back news."

"What do we do then, sir?"

"Go back to that farmhouse. Give what help we can to the survivors. And gather as much information as I can."

That evening Magnus, tired and weary, reported back to Aetius at his headquarters, a requisitioned villa. Aetius was sitting in the shade of the colonnaded courtyard. "Yes, Magnus?"

"We encountered enemy foragers, sir. We drove them off. Then we came across a lot of refugees. The Huns are looting every villa and farmhouse east of the river Piave. It seems that many of the citizens have fled to the surrounding countryside."

Aetius grimaced. "Have their army reached Treviso?"

"No, sir. It's just foragers. The army hasn't crossed the river. Or not yet, anyway. The refugees say that the Huns are losing men to disease."

"Excellent," Aetius said. "If these rumours are true, they're too weak to face up to a proper army."

"Sir, if you sent some heavy cavalry forward, you could drive off the foragers and protect all those farmhouses from looters."

"And risk losing good men in an ambush?" Aetius waved this aside. "Thank you, Magnus. You've done well." The words were clearly a dismissal.

"Thank you, sir." Magnus went away satisfied. His suggestion had been ignored, but tomorrow it was Nectaridius's turn to scout ahead.

*　　*　　*

Padova

Aetius, standing on the makeshift podium, surveyed the men assembled in the forum. Magnus stood on the podium beside him. It was still an hour until noon, but the heat was already building up.

The Italian authorities, as usual, had taken no steps to defend Padova. Aetius felt obliged to take action, even if it only delayed the Huns for a couple of days. People with means of transport were being encouraged to send their dependents to safety further west. He had asked the citizens of military age to stay, but he was not hopeful.

All of the slaves in the city had been rounded up. Now they glared back, sullen. A detachment of heavy infantry stood round the group, weapons ready.

"Listen up! Lord Majorian's worried that you might seize the opportunity to run off. A threat to society. I was going to offer you freedom if you agreed to defend the city. But Lord Majorian has informed me that, in law, slaves can't be freed before they're thirty." Most of the wretches here were under twenty. "So, instead, I'm going to conscript you into the army of Gaul."

Magnus had advised him that this was perfectly legal, with several precedents. More than one would-be emperor had created his army that way.

They didn't like that at all. One man stepped forward. He was scrawny and looked half-starved. "You're sending us against the Huns? My lord?"

"No. Of course not. Training you'd take months, and the Huns'll be here before the week's out. If we put you into the front line, you'd be slaughtered." He gestured to the city walls. "So, for the time being, we're going to put you on the walls." That had been Magnus's idea. That young man was too inventive for his own good.

"You'll send us to Gaul, afterwards?" the scrawny man asked.

"Show more respect! What happens next depends how long this campaign lasts. Gaul can't afford a standing army. If we defeat the Huns, you'll be discharged."

"But - we'll be free?" the man asked.

"Of course, boy. All discharged soldiers are free. No matter how short their term of service." Majorian would probably have a seizure when he heard about it.

The man suddenly grasped what was going on. "That's legal?"

"Don't you dare question me, boy," Aetius snapped. He turned to Magnus. "This fellow's too clever for his own good. We'll end up hanging him for insubordination. Pity," he said in an undertone.

"We could promote him to sergeant," Magnus said, under his breath. "Keep him busy."

Aetius choked. "You're getting insubordinate too."

"Sorry, sir." He did not sound sorry at all.

Well - why not? Aetius turned to the scrawny man. "You've been billeted in the basilica. Take your men there, then draw rations for them."

* * *

Magnus Vitalinus, Commander of the Numerus Britannicus, writing from Asolo, north of Treviso, to Lady Claudia, greetings.

My lady, you asked me to let you know of any developments here in Italy. So far, we have retreated west and avoided battle.

The infantry grumble about doing nothing but Lord Aetius and Lord Majorian, knowing we are outnumbered, keep the army where it is. They have a good defensive position close to the mountains. From this location west of the river, we could attack the Huns if they moved against Milan and at the same time guard the road south. Camp rumour is that Lord Majorian has been reluctant to fight.

However, the Pope has sent a legate on a diplomatic mission to our generals, imploring them to act and save Rome. His Holiness wished to know whether he should intercede in this conflict. He was prepared to travel north and speak with King Attila if that was the only way to save Rome. Lord Aetius refused to allow the legate and his companions to continue any further east.

The legate responded by saying that his holiness had decided that he must act to save Rome, since the army seemed unable to do so. While the army remained indecisive, the cities of the Padus valley burned.

The legate accused the army of abandoning Padova to the Huns. Lord Aetius denied this, saying that the city was holding out. The Huns had ignored the city and instead devoted their attention to us. The legate was doubtful, but all of our information confirms this.

Lord Majorian said that by staying here, the army guarded the road to Rome. Aetius promised that he would lead his army against the Huns at once.

When the Huns invaded, the Eastern Emperor Marcian promised to send us aid. A courier arrived here yesterday with the news that Emperor Marcian has indeed kept the promise he made to Lord Aetius. The first consignment of troops from the eastern empire has arrived in Italy.

Your obedient servant, Magnus V.

Claudia stopped reading and cleared her throat. Her husband was surprised, even suspicious. "Why should Emperor Marcian want to help Emperor Valentinian?"

Her father smiled crookedly. "Two years ago, Emperor Marcian refused to continue to pay tribute to Attila. It was a brave thing to do, and he was lucky. Attila marched west instead. Now he fears another attack by the Huns. Sending reinforcements to Italy is a way to keep the Huns from attacking Constantinople."

"Let's hope they arrive in time," Claudia said.

Her father ignored her and turned Ambrosius. "The Pope is begging for help. He even suggested dealing with the barbarians."

"It seems cowardly of Aetius to retreat like that," Ambrosius said.

"Don't you see it, Ambrosius?" Her father was scornful. "While the army remains intact, Attila daren't turn his back on it."

Claudia could not remain silent any longer. "But if the army is destroyed, father, Attila can demand a ransom from every city north of Rome."

"Yes, indeed, girl. And why stop at Rome? What's going on? How old is that letter, girl? Two weeks? Has there been a battle since then? Write back. Ask."

"Yes, father."

*   *   *

The air had been hot and windless for three days now. Everybody was bad tempered; this led to quarrels, which often escalated into fights. More than once, knives had been drawn.

225

Aetius's secretary escorted Magnus into the villa's sumptuously decorated dining room. Aetius and Majorian were sitting on opposite sides of the dinner table. Both men were wearing comfortable white woollen tunics, lavishly decorated in purple. Each man had two bodyguards standing behind him. They ignored the servants who were preparing the meal.

Magnus stepped forward to make his report. He felt very, very tired. He kept his report concise.

"They've crossed the river, my lord. I caught up with their scouts, north of the road to Mantova. I'm certain that Attila's already across with half his army and is heading west."

Majorian's eyes widened. "So, he'll come after us? He'll get here – when? Noon tomorrow?"

"No, my lord. He's south of us, marching west, towards the river Mincio -."

Aetius heard Magnus out in a stony silence. He had already started drinking. "The Huns are on the march? This is a disaster. The Huns outnumber the imperial army - our combined forces. Now the barbarians are threatening a Roman city. Unless they're stopped, they'll march on Rome itself."

"Yes, sir."

"Mantova's on the river Mincio. We'll have to march south to protect it."

Majorian shrugged. "Can we, though? They outnumber us."

"My guess is that Attila will head for Mantova and demand a ransom. He must have realised how weak we are," Aetius said. "I had been counting on the aviators to locate the enemy. Now I have to work blind. Our only advantage has gone."

226

Majorian turned to Magnus "You cannot say for certain which direction the Huns have taken?"

"Their scouts were too numerous to allow me to allow me to get close. But it's obvious that Mantova is their -."

"Silence, boy. I am not interested in the guesses of inexperienced subalterns." He turned to Aetius. "The Huns are marching to attack us. We must prepare a defensive position, in the hills, and fight a defensive battle. It worked in Gaul."

Aetius was angry. "The Huns aren't threatening us! While we do nothing, the Huns will destroy Mantova!"

"We've already lost too many men! We must keep the army intact! We have to save the rest in case the Huns marched on Rome."

Magnus, listening in fascination, grudgingly admitted to himself that for once Majorian had a valid argument.

Aetius got to his feet. The chair scraped across the marble floor. "What's the use of keeping the army intact if we do nothing?"

There was a sudden hush. Everyone in the room was trying to pretend that he was invisible.

Majorian stood too, his chair going over with a crash. For a moment they glared at each other, then Majorian turned and stalked out. Men blocking his path scrambled to get out of his way.

*   *   *

Messenger station, Mount Noroni, Dawn.

An hour after dawn, everyone at the messenger station gathered on the meadow. Captain Dumnorix, as was his custom, plucked some dead grass and threw it into the air.

Everyone had been up at first light and now they paused in their work to watch the result. Not just the aviators and the ground crew, but the artificers as well. Even the local men recruited to haul on the ropes knew how important this was.

Dumnorix watched solemnly as the stalks were blown up over his head. He sighed.

The sky was clear, with not a cloud in sight. It was going to be hot down on the plain.

"Is it strong enough to get us into the air?" Young Orgetorix asked. After his spectacular stunt at the Bavaria Pass, the boy had been sent to Italy as a punishment. He was a hot pilot, sure enough, but Dumnorix wished the boy had been sent somewhere else.

"Oh, it'll keep you in the air. Whether it'll let you travel any distance is another question."

"I think it's worth trying, Captain."

Dumnorix nodded his agreement. He raised his voice. "Let's get to work. You know what to do." The ground crew scattered to their tasks.

He turned to the aviators. "I want you to get as high as you can, then head south. One of you might get lucky. As soon as you've lost half your height, turn back here. Don't take any risks."

"We're not likely to see anything of value," Orgetorix said.

"You never know. That slimy toad Majorian thinks the Huns are marching north to attack Aetius. So, if you reach that road and see it's empty, that itself is valuable military intelligence. Very useful to Aetius, that would be."

Orgetorix's face lit up as comprehension dawned. "Yes, Captain."

"Don't take any risks," Dumnorix said again. "Getting back with meagre information is better than trying to get more and not getting back at all."

The boy was not convinced. "We've got to stop Majorian, Captain."

"What if we find wave? Can we use it?" Acco asked.

"There's no chance of wave today," Orgetorix said. "The wind's coming from entirely the wrong direction."

"Yes, the wind down here's wrong," Acco said. "But the wind direction at six thousand feet is often blowing in a quite different direction."

"I know that!" Orgetorix retorted.

"If the upper wind is from the north, we could get wave."

Dumnorix glanced up, but of course there were no clues. "If you can find wave, then use it. But don't take any chances."

* * *

To the relief of everyone in the army, the weather had improved during the night. On the march west, the strengthening breeze offered some relief from the heat.

Magnus and his men had the task of riding to the south of the column of infantry. The light cavalry had been ordered to keep enemy scouts at a distance and to guess the enemy's movements. He had succeeded in the first task but the second had proved to be impossible.

Dusk was falling as Magnus led his men to the new camp that Aetius's staff had organised, south of a modest farmhouse. It had been a long, trying day and both the men and their horses were exhausted.

He led the way to the horse lines and dismounted. He was as tired as anyone, but his horse came first. Wearily, he unbuckled the saddle straps. He would have to report to Aetius next, and he was the bearer of bad news.

His servant, Conwyn, dropped the leather bucket he was carrying and stepped forward. He helped Magnus to pull off the saddle. "Let me do that, sir."

He grunted. "Thanks."

Then Alban joined them. "Welcome back, sir. You're late. How did it go?"

Magnus grimaced. "Attila's scouts prevented us from getting a view of the army." He felt that he was wasting his time. Even if he discovered something worthwhile, he knew that Majorian would ignore any evidence that contradicted his theory.

"At least the weather's improved," Alban said. "Although some are hinting that there'll be a storm by dawn."

"Pessimists," Magnus said.

"My men are on picket duty," Alban said. "In an hour I'll have to ride the rounds."

Conwyn turned his head. "What's that? Somebody's asking for you, sir."

"Perhaps it's one of your aviators," Alban said.

Everyone looked round. A pair of Alban's troopers were escorting a civilian, leading an exhausted horse, to the horse lines. The man was dressed in civilian riding clothes. Magnus guessed that he was a local man.

Alban's troopers led the man to the officers. "They told us you were 'ere, sir. This 'ere's a courier from the aviators."

The courier was delighted. "You're officers? I can't make these men understand me. I've brought a message from the aviators at Mount Noroni. I must deliver it to the General at once."

"Aetius has commandeered another farmhouse," Alban said.

Magnus nodded. "I'll take you to Aetius at once. My men will see that your horse is cared for."

They found Aetius still dressed for riding, studying a map. Majorian was there too, wearing a military cloak over a fresh tunic, but he ignored the newcomers.

Aetius looked up. He noted the newcomer. "Yes?"

The messenger blurted out his story. "The aviators were able to locate the Hun army, sir. The barbarians are twenty miles south of the general's position, heading west. The aviators say they estimate that the main body of the army was covering ten miles a day."

Majorian looked sour but said nothing.

Aetius was delighted. "Excellent!" He put his finger on the map. "So - I know where Attila is, while the barbarian can only guess about the imperial troops. And tomorrow he'll move to *here*, along *this* road."

Majorian, stood up and peered over his shoulder. "You want to risk everything on a single throw? Well, it's the best chance you'll get."

Magnus nudged the courier. "Let's go."

When Magnus led the courier back to his unit, he found that the officers had already begun their meal. "What's the news?" Alban asked.

"Aetius said that tomorrow we're going to ride across country and catch up with the Huns. They're going to be strung out along the road. We'll catch up with them before they can make camp, before they can form a battle line. We're going to run right over them."

"If the Huns follow Aetius's script," Alban said.

Magnus grinned. "Tomorrow, speed will be everything. Any man who can't keep up, any horse that goes lame, will be left behind. Attacking them a hundred men short will be preferable to attacking them an hour late."

Everyone nodded.

"You all know what to do," Magnus said. "But Ricimer's light cavalry has demanded the honour of scouting ahead tomorrow."

"Bah. Where will Ricimer himself be?" Alban said.

"Oh, with his men. He persisted until Aetius gave in. Hopefully, they'll send a message back if Attila does anything unexpected."

"If they can find him," Alban muttered.

"Now, now. So, I'll be with Aetius. Cynon, you and your troop'll come with me."

"Yes, sir."

"Alban, Nectaridius, you and your men will be part of the advance guard."

Alban nodded. "Yes, sir."

"What happens if the Huns stop where they are and wait for us?" Nectaridius asked. "Form a battle line?"

Magnus hesitated. "Aetius will probably cry off. If we attempted a set battle on level ground, we'd probably lose."

The next day, the imperial army broke camp at first light and took the road south. The Magister Militum, with his staff officers, rode just ahead of the main force.

Magnus, with his two troops of cavalry, were a quarter of a mile behind the advance guard, choking on their dust. He was aware that Aetius was following closely enough to monitor his troops' performance.

The road led steadily south through farmland. The view ahead was obscured by a shallow rise, covered with bushes.

Magnus watched with mounting annoyance as each unit in turn made its way to the top, cheered, and dashed forward, out of sight. He cursed their unprofessional behaviour.

When Magnus and his troop climbed the rise in turn, they could see the countryside below. South of them was the main east-west road. And spread out along it, from one horizon to the other, were the Huns.

"Hell! Look at that. And all at our mercy!" Sergeant Madog blasphemed in surprise. "At them! At them!"

"Hold! No man moves!" Magnus shouted. He cursed the fact that Aetius was too far away to keep these militia units in order.

The imperial troops ahead of Magnus, their discipline gone, were dashing down the hill.

"Stand firm. We'll wait until Aetius gets here," Magnus said, and was relieved when they obeyed. "This is a disaster! The Huns outnumber us four to one. When the Huns pull themselves together and counterattack …"

"Where are the enemy scouts? Why didn't they give warning of our approach?" Cynon said.

"My guess is that they must be to the south, watching for Emperor Valentinian's army."

The Huns down below were not given time to form a battle line. Magnus watched as the leading units of the Field Army charged right across the road and cut the enemy force in two.

A few minutes later Aetius rode up, attended by his staff officers and Majorian. They stopped to take in the scene below.

Majorian looked sour, as usual. Aetius, in contrast, was unusually cheerful. "Good morning, Magnus."

Magnus was too angry to give a polite response. "Sir – look! This is a disaster. The Huns are going to crush us."

Aetius glanced over the battlefield. "It looks a splendid sight to me, Magnus."

"But - when Attila's advance guard and his main force get their act together, we'll be caught between the upper and nether millstones."

Aetius, unperturbed, looked over the chaos below him. "I was hoping for something like this, you know. I was going to draw up the army in a line, north of that hill, and charge over the top and sweep the Huns away. But that plan was far too complicated, you know? Something was bound to go wrong."

"Yes, sir," Magnus said.

"We caught them off balance and off guard. Mainly by luck, I admit. At the moment we have the initiative, Magnus. Our only hope is to press our advantage. Give them no chance to discover how weak we are."

"But when Attila realises -."

"It's quite likely that Attila doesn't know how serious things are, because nobody dares to tell him." Aetius smiled. "It is even possible that none of his subordinates have grasped the peril they are in."

Magnus was subdued. "Yes, sir."

"But you're right. We must try to save the day. Lord Majorian, you and I will head east with the men we have here, and take command of the troops attacking Attila's main force. Magnus, I want you to take your men and head west, to take charge of the forces attacking his advance guard."

"That is a task best suited to Count Ricimer," Majorian said.

"Very likely," Aetius said. "But unfortunately, he isn't here. He's down there somewhere, with his men. Magnus, your main task is to prevent the Hun advance guard from turning back and reinforcing their main army. An impossible task, I know, but do what you can."

He gulped. "Yes, sir."

"I will send Count Ricimer and his cavalry to join you as soon as I can. Until he arrives, you're in charge of the operation."

Half an hour later, Magnus caught up with the imperial troops harrying the Huns' advance guard. He found that the imperial troops were a disparate mixture, each unit with its own officer, each uncertain what to do next. The Huns, in small groups, spread over several hundred yards, were trading arrows at maximum range with their enemies.

The Imperial troops held the advantage, for the time being, and blocked the road east, but that was unlikely to last. If the Huns decided to break free, nothing could stop them. Magnus knew that he must somehow keep the barbarians from rejoining the main force.

The Huns remained at maximum bowshot range, continually moving, sending the occasional arrow and insults. Very few of them wore armour, but that gave them the advantage of speed and endurance.

"At first it was easy," the German mercenary commander said. "We took them by surprise. They didn't know how to respond. But now - I think they've realised they outnumber us."

"We must stop them from rejoining the main force," Magnus said.

The German mercenary commander, sweating under his helmet, was not impressed. "What is your authority, young man?"

"The Magister Militum sent me. He has asked us to prevent the enemy advance guard from moving east and reinforcing the main force."

"At least someone knows what to do," the Gaulish militia officer said.

The German was impatient. "So far, they haven't tried to turn back."

"But their commander needs them."

The Gaulish militia officer smiled. "But they don't know that. They're the advance guard. They were told to advance. And Attila doesn't like it when men disobey him."

"I see." Magnus grinned "Of course, if they learn that their main force needs them, I've lost."

The commander of the Gaulish militia cavalry had a more practical question. "What if they split up? You know how Huns fight. It's like tackling smoke."

That was Magnus's greatest fear. "We'll just have to concentrate on the biggest group," he said, trying to sound confident.

The individual commanders were happy that Magnus had an agenda that they could follow. As the German commander said, Magnus would take the blame if his tactic failed.

Before Magnus could explain further, a group of over a score of Huns broke away from the main force and charged the British contingent.

Magnus shouted to his own men to follow and led them to cut the barbarians off. Could he get there in time?

He expected a brutal melee, but instead the Huns scattered in every direction, some of them shooting as they retreated. Magnus, riding with his shield up, took an arrow in his shield, a couple of inches from his face.

Five of the Huns broke away and fled east, firing over their shoulders as they went. Magnus shouted at his men to let them go.

Then another group of Huns charged their enemy. This time it was the Gaulish militia who rode to intercept them. The Huns turned back.

For the necessary few hours, the Hun advance guard kept moving west. For these barbarians, the battle was a confused melee, but their attackers had a clear purpose.

Magnus had a stroke of luck an hour after noon, when the Huns decided their horses needed water and withdrew north to find a stream.

Ricimer and his cavalry arrived that afternoon, too late to contribute anything of value. He bluntly told Magnus to report to the Magister Militum.

"But what about Attila's army, sir?"

"You don't have to worry about them any more. You have your orders. Go."

"Yes, sir." As Magnus rode across the battlefield, he realised what Ricimer had meant. A great victory had been achieved here.

* * *

Britain, September, 452 AD

Magnus Vitalinus, Commander of the Numerus Britannicus, writing from Milan, to Lady Claudia, greetings.

My lady, you asked me to let you know of any developments here in Italy. We have fought a great battle and defeated the Huns. In the days that followed the battle, Attila's allies abandoned him and fled to the east, towards the Alps. The main component of Huns stayed to protect their king. The Imperial Army, now full of confidence, attacked them head on. Attila and his closest companions were surrounded and fought to the last man.

Lord Aetius has led his expeditionary force back to Milan. He clearly intends to enjoy the fruits of victory.

The Roman Emperor Valentinian fled to Rome at the start of the campaign and took no part in the fighting. Men now say openly that Lord Aetius, with another victory to his credit, is now the effective ruler of the Roman Empire.

Italy is now at peace. I assure you that I am in good health.

Your obedient servant, Magnus V.

"Interesting. Your father will want to know more, of course. But it must cost that fellow a fortune to send all those letters. How can he afford it?" Ambrosius said.

"Perhaps he has a friend in the messenger service," Claudia said. She remembered his earlier letter where he said he was learning to fly. Had he called in some favours?

"Nonsense, woman. He must have friends in high places, that's all. This is important news, though. Your father will be delighted to hear it. Send a copy of this to him at once."

"Yes, my lord."

*   *   *

Milan, late September

The day was drawing to a close. The officers of the Numerus Britannica gathered in Magnus's lodgings, to share a meal and discuss Aetius's announcement.

Magnus had set about the task of rebuilding his company. They had suffered steady losses. Damaged, under-strength teams had to be merged and re-formed. On top of that, he had to catch up with the inescapable paperwork.

Magnus had found quarters for his men in the barracks at Milan. Using the last of his pay, he had found an apartment in the city, to serve as quarters for himself and his groom Conwyn.

The lodgings consisted of three rooms on the upper storey a patrician's town house, just a street away from the barracks entrance. The compact rooms were up a rickety flight of stairs, but they were his own. His servant did the cooking and all the other domestic chores of the household.

"What did lord Aetius have to say?" Alban said.

That afternoon, Aetius had summoned his military commanders to the palace and made an announcement. "He intends to spend the winter in Milan." That created quite a stir among the British officers.

Magnus's servant handed out servings of bread, olives, cheese and sausage. The guests ate standing up, their plates in their hands. "The Magister Militum wants to stay near the centre of power," Alban said darkly.

"Well, the Huns embarrassed him at the beginning of this year," Magnus said reasonably. "When they invaded, he was several hundred miles away, on the wrong side of the Alps. He doesn't want to get caught out again."

239

"Unfortunately, Count Ricimer doesn't like the Magister Militum breathing down his neck. He likes his independence," Alban said.

Nectaridius coughed. "Sir, did Aetius mention when we're going to receive our back pay? Some of my men have been asking me."

Magnus had not been paid either. "I'm afraid not. But that reminds me. Aetius said the Master of Cavalry in Gaul has asked for reinforcements. Aetius may decide to send us."

Nectaridius rolled his eyes. "Wonderful. So we have to cross the Alps again. With winter coming on."

"So, this way, the chancellor in Vienne will have to pay us?" Alban asked.

Magnus grinned. "You're too cynical for your own good. But If the order comes, we'd better get across the high passes before the first snows."

"I hear you got another letter from home. Some people have all the luck."

"It's news about my parents, that's all," Magnus said.

Claudia Ambrosius to Magnus Vitalinus, commander of the Numerus Britannica, greetings. I thank you for your letter. It was very kind of you to write to me. Are you well? I am concerned about you and the situation in Italy. Will you and the British troops remain in Milan? Is the Roman Emperor Valentinian safe? Did the cities suffer terribly from the Huns?

Your parents are in good health. Farewell, commander. I hope you prosper, and I salute you. Claudia A.

He was disappointed by how short the letter was. But she probably could not afford long letters. She had asked him to describe the political situation. How could he do that in a single letter? An interesting challenge.

He drafted a cautious reply, trying to explain the political situation, carefully phrased on the assumption that her husband would read it too.

Magnus Vitalinus, writing from Milan, to Claudia Ambrosius, greetings.

I confirm that I am in good health.

I am pleased to say that the situation in Italy is now stable, although the Roman emperor has not yet returned to his capital. The Huns and their allies have retreated east of the Alps and so far remain quiet. The landowners in Italy complain that the damage done to their northern estates will take a generation to repair.

The Magister Militum has decided to remain in Italy for the time being. However, he is confident enough of the situation to transfer several units back to Gaul. The Numerus Britannica was one of those units ordered to Vienne. We have been ordered to leave Milan within a month. You will see that we are required to cross the Alps once again.

I pray that you are enjoying the best of fortune and are in good health. Farewell, my lady."

* * *

Britain, April, 453 AD

In the new year, shortly after the sailing season opened, Claudia received another letter from Magnus. She was surprised at how bulky the envelope was. As usual, she took the letter to husband.

Ambrosius was unwell and had taken to his bed again. He was lying on the couch, propped up on pillows, uncomfortable and bored. Carefully, she explained that a courier had brought a letter.

"Read it, woman."

"Very well, sir." She sat down on the chair next to his bed, cleared her throat and began to read.

"Magnus Vitalinus, writing to you from Vienne, in Gaul, greetings.

I thank you for your most recent letter. My unit has been transferred to the capital of the Gallic Empire, on the Rhone. The city is the headquarters of Lord Avitus, Commander of Cavalry. It is also, for the time being, where the Numerus Britannica is stationed.

The city often receives snow in winter and the river is frequently misty in the morning.

With its riverside position, Vienne once prospered as the empire's major wine port on the Rhone. Many imperial monuments survive to mark this past glory.

The city is also home of the bishop of Southern Gaul and -."

"Why's he wasting his time writing about the bishop?" Ambrosius demanded.

Claudia looked up. "Perhaps he has nothing more interesting to write about. No invasion, no revolt."

"Hah. Mark my words, there'll be a mutiny before long. Does he say anything about politics?"

She skimmed the letter. "Yes. 'The emperor's palace, on the west bank of the Rhone, is a grand affair ...' perhaps he's seen it... 'But the emperor is ill, and the palace is ignored by those people interested in power ...'"

"That sounds a dangerous thing to say. Go on, woman."

"The chancellery is on the east bank. The building is functional, lacking any ornamentation, made of brick, not stone.

General Avitus, Commander of Cavalry, is responsible for the defence of Gaul. General Avitus is an elderly gentleman, who owns a large estate in southern Gaul.

I will be working alongside Edeco, the commander of the German mercenary troops here. He is glad to see us. According to rumour, he's been begging for more cavalry for months.

However, things are fairly quiet at the moment. Italy also is quiet. I hope we won't have much to do.

A month after our arrival in Vienne the men of the Numerus received their back pay. I used this opportunity to find lodgings, in the old town, halfway between the forum and the old theatre.

"I have to visit Commander Avitus almost every day. You may ask what Avitus is like to work with. After working so long with Lord Aetius, I find Avitus very straightforward and direct. Refreshingly so.

"But he doesn't have much military experience. This could be considered a major handicap. However, he has enough mercenary officers around him to give him advice. I think he's astute enough to keep his captains in line. And if we have a major military crisis, the Magister Militum can always come up from Italy."

Her husband was angry. "He's in Gaul! What use is that?"

"He says things are quiet in Gaul. He says Italy is quiet too. So presumably he won't be sent back there."

"You assume too much. The Huns invaded last April, didn't they? They could do it again. What news does he have of them? Your father will want to know. Perhaps he'll pay the postage."

"Yes, my lord."

Chapter 14: Homecoming

Britain, September, 453 AD

The old road, the Akeman Street, built by the legions three hundred years before, ran west from London to Corinium, on the southern fringes of the Limestone Edge.

Magnus turned off the old military road at last. The narrow country road followed the contour of the tree-covered hills.

The familiar apple orchard came into view, then the red-tiled roofs. The farm looked comfortable, with its kitchen garden and smell of freshly-baked bread, but it was more modest than he had remembered. He was fond of the place where he grew up. It was safe, in the heart of Britain, untouched by the storms that racked the rest of the empire.

He told himself that he could have stayed and worked for a share of this. But the farm was a modest one and getting poorer. If it were divided between three brothers, his portion would be negligible. He preferred to make his fortune elsewhere.

As he rode into the farmyard, his mother came out of the buttery to see who the visitor was. Her dress, of the rich local wool, was dyed a rusty red. "Magnus! Welcome home," she said warmly. "Will you be staying long?"

He dismounted. "No, mother. I'm going to Deva, to help the garrison commander. How's father?"

"So, you've left the general's service? Your father won't approve, you know."

This oblique answer told him all he needed to know. He led his horse to the stable. Caring for his horse would postpone his meeting with his father.

He went to the cramped room he used to share with his brother and was busy stowing away his sword when his father walked in.

Father, grave and dignified, was tall, with greying hair. He looked stern. "Your mother says you can't stay."

Magnus looked up at his father. He had long ago given up hope of growing any taller. "No, sir. The governor here asked the emperor for experienced officers. My application was accepted."

"The army's a foul trade, best left to barbarian mercenaries." Magnus was reminded once again that his father was a rigid moralist.

"But I've been promoted, father. It's an executive post. Adjutant to the commander at Deva."

Father was unimpressed. "Adjutant? To a barbarian commander?"

"I'll be learning how to run a major fort. And a count's headquarters."

The old man asked a series of sharp questions about the situation in Italy. "I'm glad to hear that you're well, Magnus. Although I disapprove of my son joining the army. Did you take part in the campaign against the Huns?"

"Yes, sir. Although I spent most of my time with the messenger corps, setting up a new route ..."

His father asked him to explain, and seemed to be amused by the story. "So, you spent most of this time acting as manager? How very wearisome you must have found it."

"Yes, sir. Although I learned to fly while I was about it."

"Indeed? That sounds more like you. But why?"

"I thought I could get the most out of my men by sharing with them, sir."

"And that of course was your only reason," father said. "Have you been in trouble again?"

"Well, not in the way you mean, sir ..."

"Never mind that. You'd better get changed for dinner. Your mother will undoubtedly prepare something special for you."

"Yes, sir."

He encountered his oldest brother, Gaius, at dinner. Gaius used the opportunity to launch into one of his grumbles. "It's getting more and more difficult to sell our produce. All the towns within travelling distance are getting poorer, the people are emigrating and no-one's taking their place. The larger estates around us can sell their crops at a lower price. Soon we won't be able to sell anything."

This rant distressed his mother, but Magnus pretended to take no notice. Gaius was always saying that. Starting an argument would just make things worse.

His visit came to an end all too soon. When he prepared to leave, his father surprised him. "I disapproved of you joining the governor's bodyguard. But defending Gaul from the Huns is different. Go with my blessing, my boy."

*   *   *

Conwyn, riding Magnus's spare horse, followed directions to the Ambrosius estate, a farm in the upper Thames valley. Taking the estate's private road, an impressive set of red-tiled roofs came into view.

The Ambrosius villa, nestled against the Limestone Edge, was as grand as he had expected. The servants were snooty towards an adventurer; even the household slaves looked down on him.

They led him to the kitchen, where things went better than he expected. The ageing steward told him to clean himself up.

"But don't rush. That letter of yours won't come to any harm from an hour's wait. You'll do better make yourself presentable first."

The cooks listened to his stories in fascination, treated him like a hero and ensured he was well fed. They told him that the old man looked sour, but he wasn't as uptight as he appeared.

The cook smiled. "You met the lady's brother – young Julian? The lad was a real tearaway. Got into one scrape after another. Caused his father no end of grief."

The steward appeared in the doorway and the chatter stopped. "You've made yourself presentable? Good. The master will see you now, lad."

The steward led him through the corridor to the master's room. He tried not to gape. The walls of the room were skillfully painted to suggest marble pillars and a gateway to an imaginary garden.

The lord and lady of the household were sitting on opposite sides of a grand room. The floor was decorated with an elegant mosaic. Lady Claudia was young, pretty, but austere. The lady's chair looked elegant in the Italian style but very uncomfortable. Ambrosius, plump and indolent, sprawled on a couch.

Conwyn, tongue tied, explained that he carried a message. "Commander Magnus is in good health and – and prospering, sir"

The austere lady nodded. "I see. Lord Magnus has been transferred to Britain, then?"

"Yes, ma'am. He had hoped to come here in person, but when we arrived in Portchester he was summoned to London by the governor."

Conwyn placed the sealed letter on the desk. "This is from Commander Magnus, ma'am."

The letter was left untouched. "Thank you. I will read it later. The fact that this letter was written is more significant than its contents."

How could Magnus imagine marriage with such a lady?

The lady changed the subject by asking politely about Conwyn. "So, you come from London? Have you served with Magnus for long?"

"Only two years, ma'am. My main task was to look after Magnus's horses. I had wanted to join the army..." But the infantry of the coastal forts, tied to the land, held no appeal for him. "You see, you could only join the mobile army if you already had some combat experience."

The lady's husband sat up. "Silence, boy. That letter -. Give it to me, fool." He grabbed the letter, ripped it open and made Conwyn wait while he read through it.

There was an uncomfortable silence. Conwyn realised that Lady Claudia was embarrassed. He had always hoped to see the inside of a patrician's mansion but just now he was fervently wishing himself elsewhere.

Ambrosius growled. "He says he's been posted back to Britain. What use is that to me?" He read the letter again. "What does the fellow mean … 'you can trust the bearer of this message?' What the hell does that mean?" he was deeply suspicious.

"I - I don't know, sir. I wasn't allowed to read it."

Lady Claudia intervened. "Perhaps it means that the young man here can explain about, ah, the commander's career in Italy." The lady was prim, but perhaps that was because her husband had read the letter – her letter - in front of her.

Conwyn did not want to overstay his welcome. "I must be going, sir. It's an hour's ride to the nearest posting inn."

Ambrosius read through the letter once more, then looked up. "You can go, boy."

"Yes, sir."

Conwyn was anxious to get away and this time no-one tried to stop him. "You're eager to be on your way?" the melancholy steward asked. "Well, perhaps it's for the best."

Conwyn walked through the streets of London to his father's house by the Aldgate. His father had bought an old decaying brick house cheaply, knocked it down and built a wooden house in its place. Coming in from the street, the room seemed full of smoke, but it was warm.

"Conwyn! How are you?" His mother flung open the door. "Come in, come in! How long will you stay?"

"No time at all, mother. I have to go on my journeys in a couple of days." Mother was distressed, which made him feel guilty.

His father, sitting in his chair by the charcoal brazier, looked up. "Where have you been, all this time, boy? Rubbing shoulders with soldiers again?"

All of his resolution deserted him. "I've been in Gaul, father. I got a job, respectable. I've been serving as a groom for an army officer. Magnus Vitalinus was part of the expeditionary force to Italy. We're leaving for the north in a couple of days."

"A groom?" exclaimed his father, gripping the arms of his chair till his knuckles shone. "You accepted a position as a servant, boy?"

"Yes, sir," Conwyn said stoutly.

"You bring shame on the family. You ought to stay at home and help your brothers."

Conwyn glanced at his brother Cynon, sitting in the chair opposite his father.

"I left because I was tired of being my brother's unpaid servant. I was tired of being stuck in London, and I was tired of this backwater province. I wanted to see something of the world." He had no useful skills. The role as an officer's groom had been the best he could hope for.

"You're a fool, boy. Why accept a demeaning role as a servant when you could train as a craftsman in London?"

"It wasn't demeaning. Magnus is -."

"The Vitalinus family is the most powerful and arrogant in Britain. Powerful enough to ignore the law. And a son of mine is serving that family."

"Magnus has no land at all. That's why he joined the army."

Cynon looked up. "The greed of those patrician families is destroying Britain."

"You've been listening to too many sermons, brother," Conwyn retorted.

Cynon sneered. "You'll spend all your time cleaning up after horses."

"That's better than staying here and cleaning up after you."

"Conwyn!" his father snapped. "Apologise to your brother at once."

Conwyn remembered all over again why he had joined Magnus. He had wanted to escape from this stagnating city and his brothers. When Magnus had been selected for the expeditionary force, Conwyn knew that he had done the right thing. He was going to participate in world-shaking events.

He slammed out of the house in a rage. He would go back to the fort and share a meal with the other servants. That would be preferable to eating humble pie in his father's house.

* * *

Chester, Late September, 453 AD

Magnus had been sent to Chester as adjutant, secretary to the Count of the Irish Shore. It was a responsible task, and a stepping stone to greater things. The city, with its imposing walls, was on the north bank of the gently flowing river. To the west and south west, visible on a clear day, were the great mountains of Britain. The nearest of those hills housed the messenger station. Magnus had heard that messages took three days to reach London, even in good conditions. To the north west was the Dee estuary, hidden by some low-lying hills.

The commander's headquarters was at the centre of the old city. The layout followed the old pattern, with the count's personal rooms built round a courtyard. A servant escorted Magnus along the colonnade to Count Waltharius's office. The study faced south, to catch the best of the sun and its warmth.

The commander of the Chester garrison welcomed Magnus warmly. He was a mercenary from Germany, who had grown old in imperial service. Magnus noted that his white tunic, embroidered at the shoulders, was of the finest wool. He had adopted the Roman fashion of hair bulked over the ears and a neatly trimmed beard.

"We have plenty of work for you, young man." Waltharius grinned. "Some of us wondered whether you were being sent out here to take command. As soon as we heard a patrician had been appointed here the rumours started growing."

Magnus was appalled. "No, sir, I was sent here to broaden my experience. I had hoped that when I return to Gaul I'll be appointed to the emperor's staff, meet the chancellor and senators. Then, perhaps, given command of some fortress or promoted to count. But ... only if your report was favourable, sir. They made it quite clear to me that I wouldn't have any men under my command. My sole task was to assist you in your duties."

The count smiled. "I understand, lad. That's become quite routine." He hesitated. "You're not married?"

"No, sir." He changed the subject. "I was also asked to look into the messenger service, but from what I've seen, it seems to be working all right."

The Count looked sour. "Those flyboys are a law unto themselves. They're always complaining about the weather. They've got a wonderful quiver-full of excuses."

"Well - those machines were designed for the Alps, not Britain. The conditions here are barely sufficient. But I'll find out whether their poor performance is due solely to the weather."

"Did they tell you I've been transferred elsewhere? I've already made my preparations for my journey for Eboracum," the count said. "Guthlaf will assume command here in my absence."

Magnus had been warned of this. "Do you expect any trouble when you get there, sir?"

"Not really. The problem was political rather than military. And the knowledge that the emperor was personally interested quietened things down."

There was a knock on the door and another middle-aged mercenary officer walked in.

Count Waltharius introduced Magnus to Guthlaf, his second in command.

Guthlaf was another immigrant from Germany, a grizzled veteran who had risen through the ranks. His tunic was decorated with two vertical woven bands. He, too, sported a neat beard.

Guthlaf's welcome was equally warm. "We've been expecting you for some time, lad."

The count intervened. "Magnus has been sent here to serve as the fort's adjutant."

Guthlaf nodded. "So, the rumours were wrong? I'm glad that's been cleared up. And I'm equally glad that somebody else will have the task of writing reports to the governor."

"Don't frighten the lad," Waltharius said. "You understand, there have been no pirate raids this year, but we have to remain on our guard through the sailing season. They haven't given up. British slaves are highly valued over there. There's no shortage of bravos prepared to take the risk."

Magnus nodded. "I understand, sir."

The old fort at Chester was half-empty, but Magnus had expected that. Autumn was drawing on, the campaigning season was over, and the part time militia had returned to their homes. The mercenaries who made up the permanent garrison took up only a quarter of the living space. The auxiliary cavalry and their horses, taken together, only took up another quarter.

That evening, all of the officers dined together in the largest room in the commander's quarters. Waltharius led Magnus around the room, introducing him to each officer in turn. "Magnus has been sent up here to serve as our fort's new adjutant."

Magnus smiled politely and did his best to remember their names. He tried to exchange a word with as many officers as he could.

"If I serve with distinction, and the count puts in a good word, I hope to be promoted to somewhere closer to the centre of things."

"Lyon? Vienne? Under the Magister Militum's eye? Rather you than me, boy," Guthlaf said. "How long do you expect to stay up here?"

"In Britain? Oh, two years at most."

Magnus tried to judge the mood of the garrison. The officers were proud that Waltharius had been given the task of repairing the situation in the north - and the promotion to duke that went with it.

Magnus knew that his duties would require tact. Most of the officers were mercenaries from Germany, promoted through the ranks. They had very little hope of rising any further, while Magnus could hope to achieve the rank of count – or higher.

When the meal was over, the serious drinking began. "Did you acquire a taste for fine wines in Italy?" Waltharius asked.

Another officer intervened. "Are you too proud to drink ale now?"

Magnus grinned. "I prefer good ale to bad wine. And Gaul has plenty of bad wine."

This seemed to please everybody. "Our beer is freshly brewed," Waltharius said. "Every few days. Can't ask the men to drink stale beer."

The conversation changed to Aetius's campaigns against the Huns, and Magnus described the role of the light cavalry. He listened to the others talking among themselves and judged that the count was running his command smoothly.

The next morning, in the Principa, the headquarters of the fort, the formal handover took place. Waltharius wished Guthlaf well, then he and his retinue departed for Eboracum. Magnus watched them go, out across the ditch and towards Delamere Forest, riding along the long road that led to Eboracum.

That evening, just before dinner, Magnus knocked on the door of Guthlaf's office. The new commander was alone.

"You asked to see me, sir? I've drafted that letter to the governor, pointing out that the garrison's pay is in arrears. It's ready for your signature."

"It isn't that, young man. I'd like a word in private."

Magnus closed the door. "Of course, sir. What is it?"

The old soldier looked uncomfortable. "The thing is, I'm too old to learn new tricks. Being promoted to count isn't just a military rank. It's political as well. You've got to visit the governor, explain yourself to the council of advisers. I'm not looking forward to that at all."

"I'm sure Waltharius has confidence in your abilities, sir."

"Well, I don't. A trip to London's more dangerous than fighting pirates. One mistake there could ruin your career."

"Well, yes, sir."

"In October I have to go to London and explain things to the Council. I'll probably make a mess of it. Waltharius should've given the promotion to one of the younger men, who could do it properly."

Magnus nodded. "Well, I can understand how you feel. I had to report to the Magister Militum during the campaign against the Huns."

Guthlaf cheered up. You've done it before? Reported to the top brass?"

"Yes, sir. But I never learned to like it."

"Well, never mind that," Guthlaf said. "I want to inspect the outlying forts along the coast before winter closes in. I want you to plan the details for me."

"Yes, sir."

*   *   *

Durovigtum, October, 453 AD

Finn, commander of the British Field Army, was known behind his back as Finn Oathbreaker. He knew this, of course, and he hated it. He had carried out the obligations of the blood feud. Hnaef had killed Finn's kinsman. But everyone ignored that and remembered only that Hnaef had been a guest in Finn's hall.

Finn and his companions had fled to Britain and joined the mercenary army. He had prospered, being used to command, and now the imperials had appointed him as commander of the Field Army, a thousand men strong. But leaders acquired enemies. He had thought the killing had been forgotten. Now his enemies reminded everyone that he had struck down a guest in his own hall. They whispered that he would strike down his own men too.

Now that the campaigning season was over, the mercenary troops had gone into their usual winter quarters at Durovigutum. The local magistrates, hoping to curry favour, had given the English commander a house in the city. Finn hated it. The place was too large for comfort and had a large courtyard open to the sky, so it was impossible to keep warm. It was built of brick, which meant it was difficult to keep repaired. He would have preferred to build anew, in wood, but that would have meant a loss of dignity.

This evening he left the house as usual and strode through the streets of the decayed city. His companions lengthened their stride to keep up. The army had taken over the town's basilica as their dining hall. Tradition demanded that the commander of the troop would share the evening meal with his men. If he were late, his enemies would claim it was a deliberate insult. Finn never even considered the possibility of dining alone.

The British leaders, the councillors, said that the field army was there to defend the land from overseas enemies. Everyone knew, though, that their main task was to protect the landowners from their enemies inside Britain. Finn despised the landowners, who were so soft that they could not even defend themselves from their own tenants.

Finn entered the hall and glanced round. Three fire-pits had been made down the centre of the hall. It was ill-lit and full of woodsmoke, but he was used to that. A few men at the benches nearest the door greeted him. He responded with a wave and a casual word or two. He judged the preparations, then relaxed slightly. The dining benches had been set up, the meat was being cooked, but the hall was not full yet. He made his way to the high table. Most of his officers and companions were already sitting on the bench. Their greetings were a mixture of respect and banter, depending upon how long they had served with him. He grinned.

"Sigeferth, you're always first to arrive! Have you left any ale for me?"

His companion grinned. "Just the dregs!"

The serving women brought in the food, the last of the men sat down, and the meal began. Over their food, his companions complained that their pay was in arrears again.

Finn was not very concerned. "What is there, in Durovigutum, in winter, to spend it on?"

Then Sigeferth, sitting to his right, pushed his plate aside. "The rations, that the landowners promised to deliver, were late in arriving. And they're barely adequate."

Finn took the horn filled with beer from a servant. "Now, that *is* serious. Remind me again in the morning and I'll send a complaint to the governor." He drank deeply and passed the drinking horn on to Ordlaf.

"Thank you, my lord." Ordlaf drank in turn. "Everyone's heard that the new count in Chester's a British speaker, a patrician. The whole troop is grumbling about that."

There was a murmur of agreement from around the table. Finn nodded. He had been angered at the news himself. "Yes. Apart from the insult, who can speak up for the English community to the governor and his Council?"

Sigeferth grinned. "You're now the senior English-speaker in Britain."

He snorted in derision. "Nonsense. Duke Waltharius outranks me, and the other counts besides."

"But he's in the north. The Empire regards that as a separate province. Waltharius can't report to Governor Gallus in London. And we can't appeal to him for aid. In the south, you're senior."

"True enough," Ordlaf said. "Finn here's the man to speak up for the English community!"

Finn knocked back some more beer. The idea attracted him. Sending a petition to the governor would strengthen his

259

authority, not just in his own troop but amongst every English speaker in Britain.

He was eager to gain status. He knew that the field army had been commanded by a count at one time, but the idea of a count commanding less than a thousand men was absurd. He had suggested to Waltharius, before his promotion, that the Council should recruit more men into the army, but Waltharius had said that the landowners would refuse to pay for it.

Finn wanted a larger army and more power. He wanted promotion to count. He was angry at the lack of respect he got from the Council. He regarded Vitalinus as his sponsor, but the old man's power was waning. Everyone knew the governor was weak, with no support from the emperor in Vienne. That might have been useful, but unfortunately Aurelianus was now the most powerful man in Britain. Everyone knew that the governor supported Aurelianus. Finn expected his own status to diminish now that Aurelianus's power was increasing.

*   *   *

Corinium, October

The aviator placed the letter on Magnus's desk with a smirk. "The lady asked me to deliver this to you in person, sir."

Magnus recognised the handwriting but the letter was unusually bulky.

Guthlaf looked up and smiled. "A letter from a lady? Don't mind me. Go ahead and open it."

Claudia Ambrosius to Magnus Vitalinus at Chester, writing from Corinium, Greetings.

You say you are bored in Chester. But you write letters to the provincial governor and his chancellor, and even the imperial chancellery, about affairs of state. How can that be boring?

Lord Ambrosius will shortly be making his annual visit to London. I will probably be asked to accompany him.

Now that the summer is over Lord Ambrosius and I have made several visits to Corinium. I have made friends with Lady Dobunnius, wife of the city's chief magistrate, and her granddaughter Julia. She is a dear girl, but she shocked the prudish this summer by visits to the messenger station, in the Vale of the White Horse, where she persuaded the commander to teach her to fly.

She was deeply upset when her parents died, of fever, and her grandfather though these lessons would take her mind off her grief. Do you think this an unacceptable pastime for a lady?

Julia is fascinated by your description of your exploits with the aviators in Gaul. I hope you will forgive her impertinence.

Farewell, commander. I hope you prosper, and I salute you.

He smiled and put the letter aside. Guthlaf, although comfortably married, was fascinated. "So it was a letter from a lady? You lucky dog!"

*　　*　　*

261

Four miles west of Corinium, the track breasted the rise and the party halted to rest their horses. The track was mainly used by pack horses, but Claudia knew it was just wide enough for the chaise.

"The horses are fine. Let's go," Magnus told her.

This was the first time she had seen Magnus since he left for Gaul. So far, the only words they had exchanged had been polite platitudes.

They began the descent into the Golden Valley. Claudia, with her friend Julia sitting alongside her, took the corners with exaggerated care.

They had seen lots of rain the week before, but the morning of the expedition had turned out to be sunny and warm. The leaves were falling, but the grass was green and lush underfoot.

The series of hills that made up the Limestone Edge were a mixture of wooded hills and farmed valleys. The scattered villages were clusters of stone-walled cottages with thatched roofs. The stone weathered to a pleasing silvery grey. The impoverished but self-reliant villages in the southern half of the Edge made an uncomfortable contrast to the sprawling villas in some of the northern valleys.

Julia had proposed this outing weeks ago. The messenger station, perched on a hilltop fifteen miles outside Corinium, was a fascinating place to visit. It was just the right distance from the city for an excursion. But Julia's grandfather Philip had refused to let Julia go, saying he was too busy to accompany them.

Then Magnus had arrived in Corinium. He had paid a visit to Philip and had volunteered to escort the ladies. He had suggested the airfield merely as a destination for a day outing, for the whole family, without betraying any other motives.

Claudia had her chaise, dainty but capable of good speed, which could accommodate both ladies. But then Claudia's younger brother, Basil, had offered to escort them too.

Basil, of course, was no help to anyone. He and his two cronies, mounted on showy horses, chatted between themselves and ignored everyone else.

"I still don't understand what Vitalinius is doing in Corinium," Julia said.

Claudia rounded the corner before replying. "He said he's on his way to London to report to the governor and the Council. But -."

They left the Golden Valley and began the long climb to the Edge. After an hour, they paused again to rest the horses. Magnus walked back to ask the ladies whether they were tired.

"No, of course not," Claudia said. She was at last able to ask the question that was bothering her. "Magnus, I thought you were stationed in Chester."

"Yes, I am. But Lord Guthlaf, the commander there, asked me to report to the Council in London."

"Is he too ill to make the report himself?"

"No. Can I trust your discretion, my lady? He's terrified of my great-uncle. And your father." She nodded.

They continued on their way. Basil had ignored the ladies for most of the journey, preferring to talk to his cronies. Then he rode ahead to question Magnus about his campaigns. Claudia could just overhear Magnus's reply.

"I can't get used to how green everything is! In Italy, everything was parched before the end of spring. You get occasional bouts of damp weather, but in the months I was there I don't think I ever saw it as green as this."

"Do you intend to go back?" Basil asked. Claudia could tell that her brother was grinning.

"To Gaul? If I want to gain advancement, I have no choice."

As the path grew steeper, Basil dismounted. Julia remarked, in an undertone, that he cared more for his horse than he did for his servants.

"Hush," Claudia said. She was enjoying Julia's company. The girl was considered to be rather wild. She had been living with her grandparents since her parents had died. Their farm was in the Vale of the White Horse, close to Corinium's southern messenger station. She visited the messenger station at every opportunity.

Basil chose to accompany Magnus on the climb. "How much further? I hear that these flyers have republican views, with no respect for their betters."

"Well – they lack social skills." Magnus sounded embarrassed. "That might be mistaken for lack of respect. They respect each others' skills more than they trust outsiders."

"It would be amusing if we could see one of them fall to his death."

Magnus's reply betrayed no emotion. "That risk adds spice to every flight."

Claudia knew from Magnus's letters that he had learned to fly. Too late, Basil remembered. "You have flown, I believe? In one of those death traps?"

"Oh, yes."

"Did you see any crashes?" Basil asked eagerly.

"I must tell you about my own, sometime. But, more than once, one of my colleagues failed to return."

"You regard them as your colleagues, then?" Basil clearly disapproved.

"I fought alongside them."

Claudia found that the messenger station, perched on its hilltop, was a curious place. Its long low wooden huts had a ramshackle, temporary air. It did not seem to be a home to be lived in. It seemed as transient as the flying machines that came and went so effortlessly.

To the west, they could see the River Severn. Beyond that was another range of hills. Magnus turned to face the wind and breathed deeply.

Claudia smiled. "I agree, the breeze on this hilltop makes a refreshing change from the stale air of the city."

A middle-aged man with blond hair stepped forward to meet them. "Good morning, ladies and gentlemen. I'm Sergeant Rhys. Welcome to Edge."

"Good morning, sergeant," Claudia said. Rhys was a commoner - he seemed to be awed by the visiting aristocrats.

Basil was tactless, as usual, but fortunately his manner was patronising rather than insulting. "Fine weather for flying, don't you think, my good man?"

"The wind's only strong enough for training flights," the sergeant said. "This breeze isn't strong enough to allow the machines to travel more than a couple of miles. Even our light training machines are struggling to stay aloft."

"Would they crash?" Basil asked.

"It's more likely, sir, they'd sink down to the bottom of the hill and we'd have to pull them up again. Embarrassing rather than dangerous."

"The wind might improve later," Magnus said.

Rhys was tongue-tied until Julia remarked that Magnus had fought the Huns. Claudia listened while Magnus discussed the campaign with the aviators. He seemed self-confident amongst these men.

She decided that he had changed since had left Britain. Now he was a man in authority, appointed to a post that offered further advancement. The campaigning season was over, but different responsibilities awaited him in London.

Magnus described his own flights in the Italian Alps. The aviators politely refused to believe him.

Magnus took all this in good humour. "Let me prove it, then."

"Can you fly in these light airs, sir?" the sergeant asked.

Magnus responded by stooping to pull up some grass. Claudia watched in surprise as he tossed the stalks into the air and watched the wind blow them away. "Yes, the wind's strong enough."

"I can't let you fly solo," the sergeant said. "But how about a flight in a two-seater?"

The other pilots grinned. Claudia suspected that they were secretly hoping that this patrician would make a fool of himself. Fortunately, Magnus's riding clothes were suitable for a flying machine.

Claudia's brother and his cronies regarded this performance as a splendid joke. The self-confident, boastful soldier would be shown up as a fraud.

"And all these hicks will witness it!" Basil said.

Magnus exchanged a glance with Claudia and winked. He had described his flying experiences in his letters, so she was in on the joke.

At last Claudia was able to witness a flying machine being launched. She had always been curious about that. A score of brawny men running down a hill, pulling on a rope, was not a sight easily forgotten.

The machine turned, parallel to the ridge. Julia was impressed. "He's got a light touch."

The flight did not last long. The machine flew in a circle and approached the field. As the machine came in to land, Claudia could see that the sergeant, in the back seat, was holding his hands above his head, clearly showing that Magnus was flying.

When the machine came to rest, the aviators clustered round. "That was your best landing yet, sarge!"

The sergeant grinned back. "It wasn't me, it was the lad here."

"How do you rate him, sarge?"

Rhys shook his head. "You won't get any flattery from me. Magnus here is only just good enough."

It took Claudia several minutes to realise that the sergeant had stopped referring to Magnus as 'sir.' But there was no doubt that the man's respect for Magnus had increased.

The aviators asked Magnus where he had learned to fly. He mentioned his first flight in Gaul, then described his first unintentional solo flight. The aviators were amused. Claudia could see that their deference had vanished.

"They've accepted Magnus as one of them," Julia whispered.

"Yes, I see that." Claudia realised that the deference they showed their guests was a barrier.

Basil, excluded from this talk, was scornful of Magnus's common touch, but Claudia was jealous. This was a community with its own hierarchy, and she was excluded. Now that she knew what to look for, she realised that Julia was included, like Magnus. This wasn't a male-only community. But Claudia's family – her relatives and her Patrician status - was a barrier.

On their journey home, Magnus described the messenger routes to Claudia. "The western mountains run north-south.

The chalk ridge runs east-west. The Bald Mountain and the Limestone Edge are in between. So Corinium is the hub for the whole network."

"But shouldn't the hub be in the centre of the province?"

"That would be preferable, yes. But the east of Britain is flat. That makes it useless for flying."

She was fascinated by freedom of flight but, regretfully, her father regarded it as being a totally unsuitable pastime for a lady.

*   *   *

London was the biggest and busiest city in Britain. The population had fallen since the crisis, some blocks had been abandoned, but the citizens were confident. The docks could accommodate the largest seagoing ships. The magistrates ensured that the major streets were kept clear of falling leaves and other refuse.

The provincial chancellery was based in the city and, every winter, the governor's council of advisers assembled here.

The upcoming meeting of the council had brought Guthlaf and Magnus to London as well. Guthlaf's first action was to pay a courtesy visit to the governor.

Magnus had not been impressed by their first meeting. Cornelius Gallus was painfully thin, a fop, his carefully oiled hair bulked over his ears in the style fashionable in Constantinople. The man possessed an easy charm that was probably a great success with the ladies.

Now Magnus asked whether he was being unfair. True, the man was ineffectual. He had not achieved anything since his arrival in the province. But could he be blamed for that? The patricians feuded endlessly with each other, but one thing they agreed upon was that they didn't want an administration with real power. They co-operated to cripple the governor.

Cornelius showed nothing of this as his visitors walked in. "Good afternoon, Guthlaf, Magnus. I heard you were on your way. But, Guthlaf, why did you bring Magnus? The annual report is supposed to be given by the commander of the fort."

The governor's tone was mild, but something warned Magnus that he should not underestimate this man.

"I have a dislike of politics, sir. I admit I'm terrified of those councillors. So I asked Magnus to accompany me and answer the technical details in my place."

"I see. But this is going to cause me a lot of trouble, Guthlaf."

I regret that, sir. But I thought it was for the best."

The sky was overcast, the wind blustery, with a hint of rain. Magnus was wearing the military cloak that he had brought with him from Italy, fastened with his best brooch. He walked across the forum towards the basilica. By tradition, the Council sessions were held in the old hall, on the north side of the forum.

The councillors met in London every autumn to exchange gossip and remind everyone of their patrician status. The formal meetings of the council were regarded as a chore. But this time they had something important to discuss.

The governor had received a petition from the English mercenaries of the mobile army. According to rumour, their main complaint was that the English speakers no longer had anyone to speak for them on the council.

Magnus knew that the basilica was over three hundred years old. It was rather grand, in an austere way. His father had told him that the great hall had been damaged in the previous century, so one of the walls had been demolished, then carefully rebuilt closer to the remaining wall. As a result, the two sides of the hall did not match and the hall was too narrow, ruining the classical dimensions.

The Councillors were standing around the large table at the eastern end of the hall, discussing the agenda. Governor Cornelius was dressed in his formal best, a richly embroidered cloak over a white tunic. He was standing at the head of the table, looking harassed.

Magnus's great-uncle, Vitalinus, had already taken his place at the table. He glared round at everyone. He was abrupt with his allies. He and Magnus carefully ignored each other.

Finally, Cornelius sat down and told his secretary to call the meeting to order. He managed to look dignified. "Gentlemen, the first item for discussion is the petition from the commander of the English troops. The fellow's name is Finn, I believe."

"Yes, my lord," the chancellor said. "Traditionally, the Count of the Irish Shore has been an English speaker, an experienced mercenary. Finn has complained that there is no English speaker here for this session. He seems to think that Guthlaf sent Magnus in his place."

"They've got a point," Vitalinus said. "The count has been their only voice on the Council."

"Count Waltharius spoke up for the English well enough," Aurelianus said.

"But he's been transferred to Eboracum. A mistake, that. His duties keep him away from London," Vitalinus said.

Cornelius seemed to be sympathetic. "Yes. We cannot ignore the complaints of our best troops."

Aurelianus interrupted. "Is it true that this man Finn demanded a seat on the Council for himself? And promotion to count into the bargain?"

"Yes, it's true," Cornelius said. Reluctantly, he asked the chancellor to read out Finn's letter. It was short and blunt.

"This is monstrous!" Aurelianus looked down his nose at the assembled councillors. "My lords, you ought to reject this request out of hand. Giving this man Finn a seat at this table is unthinkable. I remind you, gentlemen, that membership of this Council has a strict property qualification. None of the English farmers is wealthy enough to qualify for a seat."

Cornelius raised a hand for silence, but Aurelianus pretended not to notice. The councillor was just getting into his stride. "I'm tired of this mercenary leader's endless demands for reinforcements. He wants to increase his own power, not defend us! Even if we recruited the men, how could we pay them? The privileges of the settlers as members of the militia should be withdrawn."

He sat down at last, amid a burst of applause from his cronies.

Vitalinus glared. "These English warriors have been insulted," he rasped. "They defend our homes and they're used to having a voice on this council." Magnus guessed that he spoke up mainly to embarrass Aurelianus.

The chancellor had been whispering in the governor's ear. Cornelius nodded. "Gentlemen, Count Waltharius made a point of voicing the complaints of the English in the past."

"But Count Waltharius isn't here," Vitalinus said. "He's in the north province. He was replaced by that fool Guthlaf."

"Count Guthlaf?" Cornelius asked. "You are acquainted with the English officers at Chester."

"I seem to have made an error of judgement," Count Guthlaf said. "I expected to answer details of the situation at Deva over the last year, not speak up for the English settlers."

"You're a fool, Guthlaf. You should never have asked Magnus to accompany you," Vitalinus said.

"For once I agree," Aurelianus said. "You gave this fellow Finn an opportunity to complain."

Magnus thought it best to intervene. "The English troops have a point, my lord. Their requests have been ignored. When I arrived at Deva, I found that the garrison's pay was months in arrears."

"That problem has now been resolved," Cornelius said hastily.

"Yes, my lord, but their other problems have not," Magnus said stoutly. But it didn't do any good.

Aurelianus stood again. "This letter from the English mercenaries is tantamount to treason. I put forward the motion that this council should ignore it."

Cornelius suggested compromise. Magnus thought it might be accepted.

But then a member of Vitalinius's faction changed sides and seconded Aurelianus's motion. Cornelius reluctantly asked for a show of hands. The council voted to reject the mercenaries' complaints.

Magnus was dismayed at how clumsily the issue had been handled. Perhaps he could persuade the councilors to change their minds at the next meeting.

Chapter 15: Mutiny

British Midlands, May, 454 AD

Lord Ambrosius's eastern estate was on the east facing slopes of the Northampton Uplands, just west of the Ermine Street. These were gently rolling hills, most of them forested.

The weather was hot and windless. Claudia was following Ambrosius across the farmyard to the buttery on a domestic chore. She was annoyed. Her husband had no right to interfere in her side of the household.

They were stopped by the captain of Ambrosius's bodyguard. He was wearing a tunic of light grey wool, made for him by Claudia's maids. A dagger hung from his belt. "Beg pardon, sir -."

"Yes, what is it, man?" Ambrosius snapped.

The captain spoke with a German accent. "My lord, you need to know that Lord Finn has declared his independence of the imperial government. He claims this territory for his own."

Claudia gasped and Ambrosius rounded on her. "Silence, woman. This scoundrel Finn deserves to be strung up."

"You're in danger, sir," the captain said. "But my men'll protect this household against this danger if they receive their back pay."

Ambrosius waved this aside. "Damn you, don't waste my time with this absurd story."

The captain hooked his thumbs in his belt. "Finn sent me a message, personal, asking us to join him. But I prefer to stay - if I'm paid."

Claudia realised that the man's story was true. They needed his protection. "My lord Ambrosius, I beg you to hand over the money. If the army has mutinied again, we're all in peril."

Ambrosius ignored her. He sneered at the captain. "You don't deserve anything, barbarian."

The captain lost his temper. "You greedy fat pig." He slapped Ambrosius backhanded. The blow took Ambrosius by surprise and sent him reeling. He slipped and lost his footing. He fell heavily against a pile of masonry stacked against the wall. He did not get up.

Everyone else gaped, unable to move. Claudia bent over him and turned him over. Ambrosius still breathed, but he was a dead man. His skull had crashed against a sharp corner of masonry, and there was a neat triangular impression in his left temple. It oozed blood, but the right side of his body was twitching.

The captain knelt down beside her, noticed the wound, and drew in his breath sharply. "Well, he was always clumsy. But I didn't intend to strike him - didn't mean to kill him."

Claudia was shocked at the man's attitude. She wondered whether she would be next. "I will testify to that."

The captain hesitated a moment, then took Ambrosius's keys. "Take your servants and leave. I want you out of here by noon."

Claudia wondered why he was letting her go. Were some of his men loyal to the legitimate government? Perhaps sending her running was the neatest compromise.

"Very well, captain." She was eager to escape before the captain or his men had second thoughts. She knew she would have to travel light.

She tried to think. There was nothing in the house that was both worth taking and portable. Her woollen dresses were bulky, so she abandoned them. She took her jewellery box, depressingly small. She chose her cosmetic case, frivolous but reassuring for being ordinary.

She was interrupted by the captain. "The strongbox was empty. That's why he refused to pay us. So I'm taking his jewellery."

"The family owes you a debt, captain. If the gold isn't enough, I have a silk dress -."

"The purple one that stinks of fish? No. take it with you."

Well, she could always sell it. She chose a heavy travelling cloak, unfashionable but very, very practical. It occurred to her that she would probably never return here. Even if order was restored, this house would go to her brother in law.

Ambrosius died an hour later, without regaining consciousness. The house steward was appalled, Claudia was resigned.

The captain gathered his men in the farmyard. He used the step as his podium. "It was an accident. But I don't trust imperial justice. We'll march east and join Finn." Some of his men protested. He raised his voice. "Finn has written to say that all of east is in the hands of his men."

Claudia wondered, desperately, whether that included London.

One of the mercenaries, a Dane named Oslaf, spoke up. He was blond, broad-shouldered, but no taller than Claudia. "Captain, you're mad to trust the oathbreaker."

The captain was angry. "Then go with the lady, then. Escort her to where she wants to go. Find out whether you can trust the governor."

She thought there was going to be a duel, right there in the courtyard.

"I'll go with the lady and be damned to you. I trust Cornelius more than I trust Finn."

Three more bodyguards sided with Oslaf.

Most of the farmhands decided to stay, something that did not surprise her. They had no liking for their dead employer. Did they think their chances would be better with Finn than with Ambrosius's revengeful family? Or did they plan to run off in this chaos?

Some of the servants, three men and two women, gathered round. "I beg you, my lady. Don't leave us here. Let us accompany you."

"Well … yes. I mean, yes, of course." She tried to hide her dismay. Now she was responsible for these people. But how could she get them to safety?

She stood by while the Germans ransacked the villa. They took everything that was valuable and portable. But there was no wanton destruction.

Then Oslaf the Dane bowed to her. "My lady, me and my companions, we have horses. We could take those servants, riding pillion. In return … we need to find an employer, a landowner. But how to find one? Warriors like us, riding across Britain alone, are likely to be mistaken for thieves. Especially in troubled times."

Another responsibility, she thought. "But I cannot pay you."

"No matter, my lady. I want to tell those in authority that I'm serving someone. Anyone will do, begging your pardon."

She could not decline this offer. "Very well. Thank you." But where should she go? Was the Ambrosius family's western villa safe? There was no way to find out.

The foreman said, "Can you protect us, lady?"

"No. I have no soldiers. You could accompany me, perhaps …"

She made her decision. "Water Newton. That's closest. The Ermine Street takes us straight there."

She asked the captain for the chaise for herself and her female companions: it was a dainty vehicle, with no room for any luggage, but it was swift.

The Captain shrugged. "The thing's a toy. I've no use for it. Take it and go."

Late that day, Claudia drove the trap under the arch of the north gate of Water Newton. She and her companions were exhausted.

There were other groups of refugees on the road, but she was certain that her little band was the strangest. She was not surprised that the men of the gate guards were suspicious. "Why're these men with you? They're barbarians."

Everyone tensed. Claudia wondered whether the Dane was about to be lynched. She knew she had to stand up for these men.

She spoke coldly. "They are my bodyguard, soldier. They are loyal servants of the Ambrosius family."

The sentry backed off. "Sorry, lady. Just doing my job."

"Very good. Stand aside." She drove under the gate arch. She felt that now, at last, she could relax. She had brought her companions to refuge. They were safe and so was she.

She drove on through the streets to the house of the chief magistrate. The gatekeeper looked up, surprised.

"I'm Lady Ambrosius. You've seen me here before," she said. "I must report to someone in authority!"

"Of course, my lady." The gatekeeper called for a servant to take care of her pony and escorted her into the courtyard. Claudia, accompanied by her companions, sat on a bench and settled down to wait.

Oslaf stood at her side. was amused. "I'm glad you don't use that tone on everyone, lady."

"I was dreadful, wasn't I?"

A few minutes later, the magistrate hurried into the courtyard. Maenol was stately and dignified, but instead of coming alone, as Claudia had expected, he was accompanied by a young woman in a stained grey dress. "My lady, I hear you have distressing news for me. Ah – my wife is not at home at present. But of course you know my granddaughter."

"We have met before, sir." Claudia wondered, too late, whether she had sounded rude.

But the girl did not seem to mind. "Perhaps we should all sit down," she said. "There's the morning room."

"Of course, of course," Maenol said. "If you would be so kind, Lady Claudia …"

His granddaughter asked a servant to serve some mint tea, and Claudia had the bizarre experience of describing the mutiny while demurely sipping at a herbal infusion.

"Thank you, this information is most useful," Maenol said. "We've heard reports, but … All of the reports agreed that the mutineers were targeting patricians …"

"It's only patricians who can afford to hire German mercenaries, sir."

"Yes, true enough. I thank you for your report. We've heard others, but none as intelligible as this. The reports were second hand, or by people who did not understand what they were seeing. I shall have to send a report to the governor..."

"I need to find a place to stay," Claudia said. "I have ten people with me."

Maenol looked blank. He was rescued by his granddaughter. "There's Gwalchmei the wool merchant."

Maenol smiled. "Excellent." When Claudia had finished her drink, she accompanied the pair of them down the street to the merchant's house.

The house was a sprawling affair, built round a courtyard. Huge sacks of wool were piled up in one corner.

Gwalchmei was courteous. "Of, course, I'll be glad to rent out a few rooms. The place is far too big, I can't afford the upkeep. My wife will be pleased to have such a gracious guest. I've been hearing all the rumours, my lady. If it's true that civil war has broken out, I'm likely to be ruined ... Horses, yes, there's room."

Claudia mentioned the silk dress and asked whether he could find a buyer for her. Gwalchmei was suddenly enthusiastic.

*   *   *

Chester, June, 454 AD

For several days, the weather had been sultry and the breeze minimal, but then a set of thunderstorms cleared the air. Magnus would have enjoyed a ride out to the messenger station. But the garrison was preparing for the campaigning season. He cursed the fact that duty kept him in his small office in the fort.

His boredom was disturbed when a pilot pushed open the door and stepped into his office. "Lord Magnus? I'm from Corinium, sir. I have to deliver a message to the adjutant." The man had a heavy west-country accent. "I was ordered by the governor to deliver this to your hand ... Everything seems quiet here, sir."

"Boring," Magnus agreed. He wondered idly what had brought the governor to Corinium. He opened the letter.

'To Magnus Vitalinus, adjutant to the Count at Chester, from Cornelius Gallus, Governor of Britannia Superior, greetings.

Finn has led a mutiny of the field army. He has proclaimed his men independent of the empire. Many of the patricians' German bodyguards have joined the revolt. Refugees concentrating on London and Corinium. Has the mutiny spread to Chester? Why has Chester stopped sending reports?

Reply at once. Cornelius Gallus, at Corinium.'

Magnus wondered what was happening in the east of the province. Chester was following its normal routine. The governor's query seemed unreal.

Magnus read the letter a second time. His father was safe. But what about his uncle? And – where was Claudia at this time of year? And why hadn't the governor written to the count? "Hell."

He stood up. "Wait here, pilot." He took it the letter to the garrison commander.

Guthlaf looked up from the report he was reading. "I hear you've received a pile of letters from the governor. What does he want now?"

Magnus handed him the letter. "Just one. You'd better read it, sir."

Guthlaf took it and scanned its contents. His reading skills were better than his writing. "Good God. So, Finn's finally done it. I'm not really surprised. He's broken his oath once already. I shall write to the governor at once." He suddenly looked very old. "I had hoped to retire with honour before something like this overwhelmed us."

Magnus coughed. "It would be better if I wrote, sir. Or we both did. Otherwise ..."

Guthlaf looked startled. "As bad as that? Yes. Perhaps you're right."

"We must inform the other officers of this, sir. If we keep them in the dark, they'll be as angry at you as you were with the governor."

"You're right, of course," Guthlaf said heavily. "Where's that courier fellow? Bring him here. I want to learn everything he knows about this disaster."

"Of course, sir."

That evening, the officers assembled in the main hall of the principia. When Guthlaf stepped up onto the podium, there was no need for Magnus to call for silence. The men waited expectantly for Guthlaf to speak. The lamps had been lit, casting grotesque shadows against the walls.

In matter of fact terms, the count explained what he knew of the crisis in the south. The officers, most of them English speakers, listened gravely.

"The Oathbreaker has no honour at all," a junior officer said. There was a murmur of agreement. No one showed any desire to join Finn.

Guthlaf hesitated. "Gentlemen, I intend to write a letter to the governor. I shall have to inform him about taking action to suppress this mutiny." Now it was their turn to be uncomfortable. "Gentlemen, if I asked your men to march against Finn, would they follow me?" He was really asking the officers if they would follow him, and everyone there knew it.

Each of the English officers told him much the same thing, that they wouldn't join the rebels but they wouldn't march against them.

Magnus needed a more precise answer. "But what if – if the governor asks me to lead a force of British troops against Finn?"

"The Oathbreaker deserves everything he gets," someone said.

Magnus glanced enquiringly at Guthlaf. "Many men dislike and distrust Finn," Guthlaf explained. "He killed a guest in his household, his own brother in law, and now he's on the run from his guest's kinsmen."

Magnus nodded. "I understand, sir."

"Well, the important thing is that we'll defend this coast against pirates," Guthlaf said.

"We're honour bound to do that," one man said. The others nodded.

That evening, Magnus wrote a concise report to the governor. If the English troops at Chester wouldn't march against Finn, the government's main hope was the coastal militia. Magnus wanted to write a letter to Claudia, to describe the situation to her. Writing to her was a habit that he couldn't break. But where was she?

He took the letter to Guthlaf. "If you don't mind reading this, sir ..."

Guthlaf skimmed the lines. "Yes, it'll do," he said. He watched while Magnus sealed his letter. Guthlaf included Magnus's letter with his own report, then summoned the courier.

"You are to take this dispatch to the messenger station in the morning. It's to be delivered to the governor in person."

"Yes, sir."

*　　*　　*

Two days later, Claudia was sitting in the shade of the courtyard, bored, when the estate foreman walked in.

"Good morning, my lady. I am glad to see you well ..."

She wondered what new disaster had occurred. "What is it, man?"

"You see, my lady, those Mutineers have fled. They were worried about retribution. So, they looted the villa and fled."

"Yes?" Her tone was sharper than she intended.

Oslaf walked across to join her.

"There's no-one, now, to protect the villa. Or your people. Could you do something to help? Protect them?" the foreman said.

"That's absurd. I have no soldiers. Oslaf and his men cannot protect the villa on their own."

Oslaf shuffled his feet. "Arm the slaves."

She was appalled. "It's illegal to free the slaves. At least, if they're under thirty. If I gave you my promise on such a thing, it would have no weight in law."

Oslaf shook his head. "I'm not suggesting you free them, my lady. I'm asking you to arm them."

She thought this was absurd. Slaves with weapons would defy their masters. They would run, wouldn't they? And if they chose to stay … "You could get away with it, perhaps for a month or so. But the next governor would overturn my request."

The foreman wrung his hands. "We're worried about the next month, not the next year."

"But I told you." As a woman, her word had no weight in law. "With my husband dead, my father in law makes the law. And he's in London, out of reach."

Oslaf shrugged. "So, write to him. And until you get a reply, act."

She went to see the magistrate and told him the news. She had assumed he would be shocked, but he took it calmly.

"These are desperate times, my lady. And you are a patrician. You outrank anyone here."

When she was a girl, the words 'you must remember you're a member of the patrician order' had usually been followed by her nurse or her mother forbidding her from doing something.

"Socially, I'm a patrician, yes. I take precedent over everyone else. But not in law. I have no authority."

The magistrate's smile was bleak. "We are used to seeing aristocrats making arrogant gestures."

All her life, she had yearned for the freedom to make her own decisions. But, right now, she would have liked to ask a man for advice. That boy Magnus, for example, would be handy.

Could she do this? Defy polite society? She smiled.

So, she told Oslaf to put her pony in its traces. Then she and her companions travelled back to the family villa. She expected to find a ruin.

But the roofs were still in place. The interior had been ransacked. All the fine furniture was smashed.

She told the foreman to assemble the field hands. Her husband's heavy wooden chair had been knocked over but has survived intact. She tried to pretend that this was a patrician's throne.

To her prejudiced eye, they looked more like sheep than wolves. She wondered what Magnus would have said about volunteers such as these.

She spoke clearly. "Are you prepared to do this? Use weapons to defend this place? Stand and fight – and risk death?"

They all said they were eager to defend her and the family property.

She sighed. So be it. "Very well. There is lots to do."

The estate carpenter said he could made shields. And each man could make his own crude spear.

Oslaf the Dane promised to show them how to fight as a team. He growled at them. "Although you're going to hate me for it."

She wrote to her father in law, in London trying to explain what she had done and asking for permission.

A week later, everyone had settled into a new routine. Then a family retainer arrived, bringing a letter. But she found that it was from her brother in law. "My lady, it is my sad duty to inform you that your father-in-law has died. From a broken heart, they say."

After the flamboyant opening greetings, there were a few brief lines. 'I cannot travel in these troubled times. Until I arrive, listen to the dictates of the bishop. Do not dishonour the family.'

She was dismayed. "What does that mean?"

The messenger shuffled his feet. "His lordship had a verbal message too, my lady. He said you should continue exactly as you are. And he said, you seem to have more gumption than anybody else in the family."

*   *   *

Magnus, with Conwyn riding his spare horse, reached the North Gate of London an hour before dusk. They were followed by an escort of twenty men. The troopers had been carefully chosen and, if the worst came to the worst, they would have no inhibitions about fighting the Oathbreaker.

The country he rode through had been quiet, although the rumours told of trouble further east.

Magnus explained who he was to the sentry at the gate. "I'm on official business, summoned here by the governor."

The man saluted. "We were told to expect you, sir. I was told to say, you're supposed to report to the governor's residence at once."

"Very well."

"All of the councillors, and their families and their retinues have abandoned their estates," the sentry said. "The city's bursting with of refugees from all over the Midlands."

Magnus escaped at last and made his way to the palace. A servant escorted him to the study, where the governor stood to greet him. The shutters were folded back to give a view over the formal garden. Twilight was already closing in.

"Magnus. So good of you to come," Cornelius Gallus said. "Sit down, sit down. Would you like some wine?"

"Thank you, sir." Magnus was surprised at this courtesy.

"I've spent the best part of the last month trying to negotiate with the rebels, but it hasn't achieved anything," Cornelius said.

"I see, sir."

There was a delicate pause while the servant carefully poured the wine. Magnus noticed that the glassware was an expensive import.

"Get out, man," the governor said irritably, and the servant scurried away.

"This situation needs Aetius," Magnus said. "Why doesn't he come?"

"Aetius is in Italy, negotiating with the Roman emperor," Cornelius said.

"You mean we're on our own?"

Cornelius was more tactful. "Magnus, I want you to take on the task of crushing the rebels. You're the most experienced commander in Britain."

"What?" Magnus had not expected this. Why hadn't the governor asked the Count of the Saxon Shore? "Caius outranks me, sir."

"The Count has no experience of mobile campaigns. You've commanded large numbers of men in the campaigns against the Huns," Cornelius said.

Magnus knew there was the world of difference between a subordinate commander in a large army and being the overall commander of a force, however small. Any failure would be his responsibility. He sipped at his wine to give him more time to think.

"Very well, sir. How many men can you give me?"

"We can't expect any reinforcements from Gaul. But the western tribal princes have offered their support. The bishop in Corinium persuaded them to help us."

"Yes, I heard about that."

"If that's true, you can ask the western tribal princes to call out their light cavalry. Over a thousand men, all told."

That sounded more promising. He had commanded British troops on the continent. "Yes, sir. But I can't expect to defeat Finn with light cavalry alone,"

"No," Cornelius said. "But there's the garrisons of the Saxon Shore forts. They can't be forced to leave their homes, but if you asked for volunteers, four or five hundred men might come forward."

"But even if they did, my force would be no bigger than the rebels."

The governor shrugged. "I suppose we could wait, while we ask the emperor to lend us some men." His tone was bleak.

Magnus glanced at the governor. "Sir?"

"We could ask," Cornelius said. "But the emperor has problems of his own. Besides, he expects us to solve our local problems without running to him for help."

"Yes, sir."

Cornelius picked up his wineglass and then put it down again. "Apart from that, is there anything else we can do?"

Magnus took a breath. "I ask you to announce an amnesty for those who disperse. The fewer men I have to fight, the better."

"Councillor Aurelianus won't like it," Cornelius said. "But I see the need for it."

"The English have a valid complaint," Magnus said. "They're the only fighting men in Britain who aren't represented on the Council. I ask you to allow an English spokesman on the Council."

"That man Finn, perhaps?" Cornelius said. "No. He and his men are in a state of rebellion. I don't want to be seen to be negotiating under pressure. If we give in now, they'll revolt every time they want something."

Magnus insisted. "The Council is supposed to advise you, sir. We need someone to tell the Council whether their decisions will provoke an uprising."

Cornelius nodded. "Yes. You've got a point there. Aurelianus might accept that argument. Very well. But I'll only announce the spokesman after the rebellion had been crushed. You must not mention it before then, Magnus."

"Very well, my lord." Magnus said reluctantly.

"Councillor Aurelianus has demanded that their leader should be dragged back to London for execution."

"What did you tell him, sir?"

He grimaced. "I said that we have to defeat them first."

"Yes, sir. Besides, Finn could accept this amnesty and surrender on terms."

Cornelius looked surprised. "He's a barbarian and a traitor. Do you object to using deceit to capture him?"

Magnus sighed. "These warriors take their honour very seriously. I've got to work with them after this is over. I don't want them calling me Oathbreaker too."

Cornelius scowled. "I can't imagine this barbarian asking for terms." He sipped some of his wine. Then he nodded. "Very well. My word on it."

"Thank you, sir."

*

British Midlands, July 454 AD

Magnus led his little army north from London along the Ermine Street. The British princes had sent only half of their fighting men, so he had four hundred cavalry with him. Besides the cavalry, he had half a hundred adventurers from London and Corinium. He had spotted four men in the colours of Ambrosius.

The weather was fine, and they made good progress. As they rode north, Magnus occasionally glimpsed flying machines to the west, monitoring their progress.

Magnus had sent a message to Gaius, the Count of the Saxon Shore, asking him to send him as many of the British-speakers from the Saxon Shore militia as he could spare.

Gaius had responded with a curt note stating that he would ask for volunteers to come forward.

When they reached Great Chesterford, where the road from Colchester met the Ermine Street, a courier met them with the news that five hundred infantry volunteers, from the Saxon Shore militia, were marching west to meet them. Magnus decided to wait. The city could feed his men and the posting inn made a useful headquarters.

The next day later, the infantry volunteers reached them. Magnus greeted the commander and called together his subordinates, including the commanders of his light cavalry, Kai of Devon and Jago of Powys.

"Gentlemen, I would like to introduce you to Alban, the commander of the troops from our coastal defences. Alban served with me in Gaul and Italy."

Alban was a professional soldier and not enthusiastic about serving alongside tribal warriors. But he was careful not to let it show.

"There mutineers seem to be sitting tight, sir. They certainly haven't moved south or west," Alban said.

"That won't last," Magnus said. "When Finn hears about us, I expect him to lead his army south to meet us. Remember, these English soldiers are professionals. If they manage to take us by surprise, the battle will over before it's begun. So it's vital that we're not taken off guard. I want the cavalry to take it in turns to scout ahead. A fresh troop every day."

Kai nodded seriously. "Very well, sir."

"We march at first light," Magnus told them.

As they made their way cautiously north, the land became flatter and the rivers wider, meandering and muddy.

On the second day the road ran parallel to the River Ouse, slowly making its way to Durovigutum and the marshes beyond. They had not encountered any opposition. It seemed that Finn was staying in the heart of his newly-won territory. They paused at noon to rest.

"I hate this land," Jago of Powys told Magnus.

"Yes, I agree," Magnus said. He preferred the limestone hills of his home. No flying machines could operate over these plains.

"We'll reach Durovigutum tomorrow," Alban said. "Have we taken Finn by surprise? Didn't he expect us to strike back?"

Magnus was growing increasingly tense. A surprise attack by Finn could destroy his force and alter the lives of everyone in the province. "Possibly. He commands the only professional troop in Britain, after all."

That afternoon, as they approached the flat fen country around Durovigutum, a galloper from Kai's light cavalry finally brought back news. "We've located Finn and his army up ahead! Three, maybe four miles. The prince told me to say, sir, they're armed and ready for trouble."

"Thank you, trooper." Magnus was relieved. At least he knew where his enemy was.

An hour later, Magnus and his army came within sight if the enemy camp, on top of a modest hill, east of the river. Magnus calculated that Finn had about eight hundred men, almost as many as his own force. He ordered his men to set up camp on the hill opposite.

At dusk, Magnus took a few bodyguards and went forward to negotiate. As they approached the rebels' encampment, Finn came out to meet him, escorted by a few of his companions. All of them were wearing chain mail, with infantry swords in baldrics. The English leader was tall and broad-shouldered.

Finn, walking slowly down the slope, stopped and shouted. "No further! This is close enough."

Magnus halted and looked up at the English group. He silently cursed the fact that he was lower down the slope, looking up.

Finn looked down at him. "And who might you be, little man?"

He growled. "Magnus Vitalinus. Adjutant to the Count of the Irish Shore."

Finn was surprised. "Magnus? Count at Chester? So this is all your fault, then."

Magnus kept his voice steady. "I was appointed to the post of adjutant, nothing more. And the count at Chester, and his men, did not seem to mind."

Finn ignored this. "What is your message, little man? Has the governor accepted my terms? Is he offering to make me count?"

"No. He offers an amnesty to all of you if you disarm."

The rebels at Finn's back jeered at this. Finn smiled broadly.

"We've already heard about that. We refuse. And what about me? Does your amnesty apply to me as well? Aurelianus wants my head on a platter, I hear." Finn was self-assured and mocking.

"Aurelianus demanded that, yes. But the governor refused. Instead, he ordered me to strip you of your command and bring you back to London. But he will spare your life."

"I will take your word on that, Magnus. But can we trust the governor? Everyone knows those patrician landowners have no honour. Once my men have surrendered their weapons and I am in his hands, will he change his mind and hand me over to Aurelianus?"

That thought had occurred to Magnus as well. "That's a problem, true enough. If you're worried, you could always leave the country."

Finn raised his eyebrows. "You would do that? Let me go, in defiance of your orders?"

"Yes. I've been ordered to suppress this revolt. If the only way to disarm your men is to let you slip away, then I'll do it." He knew that Aurelianus would hate that. Would the councilor take his revenge in some way?

Finn shook his head. "I'm not going to run away a second time. If you won't make me a count, I want independence for my men. I'll create my own kingdom here in Britain." His companions grinned.

Magnus, dismayed and saddened, retreated with as much grace as possible. He knew there would be a battle the next day.

The next morning, Magnus made sure the men were up early. The soldiers helped each other to pull on their chain mail shirts. Conwyn helped Magnus into his own mail. The sky was cloudless, with a gentle wind blowing.

To Magnus, it seemed almost sacrilege to spoil it with a war. Nobody else seemed to share this view. Finn's men, on the opposite hilltop, formed their line of battle.

The British militia, led by Alban, formed their own line facing the mercenaries. They looked relaxed and confident. But Magnus knew they could not win the battle by themselves. He began by sending the tribal cavalry to harry the enemy's flanks, but Finn gave an order and the mercenaries neatly transformed their formation into a shield ring. Spears bristled aggressively outwards at the cavalry.

Magnus was standing at the foot of the hill, close to the horse that Conwyn was holding for him. He told himself that he should have moved faster. He ordered the archers forward, to shake up their opponents' formation and morale. The tribal warriors despised such men, but Magnus considered them the most useful part of the army.

The archers moved up to within a hundred yards of the English line and loosed with their short bows. But the English stood firm and most of the arrows struck the heavy wooden shields. The British archers began to run out of arrows and the rate of shooting slackened.

The next step in the battle was set out in the textbooks. "Alban, I want you to send in your militia infantry. I want your men to open up the English line, so the cavalry can exploit the breaks and drive the English into flight."

"Yes, sir." Alban saluted and hurried away.

Magnus and the rest of the army watched as the British infantry made their way up the hill. Alban's troops made a brave attempt at it. But as they advanced, they were met by a hail of missiles of all kinds, which shocked them with its ferocity.

The British persevered. They formed their own shield wall and charged forward. They opposing lines came together with a crash, but the militia were no match for Finn's experienced warriors. Their mail and shields could not resist the English two-handed axes, and they could not break through the shield wall.

As their losses mounted it became clear to Magnus that the charge had failed. He was relieved when Alban ordered them to retreat.

Most of the British militia drew back in good order, but the men on the left panicked and fled. The English warriors facing them broke ranks. Cheering madly, they chased down the hill after the militia.

The cavalry had trained for this. Without waiting for orders, Jago led his men across the battlefield and charged the scattered English warriors. Some of them were cut down. A few threw away their shields and scattered. But most turned about and retreated ran back up the hill.

All but a very few of them made it back to their own line. Those who could not run fast enough threw down their weapons and tried to surrender, but the tribal cavalry ignored their gesture.

Magnus watched this with rising anger. His best hope, still, had been to persuade the English to negotiate, but this act wrecked his hopes. The English on their hilltop shortened their shield wall but stood firm.

Alban came to report. "My men are tired, but I ask to be allowed to try again. We hurt them, Magnus. They suffered heavily." He was as weary as his men.

"Yes, you hurt them, but your men suffered more. How many men did you lose?"

Alban hesitated. "Fifty killed or wounded, sir. But my men are eager to try again."

One in twenty of his army. Magnus was dismayed. "If I lose all of you, Finn will still have most of his force." He knew that Finn could fight a defensive battle and hold his enemies off for ever, just as Aetius had done. Tell your men they fought well."

Alban nodded. "Right. Thank you, sir."

Magnus had to decide what to do next, for things had not gone at all according to plan. He asked his cavalry leaders, Kai and Jago, whether their men could break through the English defence.

Jago refused. "You know that the main role of the cavalry is to pursue a retreating enemy."

Alban begged to be allowed to try again. "Perhaps you could order your archers to concentrate on a small part of the enemy line."

Magnus was reluctant, because he knew that the heart of his little army was the five hundred militia infantry - four hundred and fifty now - and he could not afford to lose them. The English on their hilltop were shouting their defiance. He tried to ignore it.

Weakly, he gave in. "Very well, commander." Alban grinned at him in triumph and hurried away.

The archers, with fresh supplies of arrows, began harassing the English line again. Alban took his place at the front of his men, saluted Magnus, then turned and led his men in their charge. Alban's men were enthusiastic. They crashed into the English shield wall, forcing the mercenaries to give ground.

There was a struggle all along the line. Magnus could tell that both sides were suffering heavy losses. Several more of the defenders fell. The English struggled to fill the gap. Was Alban going to succeed?

But then Finn and his companions rushed to the spot. The gap in the shield wall was filled and the British were forced back. The attack ended in a sullen withdrawal.

Then the English gave a cheer. A formation of rebels detached itself from the shield wall and advanced steadily down the hill after the retreating militia. What had appeared to be a humiliating withdrawal looked like tuning into a crushing defeat.

Magnus did not hesitate. Knowing Kai and Jago were watching, he drew his sword and held it up to the sunlight. "Warriors!" He roared. "With me."

He gave his mount a hint of the spurs. It sprang forward, almost causing him to lose his grip of the reins. He rolled in the saddle as his mount increased its pace, hooves hammering, the muddy turf flying by beneath him. He was dimly aware of his escort following, some distance behind, but his attention was drawn to the ever-increasing body of English soldiers directly ahead.

His horse carried him forwards with gut-churning speed, directly at a man at the very front of the crowd, a warrior screaming his defiance at the enemy. He was moving effortlessly despite the heavy weight of chain mail he bore. The man's bad luck, Magnus supposed, to have given way to impetuosity. The man's eyes went wide as he turned to face this new danger and saw an enormous weight of horse bearing down on him. He tried to throw himself aside.

The edge of Magnus's sword came down on his armoured shoulder. The edge failed to cut the chain mail, but the blow had the full force of the charge and flung the man onto his back. The force of the blow travelled up Magnus's arm. More men went down screaming under the hooves of his mount as it crashed into their midst, he could not have said how many.

Then all was chaos. He sat above a mass of snarling faces, glinting armour, jabbing spears. Wood cracked, metal clanged, men shouted words he did not understand. He hacked around him. On one side then the other, yelling mindless curses. A spear tip shrieked along the chain mail covering his thigh. He chopped at an arm as it reached for his reins. Something crunched into his side and nearly threw him from his saddle. His sword crashed into an iron helmet and knocked the man wearing it down into the press of bodies.

Magnus's horse gave a shriek, reared up, twisting. He felt a terrible lurch of fear as he came away from the saddle, the world turning over. He crunched down, dust in his eyes, dust in his mouth, coughing and struggling. He rolled onto his knees.

Hooves crashed against the broken turf, close to his head. Boots slid and stomped. He fumbled for his sword. He plucked weakly at the grass, turned over a flat stone.

He had forgotten what he was looking for. His fingers found the pommel of his sword and he stumbled up, something caught at his foot and snatched it painfully away, dumping him on his face again.

He waited to have the back of his head broken, but it was only his stirrup, still strapped to his horse. He dragged his boot free, gasping for air, and reeled to his feet the weight of his armour, his sword dangling from his hand.

Someone lifted a blade and Magnus stabbed at the chain mail covering the man's chest. The man grabbed at Magnus's sword but then fell. Something thumped into Magnus's chain mail with a dull clang and knocked him sideways, right into an English soldier with a spear. The man dropped it and they clawed at each other. Magnus was getting terribly, terribly tired. His head hurt a lot. Just dragging the breath in was a tremendous effort. The whole heroic charge idea seemed as if it had been a bad one. He wanted to lie down.

Magnus, swaying numbly back and forward, almost felt sorry for the English. Their numbers might have been impressive from a distance but close up these men were badly equipped foot soldiers, following a few impetuous leaders in a reckless endeavor.

But then something hit Magnus on the side of the head, and he slid to the ground for a second time. Someone trod on him, probably by accident. He was going to be trampled to death.

"Magnus!" Conwyn shouted. "Vitalinus!"

Conwyn hacked his way through the English warriors, growling as his scything sword knocked splinters off shields. Other men, equally determined, followed him.

Another English soldier leapt towards Magnus, a short sword raised. Before he could strike, Conwyn's heavy blade crashed against his helmet. An axe clanged into Conwyn's heavy wooden shield and he shrugged it away as if it was a fly, then chopped at the man who had swung it.

Other armoured figures crowded in after Conwyn, shoving with shields, chopping with their bright swords, clearing a space around Magnus.

Conwyn's hand slid under Magnus's armpit and dragged him backwards, his heels kicking at the grass. He was vaguely aware that he had dropped his sword somewhere, but it seemed foolish to go looking for it now. Some scavenger would no doubt receive a priceless windfall while he hunted among the bodies, later. Magnus saw a warrior still mounted, his long sword chopping around him.

He was half-carried back, out of the press.

The medic inspected the head wound. "Sit still, boy. You're lucky. There's two kinds of head wounds – the kind that look worse than they are, and the kind that kill you. This wound looks spectacular, but the damage is superficial. Hold still."

The man washed the cut with something that stung enough to make him yelp. "Hell."

"Excellent. That will heal cleanly." The medic applied a bandage.

Magnus was finally able to turn to face his subordinates.

The English charge had been broken, but the advantage had passed to the mercenaries. Now it was the British who were on the defensive.

Magnus drew a breath. "Alban, I want you take half your men back up there. Keep pestering them. Don't take any risks, but don't give them a chance to rest. Look for weaknesses in their defences."

Alban was apologetic. "I'm sorry, sir, but they say they've taken too many losses."

"What do you mean? The militiamen have fought bravely, but they've taken light casualties."

"You don't understand, sir," Alban said. "The Militia are volunteers from the coastal forts. They can't afford further losses because, you see, after this battle is over, they have to go back and defend their homes."

Magnus was angry. "How can they defend those coastal forts against the combined force of the enemy? Their only chance is to defeat Finn, here, today."

Alban wiped the sweat from his face. "True, but ... they think of their families first."

Magnus knew that sacrificing a small number of men to win the war would make perfect military sense, but he could understand that for these men their priority was to defend their homes.

This was mutiny, but he realised there was no option but to withdraw and report his failure.

Prince Jago demanded the right to attack again. "We cannot let these pagan foot-soldiers defeat us."

Magnus shook his head. "No. We would lose too many men." The commander glared. Magnus wondered if this man would obey him. He realised that Alban and everyone else was watching him.

"You must do something!" Jago said.

Magnus was blunt. "You failed last time. Why would it be different a second time?"

"We weakened them. Yes, and your infantry weakened them too. My men are prepared to try again. My lord."

Magnus knew that the cavalry had no chance of winning this battle on their own. "I know they are prepared to try. Their bravery is commendable. But the cost would be too high."

They stared back at him, each man hesitant to speak. He swallowed. "Gentlemen, we are going to have to withdraw." He saw agreement in Alban's expression, and relief. Someone had been able to mention the unthinkable.

"My men are prepared to fight to the last," Jago, said.

Magnus could see that he meant it. "But I don't want your men dead. I want them to defend Britain next year."

Chapter 16: The aftermath

London, July, 454 AD

Magnus stood in the governor's study in London. He stared at the wall behind the governor's head. He found it difficult to meet the man's gaze.

He had gone first to his quarters at the fort. Even in the face of disaster, he could not enter the governor's presence in shabby riding clothes. While he had taken a sponge bath, Conwyn had pulled out his best tunic and boots and checked they were clean.

He had left his sword at the gate and now he faced the governor, his best cloak neatly fastened. He had to report disaster but at least he could do it in style.

The governor might be a fop, but he was no fool. "So your casualties were heavy, Magnus?"

"Yes, sir. I accept full responsibility for the decision to withdraw. But I felt it was better to keep our forces intact than to risk destroying them in another charge. We can protect our farms and discourage the English from advancing too far."

Magnus's wound was troubling him. The pulse felt like a hammer blow. It took an effort to think.

The governor, who usually looked free of all cares, now looked worn. "I am sure you did everything you could, Magnus. I sent you out with inadequate troops." His tone was sympathetic, which Magnus hated.

Magnus regarded the battle as a personal defeat. It was all his fault. He had already decided to return to Gaul.

"This situation needs Aetius. Why doesn't he come?" Magnus asked.

"To him, this is just a mutiny. Less than a thousand men, not worthy of his attention."

"It's more than that, sir."

"Yes, I know." the governor hesitated. "The emperor is too ill to leave the capital. Aetius is in Italy, negotiating with the Roman emperor."

"You mean, we're on our own?" he remembered saying that before, somewhere.

The governor did not bother to reply. "Where's your army now?"

"I left them in Cambridge, sir, guarding the road south. Prince Jago and his cavalry had acted as rearguard, hoping to ambush the enemy and turn defeat into victory. But Finn and his men did not follow us." There was no need. Everyone in the British army knew that the English had won.

"You say they didn't follow you south? It was a draw, then. You fought them to a standstill."

He waved this aside. "I feel I must – I must resign my command, sir."

"Yes, that might help me with my critics, a little. Have you any ideas about what to do next?" The Governor asked.

"Only that we need to raise a force to protect the frontier, but we have no money to pay for such a force, sir."

"You can leave that to me. I shall announce that circumstances have forced me to accept English as 'allies' of the empire and to establish a formal frontier. It's a sham, of course. But the pretence suits both sides."

"Yes, sir."

"The circumstances, of course, are the stupidity of the patricians in hiring barbarian bodyguards and their greed in not paying taxes. Magnus, I'll write to Aetius. He'll find a task to keep you busy."

"Thank you, sir."

Magnus was devastated by this defeat. He had thought that he only needed to defend the frontiers, that all of the empire's enemies lay outside, and all he had to do was keep them out.

Now he realised that the empire was rotting from within. Each sector of society blamed the others, but the worst were the great landowners. They were greedy for power and in their greed, they weakened the civilisation they claimed to lead. Vitalinus, his father's uncle, was the worst of them.

* * *

London, late July, 454 AD

Claudia was staying in her brother-in-law's house in London. The panic had receded, and she had travelled south in a dignified manner. Her brother-in -law had taken her in.

She had heard that her father had fled to the city, bringing his family with him. Instead of finding a house in the city for himself, he had simply moved in alongside his brother.

Several other refugees from other families were all squeezed into the Ambrosius house too. But the situation in the countryside seemed to have stabilised. The rebels had promised to respect the boundary. She wanted her brother-in-law to return to his estate in the Limestone Edge, but he refused to discuss it.

The house had a tiny ornamental garden, with high walls to protect the delicate plants from north winds. This afternoon she was sitting on a stone bench in the middle of the garden, enjoying the weak sunshine, discussing events with her mother-in-law.

The city had been anxious ever since Magnus had led his little army north. Then the news from London unsettled everyone. The army had suffered a defeat and had retreated towards the capital. Then the governor returned to the city after one of his regular visits to Corinium.

Claudia was not surprised when the governor, still in travelling clothes, was escorted into the garden by her brother-in-law. "This isn't as stuffy as indoors, my lord, and the walls protect us from the wind."

Her mother-in-law caught Claudia's eye and together they stood and withdrew to a corner. Her cousin stayed to listen. Claudia strained to hear what the governor was saying.

"I wish to assure you, Lord Ambrosius, that the army is still intact. The battle has achieved an agreed frontier."

"And where's that fool Magnus?"

"I sent him off to Colchester. He'll be back any day now. My lord, I came here to ask you to make a gesture to reassure the populace. I want you to return to your estate. Gestures matter a lot in times like these."

"I'll think about it, Cornelius."

"Thank you, my lord," the governor said.

Claudia's sister-in-law stepped forward to offer refreshments to her guest.

Cornelius politely refused. "I'm sorry to rush, but I have to visit another household ..."

"Of course, of course." Her brother-in-law and his wife escorted their guest to the door.

Claudia, determined, tagged after them. She could tell that some members of the family were not assured by the governor's visit.

She knew her father, too, was afraid to return home.

Claudia went off to the little garden to brood. She was sitting on the stone bench when her brother-in-law entered the garden. She was surprised. What brought him back here?

"So here you are, Claudia. That fellow Magnus is here. Asking to see you."

She was startled. "Magnus? In London?"

"He's standing in the street outside. He says he deeply regrets this failure. He's taking it hard. But he was asked to do the impossible. I blame that fop Cornelius. The governor should have written to Vienne, asking for help."

"Yes, sir."

"And those tribal warriors are untrustworthy. Those tribesmen have no notion of discipline. Young Magnus did the very best he could with the forces the governor gave him ...

"Well, sister? Do you want to speak with him?"

She had been given a choice. Magnus was outside, waiting to speak to her.

"Shall I tell the servants to let him in, Claudia?"

She felt a moment's panic. What could she say to him? She decided against it. She was shocked by the British defeat. She felt unable to give comfort to the man at the centre of it all.

"No, my lord. Not yet. Perhaps later."

"Very well, my dear."

*   *   *

Back in his quarters, Magnus drafted a letter to Claudia, trying to put down all of the ideas that he had planned to say directly.

Magnus Vitalinus, writing from London, to Lady Claudia, greetings.

'My lady, I cannot protect the provincial government or the people of Britain. The populace is going to panic. Order is going to collapse here. You must escape to the continent while you can.

I am ashamed of my failure. But I can achieve nothing by remaining in Britain. Perhaps I should explain that the governor agrees that the troops at Chester will be more loyal, and the task of their English commander less difficult, if I leave. He has given me permission to rejoin Lord Aetius in Italy.

I ask you to come with me. I offer to escort you to your family estate in Gaul. Bring your family with you.

I offer to atone for my past conduct by escorting you to the Aurelianus estate in Gaul.'

Your obedient servant, Magnus V.'

* * *

Claudia read Magnus's letter, astonished. If she had known he was going to leave Britain, she might have agreed to speak to him, to bid him farewell. But it was too late now.

She decided that Magnus was taking his defeat very hard and was over-reacting. And even if things were as bad as he claimed, she must stay.

She looked round her room. The wall-hangings, designed to keep out the cold, were pushed aside in this warm weather. Her sister-in-law had woven them in the cheerful native British style, quite unlike the formal Imperial style her mother would have chosen. That made her think of the green hills just outside the city.

307

The very suggestion that she might leave crystallised her decision. Britain was her home.

She wrote a letter in reply, working in haste, to endure that he received it before he sailed. In her haste, she used terms that she later regretted. A young man, shocked by a personal disaster, might misinterpret them.

To Magnus Vitalinus, greetings.

I regret to hear that that you are leaving Britain. I had thought that you had a duty here in the land of your birth.

My brother-in-law has assured me that you did the very best you could with the forces the governor gave you.

However, I am surprised at your decision to leave.

I feel that I cannot leave. No, for Britain is my home. Farewell, my friend. Claudia Ambrosius

* * *

London, early September, 454

The death of Claudia's husband was as devastating in its own way as the mutiny had been. As tradition demanded, she had gone into formal mourning. Until her mourning was over, she technically belonged to her husband's family.

She asked her maidservant and one of the footmen to accompany her to the governor's palace. Once there, she asked to speak to Cornelius' sister. She told the doorman that it concerned 'matters of state'. The governor had asked his widowed sister staying with him, to manage his household.

Cornelius' sister had agreed to see her, but her manner was cold. "This is most unladylike. Affairs of state, indeed!"

"I know. But let me speak." She set out her proposal.

308

"So, it is serious after all. Wait here. I'll speak to Cornelius."

She returned five minutes later and led her to Cornelius' study. "Tell my brother what you told me."

She started over. "You asked my brother-in-law, and my father, to return to their country estates. To reassure the populace. My father refused." She swallowed. "My lord, I would like to return to my husband's estate by Water Newton. That would reassure the populace, surely?"

"Do you have your father's permission for this?"

"I don't need it. I'm married. I spoke to my brother-in-law. He gave his permission."

"Did he, indeed? And do you have this letter?

She opened her bag, pulled out the letter and handed it over.

"This is very dramatic," Cornelius said.

"What really decided me was that my brother, Basil, is going to the continent. He says he's going to inspect the family's estate in Armorica."

"I see." Cornelius read the letter twice. "This is very vague. It could mean almost anything."

"Why, I thought that was my brother-in-law's intention."

Cornelius scowled and read the letter again. Then he laughed. "Yes, very clever." He turned to his sister. "Would you regard this as improper?"

She pursed her lips. "No, brother. Of course, if she were unmarried, it would be impossible. But as a widow – you would be chaperoned?"

"Of course," Claudia said, at her most frosty.

*   *   *

Ravenna, October, 454

The palace dining room was magnificent. The mosaics displayed the newly-fashionable variety of terrestrial beasts, fruits, flowers and trees - designed to depict the bounty of God's creation. The mosaic was matched by embroidered wall hangings.

Today the room was full. Aetius had presented himself at court in Ravenna to deliver a financial account for the field army. Emperor Valentinian had responded by arranging a banquet in the general's honour. The emperor's most powerful generals and courtiers - and their ladies - had been invited.

Aetius was at the high table, at Valentinian's right hand. A poet was reciting a eulogy to the emperor's achievements. It was all lies, of course.

Magnus was positioned halfway down the table. His partner, a lady named Fausta, was wearing a double-dyed blue silk dress. She was eager to tell him all the court gossip.

"Aetius is planning to marry off his son Gaudentius to one of the emperor's daughters. My husband says he's pushing his luck."

Magnus was surprised. "There was no objection when Aetius arranged the betrothal of his other son to Lady Placidia."

Fausta lowered her voice. "No, but Valentinian feels intimidated by Aetius. His cronies are telling him that as soon as the marriage takes place, Aetius will push him aside and place Gaudentius upon the imperial throne."

"Aetius isn't like that."

She simpered. "You're on Aetius's staff. Is he as difficult as they say?"

He did not want to talk about his commander, so he tried to distract her by mentioning his liaison work with the aviators.

As he hoped, the lady was diverted. "Really. How *fascinating*. Is it true what people say about aviators?"

He smiled. "If you visit a messenger station as a guest, they're perfectly decorous. It's only on journeys to other cities that they become dangerous."

"Really? How fascinating -."

Everyone was surprised by shouting at top of table. Magnus looked up, just in time to see Valentinian leap to his feet. A chair went over with a crash. Everyone, from Aetius to Magnus to the guards standing against the walls, was too surprised to move.

Valentinian shouted again. Damn you!" Magnus saw that he was holding a dagger. Magnus jumped to his feet.

Valentinian held Aetius down and struck, again and again. Lady Fausta screamed.

The emperor's bodyguard, too late, rushed forward. Valentinian threw the dagger aside as if it had suddenly become red-hot. He looked half-angry, half ashamed. "Clean that mess up. And take care of *them*."

Only five of Aetius's bodyguards and companions had been allowed to accompany him. In silence, they were checked for weapons and herded into a corner.

The emperor's men noticed Magnus, standing alone. Two soldiers pulled him forward. "You have weapons?"

"Only my knife -." It was taken and his cloak, with its courtier's purple rectangle, was torn off. The courtiers and their ladies look on in horror.

He was pushed into the corner along with Aetius's bodyguards. He recognised two Hun companions of Aetius, Optila and Thraustila.

Sidonius Apollinaris angrily addressed the emperor. "I am ignorant, sir, of your motives or provocations. I only know that you have acted like a man who has cut off his right hand with his left." The emperor ignored him.

An Italian courtier began questioning the prisoners. He was brisk. "Magnus? From Gaul? You're harmless. Go back there. Collect your belongings and be gone."

"Should we give him his horse, sir?" a soldier asked.

"He doesn't own any land. He has no right to a horse. Give him a pair of boots. He can walk home." The soldiers laughed.

Magnus, angry and humiliated, tried to decide how to respond.

The Hun, Optila, spoke in an undertone. "Get out of here as fast as you can." He spoke in clumsy Gaulish, a language they shared but was unlikely to be understood here. "Another death here today would embarrass them. But they can't let you reach Gaul alive. They'll murder you on the road home."

Thraustila agreed. "They'll be waiting for you at the west gate."

Magnus tried to think. "Thanks for the warning. And you?"

"We can take care of ourselves," Optila said. They think we're mercenaries. No honour. Prepared to accept their gold. But we have sworn revenge."

Thraustila nodded. "We must stay. Blood feud."

If the gates were watched, how could he escape? But Ravenna was a naval base. If he could get down to the port, he might be able to find a ship. Perhaps.

*   *   *

312

Castle Newton, December 454

Lady Calpurnia sipped herb tea from Claudia's best cups. The lady was polite and gracious. "Nettle is such a soothing herb, my dear. Your dinner service is very elegant."

In the world outside her new home, the panic had ended, and life had returned almost to normal. The governor had asserted his authority over the landowners. In this crisis, they were prepared to accept his leadership.

Her father had disapproved of her decision, of course, but her mother had quietly approved. He had reluctantly consented to the arrangement, on condition that she was accompanied by her aunt Placidia, who had also been widowed in the mutiny and was without a home.

"Thank you, Lady Calpurnia," Claudia said.

"But why do you not use silver?"

"Metal would heat up too fast. Porcelain is more comfortable to hold."

"Yes, that is true."

Claudia decided it was time to hint at the real reason for this meeting. She had thought long and hard about the political and strategic situation.

She put down her cup. "A woman can achieve very little in these troubled times."

Lady Calpurnia sipped at her tea. "True, my dear."

"But men are also adrift in the current. They are eager for advice, from any quarter... I am convinced there is no need to panic -."

"Some men have done so," Lady Calpurnia said dryly.

Claudia tried to hide her irritation. "Quite true, my dear. But a word of encouragement might prevent it."

Lady Calpurnia was amused. "Do you imagine you can change the destiny of this province, child?"

"If I don't make the attempt, my lady, I will achieve nothing. That is why I returned to my husband's estate."

"Indeed."

"If the men on the council are devoid of ideas, perhaps their ladies can fill the gap." Claudia poured more tea for herself.

Lady Calpurnia took a delicate sip at her tea. "As you say, a woman can achieve little in these troubled times."

"The fate of Britain hangs in the balance. The scales are evenly balanced. Even advice from a woman could make the difference."

"You do not lack ambition, my dear," Lady Calpurnia said. She looked down at her cup. "And is Britain dying?"

Claudia was surprised at this bold statement. "It will if we leave it to those fashionable fribbles in London."

The lady was amused. "No, supercilious insults are not your style at all."

"I'm sorry, I usually guard my tongue."

"There is no need to apologise, my dear. Sometimes blunt speaking is necessary. I am honoured that you trust me enough to speak openly."

Was that praise also a subtle insult? She was flustered. "Thank you, my lady."

Lady Calpurnia put down her cup. "My husband's biggest estate was in the Fens. He has lost it, and also his place on the council. He is no longer a patrician. He wants to emigrate to Gaul and start over."

"If you go to Gaul you will have nothing, not even the respect due to a land-owning family."

"True, my dear." Lady Calpurnia took another delicate sip at her tea. "I hear that you have befriended the magistrate's granddaughter."

Was that a challenge? "Yes. She comes from a respectable family." Claudia knew how much her guest valued that.

Lady Calpurnia mellowed slightly. "The news from Ravenna is shocking, isn't it? The Italian emperor has murdered general Aetius, with his own hand, they say."

Claudia nodded. News had just reached Britain that Aetius had met a violent death. She knew that Magnus had been sent to join Aetius's staff. Had he been killed too? Perhaps Magnus had dawdled on his way south and had missed the disaster. But Magnus was not the sort to dawdle. She wished now that she had spoken to him before he sailed. But it was too late for that. She would never receive another letter from him.

"You seem upset, my dear," Lady Calpurnia said.

"An acquaintance of mine was in Ravenna ..."

"A young man? How terrible for you, my dear."

Chapter 17: Gaul

Vienne, February, 455 AD

Vienne was built on the east bank of the river Rhone. The old city was narrow, squeezed between the shoreline and the cliffs behind. Several streets that made their way up the hill were forced to resort to steps on the steeper slopes.

Magnus and Conwyn walked north through the streets towards the city centre. They were both tired, thirsty and footsore.

The city had become capital of the Gallic Empire, thanks largely to its position at the heart of the messenger network.

The high hills on each side of the river channelled the wind, so that it either blew up or down the valley, but never across it. The messenger station was based on Mount Heracles, to the north of the city. The aviators had chosen that spot because the mountain was on a bend in the river, so it caught the wind whatever direction it was blowing.

The west bank had once been the commercial quarter, but the warehouses and workshops had been abandoned after the crisis. Now only a few patrician residences and the palace remained. The emperor's palace consisted of a series of elegant courtyards, with ornamental gardens. But these days power flowed around the palace rather than through it.

Everyone knew that the health of the Western Emperor, Vindex, was failing. He was content to delegate authority to his army commander, Lord Avitus, and the imperial chancellor.

The Rhone valley grew the wheat that provided Rome with its bread. At harvest time, the barges journeyed downstream to Arles. In return, incoming ships brought all the luxuries of the eastern empire.

All of this bustling activity was an irritant to Magnus as he walked through the city. He and Conwyn had crossed the Alps from Turin three days before. Their clothes, travel-stained tunics and homespun cloaks, were covered in dust. Magnus tried to avoid catching the eye of passers-by. He was nothing to them, a ghost. The pedestrians avoided him. What did he look like to them? He dreaded the thought that one of them would recognise him. He had lost his honour and, with it, his place in society.

He was full of remorse at his failure to save Aetius, but once again pushed the thought aside. What could he possibly have done?

Magnus had planned to buy a night's bed in an inn with the last of his coins and present himself to the garrison commander in the morning. Suddenly, he changed his mind.

"I'm going to the barracks."

Conwyn was surprised. "Now, his evening?"

"Yes. Come on." He would climb to the barracks and find whether he could claim refuge or not. Before the light faded. Before his heart failed him.

The hill was on his right hand, glimpsed between houses. On his left was the gentle slope down to the river, sometimes obscured by houses built on the slope. The road he was following led gently upwards.

As he climbed the last slope to the main garrison gate, Magnus regretted he did not have his uniform cloak with him. But he had been forced to abandon his possessions and to travel light. He had left behind his court clothes, his armour and everything else of value.

The two guards in imperial livery and chain mail watched his unarmed approach without alarm, but also without any of the alert interest that might imply respect. Magnus saluted the senior man, obviously a sergeant, only with an austere, calculated nod.

"Good evening, sergeant. I am here to see the officer of the day. I am Magnus Vitalinus." That left the sergeant to guess, preferably wrongly, if he'd been summoned.

"On what business, sir?" the sergeant asked, polite but unimpressed.

Magnus's shoulders straightened; he didn't know from what unused lumber room in the back of his soul the voice came, but it came out clipped and commanding, nonetheless. "On his business, sergeant." Then he felt ashamed of himself. He had no right to bully the man. He could not pull rank because he had none.

Conwyn recognised his cue and took a step backwards. In a moment, he ceased to be a companion to a vagabond and became a mistreated servant.

Automatically, the sergeant saluted. "Yes, sir." His nod told his companion to stay sharp, and he gestured Magnus to follow him through the open gate. "This way, sir. I'll ask whether the commander will see you."

Magnus's heart wrung as he stared round the broad cobbled courtyard inside the gates. Once, this had been home.

The sergeant escorted him to the inner courtyard that he knew so well. Magnus wondered whether the officer of the day would condemn him as an impostor and order him to be thrown out into the street.

To his surprise was taken to someone he knew. The man leaning back in his chair was the British officer, Cynon. He had served as Aurelianus's sergeant before his promotion.

He sat up. "Magnus! What brings you here?"

He tried to explain in dry, concise terms. "I was with Aetius in Ravenna. After he was cut down by Emperor Valentinian, I was kicked out. So I made my way west."

"Ravenna? God's truth! You mean you were there when he died?" Cynon was eager for news.

"Yes. I was halfway down the table." Magnus knew that if he had been any closer, he might have tried to intervene, and been cut down too.

He was blunt. "Aetius was murdered. Valentinian did it himself. All of Aetius's associates were rounded up, under suspicion. Some of his Italian staff were persuaded to change sides, but I was a foreigner, only an adjutant, not worth bothering about. So they let me go. His Hun bodyguard swore revenge, but they didn't want me getting in their way. I decided to make my way west."

Cynon considered this. "What are your plans?"

He shrugged. "Find a role here. Or make my way home."

"I owe you a debt, sir. You promoted me. You trusted me with command." He paused. "Here – sit down, have some wine." He picked up a spare goblet, gave it a superficial wipe with a cloth and poured the wine.

"Thank you." He accepted the wine and took a cautious sip.

"Tell us more. All we have to go on are official reports and travellers' tales. What was the cause of the quarrel?"

"Oh - Aetius arranged a betrothal between his son and the emperor's daughter. Valentinian was not keen. Neither were his advisors. But Aetius didn't notice. The Roman senator Petronius Maximus and the chamberlain Heraclius persuaded Valentinian that Aetius wanted to put his son on the throne. So, when Aetius visited Ravenna, he was invited to dine at the palace – and cut down by Valentinian in person."

"Go on," Cynon said.

"I think Maximus expected to be made army commander in place of Aetius, but was blocked by Heraclius." He took another, longer, sip at his wine.

"But Aetius saved the empire!"

"Aetius wasn't liked in Italy, you know. Most people in the west thought Aetius was the only person who could save them from the Huns. But the Italians were afraid he would take Italy into the Gallic Empire."

"You travelled here alone?"

He took a gulp at his wine. "Yes. Except for one servant. I was forced to abandon everything. My other servant disappeared. Perhaps he'd been murdered. But I was unable to protect him."

"Your concern does you credit." Cynon stood up. "Avitus will want to hear this. Come on."

Magnus was tired and wanted only to rest, but he followed as Cynon took him through the streets to the town house of Avitus.

Avitus was a patrician, but he looked more like a country gentleman than a commanding general. He was lean, below average height, with a dignified air. Now he listened gravely as Magnus repeated his story.

"So, it was murder in cold blood. We had doubted the tales. This changes nothing, you understand. Valentinian is a reigning emperor. He accused Lord Aetius of treason. We cannot act."

"I understand that, sir."

"What will you do now, Magnus?" Avitus's tone was avuncular.

"Make my way home, I suppose, sir. Or find out whether there's a post vacant here. anything would do." He would not beg.

"Oh, I think we can find something." Avitus glanced at Cynon. "We can make use of your talents. We have a need of officers with combat experience."

*   *   *

Water Newton, March 455

Claudia had escaped from her father's presence and returned to her husband's estate. The country life was dull, but she never felt that she was in danger. She occasionally received notes from her friends in London, but she was surprised when a messenger brought her a dispatch.

"I'm from the messenger station on Beacon Hill, in Charnwood Forest, my lady."

"That's a long ride," she said, with sympathy.

He grimaced. "Two days, my lady. But the sergeant said there was good weather for it."

"Yes. But what brings you to my home?"

He held out a letter. "This is for you, my lady. From the continent."

Claudia recoiled. A letter from Vienne could mean only one thing. "But – but he's dead. He was with Aetius when he was murdered."

The young man shrugged. "Perhaps his commander thought it best to write to his family ..."

She ignored this witless utterance. She tore open the letter and read the introduction. Magnus. It was him. She read it through. He said he was safe in Vienne. He wasted space describing the Vandals in North Africa. But he did not say *how* he got to Vienne. The man was infuriating.

*   *   *

Vienne, April, 455 AD

Magnus had been given a tiny room in the fort as an office. Already, at the beginning of the campaigning season, the room was uncomfortably hot at noon. He hated to think what it would be like in the middle of summer.

Magnus leaned back in his wicker chair, which creaked, and broke the seal on the letter that his friend had given him.

"Claudia Ambrosius to Magnus Vitalinus, on the staff of Lord Avitus in Vienne, greetings. I thank you for your letter. I am glad to hear of your success on Lord Avitus's staff.

I sometimes visit the nearest messenger station, but it is a long journey. Do you ever visit your aviator friends?

I have asked my new nephew, Gaius, to bring you this message. Give my greetings to him. I commend him to you. Please write to me about the situation in Vienne, in Gaul, and in Italy. How were you able to leave Ravenna?

Farewell, my friend. I hope you prosper, and I salute you."

Writing from Water Newton.

Magnus showed Gaius the letter. His friend was amused. "So, I'm promoted to nephew, am I? When I was merely a ne'er-do-well guardsman, my Uncle Brutus barely acknowledged my existence."

"So, what's changed? You're an impoverished ne'er-do-well cavalry officer."

"Magnus, my friend! You're so naïve. Now, of course, I'm the best friend of the famous Magnus, erstwhile commander of the Numerus Britannica, who was the drinking friend of the great Aetius and is, at the very least, acquainted with Lord Avitus."

Magnus was shocked. "They're not saying that in Britain, are they?"

"No, I picked up that story when I asked about you in Lyon."

He glanced at the letter again. "She calls me her friend."

"That's just good manners," Gaius said gently. "I wouldn't build too much on it."

"No, of course not." He put the letter down. "But enough of me, Gaius. What's been happening back in Britain?"

"Oh, the frontier is holding. The governor is doing better than anyone expected. Did news of that reach you?"

"Yes."

"But then the lady Claudia, my aunt by marriage, asked to see me before I left." He grinned. "She's quite an eyeful. She was wasted on my uncle."

"I know about that," Magnus growled. "Gaius, did I make the wrong decision?"

His friend was suddenly totally serious. "Personally, I think you over-reacted. You should have stayed and defended the new frontier."

"My presence was an embarrassment to everybody. The best way I could help out was to leave."

His friend waved this aside. "But when lady Claudia heard I was on my way to Gaul, she asked me to bring you that." He grinned. "She asked me to tell you, privately, that she's most annoyed. You didn't tell her how you escaped from Ravenna and how you reached Gaul."

"Well, I can describe my hike across Italy, if that's what she wants. Take a seat. I wondered how the governor would get rid if you."

His friend relaxed. "You've done well for yourself."

Magnus shrugged. "I survived a couple of disasters. More by luck than by judgement."

"You were never so modest back home. Is the responsibility of command getting you down?

Magnus ignored this. He was looking for some cups. "My main problem is dealing with the general. Although he's a lot easier to deal with than Aetius was."

Gaius sat in a wicker chair. "You talk very casually of governors and generals, Magnus. And what's Avitus like?"

"Oh, he's sharp enough. He's a patrician. The Visigoths respect him . . . here, have some wine. From the Rhone valley. Excellent quality, a real bargain."

"I was warned about cheap wine."

"Quite right. But this is safe enough." He took a sip. "My unit was stationed in Lyon, but with the news from Rome, we were transferred back here."

Gaius was suddenly a lot more serious. "These are difficult times, Magnus. Just before we sailed, we heard that the Roman emperor had been murdered. Is it true?"

"Yes. By two of Aetius' bodyguards. Those Huns were loyal to him."

Gaius sat back. "Well, the emperor murdered Aetius last year, so you can say he got what he deserved. Who's the new emperor in Italy?"

"Petronius Maximus. He was proclaimed emperor the day after Valentinian was killed."

"You make it sound as if he was party to the murder."

Magnus sipped at his wine. "Plenty of other people have made the same assumption. Particularly as he was one of the men who persuaded Valentinian that Aetius was plotting treason."

"How did Avitus take the news of the new emperor?"

Magnus raised his eyebrows. "He expressed his regret at the death of Valentinian, what else?

"I see. I think." Gaius' usual exuberance returned. "Don't you want to know the London gossip? No, perhaps not. What else is there? The frontier's holding, did I say that? The governor's trying to recruit a militia to defend it. The old men on the council hate that."

"Nothing new there."

"But enough talk of me and Britain. What's happening at the heart of the empire?"

"Apart from assassination in Rome? Well … when the Vandals invaded Tunisia, they captured the Roman fleet based in Carthage. Now they've attempted an invasion of Sicily."

"That's reckless. The Romans will soon throw them out again."

"Of course."

*   *   *

Vienne, Gaul, June 455

Lord Avitus had called for a staff conference. His house, large by the standards of Vienne, was halfway up the hill. The senior army officers had been bickering over the right to attend, so Magnus was surprised when he was included.

Avitus's secretary had shown the officers into the meeting room. Now they were waiting, with growing impatience for Avitus to arrive. All the shutters had been folded back to improve the ventilation, but despite that the room was hot and uncomfortable.

The room gave a fine view over the city on the riverbank and the mountains beyond, but nobody had time for that now. Such a calm room for such violent news, Magnus thought.

The atmosphere was emotion-laden. The officers knew that the emperor had taken a momentous decision. Some of them relished the idea of marching on Rome. Some had hopes of advancement, wealth or, simply, loot. Others were quieter, reluctant to speak their fears. Magnus tried to ignore the gossip.

He was standing behind two Italian officers. One was an exile from the Emperor Valentinian's feuding.

"Is there no end to the bad news?" he said to his companion. "First Aetius was murdered, then Valentinian. Now they're asking us to invade Italy."

"If you ask me, Valentinian deserved it. He murdered Aetius," the mercenary said.

"Maybe so, but then Rome got that fool Petronius Maximus."

"You haven't thought it through. If this gamble fails, the Imperial authorities are likely to execute us for treason."

"But we aren't Romans. We're subjects of Gaul. That isn't treason."

"Would that stop the Italians?"

Magnus wondered idly whether he was junior enough to escape this fate. He had already escaped from Italy once. Or, if a battle was lost, could he escape? At least he had somewhere to go, back to Britain.

The door was pushed open, attracting everyone's attention. Avitus walked in, accompanied by his son in law, Sidonius. They were followed by Avitus's secretary and Edeco, the commander of the German mercenary troops. All were dressed in richly-embroidered court robes.

Avitus turned to face the room, the gesture of a skilled orator, and everyone automatically fell silent.

"Good morning, gentlemen. I assume you have all heard the latest news from Italy?"

There was a murmur of agreement.

"The chancellor has received reliable news from Rome. It confirms that the earlier stories were true. I can confirm that the Vandals have indeed sacked Rome."

The Italian exile groaned.

Avitus raised his hand for silence, and once again he got it. He was a shrewd politician and a skilled orator, and his men respected him.

"But there have been no casualties and no destruction. Pope Leo pleaded with the Vandal king, Gaiseric to spare the city. The king promised that there would be no killing, no torture, and no destruction of buildings. And he kept his promise. If any of you have kin in Rome, I assure you that they are quite safe."

Avitus was a nobleman and a gentleman, a politician rather than a warrior. It occurred to Magnus that the Empire had a surfeit of warriors. Perhaps a talented politician was exactly what was wanted.

"His majesty and the Senate of Gaul have asked me to lead an expeditionary force on Rome and drive out the Vandals.

"Gentlemen, we have been asked to restore order in Italy," Avitus said. He turned to Edeco. "I would welcome your opinion, sir."

"Speed is of the essence, my lord," Edeco said. "Now that we have our orders, I recommend that we should take all the troops under our command and march on Rome at once."

There was an uncomfortable silence. Most of the officers knew that such a move would leave northern Gaul open to the Franks.

The mercenary officers were impatient at this. Rome was the only thing that mattered to them.

Magnus decided to break the silence. "My lord, the Franks were quiet last year. It should be safe to withdraw troops from the frontier for a few months. The messenger service can send you news if the Franks decide to act. Of course, if we're away two years, or we lose a battle . . ."

"Yes, I see. Thank you. But I am reluctant to leave our northern frontier undefended. Edeco, please make arrangements to leave your most dependable troops to watch that frontier."

Edeco nodded. He knew how to interpret that. "Yes, sir. But that will leave us short. How do we make up the loss?" The room fell silent.

Avitus looked round. "Gentlemen, the king of the Visigoths has offered to lend me some men for a single campaign. It is my intention to ask him."

Avitus turned to Edeco. "I agree that we should take every man we can spare, and that we should leave as soon as possible."

"Yes, my lord."

"Gentlemen, I want you to begin preparations for a march on Italy."

Avitus asked each commander in turn how soon his men would be ready to march. Most of them had anticipated this question and had their answers ready.

Finally, Avitus summed up. "Five days from now? Are we agreed, gentlemen? Very well." The room began to empty, but Avitus told Magnus to stay. "A word with you, please. Young man, I want to appoint you as the commander of communications. I want you to set up a series of messenger stations."

"But - why use the messenger service, sir? The Roman courier service, on the main roads at least, is faster and more reliable than our messengers."

Avitus raised his eyebrows. "Didn't you know? The chancellor has told me that the Roman courier service has collapsed. Half of the horses have been stolen." He smiled. "At the moment, our messenger service is faster than the Roman couriers."

"That won't last, sir."

"No, of course not. As soon as order is restored, the courier service will be rebuilt. But in the meantime, I will have to rely on your aviators."

"Yes, sir." Magnus swallowed his shock. A huge task lay ahead. He would command a hundred men at most, but this post held as much power as any of the others discussed today. He would control access to the general. He realised that he had been chosen mainly because he would also be on Avitus's staff. Most of the other officers here were barbarian mercenaries and, apart from Avitus and his secretary, Magnus was probably the best-educated person in the room. Magnus remembered wryly that he had hated his school lessons.

* * *

Magnus had decided that the quickest way to get to the messenger station at Lyon was to ask for a lift in one of the flying machines. The weather was favourable and they touched down at the messenger field outside Lyon without incident. Magnus complemented his pilot on his landing and went to look for the captain.

Commius was surprised, but politely invited Magnus to his quarters. "I'm glad to see you again, of course. But I have a bad feeling about this. What brings you here, sir?"

The captain was a southerner from a poor family. He was tall, with black hair. He was intelligent and had educated himself, but he lacked self-confidence. Aetius had despised him as a commoner, but Magnus respected his skills as an organiser.

"You're right to be apprehensive, captain. You've heard of the expeditionary force to Italy, of course. I've been given the task of creating a series of courier stations to link Vienne with the army as it marches south." He told himself that at least he knew what to do.

"Our task is to set up a courier service from Turin to Rome. I want you to hunt down the men you recruited during Aetius' campaign against the Huns."

"I need a beer. You'll have one too? Freshly brewed ..."

"Thank you, captain."

"I don't like it, sir. We can pull a team together, I suppose. We've done it before. But ..." He took a pull at his beer. "Italy's nothing but trouble. When the Huns were marching across Italy, the Italians welcomed us. They knew we would leave as soon as the campaign was over. They were happy to haul on the launching ropes for us. But this time - we're coming to stay. They won't like that."

Magnus took a sip at his beer. He had not thought of that.

"You may be right, captain, but we have our orders. We'll only need the messengers until the courier service is restored. That should only take a couple of months. Then we can send everyone home."

"That sounds optimistic to me, sir. I – I apologise if I seem obstructive, sir."

"Not at all, captain. I need to know about the problems we face. I welcome any advice. But we can't ignore an order from Lord Avitus."

"No, sir." Commius took a long pull at his beer.

"I want you to send out a request for volunteers. Tell them it's for a tour of six months. Offer them a temporary promotion. A chance to prove themselves."

"Very well, sir. Some of them'll volunteer just for a break in the routine. D'you want Sergeant Dumnorix from Trier again, sir? He'll relish something like this."

"Not this time, Captain. We're not fighting the Huns now. We need someone who knows how to be diplomatic."

* * *

Tuscany, June 455

Julius Valerius Majorian belonged to one of the most powerful families in Italy. Four years before, his family connections had won him a commission in Aetius's army in Gaul and then appointment as his financial officer. As a result of careful peculation in Gaul, he was now one of the wealthiest men on the senate.

He was now using some of the money to refurbish the family villa in lavish style. He, like his ancestors before him, appreciated that emphasising his wealth was a way of translating it into power.

He wanted a new mosaic and had chosen to interview the craftsman in the colonnade of the outer courtyard. He eyed with dislike the man bowing and scraping in front of him. But this was an important commission and he had summoned the craftsman personally.

The family's principal villa was in the hills to the north east of the old city of Florentia. The main axis of the villa was carefully aligned so as to give a view of the city below.

"I commissioned a new dining room some time ago." Before the political troubles began, he meant. There was no need to say so. "Now the time has come to complete the project. The room is designed in the classical style, you understand, where the guests can recline on three couches in the traditional manner."

"Yes, my lord. I have worked on several such rooms."

His friend Libius Severus, leaning against a column, saw no need to be tactful. "Do we really have to tolerate this sniveling fool, Julius?"

"The man claims to be a master craftsman. If he is as good as he claims then, yes, we shall have to tolerate him." Majorian turned to the craftsman. "The builders have finished their work, behind schedule of course, and now I have summoned you to provide a mosaic for the floor."

The man bowed again. "I shall endeavour to give satisfaction, my lord."

"Shut up and follow me." He chose to personally escort the craftsman through the courtyards and gardens of the villa to the new room. He felt that a matter of this importance had to be dealt with personally.

Libius chose to accompany him along the colonnade. To the left, a courtyard held a formal pool. To the right was the doorway to the unfinished dining room.

A slave was sweeping up the loose plaster. He looked up, recognised his master, and hastily stood aside. Majorian eyed him with deep disfavour. A damned fool, this one. Two years ago, he had been a tenant, deep in debt, but with hopes of paying it off. Then the harvest had failed, and he had been unable to keep up the payments on his loan.

Majorian's bailiff had enslaved him, in lieu of the debt. The bailiff should have set the man to field work, but instead had sent him to help the carpenters here in the villa.

"Out of my way, fool!" Libius snapped, and the slave scurried out into the courtyard.

Majorian turned to the master craftsman. "This is the room. What can you make of it?"

The craftsman tactfully ignored the slave. "A very large room, my lord. Impressive, if I may say so. And it faces west, so it'll catch the evening light. I have brought several designs, my lord, if it pleases you ..."

Majorian made a pretence of looking through the designs carefully, while the craftsman dithered anxiously. "I want a traditional design, very formal, but without any pagan symbols."

"Yes, my lord. An interesting challenge."

Libius smiled. "The Church seems to have borrowed a lot of pagan symbolism, Julius."

"Well, no overt pagan symbolism, then. I want plenty of gold in the design," he told the craftsman.

The man glanced at Majorian's embroidered robe. "Yes, my lord. And perhaps some purple?" The craftsman was obsequious.

"Not in my home. I don't want the priests accusing me of hubris. But I plan to redecorate the local Church. I could include some purple in that, as long as everyone knew who paid for it."

"I see, my lord. The purple would indicate Christ's majesty, of course. An excellent scheme."

Majorian ignored this. "When can you begin here?"

"Next month, my lord. Unless the troubles spread north."

"They will not do that. My bodyguard will see to that," Majorian said flatly. A few bribes in the right quarter had helped as well. "You may leave now."

"Ah – I have no gold in stock, my lord. I regret that you would have to supply it before I could begin."

Libius turned to his friend with weary politeness. "I thought that payment on delivery were the usual terms?"

The craftsman wrung his hands. "These are difficult times, my lord . . ."

For once, the man was not exaggerating, so Majorian refrained from issuing a crushing rebuke. "Very well. Go and see my steward."

"Yes, my lord. Thank you."

Majorian gestured to the slave. "You! Show him the way."

"Yes, my lord." He escorted the craftsman away.

Libius watched him go. "That craftsman defied you! I'm surprised you could tolerate the fellow!"

"He represents the best mosaics workshop north of Rome. Perhaps the best in Italy. I'll put up with a lot for that."

"Ah. I see. The commission will be expensive, then."

"My family is an ancient one. We must maintain appearances," Majorian said. "In these troubled times, it's necessary to remind everyone of that."

That had become more difficult lately. The emperor had rewarded him by giving him the title of honorary commander of the palace guard. That had been gratifying. Unfortunately, the complement had turned sour when the guard had murdered the last emperor and had then done nothing to protect Rome from the Vandals. Instead of raising his dignity, the title had diminished it.

"I hear that you're using part of your fortune to build up your personal bodyguard," Libius said. "According to some, you're turning it into a private army."

He shrugged. "Rumours always exaggerate," It was true that he was recruiting foreign mercenaries. They were uncouth barbarians, and the demands their officers made were exorbitant, but he knew that you got what you paid for. If he wanted a decent force he would have to put up with their demands. He was determined that his own force would be more useful than the emperor's decorative palace guard.

"Is it too early for some wine, Julius?" Libius asked, with easy familiarity. He was the younger brother of another powerful senator, fully his social equal. They had known each other since childhood.

"Not at all, Libius. Come this way."

Libius followed at his shoulder. "My brother tells me there are rumours in Rome that you plan to make yourself emperor."

"Rome is always full of foolish rumours. How could I possibly do that? Only the emperor in Constantinople can appoint a co-emperor, and how could I influence him? Without that recognition, I would merely be an usurper ... I sometimes feel that Italy doesn't need an emperor any more. The senate could run things, just as they used to."

"With yourself as the most powerful man in the senate?" Libius sounded amused.

"Of course," Majorian said serenely.

He had fled Rome, along with everyone else, when King Gaiseric and his Vandals arrived. It was humiliating, for himself and for Rome, but there had been no alternative. Standing up to the Vandal army would have been suicidal.

"You have an army now," Libius said. "Can't you drive Gaiseric out?"

"If I ordered them to march, it would be a magnificent gesture," he agreed. "A victory would bring me to the attention of the eastern emperor. But the casualties would be heavy."

"Mercenaries can always be replaced," Libius said.

"Yes. But if the attack ended in failure, my standing would be diminished. I can't risk it." He paused. "Some of the other senators have bodyguards too. If we acted together, combined our forces, we could drive the Vandals out. I've approached some of them, asked them to add their forces to mine, but they've either prevaricated or refused outright."

His guest looked uncomfortable. "They treasure their independence too much. Majorian, I'll write to my brother. But he'll be reluctant. I can't promise anything. I'm sorry."

"They all treasure their independence, my friend," Majorian said tactfully. "But if Gaiseric stays in Rome much longer, the patricians will be more afraid of them than they are of me." When his power was recognised, he would have to take revenge for the insult the Vandals had given Rome. He was determined that he would have to invade Africa and destroy the Vandal kingdom.

He led the way to the dining room and gestured to a servant. "Come, let's sample some wine. I've bought some from Gaul. The Rhone valley. It doesn't match our best, but at least it's different."

*　*　*

Rome, end of July

The via Aurelia, west of the Tiber, topped a low rise and Avitus and his staff came within sight of the walls of Rome at last. Avitus and his staff were riding immediately behind the advance guard. Behind them, on the old military road, marched five thousand infantry, less than one of the old legions, but the best that Gaul could provide.

On the horizon, away to the west, Magnus could see an aqueduct, an immense structure that strode across the landscape. He had heard there were ten of them, built by earlier emperors to provide water for the citizens. It was a vast undertaking, far beyond the abilities of the empire today.

He had been told that this city was bigger than all of the cities of the Gallic Empire combined. It was also far richer. Looking at those walls, he realised it was true.

Gaius Ambrosius rode back to join Avitus. "My lord, the scouts tell me that the Vandals are withdrawing from the city. They must have got wind of our approach. They're retreating towards the coast."

"In good order, I suppose?" Avitus said. He was wearing chain mail and looked exhausted.

"They're taking the Via Portuensis to the new harbour. The 'Portus Augusti'."

All Magnus knew was that Portus was on the north bank of the Tiber.

"Their rearguard is blocking the road. Eight or nine hundred men," Gaius said. "The road to Portus runs over the hills for the first half of the journey."

Avitus squinted at the road ahead and the city walls beyond. "Then we must dispose of them. We could just brush them aside ... But that would take too long and cost us too many men. Magnus, write a note for General Edeco. Tell him he is to deploy his men. He must outflank this rearguard and prevent them from rejoining their brethren. He is to harry the main force and ensure they continue to retreat. Have you got all that?"

Magnus had dismounted and was struggling with a message pad and stylus. "Yes, my lord." He was impressed. Avitus, in a couple of minutes, had come up with a workable plan of battle.

The army outflanked the Vandals' rearguard and turned south, towards the Tiber. Avitus was cautious, sending the cavalry forward against the enemy's main force to test their reaction. To everyone's surprise, the Vandals went on the defensive.

In the skirmishing that followed, Avitus managed to gain the tactical advantage. The Vandals, faced with a skilled opponent, who commanded a determined force of troops, were forced to give ground. Avitus became more assertive and, by careful maneuvering, he forced the Vandals to abandon the wagons containing their loot and retreat back to their ships.

The Vandals' rearguard, cut off, with no hope of escape, grudgingly surrendered.

The troops were pleased by this success but Avitus remained cautious. Although the Vandals had suffered casualties, Avitus knew they were still a threat.

Magnus wondered whether the city would defy Avitus. But as the army approached the walls of the city, magistrates and dignitaries of the city flung open the Porta Aurelia. They walked out in their showy robes and in, with proper formality, welcomed Avitus as their saviour.

Avitus accepted this performance gravely.

At the heart of Rome were the Capitoline and Palatine Hills with their great mansions and stone temples. But as Avitus and his colleagues approached the centre of the city, they entered a maze of streets and the wider view was lost.

The closer they got to the centre the more crowded the buildings were, and the taller they seemed to grow. They were rickety heaps of brick and crimson-red tiles, three or four stories high. The stink was remarkable, of rotting waste, sewage, and cooking food. And the noise of the city seemed to engulf the newcomers, a constant clamorous racket.

Magnus was appalled at the damage he saw. The Vandals had stripped the city of its wealth: the gold and silver ornaments from the churches, the statues from the palaces. Even the Temple of Jupiter Capitolinus had lost half of its gilded copper roof.

The buildings of the imperial residence were spread all over the Palatine hill. Avitus walked through the private rooms of the palace, accompanied by his secretary, Magnus, and a couple of troopers. The rooms had been tidied up but still had a neglected air.

They found the Master of the Chancellery, Severus, and a couple of his associates, waiting for them. Severus, an old, gaunt man, gave an ostentatious bow.

"Congratulations, my lord. You have achieved a great victory. The populace regard you as the hero of the hour. The city magistrates are talking of erecting a series of statues to commemorate your victory."

Avitus was appalled. "They're too fast. All I did was oversee a series of skirmishes. This war isn't over yet."

"You are too modest, my lord. You have driven the Vandals from our shores."

"Modest?" Avitus lost his temper. "King Gaiseric has *not* been defeated. His army is still intact. He could invade us again, at *any* time. I had to send half of my army in the south, to drive the Vandals out of Naples."

"But you have taken a thousand prisoners! When we sell them, they'll bring in a tidy profit for the government. We could do with it."

"That was not part of their surrender terms," Magnus said.

"Who cares about promises made to barbarians?" Severus said.

"I doubt if they would make good house servants," Avitus said dryly. "And when they're told their fate, they might turn violent."

Magnus interrupted. "We could ask them to volunteer for the army, sir. Send them to protect the northern frontier against the Huns."

"That seems a neat arrangement," Avitus said. "But can we afford to pay them?"

Severus ignored this and changed the subject. "We must ask the court poet to write a panegyric, celebrating your accession to greatness, your highness."

"I suppose we must." Avitus did not sound enthusiastic. "And the correct form of address is 'my lord duke', not 'your highness'."

The Master of the Chancellery grandly ignored this remark. Magnus realised he had his own agenda and would not let Avitus challenge it.

"Elevation to a suitable rank will surely follow. I have found some rooms in the palace that I consider suitable for your highness and your companions."

The palace institutions were apparently more robust than mere buildings. Severus, with unshakeable dignity, showed them round the palace complex.

Avitus followed the chancellor gloomily, accompanied by his secretary and a couple of bodyguards. Magnus tagged along behind. They found that the palace too had been ransacked. Some of the landscapes painted on the walls had been scored with a knife.

Avitus shrugged. "It'll do for now. I was never fond of ostentation anyway."

"The palace complex is not restricted to the imperial residence," Severus said. "The palace bodyguard is housed in one quarter, while the Chancellery staff takes up another. His highness Petronius Maximus was pleased to occupy the imperial palace."

"Indeed?" Avitus said. "But perhaps my residence here would send the wrong signal to the people of Italy."

Severus chose to ignore this. "The populace needs a new hero. We must not let them see any sign of weakness in you. So, we must rebuild the imperial palace."

Avitus waved this aside. "The government can't afford it."

Severus took no notice. "The audience rooms are the biggest problem, your majesty. They contained the greatest wealth and, of course, suffered the greatest damage. All of your guests are going to be examining those rooms. You will have to be mindful of your dignity. And faded wall-paintings are worse than no paintings at all. We must start at once."

"Wall hangings and tapestries can cover those," Avitus said. "But you're right. I'm going to be interviewing a lot of people over the next few days. Starting with Count Ricimer."

He turned to his personal secretary. "Please send a formal invitation to the count. I want to see him as soon as possible."

The secretary made a note. "Yes, my lord."

"Surely that is my responsibility and my duty," Severus said.

Avitus fobbed him off. "The main problem now is the corn supply. Do you have any plans for that? Now that the Vandals have cut off the supply from Africa, the main supply is Sicily. But the Vandals can threaten that too. I hope that Ricimer can help with that."

The chancellor seemed to be surprised. "Surely the emperor in Vienne can send us some aid? The populace assumed he would do so."

"That was foolish of them. But I will write to the emperor at once," Avitus said.

Severus finally took the hint and departed. Avitus's secretary waited until the chancellery officials were out of earshot. "How long do you intend to stay here, my lord?"

"There's still the Vandals to deal with," Avitus said. He had no delusions about his victory. The Vandals' fleet was intact and could threaten the entire coast. Avitus, without a fleet, could not hinder them. Although he had sent half of his forces to drive the Vandals out of Naples, he was forced to keep the remainder in the north to protect Rome.

Avitus turned to Magnus. "What's your opinion of the palace guard?"

"Lord Edeco and I looked them over. Edeco said the men were useless. When the Vandals attacked, they made no attempt to fight."

"Do you think that the men we brought with us would be more effective? Despite their small number?"

"Yes, my lord."

Chapter 18: The Struggle for Italy

Rome, August, 455 AD

Julius Valerius Majorian was determined to increase the power of his family. He also had plans to restore the majesty of the empire. But those plans had just suffered a severe setback.

He stood in the courtyard of the family's house in Rome, accompanied by his steward. He was shocked at the damage done to the building. The house in Rome had been one of the most lavish in the city. But the Vandals had stripped it of anything that looked valuable. "The bronze statues?"

Dragged off to be melted down, my lord. They tipped the marble statues over too, but then abandoned them. The barbarians probably realised they weren't worth the effort of dragging off."

"Those statues were works of art. Valuable beyond price!"

"Yes, my lord. But at least they didn't do any structural damage," the steward said. "You'll be able to move back in without too much discomfort."

Majorian grimly totaled up the extent of the damage. "This is an insult to the family honour. The repairs will take years."

"Yes, my lord," the steward said. "Although the mosaics are undamaged, my lord. And the wall paintings."

"Except for the gilding. Which totally ruins the whole design."

The Majorian family had always been determined to emphasise its power. The damage to the family's wealth was bad enough. The damage to his dignity was far worse.

"Have my clothes been unpacked? I must change. And then I must begin the task of visiting my allies."

"Of course, my lord," the steward said. "Will you visit the palace as well, my lord?"

"Shut up." He was furious at Avitus's arrival in Italy. That sanctimonious prig had made himself the master of Italy! And that threatened all his plans to dominate Italy.

When the Gaulish army had arrived, Majorian had expected the Vandals to destroy the upstart, just as they had destroyed everyone else. He was outraged when the Vandals had meekly abandoned Rome. Of course, he could see now that the pirates had come to raid, not to conquer, and saw no need for an unnecessary fight.

If he had realised that a month ago he could have led his little army against them and could now be posturing as Rome's saviour.

Majorian looked round the courtyard again. "Yes. I shall have to swallow my pride and congratulate the Gaulish general for his daring."

"Lord Avitus describes his victory as nothing more than a series of skirmishes, my lord."

"And quite right too." But, in Rome, appearance was everything. And the provincial upstart now had the appearance of a conquering hero.

And the worst of it was that the Vandals remained in Italy, and threatened Rome. For the time being, Avitus and his barbarian allies were Rome's only protection. Politics dictated that the Majorian family had to lend the fellow his support. All he could do was smile politely, try to prevent the fellow from gaining too much support, and bide his time.

"What senators are in Rome? I shall have to write to them."

"Only five at present, my lord. But I have their names."

"Good. I must start this campaign at once."

* * *

Now that it was safe, the senators returned to Rome and tried to pretend that nothing had happened. All of them demanded, as of right, an audience with Avitus.

The Senate reconvened and its members prepared to continue its debates as if they had never left the city.

Avitus, eager to show respect for Roman traditions, dutifully accepted their invitation to attend their meeting. He sat between the two consuls, as tradition demanded.

Magnus was standing in the doorway, clutching the latest dispatches from Vienne in case they were called for.

The building was plain, almost austere, the benches were cold marble, but for centuries this room had been the centre of power for the empire. All of the Senators were dressed in richly embroidered togas, a garment that been unfashionable for centuries and was reserved for formal situations such as this.

The senators showed Avitus the deference he was due. One of the senators gave a speech accepting Avitus as one of their number. He ignored the fact that he did not own any land in Italy.

Avitus thanked the senators and explained that he was merely acting as the Gallic emperor's viceroy and was not claiming any rights within Italy.

Magnus had quickly learned that Rome was all about social divisions. There were rigid barriers between social classes, from the ancient senatorial families down to the slaves. And the gulf between rich and poor was vast. There were rich and poor in the Gallic Empire too. But Gaul was a lot poorer than Italy and the men who did the fighting were not prepared to grovel to the landowners. Here in Rome the rich seemed to be a lot richer and prouder. It was said that just one thousand families owned almost all the cultivated land in the Roman Empire. Magnus had been made painfully aware that his own family would have been excluded from that inner circle. By Roman standards his great-uncle, one of the richest men in Britain, was of little more than middling rank. Avitus did not rank much higher.

Magnus could see Majorian there in the front row, sitting opposite Avitus, dressed in a toga with an elaborate gold decoration woven into the cloth, saying nothing but remembering everything. His expression was neutral, but Magnus could guess how angry he was.

Magnus's indignation mounted. These men had been sneering at the Gallic Empire for years, despising it as an impoverished backwater or a rebellious province. Now they welcomed a Gallic nobleman as their saviour.

Majorian asked to speak. "The Vandals remain a threat to Rome. I demand that I be given command of the army so I can drive the Vandals out of Sicily." He sat down amid widespread of applause.

Avitus stood to reply and the house quietened. "I agree that the task need to be done, and that a general of Lord Majorian's experience is just the person to do it. But may I point out that the treasury is empty? I ask the senate to provide the money for this campaign."

The senators, the richest men in Italy, discussed this in a half-hearted manner. One senator suggested, in pompous terms, that the Empire of Gaul should pay for this Italian army.

Avitus retained a grip on his temper and replied, in equally pompous terms, that the Empire of Gaul had no money.

The senators then promised to consider the matter at a later date. Majorian was indignant at this weakness but chose to accept the decision.

Avitus rose to his feet. "As a campaign is impossible in the short term, I suggest that we send ambassadors to the Vandals to negotiate a truce for the winter."

Some of the senators regarded this as a sign of weakness, but this time Majorian supported Avitus. "A truce for the winter? That would allow us to prepare for a campaign in the spring."

Some senators wanted to discuss the matter further. The debate grew heated. Magnus wondered whether the senators would come to blows until he realised that the anger was merely show. The house turned out to be equally divided on the issue. With a quick show of hands, the senators agreed to accept Avitus's proposal.

Then Senator Paulinus created a distraction. "We believe that the palace has received dispatches from Constantinople. We hope that Emperor Marcian has chosen to acknowledge his majesty as co-emperor."

Avitus tried to hide how embarrassed he was. "We have indeed received some letters from Constantinople," he said. "Emperor Marcian's officials acknowledged my position as ruler pro tem of Italy, but he does not in any way suggest that I am his equal in rank."

Magnus tensed. He had seen that letter too.

"Does he suggest that you are his subordinate?" Majorian said. "This is monstrous! It is an insult to us all."

"Oh, I agree, my lord," Avitus said. "We must send an embassy to Constantinople, asking for an apology.

However, I am reluctant to be more aggressive, because Emperor Marcian is doing his best to reduce the influence of the Vandals."

Majorian suggested that Avitus should not reply at all. To do so, he argued, would suggest that Rome was subordinate to Constantinople.

Magnus thought the idea was absurd. He wondered how many senators would vote against Avitus's proposal. It would indicate how unpopular Avitus was.

The vote was close, but Avitus's proposal was accepted. But Magnus knew that this was just the beginning.

*   *   *

Tiburtini Hills, Late August

Magnus had ridden out to the Tiburtini Hills, east of Rome, to visit the new messenger station. The climb was steep and for the last stretch he had chosen to dismount and lead his horse. Now he looked back across the valley floor, with its fields and woods. The sprawl of Rome, and the smoke from its innumerable hearth fires, was just visible in the distance.

The messengers and their ground crew had already made their mark on the hilltop, building the long narrow buildings that stored the dismantled flying machines. Further down the hill, vines grew on the rich volcanic soil.

The messenger station was a refreshing change from the capital; the place was quiet and well run. The blue sky was free of dust and smoke from fires, its perfection marred only by a few wispy clouds.

Magnus had arrived just as the ground crew were packing up for the day. He asked Captain Brennos for a word in private, so they walked to the edge of the meadow. He had dragged the captain from his backwater in Argentorate to take command of this key post, but the captain seemed to bear him no ill will for it.

"Any messages today, captain?"

"None, sir. A pilot we sent off four days ago ran out of updrafts and landed in a field, twenty miles short of Turin. He wrote to say he had to walk the rest of the way."

"I see." He turned to face the wind. "I'm glad to escape the city, captain, if only for a couple of days. It's like a brick kiln back there!"

Brennos's usually dour expression relaxed into a smile. "As bad as that?"

"As hot as hell, and no wind at all. Do you always get a breeze here?" Magnus noticed that the captain had stopped bleaching his hair. It had lost its spiky appearance and now looked more white than blond.

"Most days, sir. That's why we chose this spot, after all," Brennos said. "Why didn't you bring sergeant Dumnorix here? He'd enjoy this."

"This is the key station in the chain, captain. Dumnorix's a good aviator but -. He'd offend some aristocrat within a week, who'd order him to be flogged. And I wouldn't be able to protect him. And before you ask, Captain Commius at Lyon is too damned obsequious. He'd never get anything done." Magnus changed the subject.

"Do you have any problems here, captain? Anything I can help you with?"

"Not really, sir. The route's functioning well. But the stations are too far apart. Pilots forced down by bad weather 'ave to abandon their machines and walk to the next station."

"Yes. I've had to do that myself. But more stations would cost money. And we'd need to recruit ground crews ..."

Brennos raised his eyebrows. "We're short of trained men, sure enough, but we could recruit men locally, no problem."

Magnus respected the way Brennos had used his drive and ingenuity to set up this messenger station. He looked round the site again.

"I can't see any living quarters here. Are your men living in tents?"

"No, no. There's an abandoned farmhouse on the other side of the hill. We took it over. You'll see it this evening, at dinner."

Magnus smiled. "It looks as if you've chosen a good site."

"It's comfortable, but we're too far from city. Almost a day's ride."

"There's nothing I can do about that, Captain. I can't ask the Master of the Chancellery to move out here. Although if the political situation settles down Avitus might like to spend the summer here."

The Captain lowered his voice, although they were alone on the landing field. "How bad is it, sir?"

Magnus reminded himself that he had chosen Brennos for his intelligence. "We can't find enough grain to feed the populace. The poor are already going hungry. When the granaries run out, things are going to get ugly. And the senators merely see this as a means to attack Avitus."

"That's what I guessed, sir."

"If you're short staffed, we'll have to recruit Italians. It worked well, last time."

"Yes, but we'll be gone soon," Brennos said.

"Nonsense. Avitus saved the city from the Vandals. He's doing his best to feed the city. He has strong support."

"I 'ave a bad feeling about this, sir. Our new emperor won't last any longer than the last one. An' don't tell me he's just a viceroy."

Magnus was suddenly alert. "Who would want to see him go?"

"The Roman mob. They think he's trying to drag Italy into the Gallic Empire. Then Italy would be as poor as Gaul."

"Nonsense!"

"It doesn't 'ave to be true, sir. They just 'ave to believe it. They point to this string of messenger stations, linking Rome to Vienne."

"I see."

The ground crew completed their tasks and strolled over to chat with the captain. Brennos, cheerful again, mentioned dinner and led the way down the hill to the station's living quarters.

"That bastard Majorian has been complaining that the aviators spy on him," Magnus said.

"That's rich," Brennos said. "His steward asked us to send a letter to his estate outside Milan."

"Oh. But that's illegal."

Brennos shrugged. "When a man as powerful as that tells you to break the rules, you do it."

"I see ..."

They reached the modest farmhouse. Magnus found that it had been spruced up with a new coat of paint.

The men welcomed Magnus as a guest. There was no hint of the deference that he hated.

Brennos introduced Magnus to the senior artificer. "I've been telling Magnus that we'll have no trouble recruiting some men locally."

The artificer raised his eyebrows. "Oh, yes, landless men, prepared to work for a pittance, or even for their keep. But it's the training that's difficult."

Magnus almost asked whether the volunteers were runaway slaves. He stopped himself just in time. A wise leader knew when to feign ignorance. If he asked a blunt question, Brennos would be forced choose between lying to his commander or sending those slaves back to their master. And Magnus had no sympathy for Roman landowners. "Do these volunteers give you trouble? Have they learned anything yet?"

Brennos grinned. "Oh, in a year or two they'll make good ground handlers."

"Good … But take care not to annoy the local landowners, captain."

"I'm sure I don't know what you mean, sir," Brennos said. Some of his listeners grinned.

The Captain's air of wounded innocence irritated Magnus. "No? If one of those senators accused you of some misdemeanor, I'd have to have you punished. They *might* be satisfied if you were stripped of your rank. Exiled to the smallest messenger station, at the very end of some insignificant route." He paused. "Argentorate, perhaps."

Brennos's expression lightened into a smile. "I see, sir."

"Avitus has asked us to take any means necessary to win this war. That is public knowledge. And I ordered you to use your initiative and not bother me with details. That might be of some help in a court of law. Just the same ...

"Don't get caught, understand? I'd hate it if a patrician sent his men up here to lynch you. Then Avitus would have to decide whether to ignore that crime and look weak or demand justice and offend the whole Patrician order."

Everyone in the room was listening.

Brennos shook his head. 'They wouldn't do that. It'd be as very stupid thing to do."

"No? The messenger service is recruited in Gaul, not Italy. Some aviators don't have much respect for Italian patricians. These Italian landowners might be angry enough to do something stupid. So be careful."

* * *

Rome, Late August

The public section of the palace, where emperors received supplicants and well-wishers, had an ostentatious outer gate. An important audition was scheduled this morning. Magnus arrived there to find that his friend Gaius had the matter well in hand.

"Count Ricimer was told to report here at the third hour," Magnus said. "But ..."

"He still has a few minutes," Gaius said.

"Yes ... Avitus wants the count to see that your men are alert. He doesn't want the count to think we're slipshod."

"Of course," Gaius said.

"But, at the same time, Avitus says Ricimer must be treated with all due respect."

Gaius smiled. "Avitus's worrying too much," But Magnus could tell that Gaius was on edge too.

They were interrupted by a sentry. "Excuse me, sir, but the German's in sight now."

"Yes. Thank you," Gaius said.

"Prompt," Magnus said.

Ricimer was walking along the gravel path, accompanied by six men from his bodyguard. The mercenary general was wearing an elaborately decorated tunic in the latest fashion, over which he was wearing a richly embroidered military cloak. This was thrown over his shoulder to reveal a long cavalry sword, worn in a baldric.

Around his neck he was wearing a jewelled gold torque, a gift from the murdered Valentinian. His bodyguards, with their cavalry trousers and bristling blond moustaches, were clearly barbarian mercenaries.

"Good morning, my lord," Magnus said. "I hope the visitor's quarters were acceptable?"

"Quite acceptable."

"Lord Avitus bids you welcome. However, I must insist that you and your men must leave all your weapons behind."

"Are we expected to accept this insult?" one of Ricimer's men demanded.

Ricimer gave no indication that he had heard him. Gaius tensed.

"Everyone visiting lord Avitus has to leave his weapons behind. Even the senators," Magnus said.

Ricimer smiled. "We can't complain if we're given the same treatment as a senator," he told his companion. He undid his cloak and slipped the baldric over his head. "Take good care of that. It's my best sword."

"Of course, sir."

One of Ricimer's men helped him readjust his cloak. It now covered his left arm completely, in the fashionable style, just like a courtier.

Magnus was annoyed at this hauteur. "If you will come this way, my lord." He personally escorted the count to the audience room.

A secretary pushed aside the heavy curtain concealing the doorway and bowed Ricimer inside, announcing his name and his rank.

Avitus was sitting on an elaborately carved chair, positioned on a dais so that he was in the same eye level as his standing guests. On his right stood his personal secretary. The Master of the Chancellery stood at his left hand. The elaborate tapestries, brought in to hide the faded and damaged walls, gave the room an opulent look.

Over the last few days, Magnus had learned much about the Master of the Imperial Chancellery. Severus was an old, gaunt man, fiercely jealous of his status in the palace administration. He expected the new ruler of Italy to listen respectfully to his advice. He was a traditionalist who regarded any change as a change for the worse.

Ricimer stepped forward and gave a perfunctory bow. "You summoned me, your highness?"

"Welcome to Rome, my lord count," Avitus said, with due formality. "I thank you for your accomplishments against our enemies. But I have a problem for you. The Vandal fleet threatens our coast. According to the rumours, they are planning to invade Sicily."

Ricimer smiled thinly. "I believe that the island is Rome's main source of grain."

"I see you understand our problem. Yes. If the Vandal fleet manages to cut off the supply from Sicily, Rome risks starvation. I have arranged for supplies to be sent from Gaul, but it cannot possibly be enough. I want you to take your men to Sicily and protect it."

Ricimer had not expected this. "But Italy is threatened by the Huns! I must keep my men in the north."

"At the moment, the Vandals are the greater threat," Avitus said. He glanced at Magnus.

"Yes, my lord. Our latest reports from the Alps, ten days old, state that the frontier is quiet."

Ricimer raised his eyebrows. "I see, my lord. But my men have not been paid since the death of the last emperor. I demand that you rectify this at once."

Avitus refused to be browbeaten. "I cannot raise the taxes to pay the army without the permission of the Senate. I have already asked them to raise the taxes we need. I suggest you ask them. I'll do everything I can to help, of course. I'm sure something can be sorted out."

"I see, my lord." Ricimer paused, but Avitus merely looked down at him.

Ricimer bowed. "Very well, my lord. I will see what I can do." He stalked out.

There was a moment's uncomfortable silence, broken by the chancellor. "The man's arrogance is appalling!"

Avitus merely shrugged. "He's the best general we have. And he's right. The army's pay is in arrears."

*

The large cargo vessel sailed grandly into the harbour of Portus. The huge square sail billowed in the wind. To Magnus, the vessel seemed unstoppable. The ship's master shouted an order and the crew, in a frantic burst of activity, hauled on ropes, spilling wind from the sail and reducing its power. This reduced the ship's speed and allowed it to approach the quay.

The emperor's son-in-law Sidonius was standing on the quay next to Magnus. He had been given responsibility for the food supply and this shipment was the first sign that his policy was working. Magnus and his soldiers had accompanied him to ensure order was maintained.

The ship was now barely moving. Magnus could see the ship's master, standing impassively at the stern next to the helmsman. These sailing masters prided themselves on their gravity. Showing signs of fear or even doubt in a tense situation was almost as shameful as losing one's ship.

The man barked an order and the ship turned into the wind, its sails flapping. At another order, sailors hauled on ropes, bringing the sail under control in a well-practised drill.

Magnus watched, impressed, as the huge vessel crept forward. This was the first cargo vessel to arrive from Gaul, bringing the harvest from the Rhone valley. The vessel had taken on its cargo at Arles, but the grain had come all the way from Vienne itself.

The sailing master shouted another order and the sails were adjusted further. The ship came to a standstill, just a few feet from the quay. Magnus had to admit that the sailing master had timed it well. With an air of nonchalance, a couple of crewmen threw lines to the dockers waiting on the quay and the vessel was made secure.

The crowd of spectators surged forward. The soldiers lining the quay snapped to attention, ready to hold the crowd back. The chancellor had told Avitus to expect trouble with this shipment. Avitus thought the chancellor was exaggerating the problem, but had placated the chancellor by sending Magnus to Portus with instructions to maintain order.

Magnus could see that his soldiers did not have to try very hard. This crowd was merely curious. It was not the mob of Rome, just the good-humoured craftsmen of Portus itself: ship fitters, rope-makers and the like. They were cheerful, assuming this ship was a promise of more to follow.

Sidonius watched with growing impatience as the sailors arranged a gangplank for him. Finally, he was able to go on board to inspect the cargo and congratulate the ship's master.

The grain would be unloaded and stored in the town's warehouses. Magnus had seen some of the storehouses in Portus and had to admit that they were impressive, with their doorways decorated with columns and marble pediments. After all, the storehouses were a reminder of imperial policy. As more grain ships came in, some of the cargo would be loaded onto river vessels for shipment to warehouses in Rome itself. But would there be enough to last through the winter?

Magnus knew that Avitus – and the chancellor – were exuberant. This shipment was proof that the new administration was doing something right. They both knew, however, that the farms of the Rhone could not supply enough grain to feed Rome on their own. They were going to need the harvest from Sicily. For the moment, though, nobody was thinking about that.

When Magnus returned to Rome, he learned that suddenly Avitus had no critics. The senators, who knew that the mob was impressed by this achievement, were all singing his praises. Magnus was cynical enough to know that would not last for long.

*   *   *

Water Newton, Britain, September

Claudia Ambrosius was taking a walk round the ornamental garden of her home.

The days were drawing in now, and the autumn equinox would soon be upon them.

Her exercise was interrupted when a servant entered the orchard, followed by a young messenger in riding clothes.

"Excuse me, my lady, but this messenger has a letter for you."

She was alarmed. "You say this letter is addressed to me?"

The messenger nodded. "Yes, my lady. I've ridden across from the new messenger station. Lord Cornelius received several letters from the continent, and one was addressed to you. The widow, Claudia Ambrosius. Here it is, madam."

So that was it. The letter was probably from Magnus, but she did not understand how he had persuaded the governor to deliver it to her.

She took the letter from him. "Thank you. Speak to the steward. You're welcome to spend the night, of course."

"Thank you, madam," the man said.

The servant led their guest away. She walked into the house, hesitated, then broke the seal. It was addressed to her, after all.

She read the letter with growing fascination. Dramatic events had taken place and Magnus had found himself at the centre of them.

From Magnus V, writing from Rome, greetings.
You will have heard by now of the death of the unlamented Roman emperor.

Lord Avitus bowed to the wishes of the emperor and the senate in Vienne to rescue Italy from disaster. The king of the Goths graciously lent Avitus some men to join the expeditionary force. The allied army drove the Vandals away from Rome, but the city had already suffered from their attentions. Although, truth to say, the decay of the last hundred years has done more damage than the barbarians. The city is crumbling into ruin.

Lord Avitus is now safely established in Rome. The Emperor in Vienne has been pleased to appoint Lord Avitus as his proconsul and his authority has been acknowledged by the army and the Roman Senate. As his duty dictates, he is endeavouring to secure the city's grain supply.

Count Ricimer, a mercenary of German origin, was requested to protect Sicily and its precious grain harvest from the Vandals. Using great ingenuity, the count manned the fleet from among the Germanic mercenaries available to him and personally led the fleet out to sea. Lord Avitus, and everyone else in Rome, anxiously waited for news. In the churches, priests led prayers for a successful outcome.

The count sent back news that there had been no battle, but the Vandals had withdrawn their blockade. The harvest was saved, and the fleet brought shiploads of precious grain to Portus. The emperor, tactfully, publicly gave Ricimer full credit for this success.

However, the Vandal fleet has not been destroyed. Everyone knows they will be back next year.

Farewell, my lady. Magnus V.

He had summed up the situation in Rome very well. Reading between the lines, it was clear that events could become even more dramatic.

That evening, she asked her Danish steward to visit her. She waited for him in a comfortable wicker chair.

As usual, he was abrupt with the proper formal greetings. "Thank you, my lady. What troubles you?"

"I've received a letter from Lord Magnus in Italy. One of the governor's messengers brought it."

"I heard about that. So it was from Lord Magnus? What does he say?"

Carefully, she explained.

He was shocked. "This is terrible. Three emperors in one year. What are we to do?"

She suppressed her impatience. "If Magnus is right, this Count Ricimer could try to depose Lord Avitus."

"You exaggerate, surely? I suppose not," Oslaf said. "Three emperors in twelve months, and quite likely to be four, if your friend Magnus is right."

"I would like to write to Lord Magnus." She wanted him to write to her again. To tell her what was happening now.

Oslaf shot her a strange look. "Letters are expensive. Can you afford it?"

"Oh, yes. That's not the problem."

She realized that 'the problem' was not something she could discuss with a servant.

He nodded. "Information on Italy would be useful, my lady."

Chapter 19: Rome

Winter, 455 - 456 AD

Rome was a city of markets and rumours. Most of the city
was covered in tenements, several stories high, forever in
need of repair. The citizens had built a maze in three
dimensions, of brick and wood. As the population declined
and the city grew poorer, tenements collapsed at regular
intervals, with great loss of life.

The walls of the tenements were brightly painted, but the
sun steadily burnt away the colours. Fading graffiti covered
the walls: obscenities and libels about the city magistrates,
other local figures, shop-keepers who charged too much,
and the previous emperor.

Conwyn was fascinated by it. No matter how long he
lived here, he would never become accustomed to the
complexity of it all.

The mob seemed to like Pope Leo. They thought he had
saved the city from the Huns. He hadn't been able to stop
the Vandals – but then, who could? But he had wrung
certain promises out of them. And the Vandals had kept
their promises.

The markets were bustling, although everyone
complained about the high prices and the lack of choice.
Crowds thronged the streets. But that was part of the
problem. Too many people and not enough grain to feed
them.

The locals said that this was going to be a hungry winter.
Ricimer's victory had secured the grain supply from Sicily,
but the convoys from North Africa were never going to

arrive. There were stories that the people who had returned to the city after the sack were leaving again. They had farms to go to or family to take them in. The people who were forced to stay hated them for it.

Conwyn instead hated the Palatine Hill, with its gossip, intrigues and power-broking. The lower city was something else again. The streets were a stew of vagabonds, petty thieves, priests, foreign soldiers, dissolute rich and tinkers, beggars, pimps, swindlers and opportunists, street-vendors, poets and informers. All of them blamed the administration for their woes.

Conwyn walked down the hill to the forum and then turned down a quiet back street. Here was the bookshop of Josephus. The bookseller loved the old classics. The books, laboriously copied and decorated, were far too expensive for Conwyn.

Josephus grumbled that most of his customers were wealthy, who cared more for symbols of wealth than for the literary treasures the books contained. But Josephus operated a reading room for those who could not afford to buy his works.

Sales were declining, and some of Josephus's rivals had shut up shop. Most sales these days, he said, were on theology. The old classics that he loved were tainted with paganism.

Then Josephus emerged from his back room. A typical distracted scholar, Conwyn had thought at first. He was a tall thin man with a scholar's stoop, much Conwyn's senior. His dry, uncut hair touched his shoulders. He spoke Latin with careful precision.

Conwyn had asked whether the shop had anything on Britain. Josephus had suggested Bishop Germanius' description of Britain, and had mentioned the price.

Conwyn, abashed, had admitted that he couldn't afford it, and Josephus had smiled.

Conwyn had never felt so understood, as at that smile. He knew then that this was a man he could trust.

Six months they had known each other, and Conwyn had learned many things from Josephus, and taught him a few. Conwyn thought of the debates in his shop and in his small back rooms. He waited to be told which patrician faction Josephus favoured. Only gradually did he realise that Josephus hated all patricians equally. And in all those political ruminations Conwyn had never seen Josephus's beliefs written down.

Conwyn had gradually come to realise that Josephus was a subversive. He hated the city authorities and their spies.

Discreetly, Josephus sold Pelagius's infamous book, 'On Free Will'. That was part of his insurrection. "The last one in stock," he would tell each customer.

Josephus, of course, had a copy of 'Free Will' in his back room. Conwyn had read Pelagius's short work in one sitting.

Josephus looked up and smiled. "And what brings you here today?"

"I read Pelagius's book last time I was here. I was fascinated. I've been thinking it over."

"That's usually bad news for vulnerable young men."

Conwyn waved this aside. "I agree with him."

"Yes, but what do you think of Bishop Augustine's admired doctrine?"

"Augustine's theory is monstrous."

"Well, yes, but I advise you not to say so openly," Josephus said. "It would be unfortunate if you proclaimed your views just as Pelagius was denounced as a heretic."

"Yes. I know," Conwyn said. But, Josephus, is it safe to own the book?"

Josephus shrugged. "It isn't illegal, as such. Right-thinking men can own it. But if the authorities find it here, they'll say it's evidence of subversion."

Conwyn knew what that meant. "Won't your high-born customers protect you?"

Josephus's look was scornful. "If they protested too much, they would attract attention to themselves. I'd probably be used as a scapegoat. The magistrates need to punish someone, you see. I'd be publicly flogged or branded. And my books would be burnt."

Conwyn knew which would hurt him the most. "Do the magistrates seek out heretics?"

"It isn't worth their while. But if you make a display of your heresy, openly defy authority, they'll have to act."

Conwyn knew better than to ask Josephus's views on Avitus. "What do you think of Sidonius?"

Josephus grimaced. "The poor man's doing his best. To do him justice, he's got an impossible job. People are getting hungry."

Sidonius had been given the task of organising the corn supply. The young patrician was honest and meant well, but it was an impossible task. As the famine worsened, disaffection grew. The latest layer of graffiti was about Avitus and his son-in-law.

*　　*　　*

Rome, early May

In Rome, as Magnus had already discovered, status counted for everything. It was certainly more powerful than money. Ricimer was probably the best general that Rome had today. But he was a mercenary of barbarian origins, so he had been interviewed by Avitus in the forbidding formality of the official reception rooms.

Majorian was a senator, a gentleman and senior public figure. He was also the head of an ancient landowning family. Accordingly, he had been shown to one of the emperor's private rooms. Although it was quite small, the wall decoration was lavish, the furniture of the finest workmanship. The door looked out upon one of the palace's miniature gardens.

Magnus stood by the door, at an aggressive parade rest, the only warrior in the room. He disapproved of this private interview, but he had no say in the matter.

Avitus was sitting in a cushioned chair. It lacked any gold leaf or marble inlay, but it was comfortable. His tunic was white, decorated with elaborate woven panels of muted red and green.

The table set between the emperor and his guest was an example of bravura workmanship, with veneers set in a geometrical pattern. A servant poured wine into two glasses and discreetly backed away.

"I think you will find that the wine is excellent," Avitus said.

"Thank you." Majorian was wearing a tunic and hose, elaborately decorated in purple and gold. "You're wasting your time, my lord Avitus, stuck here in Rome," he growled. "Rome is dying, now that the supply if African grain is cut off. Can't you see it? You ought to be planning an invasion of Africa, not encouraging your Goth allies to attack the Suevi in Spain."

Avitus ignored this display of bad manners. "An invasion would take too long. The challenge is to keep Rome alive until we can ensure the supply of grain from Africa."

"We must invade at once!"

Avitus sipped at his wine. "I discussed this with Count Ricimer. He says an invasion would take three years to prepare. I trust his judgement."

"You've asked him?" Majorian considered this. "Three years, you say?"

"At least three years. He says that if we tried it earlier, without enough ships, failure would be certain."

Majorian stared at the table as if it was a chessboard and his wineglass was his most valuable game-piece. Avitus, confident that he had the upper hand, did not interrupt. Magnus hardly dared breathe.

Finally, Majorian looked up. "If Count Ricimer does all the preparation, he'll want command."

"Very likely," Avitus said. "He's done enough to deserve it, don't you think? But something as big as this would need several commanders. Responsibility would have to be divided. Ricimer could command the fleet; you could command the army."

Avitus took another sip at his wine. "The biggest problem, as always, would be paying for it. Perhaps you could help persuade the Senate with that."

Majorian took a mouthful of wine, then set his goblet down on the table with a click. "Ricimer wants to make himself emperor. Did you know that?"

"He wants power, certainly," Avitus said. "But if he gains the throne, he'll make so many enemies his power would be diminished. He knows that, and he's intelligent enough to content himself with some lesser title."

"Do you think you're powerful enough to oppose him? I doubt it."

"He and I want different things. He wants to lead a victory parade, I want to protect Gaul – and feed Rome. I can give him what he wants without conceding hold on power."

"He's going to walk all over you," Majorian muttered. He took another gulp at his wine. "If I won a victory in Sicily, it would increase my standing here in Italy, your *highness*. You must know that."

Magnus, listening by the door, heard the implied challenge and was shocked. How would Avitus respond?

But Avitus seemed unperturbed. "If you can achieve a victory, and renew the supply of grain, I will be satisfied. I'll risk your increased prestige."

Majorian smiled. "That can work." He took a gulp at his wine.

Magnus, listening to this interchange, was indignant. Avitus had offered a deal, and in a moment Majorian had changed his whole viewpoint.

*   *   *

Rome, May, 456 AD

Rome was a city of rumours and intrigues. Conwyn was fascinated by the city but was forced to admit that he hated the place. It was warm that spring, gamy. Visitors complained that the rivers stank, although the natives did not notice. The city was hot, and spring had only begun! The place ground to a halt at noon. The city slept for a couple of hours.

Now, two hours after noon, the place was coming to life again. The markets were showing signs of activity.

Conwyn was going to visit Josephus again. Making his way through the crowds to the forum, he found that the street ahead was blocked. A man was hectoring the crowd and the pedestrians had stopped to listen.

He made his way through the crowd to get a better view. Unauthorised assemblies were illegal, of course, like so many things in this city. The city magistrates disapproved, but they could not do much about it. Criticism of the city authorities was a popular pastime.

There was a burst of laughter in the front row. Conwyn tensed. Was the subject Avitus or Magnus? He always hated that. He pushed his way forward for a better look. No. This time the target was the previous emperor. The jokes were bawdy and effective.

The satirists occasionally picked on Magnus because he was a foreigner from the fringes of civilisation. But he was a minor figure. The mob strongly disapproved of the Visigoths that Avitus had brought with him. The entertainers' favourite target, though, was the Chancellor. He was a remnant of the previous regime, and so shared the blame for the sack of the city. The populace suspected he was touchy about his dignity. And they were right.

The speaker made a joke about an emperor's bodyguard who murdered their emperor instead of protecting him. Then they criticised the pomposity of the bodyguard's honorary commander, Majorian.

Somebody at the back shouted his disapproval. Majorian's faction had widespread support. Majorian wanted Avitus to invade Africa and force the Vandals to re-introduce the corn supply. Conwyn grimaced at the thought. And some city-born fools thought that was a workable strategy.

The speaker claimed to admire Majorian's paunch. That got a laugh. In a city on the edge of famine, anyone who was overweight was hated. Avitus's asceticism gained him points.

Somebody threw a rotten fruit. Catcalls followed. The dead emperor, after all, was the person who had appointed Majorian. Then someone threw a stone. It missed its target and bounced off the far wall. A woman screamed.

Conwyn decided to make himself scarce. Getting caught in somebody else's fight was not his idea of fun. And the watch might put in an appearance. The watch was on short rations too, which made them unpredictable. Getting himself arrested would be embarrassing. And they would probably beat him up before he could explain who he was.

He turned and hurried away westwards. He would double back later. Now that he wanted to hurry it seemed that the streets were full, and everyone seemed determined to obstruct him. Conwyn jostled shoppers and people hurrying on errands. At the next crossroads he came across a squad of the watch, looking bored. Someone was talking excitedly to their captain.

Conwyn, eager to avoid attention, slowed down and carelessly ambled past. Behind him, the noise of riot was growing. The captain shouted an order. His men grabbed their weapons and followed him towards the noise.

Conwyn turned north. He did not want to get too close to the river. Unfortunately, the tenements were more squalid here. The only fresh paint was the markings on walls. Brothels and wine shops, artists' lodgings, teachers of rhetoric, signposted by graffiti for those who could read it. The brickwork of the tenements buckled and sagged out over the street, repaired in a patchwork of wood and cement. The crowds were increasing as the afternoon drew on.

He seemed to have left the riot behind. Conwyn turned east and headed back towards the forum, carefully avoiding the street where the riot had begun.

He made his way to Josephus's bookshop in its quiet back street. "Good afternoon, Jusephus. I was worried about you. Did the riot pass you by?"

Josephus waved a hand to indicate the shelves of unread books. "As you see," he said, his voice impassive.

"Thank God for that." Conwyn felt his indignation mounting up. "I used to have sympathy for these rioters. But not any more. These thugs are complaining about the magistrates. But who suffers from their protests? Not the magistrates! No, it's the townsmen who suffer!"

"They have a lot to complain about," Josephus told him. "If Avitus can't resurrect the grain supply, Rome as we know it is ended."

Conwyn was shocked. "It isn't as bad as that!"

"No? What's Rome without the dole? We will have to wait and see."

*   *   *

Britain, 456 AD, Late May

Claudia had travelled across the country to visit her parents. The messenger station, on the western slope of the Limestone Edge, was not too far from Corinium and made an interesting day out. Claudia's aunt Placidia, conservative in many ways, was an enthusiastic horsewoman, and was easily persuaded to give her consent to this outing.

Claudia and her aunt took their places on a blanket spread across the grass, with a food basket between them.

The west country had received plenty of rain over the last few weeks and the grass in this meadow was rich and green.

Up above, a skylark had started its song, a male calling to its mate or trying to impress a new one. Claudia knew that later in the year the display could last for several minutes, but this early in the season the display would be as brief as it was spectacular. Claudia squinted, trying to see the bird so far above. To look at, it was plain, dull, and boring. The bird was delivering its song in hovering flight 150 feet above the ground, so the singing bird appeared as just a dot in the sky.

Claudia had spent the last hour wheedling the station sergeant. Her patience had borne fruit and the instructor had agreed to give her a lesson.

The skylark ceased its performance and Claudia turned to watch as the men assembled the flying machine. The notion that a girl could learn to fly had shocked the moralists, but Lady Placidia was more interested in her food than the antics of the fragile machines.

Placidia glanced round at the flying machine. "I hope you remember to keep within sight of the station, my dear."

Claudia smiled. "Yes, if I run out of lift, and land in a field, I'll have to walk back."

"I wasn't thinking of that, my dear. I promised your mother that I'd act as your chaperone."

"Well, yes. I promise to be careful. I won't fly out of sight of my friends."

Placidia turned to her food. "You should eat more, my dear."

"The sergeant said that some women are natural pilots," Claudia said.

Placidia sniffed. "He also said that it was a waste to teach a woman to fly because she'd be grounded most of the time."

What she meant was that women were forbidden to fly while they were pregnant. Claudia ignored this. She had long ago decided she wanted to learn to fly.

After a while, Claudia tired of her aunt's conversation, so she got up and walked across the meadow to talk to the ground crew. On her first visit, the pilots and craftsmen had been polite, but tended to assume that a lady would not be interested in their bizarre hobby.

Claudia smiled. She had been taught that a lady should politely discuss topics that interested her listener, rather than bore him with her views. She applied the same theory today. Trying to find a common interest with these strange men, she asked about the routes they flew.

They were flattered by her interest, so she asked about the limitations of their flying machines. The best route, they said, was up to Chester. The most difficult section was from Corinium to the White Horse. On bad days they had to admit defeat and send a horseman across the gap.

She discovered that these men would talk to anyone who showed intelligent interest. She had learned to see the hills of Britain from a new perspective.

Magnus had been right. The messenger service held civilisation together. The Limestone Edge and the Chalk Ridge formed the backbone of the province.

For flying, Claudia had taken to wearing an all-concealing leather coat. She was told it was a new fashion among the Alpine aviators.

The instructor told her to get into the front seat, so her weight would prevent the wind from blowing the machine over. This two-seater had a control yoke at waist height rather than a joystick. That allowed her to control the aircraft while still wearing skirts. She climbed in and tested the controls.

The men pulled the flying machine to the edge of the hill. The instructor took the rear seat. "You've handled a launch before. You can do this one."

"Thank you."

The men ahead pulled the ropes taut; the men holding the glider down let go; and the machine shot forward into the rising air.

The instructor had warned her that conditions were marginal. But she managed to gain enough height to venture out over the valley – and get back again safely.

When she landed, she found her aunt waiting. She was contrite. "I'm sorry I kept you waiting, my dear. I was having fun. Then I remembered – don't you have a dinner invitation with my mother tonight?"

"Yes. We ought to start back at once. Hurry up."

Back in her father's home, Claudia changed her dress and made her way to the atrium.

Her mother waited at the door of the dining room to greet her guests. "Good evening, my dear Claudia. May I introduce you to another of my guests for this evening? Lady Claudia, this is lord Vitalinus."

The gentleman was smiling at her. He was not old enough to be the head of the Vitalinus family. After a moment's panic, Claudia realised that this must be Magnus's father. His tunic, of the finest wool, bore a modest amount of tablet-weave decoration. Perhaps his wife was an expert.

He smiled. "We don't see you in Corinium very often."

"My home these days is on the east coast. I came to visit my mother."

"Of course. I hoped I would meet you here, my lady. I've been hearing the most extraordinary tales. You've formed an interesting political clique."

She blushed. "I wouldn't call it that, sir. We just meet to drink tea." In response, he gave a mocking smile.

Her mother gave her an I-told-you-so look.

Claudia was dismayed. "I thought I was being discreet, sir."

"Oh, you are. My uncle, for example, would think your activities beneath his notice, even if he heard of them. But my wife heard of your doings. She thinks I'm intelligent enough to listen to good advice. And I'm intelligent enough to listen to her." He winked at her.

Her mother sniffed her disapproval.

Claudia was not sure how to respond. Was he mocking her? "Do you disapprove, sir?"

"How could I disapprove of an attempt to save the empire, my lady?"

She blushed. "It's hardly that ..."

"Why not? If the senior landowners panic and flee abroad, Britain will likely collapse. And if it can happen in Britain, why not Armorica?"

"Dinner is about to be served, my lord," her mother said. She led the way into the dining room.

Claudia found herself seated at the head of the table, between Philip the magistrate and Lord Vitalinus. Disconcerted by his praise, she sought refuge in modesty. "My – my activities are only a trifle, sir."

"Perhaps. But for a while there the scales were very evenly balanced. He held out his hand, palm down. "Things could have gone either way. A trifle could have made the difference." He glanced up. "I was determined to stay on if the worst happened. I'm glad I didn't have to make the choice."

It was strange that he had picked upon the same metaphor that she had used.

Philip addressed Lord Vitalinus. "Your son made things worse by going abroad."

Lord Vitalinus hesitated a moment. "He stopped the pirates from seizing more territory. And he managed to keep the army together. He had done all he could. By leaving, he could allow someone untainted by defeat to take over."

"Have you heard from him recently?" Claudia put in. "I hope he's all right."

"He's a lazy fellow. All he ever tells me is that he is in good health. But he's at the heart of civilisation. What could possibly happen?"

* * *

Rome, Early June, 456 AD

The crowd on the Aventine docks was baying for blood. The protesters were squeezed together in the narrow street. Conwyn had been swept into the chaos.

He was trapped in the baying crowd and knew that if he fell, he was likely to be trampled underfoot. The protesters ignored the barges tied up against the quay and concentrated on the warehouses.

The stevedore on Conwyn's right was carrying a flaming torch. "Bread! Give us our bread!"

Conwyn was shocked. "But Avitus promised -."

The other stevedore, with a broken nose and a shaven head, was more restrained. "We're going to starve before winter, lad. The news from Sicily is terrible."

"But Ricimer defeated the Vandals' fleet," Conwyn said.

"D'you think I'm stupid? Did Ricimer sink the Vandal fleet? No. The barbarians can attack anywhere in Italy.

They'll attack the grain fleet as soon as it leaves harbour. There's going to be another famine."

The shouting was getting more exuberant. "Bread! Bread or blood!"

Conwyn had delivered a message from Magnus to the warehouse authorities. Then he had decided to make a trip to the dockside to observe the protest. He told himself that had been a mistake.

Instead of witnessing the protest, as a disinterested outsider, he had been swept inside it. If he tried to force his way out, he knew that the mob would likely turn on him.

"I lost my youngest son to hunger, last winter," the stevedore said. "When you're weak from hunger, the slightest disease can carry you off."

"Yes," Conwyn said. Most people in Rome had lost relatives to malnutrition or disease.

"We all depend on official handouts. And the granaries are running low. They'll be empty before the next harvest."

"Yes." Avitus, hearing the news from Sicily, had been forced to reduce the free ration of grain to the populace. The outraged citizens had protested. Unfortunately, what had started out as a formal, symbolic protest turned into a riot.

Night was closing in and more of the protesters had acquired flaming torches. The red glare was contrasted by shadows that jumped and wavered as the torches flickered. When people turned to face Conwyn, their eyes took on the same red tinge. It was easy to imagine that he was surrounded by devils.

Then the protesters found a roof beam to use as a battering ram. It would have been easier to find an axe, but the teamwork needed to use the ram had a symbolic meaning for everyone in the crowd. The work crew set to with enthusiasm, urged on by shouts of encouragement from the crowd. The doors gave way and the crowd roared its approval.

The greedy and the desperate were forcing their way to the front. "Come on!" the bald stevedore said.

Conwyn was left behind in the rush. Suddenly inspired, he allowed himself to be elbowed aside. Everyone was ignoring him. He seized the opportunity and made his way down a side street.

Walking down the badly lit alleyway, he realised that he had a second problem. Besides having to avoid the mob he now had to avoid the authorities. And if he managed that, he had to report back to Magnus. He wondered whether the city magistrates had pulled themselves together yet.

*

Conwyn accompanied Magnus to the granary the next morning. Magnus stood in the middle of the empty hall, counting the damage. Conwyn looked around, curious. The rioters had certainly tried to do as much damage as possible. Graffiti, political or obscene or both, had been scratched on the walls and roof-pillars. All of the arcades were empty. A few sacks had split open and had simply been abandoned. In one corner, someone had made a hurried, futile attempt to start a fire.

His boots crunched on the wreckage and Magnus looked round. "Oh, it's you." He was angry.

"Yes, sir." He kept his voice even.

Magnus ignored him. "This is folly. Look. They spoilt more grain than they stole."

Conwyn realised that the grit under his feet was actually loose grains of wheat. "Yes, sir."

"Anyone would think they wanted the city to starve."

379

"You could allow the gleaners in here, sir," Conwyn suggested.

"To pick up these grains by hand? Is anyone in this city that desperate?"

"Yes, sir," he said simply.

Magnus bit his lip. "Very well. I'll see to it."

*

Rome, June, 456 AD

Conwyn made his way through the streets to Josephus's shop. Anyone who got in his way was brushed aside. Rome was an old town, but it seemed a tired old town these days. Grass sprouted between the paving stones on some of the side streets. People moved slowly now. They ambled across the open spaces, shuffled in and out of the shops lining the streets, took their time about everything. A day was twenty-four hours long but seemed longer. There was no hurry, because there was nowhere to go, nothing to buy and no money to buy it with.

The cost of bread had doubled and doubled again. Men who spent everything on food had no money for anything else. Some men were weak from hunger but defeat and despair were just as destructive. The only exception to lethargy was occasional bouts of anger and wanton destruction.

Last night had seen another riot. The angry crowd had run through this quarter of the city and more than one property had been looted or set on fire. But surely the rumours were false. His friend was not dead.

Conwyn turned the corner into the little street and his worst fears seemed to be true. The shopfront was a burnt-out ruin.

As he drew closer, he could see that the destruction was not total. The building still stood. It was only the outer room that was burnt out. But that room was Josephus's cherished shop. He hesitated for a moment, then pushed the charred remains of the door aside. The shelves had collapsed, and the floor was covered in blackened fragments of parchment.

Then he heard movement in the back room and his hope revived. "Josephus?"

His friend appeared in the inner doorway. He was holding a stone inkpot. "Hello, Conwyn." His voice was as calm as ever.

"What happened? I mean – why you? Why did they pick on you?"

Josephus shrugged. "Everyone knows that only the rich can afford to buy books. So, a bookseller must be rich too. He's an enemy of the people, so he deserves to have his shop burned around him."

"Are you all right? You look – unharmed." Josephus merely shrugged in reply. "And your books? Did you lose everything?"

"Everything in my front room. The theological works. The stock that sold the best."

"I see."

Josephus threw the empty inkpot aside. "Conwyn, I've decided to leave Rome. The price of bread increases with every bit of bad news from Sicily. No-one can afford to buy books any more."

Conwyn was shocked. And not just because his friend was abandoning him. "But this is Rome! The richest city in the empire."

"Not any more, it isn't," Josephus said sharply. "And the city is getting poorer by the day. The only books that're selling are theological ones. And the Church authorities are taking more interest in which texts are being sold. I thought that a man of my talents had more chance in Milan."

"You would do better going to Constantinople. It's richer than Rome and Milan put together, so they say."

"Too much of a change. How could I survive amongst the rivalries of Constantinople?

"And that city has its theological disputes too."

Josephus ignored him. "At least, if I leave, there'll be a bit more food for those who remain."

*　　*　　*

Magnus and his friend Gaius made their way to Avitus's study, a small homely room in a corner of the palace. Avitus had called for a meeting of his closest advisers. He had told them to arrive at nightfall. Magnus could guess why.

The members of the senate were growing in confidence growing every day. With Majorian acting as their spokesman, the senators had presented a formal challenge to Avitus's authority.

There were protests in the streets every week now. The events now followed a recognisable pattern. The magistrates would send in the watch with orders to restore order. The watchmen would arrest the noisiest protesters and some petty criminals and drag them away for trial. As often as not, a protester would be killed, either by an over-energetic watchman or in some sort of accident. The victim's funeral, the following day, would turn into another protest.

Sometimes the protest would develop into a riot that the watch could not control. Twice, now, the magistrates had been forced to ask Avitus to send in his troops.

Avitus had become sufficiently alarmed to summon his closest companions. The room, looking out over one of the palace's formal gardens, was lit by half a dozen lamps. It was barely large enough to hold them all. The chancellor, being an Italian, was excluded.

Avitus, sitting behind the low table, looked worried. Exhausted, Magnus thought.

"Gentlemen, the populace has realised that the next harvest may not reach the city. Our popularity is declining. The senate has always hated me, but in the past they kept their opinions to themselves. But they are no longer afraid to criticise me openly." He looked round.

"The senate have offered us a devil's bargain. They will pay a one-off tax to pay Ricimer's mercenaries if I send the Goths home."

No-one cared to reply. "Gentlemen, I ask you whether I should send the Goths home. The situation is getting worse."

Magnus nodded. The senators knew that the people of Rome resented the presence of Avitus's Visigothic allies in the city.

"That fellow Majorian is putting on the pressure. And the master of the chancellery has made it clear that it's impossible to pay the army."

"You could send the Goths to Milan," General Edeco said. "They wouldn't be eating Rome's food supply then."

Avitus's son in law, Sidonius, disagreed. "We need them here to protect your throne."

"Nonsense," Edeco said crisply.

Avitus ignored this. "Gentlemen, the question needs to be asked. Should I leave Rome?"

His son-in-law nodded. "Yes, my lord. Everyone in Italy knows that the campaign against the Vandals has failed. The famine is worsening. The city's hostility is growing ..."

Avitus nodded. "Go on."

"The palace guard are Majorian's men, sir, worse than useless. The landowners have their bodyguards. Together, they outnumber your own men."

The emperor looked round. "Gentlemen?"

Magnus hesitated, reluctant to be the first to speak.

Gaius, commander of the bodyguard, shook his head. "I would not advise it, my lord. Most of the landowners want stability above all else. And they are incapable of acting together. My men can protect you. Unless there's a general uprising, you don't need more men."

"And my departure to Gaul might trigger that uprising. Yes, I see."

*   *   *

Rome, five days later

The demonstration by the populace began peaceably. The pope had announced a day of prayer. At noon, the poor of the city marched to the basilica and prayed for God's mercy and food. As the afternoon drew on, most of them went home.

But, as evening drew closer and the light began to fade, things turned ugly. The crowd had thinned, but those remaining became more noisy. They were no longer satisfied with prayers.

The city was gratified that the Visigoths had finally been sent home, but some were angry that Avitus had not sent the barbarians home empty handed. He had arranged for a number of bronze statues to be melted down to pay the soldiers' outstanding wages.

Magnus had discussed the problem with his friend. Gaius was expecting trouble and had made sure that his men were fully equipped with armour and shields.

The mob abandoned the open space outside the basilica and advanced towards the Palatine Hill, with their chant of 'Bread, bread, blood or bread.' None of them were carrying edged weapons, but most of them carried sticks or cudgels.

Magnus, by now wearing his armour, watched the situation develop. The city watch made no attempt to stop the protesters and simply fled. Magnus had predicted that. The men of the ceremonial palace guard, entrusted with the task of blocking the road up the palatine hill, were not much better.

But the men that Magnus had brought from Vienne stood firm. He led his men forward and took over from the palace guard.

At his order, his men formed a shield wall, blocking the road leading to the palace. They were outnumbered and the protesters might have overcome them with a determined rush. But the mob was not disciplined enough or desperate enough, and kept their distance. They resorted to throwing stones, so the soldiers in the second and third ranks held their shields up to protect their companions. This was a drill that they had practised regularly. Magnus was confident that his men cope with this problem. But it was going to be a long struggle.

The protesters eventually realised that their tactics had no effect. After a couple of hours, they tired of the exercise and drifted away.

Magnus left Gaius in charge and went to report to Avitus. "I've left half my men on watch, just in case. You can't really call it a riot, sir. It was too well organised."

Avitus looked bleak. "So, you think it was arranged by my enemies?"

"Yes, sir. Those bully boys weren't starving. They were too healthy. They were probably brought in for the occasion."

"Well, they didn't achieve anything."

"Not this time, sir."

"No. But this is the second time this month. We can expect more in the weeks ahead."

*   *   *

Alban Hills, Late June

Late in the day, two hours before nightfall, Captain Brennos received an alarming message from Rome. He was on the hilltop, watching as a flying machine was dismantled.

As soon as he read the message, he called his team together. There was no time to walk down the hill to their quarters, so they met in the open, next to a pegged-down flying machine.

He held up the folded message. "I've received this from the little patrician in Rome, brought to me by Magnus's body-servant here."

"I'm his groom," Conwyn interrupted. "I'll curry his horses for him, but I won't scrub him down." The man was gaunt, as most Romans were these days. Brennos realised the man was also afraid.

"Who's the message for?" one of the novice pilots asked. "Vienne or Turin?"

"The message is for the captain here," Conwyn said.

The pilot was surprised. "Are you sure?"

The boy's smile had no humour in it. "For the captain's hand alone. That's what Magnus said."

Brennos judged that the young Briton hated the patrician order as virulently as the most passionate aviator. Yet he loyally served that young patrician Magnus. Life was strange.

Brennos unfolded the letter. "Shut up and listen, everyone."

'To Captain Brennos, Alban Hills. From Magnus Vitalinus, at the Viceroy's court, greetings.

Lord Avitus, consul, has decided to temporarily abandon Rome and march north in order to recruit more troops with which to defend Rome. He has sent a message to the loyal garrison at Ravenna, requesting their aid. Lord Avitus will move north and join forces with the garrison.

Civil disturbance may break out in Rome as soon as treasonable elements realise the Viceroy has gone. That disturbance may spread. You are authorised to withdraw immediately. Abandon any equipment if you have to, but ensure the safety of personnel. Italian staff at the messenger station may turn hostile. Exercise discretion. Magnus V'

The assembly burst into an uproar. Conwyn, standing at the back, smirked.

"Shut up!" Brennos shouted. "I guessed this was going to happen. I want you to pack your belongings. We leave at dawn. Abandon everything you can't carry. We've got to travel fast."

"Do you suspect the local people, cap'n?" an old pilot asked.

"No. What worries me is a lynch mob marching out of Rome, determined to get their revenge on us because Avitus is beyond their reach."

The senior craftsman spoke up. "Some of the ground crew might want to come with us, sir. They've nothing to stay for. Runaways."

Brennos hesitated. Some of the volunteers they had collected were slaves running from harsh masters. The runaways had not volunteered any information about their background and Brennos had not been stupid enough to ask. It those men were reclaimed by their patrician masters, a harsh future awaited them.

"Wake them at first light. Tell them they've an hour to make their choice."

"And if they decide to run to Rome, spread the news?"

"Let them go. It's their choice."

"Should we burn the machines, rather than let the Romans have them?" the craftsman asked.

Brennos glanced round and sniffed the air. "The wind's favourable … there's just enough light to make it to the next station."

"You could warn them, too, captain," Conwyn said.

That decided Brennos. "Yes. Jump to it! I want those machines in the air while there's still enough light."

*   *   *

Padus valley five days later

The heat beat down without mercy. The farmland of the Padus valley, the richest in Italy, was turning to dust. The cavalcade rode along the military road, north across the flat flood plain. Just a few miles ahead, Magnus could make out the walls of Piacenza. Beyond that, far to the north, they could make out the peaks of the Alps.

General Edeco was shouting orders. "Infantry will deploy! Face – right! Form shield wall." He turned to look up at Avitus and spoke in an undertone. "We'll look foolish if this is our reinforcements from Ravenna."

Avitus leaned forward to pat his horse's neck. "There's little chance of that, general," he said. "And better look foolish than be overwhelmed."

Avitus was wearing comfortable riding clothes and a very unfashionable wide-brimmed hat to protect him from the sun. He also wore a long cavalry sword at his hip, but Magnus doubted if he was still in practice.

Everyone had known from the start that this was the most dangerous part of their journey. The highway to Milan crossed the river Padus here. Avitus must either use the bridge or make a huge detour, and everyone in Italy knew it.

Gaius's cavalry scouts had reported armed men to the east, marching along a side road. Magnus turned for another look at the enemy. He judged the force to be smaller than their own, but well disciplined. He decided that they were not as terrifying as the Huns had been, but Avitus's army today was a lot smaller than Aetius's had been.

"Who sent them?" Magnus said. "And how did they know how many troops to send?"

"When this is over, we can ask them," Gaius said. "The worst of it is the heat. And the dust. And we're short of water. We'll have to give all we've got to the horses."

"It'll have to be a short battle, then."

Syagrius, the emperor's son-in-law, was quite sure of the identity of the man behind the attack. "Count Ricimer. He was thwarted in his aim of bullying you to abdicate, so he's tried to assassinate you instead."

Avitus looked tired. "Yes, it's possible."

Edeco was bellowing orders to the infantry, getting them in position to the east of the road. The archers ran forward to take their places behind the spearmen. Edeco pointed to the squad closest to him. "You! Stay with the viceroy."

The men singled out were not happy. "We can fight too," Eli said. Fortunately, he spoke in Brittonic.

"Shut up," Magnus said, in an undertone.

The rebel forces abandoned their road and advanced across the dusty fields towards Avitus's troops. They were making good time. The dust they were kicking up obscured any detail.

Magnus dismounted and was standing next to Avitus. Conwyn stepped forward to hold his horse for him. The young man seemed to be unworried.

Edeco's infantry, moving with a minimum of fuss, had formed a line in front of the Avitus's position. They were just in time – the rebels were already within bow-shot range.

The enemy infantry responded by halting their advance. In the still air Magnus could make out the shouting of the sergeants as the rebel troops formed up into a straight line.

Avitus checked that his sword was loose in its scabbard. "What are our chances?" he asked quietly.

Edeco said nothing. The general was sweating under his iron helmet. He glanced helplessly at Magnus.

Magnus drew a breath. "I'd say our chances are about even," he said quietly. "They've the advantage of training, we've the advantage of numbers, perhaps. And Gaius's cavalry."

The rebel infantry gave a great cheer, obviously a preparation for a charge. Magnus tensed.

The rebels charged forward. The front rank of Avitus's troops leant their shoulders against their shields and braced themselves for the blow. The two lines met with a crash. A couple of Edeco's men fell, but the remainder held firm.

Magnus, standing besides Avitus together with Gaius and Edeco, had nothing to do. He remembered what Gaius had said about water. His own mouth was dry. This battle was going to be won, not by the strongest, but by the side that persevered the longest.

Magnus could make out a squad of cavalry behind the straining infantrymen. Their commander was distinguished by a plumed helmet. Ricimer, perhaps?

The commander, whoever it was, must have decided that his infantry had met their match and were not going to break through. The man shouted an order, waved his hand in a signal and led a troop of fifty cavalry forward.

"They're going to outflank our line!" Gaius said.

"Stop them, Gaius," Avitus said.

"Yes, sir!" Gaius said. He urged his horse forward and shouted an order to his men. Together, they set off at a gallop.

The enemy cavalry made no attempt to assist their infantry. Instead they trotted round the end of the infantry line and headed for Avitus.

Magnus, standing beside Avitus and Edeco, could only watch as his friend rode eastwards. The two cavalry forces met in a confused melee. The British skirmishers closed in to throw javelins at their opponents and then dashed away again.

Horsemen circled each other, trying to gain the upper hand. Men fell from their saddles, but Magnus could only guess who they were. Neither side had the advantage, but the British cavalry had stopped Ricimer's troop.

Then a few mercenaries, no more than seven or eight, broke through and headed for Avitus at a gallop. Magnus realised that if they got through it would all be over. Everything hung in the balance. One or two men would decide the outcome of the battle.

Edeco urged his horse forward, placing himself between the rebels and Avitus. "Get back, sir!"

Magnus drew his sword and stepped forward. His cavalry shield was too light for this, but it was all he had. Behind him, he was aware of the archers notching their arrows. Magnus had just enough time to wish he had not dismounted.

Behind him, Eli the archer let loose an arrow. He scored a hit and one of the cavalrymen slumped in his saddle. His horse shied to the right, forcing his neighbour to swerve to avoid him.

The lead horseman was riding straight at Magnus. He waited as long as he dared, then stepped nimbly to his left. The cavalryman's sword cut through Magnus's shield but missed his arm. Magnus struck back at the horseman as he rode by, but his sword slid off the man's chain mail. The horseman reined in his horse, forcing it to rear up. Magnus stepped aside to avoid being trampled.

Conwyn seized the opportunity, lunged forward, and stuck his dagger in the horseman's thigh, just below his mail shirt. The man screamed and turned his attention to

Conwyn, but before he could strike his horse reared up again. He was taken by surprise and fell from his saddle.

Edeco had also disposed of his enemy. Magnus looked round for his next opponent. But three of the riders had been wounded by archers and one more had lost his mount. One horseman had turned against the archers instead of Avitus.

Eli was fumbling for his next arrow. The horseman cut him down and turned against another archer. Before he could strike, he was shot by another archer at close range. The arrow did not penetrate his armour but he was distracted and missed his stroke.

The remaining horsemen decided they had no chance of success. They turned their horses and galloped away. The archers tried their luck with another volley but missed.

Magnus turned to Conwyn. "Thanks."

"All in a day's work."

"Go and help Eli, will you?"

"Right." Conwyn hurried towards the injured archer.

Magnus turned to see that the British cavalry had driven the enemy horsemen from the field. Gaius was shouting orders at his men. A few of his men broke ranks and chased after the retreating horsemen, but most followed Gaius and turned towards the rebel infantry. But Magnus knew that light cavalry could not achieve much against determined infantry.

The rebel infantry seemed to realise that their cavalry was not going to help them. The sergeants bellowed orders and, step by step, they sullenly withdrew out of bow-shot range. Magnus had to admit that their discipline was admirable.

Edeco was shouting. "Don't drop your guard, men. The bastards may try another charge!"

Avitus patted the neck of his horse to reassure it. "What are they doing, Magnus? Is it a trick?"

"I don't know, sir." His dry mouth made talking difficult.

But the enemy seemed to have given up. They continued to retreat eastwards in an orderly, disciplined fashion.

Edeco, suddenly full of enthusiasm, wanted to use the cavalry to chase after the rebels and cut them down. But Gaius did the sensible thing and let them go.

Chapter 20: The new frontier

Milan, July, 456 AD

The dinner party was more restrained than anything Aetius would have arranged. There were musicians and dancers but, as was usual with Avitus's dinners, the conversation was decorous. The shutters had been closed to keep out the rain. A multitude of oil lamps had been lit but they were inadequate.

The guests were sitting round three sides of the table, allowing everyone a view of the decorous dancers. Magnus, the junior guest present, kept quiet, listened, and pretended to devote his attention to his food and the dancers.

Magnus had been enjoying the food and the music. Unfortunately, the subject of conversation turned to politics. The guests were soon discussing the latest news from the south.

News had reached Milan that Majorian had seized power in Rome, and had proclaimed himself emperor, with Ricimer's backing.

"Italy isn't big enough for the pair of them," Avitus said. "One day, one of them will kill the other."

"You may be right, sir," Sidonius said. "Rome has a tradition of foolish emperors murdering their best generals."

"But Ricimer knows that too," General Edeco put in.

"So you think he may be tempted to strike first?"

"Yes, my lord," Edeco said.

There was an uncomfortable silence. All of the news trickling north seemed to be bad. Ricimer and his mercenaries were in the south of Italy, confronting the Vandals, and winning glory for themselves. Majorian's private army was the biggest force in central Italy. One city after another had accepted his authority.

Then the door at the back of the hall was pushed open. Magnus turned to watch as a palace functionary escorted a messenger, dressed in a long leather coat, into the room. Magnus noted that the messenger had chosen to bleach his hair, in the defiant gesture fashionable amongst the Gallic aviators.

Everyone else in the hall turned to watch as the functionary led the messenger forward to the high table. The dancers came to an uncertain stop.

Magnus noticed that the messenger's coat was wet. He had ridden all the way from the messenger station through this drizzle.

It occurred to Magnus that the aviator, in his long black flying coat, looked like a messenger doom. The man's dour expression added to the image. No doubt he was uncomfortable among these patricians and generals. The aviator's spiky hair failed to look jaunty in the flickering lamplight.

The aviator approached the dining table and paused. "I apologise for intruding, sir."

Avitus waved this aside. "I gave an instruction that all messengers should be brought to me at once. What is the news, my friend?" he said. The messenger still hesitated. "Why, what's wrong? I trust all of my companions here. You may speak out."

The musicians chose that moment to bring their tune to an end. The dancers, already forgotten, filed out.

"My lord, I travelled all the way to Tolosa. The officials of the court informed me that a month ago the king of the

396

Visigoths called up his army and led them in an invasion of Spain."

The room was hushed. Magnus realised the implication at once. There was no chance that the king had any troops to spare for Italy. Judging by the expression on Avitus's face he had come to the same conclusion.

The aviator coughed. "Before the king marched south, he issued an announcement that he intended to crush the Suevi, who were in revolt against the empire, and restore their -."

Avitus cut him short. "Yes, we've all heard the official version. Thank you, young man." He turned to the servant. "This messenger has travelled a long way. Find him some food and a room."

General Edeco found the courage to speak. "Perhaps, my lord, we can recruit some men from other parts of Gaul."

"Where would we find the men we need, general? What incentive can we offer them? We cannot pay them unless we regain control of Rome."

"Yes, my lord."

"Majorian has persuaded Tuscany to accept his authority," Avitus said. "He's a hundred miles away. And as soon as he hears this, he'll move closer. We'll have to treat Milan as a frontier post. We may have to consider moving our headquarters to Turin."

"I'd recommend against that, my lord," General Edeco said. "It'd be an admission of weakness."

"Yes. But I would rather be realistic than trapped in Milan."

*   *   *

Ambrosius family estate, Water Newton

The servant, a north country man, explained to Claudia that he had brought a note from the senior magistrate's household. "The letter, it's from the lady of the house, Lady Julia."

"And what was this message?" Claudia tried to hide her impatience. The man was nervous enough already. Shouting at him would only make him more tongue-tied.

"Lady Julia said, my lady, that the governor has returned to Water Newton. And Lady Julia has invited you to dinner. She implores you to accept."

"I see. Thank you. Ask the cook to give you some refreshment."

"Thank you kindly, my lady."

She was not surprised at the message. The governor had visited all of the towns on the Ermine Street that summer and, last time he passed by, he had spent the night at the magistrate's house.

Claudia opened the letter from Lady Julia. It was an elegant invitation to a small dinner party that evening. Lady Julia was eager for a member of a powerful patrician family to fill out her guest list.

For once Claudia had no hesitation in exploiting her class privileges. She wrote back at once. She wanted to discuss the political situation with the governor, although she was not tactless enough to mention that.

She went to find Oslaf and told him that he wanted four of his men to accompany her. He had anticipated her request and the men were already checking their uniforms.

Claudia took some time in choosing what to wear. As a widow still in mourning she must not wear anything too cheerful. But Lady Julia would be disappointed if her senior guest looked stodgy. And she couldn't wear her best outfit, because she had worn it for her last visit ...

She was careful to arrive early. She was met at the door by the magistrate and Lady Julia. The magistrate's tunic, and the lady's dress, were of the finest wool, embroidered with Lady Julia's best tablet weave. There was no sign of the daughter of the family.

Claudia smiled. "Good evening, sir. Has lord Cornelius arrived yet?"

Lady Julia tended to be very formal towards her social superiors. "He's in his room, my dear, changing for dinner."

Claudia was continuing her campaign to encourage people to stay in Britain. But the magistrate, Maenol, was getting tired of her intrigues. "I am glad you could visit us, my lady. But please don't pester my guests with your questions. There's no risk of the patricians abandoning Britain."

"That was not certain a year ago, sir."

"Perhaps so. But please remember that it's considered bad manners for women to meddle in public affairs."

She smiled sweetly. "Of course, sir."

"Do not mistake me, madam. I admit that the province is in trouble." He scorned the theory that women could not understand political problems. He was prepared to discuss the crisis with anyone, including the ladies. He would tell anyone who would listen what he thought was necessary to improve Britain.

Over the past few months, Claudia had listened to him expound his views and had discreetly encouraged him. She had decided that, although he was too fond of his own voice, his measure of the situation was reliable.

Before Maenol could say any more, the governor walked in. The magistrate stepped forward to greet him, and polite formalities replaced interesting conversation. The governor was thin, blessed with an easy charm. This evening his hair had been carefully oiled in the fashionable style.

Maenol led the way into the dining room. "This evening, lord Cornelius, only the family and a few close friends will be present." Cornelius murmured something in reply.

Claudia judged that the dining room was carefully proportioned, although the wall paintings were a bit faded. They had been repaired rather too often.

There was very little silverware at the table. Had the family been forced to sell it? She noticed that the glassware was an expensive import. In its way, that was even more impressive.

Claudia had been formally introduced to the governor before the mutiny, during her visits to London. He was broad-minded about the place of ladies in society. So, providing the conventions were honoured, talking to him about politics caused no problems.

The main course was venison. Cornelius had mentioned once that he liked venison, so lady Julia was always careful to serve it when the dined in her house.

Cornelius talked business over his meal. This was a breach of good manners, of course, and Claudia's mother would have been shocked. In her view, civilised people should discuss genteel subjects over a meal. Lady Julia, poor woman, was uncertain whether she should criticise her guest or remain silent. Claudia, though, was fascinated and did not hesitate to encourage him.

Cornelius, despite his foppish appearance, was a very determined man. He had been passive before the revolt, while the patricians held the upper hand, but now he had a mission and was fighting to bring the situation under control. He visited every place that needed help. Water Newton was just one of the places on his schedule.

This evening Cornelius was fussy, worried. "I am negotiating with the mutineers. But I admit that the negotiations are going badly. I find the challenge of coping with this rebellion stressful."

"May I say, sir, that you seem to have made the right decisions," Maenol said.

"It's not the decisions, sir, it's the stress. But I am determined to do my duty nevertheless. The rebels are claiming all of the land that we have abandoned."

Maenol snorted. "The councillors haven't abandoned their estates, they've been driven off by Finn's bravos."

"Well, yes. The rebels have promised to respect the frontier, once it's agreed between us. But there's a sort of unspoken threat that they'll lay claim to all the territory that our government can't reach."

Maenol raised an eyebrow. "Anywhere beyond the reach of a messenger station?"

Cornelius shrugged. "They're thinking of horse couriers, but I could stretch the claim. My hope is that we can establish a frontier along the Ermine Street. It's a clear marker, after all."

Claudia leaned forward. Her manner was quite decorous and only her voice betrayed her excitement. "I think you need a messenger station here."

Maenol was bleak. He turned to Cornelius. "Could we establish new stations to fill the gap?"

"We would have to be quick," Cornelius said. "But I can't talk to those messenger people. They clam up if I try. They seem to be terrified of the patrician class, have you noticed that?"

"They're polite enough, sir," Maenol said.

"Yes, but if you go beyond courteous chit chat, they become terrified and clam up. It'd take me a couple of days on their hilltop to persuade them to open up … I wish that young fellow Magnus were here. He seemed to know how to understand those flyboys."

He smiled at Claudia. "And we can't ask you to go running off to that hilltop." The governor's tone indicated that there was too much gossip about her already.

Claudia thought it through. "We would need to know where we could establish new stations. We would need to ... identify minor hills. But most of them are worthless. They could only support flights under ideal conditions..."

Cornelius smiled. "One flight a month would do. I could bluff the rest."

"Ah." She smiled back.

Claudia was confident that she had the information that the governor needed. "My lord, I've spoken to an old aviator who's most courteous to ladies. He was quite eager to tell me all he knew."

"He sounds an insufferable bore," Maenol said.

Claudia ignored this. "The old pilot told me once that if you start out from the Long Mountain, on a clear day you can see both the Pennines and the Bald Mountain. He could tell me about the minor hills in between." She shrugged. "He said something about wave flying, but he didn't explain further."

"They like their mysteries," Cornelius said. "Could you perhaps prepare a sketch map for me?"

"Yes, sir."

"It's a quite improper way to end a meal," Maenol said.

"Duty calls, duty calls," Cornelius said. He winked at Claudia. "But I've sat through some very boring after-dinner entertainments."

"I have a sketch map in my study, sir," Maenol said. "It shows the roads but leaves out the mountains. If you will excuse me, I'll fetch it." With impregnable dignity, he stood and walked out.

The governor covered the delay by gallantly pouring more wine for the ladies. Maenol returned and unrolled the map. Everybody, except for Lady Julia, leaned forward. The Ermine Street, from London to Lincoln, was clearly marked.

"Thank you, sir. You are most kind." Claudia said.

She picked up a piece of charcoal and glanced at Maenol. "If you will excuse me, sir?" She marked the hills that she knew. "There's the Chalk Ridge and the Pennines. Both are excellent sites. Most of the Ermine Street is within a two-day ride of one of these hills," she said.

Cornelius was unhappy. "Not enough, I'm afraid."

"What's wrong, sir?" Maenol asked.

"Unfortunately, the English are being very specific in their demands. They're laying claim to all territory more than a day's march from any of our castles – or from a messenger station."

"Twenty miles?" Claudia was appalled. "That makes things more difficult, sir. There are hills the aviators could use as bases, but ..."

The governor was plaintive. "Is there no way for a flying machine to reach a city in the Midlands and deliver a message?"

Claudia hesitated between politeness and honesty. "A machine can land anywhere, sir. The difficult part is getting the machine back into the air. For that, you need a high ridge and a steady wind. Once a machine is down, in the flatlands, it's trapped."

"Ah." Cornelius smiled. "You mean I could arrange a five-day meeting in the flat midlands, the machine could land in some field there on the third day, and the meeting would break up before they realised it was helpless?"

"Well, yes, sir. But the machine would be lost."

Maenol interrupted. "Saving civilisation is worth one flying machine, surely?"

Claudia thought it best to change the subject. "Further north, there's only one half-decent site between the Watling Street and the Pennines."

"Where?" Maenol demanded.

"Um … Here, sir, Charnwood Forest, west of the Foss Way. About ten miles west of Leicester."

Cornelius frowned. "Finn will not like that. He's laid claim to Leicester."

Maenol stroked his chin. "But Leicester is about twenty miles west of here."

Cornelius was unhappy. "Yes. So I can't accept their 'day's march' demand."

He managed a polite smile. "Thank you, my lady."

*   *   *

Chapter 21: Italy

Turin, Early August

Aviator Orgetorix regarded himself as a hot pilot, but his present mission did not appeal to him at all. He was flying a clumsy two-seater machine east towards the plain of the Padus. The machine was steadily losing height. And Magnus the patrician was in the front seat.

Magnus had ridden into the Turin messenger station, in the hills ten miles west of the city, just after dawn. The aviators – the station captain included – had been awed by the rank of their guest and flattered by Magnus's courtesy. The captain had introduced Magnus to his aviators.

But then Magnus had asked Orgetorix to act as pilot for him. The little patrician had asked politely, but you didn't turn down a request from a member of the viceroy's court. So, he had volunteered at once and said he was honoured.

Magnus had asked to take the front seat. That made flying the machine more difficult, but he hadn't dared object.

"We're over Turin, sir." Only five days before, Lord Avitus had taken up residence there, after Majorian had led an army north and chased Avitus out of Milan.

"Yes. We're making good time."

Orgetorix turned his machine north east to follow the river. The skies were clear, the sun blazed down without mercy and, despite the cold air, Orgetorix was sweating inside his leather flying coat. Did Magnus still bear a grudge because of his flight to the Brenner Pass - in defiance of orders? The patrician had never mentioned it, but still …

Five minutes went by, then six. They were five miles north-east of Turin, trying to find the road to Milan.

"The road follows the river ... That's the road there, sir." Orgetorix raised his voice. "The thin white line. Do you see it?"

"Where?" Magnus shouted. "Ah, yes. But how can you see something so narrow?"

"I don't know. But long straight lines are always easy to spot, sir. If an army was using that road, it'd look black. It looks as if Majorian isn't going to attack Turin today."

"No. Can we get any closer to Milan, aviator?"

He *would* ask that. "You know what Milan's like, sir. Stuck in the middle of a flat skillet. No hills to create up-drafts for us."

Magnus half-turned in his seat. "No chance of wave, aviator?" The little patrician did not sound optimistic.

Orgetorix looked up at the clear blue sky. "I can't see any signs of it today, sir. Of course, it could be there, I could go blundering about, trying to find it. But if it isn't there, sir, we wouldn't get back to Turin."

"Then don't risk it, aviator." Magnus sounded decisive. "If a machine or an aviator fell into Majorian's hands, he would stop thinking we were infallible. At the moment, he thinks we keep watch on him night and day. If he realised we made mistakes, he might even take the risk of attacking Turin."

Magnus leaned over to take one last look at the empty road. "This gives us a few more days to prepare. Take us home, Orgetorix."

"Yes, sir."

* * *

Julius Valerius Majorian, riding a showy white gelding, followed the main force of his army up the valley of the Padus towards Turin. He was with his reserve, close enough to direct operations but safely out of bowshot range. His horse was nervous, but he controlled the brute with ease.

The river valley turned south here and so perforce did the road. The valley was broad, with low hills on either side. The hills obscured his target, but he knew the walls of Turin would come into sight when the road turned west once more. The peaks of the real mountains were visible in the distance.

Ahead of his own advance guard he could just make out the enemy force. They were light infantry, vastly outnumbered by his own army. They seemed to be making no pretense at resistance. The men of the front rank would simply wave their spears, shout something unintelligible, then turn and run behind their colleagues. Then the new front rank would repeat the performance.

"I hear that Avitus raised a militia to protect the city. Landless peasants and runaway slaves." He was angry. How could Avitus betray his patrician heritage by arming slaves?

General Ricimer, riding at his left, sniffed. "They're spread too thin. They're too far apart to form a shield wall. Our infantry charge will go straight through them. And then Turin will be ours."

"Yes, general." Majorian was sweating under his armour and he could not be free of it for five hours at least. Yet he was confident. He had more men that Avitus and his mercenaries had gone from one success to the next. Avitus had managed a draw at the battle of the bridge, but since then his men had been retreating without pause. And that would destroy an army.

He looked up. A machine was circling overhead, fragile but untouchable. "I hate those bastards. They can see everything. Avitus knows the precise location of every unit of the Roman army. And our lack of reserves. While we're left to guess at his disposition."

Ricimer sniffed again. "There's no way that fellow can get that information to Avitus, is there? No matter. We can deal with the aviators when this battle's won."

"True ..." But the machine's course was strange. It would fly over the minor hills on one side of the valley, then turn back and fly over the valley, but then continue on to the opposite hill. Why? Checking for ambushes? Or additional columns of the Roman army?

Could the aviator get his information to Avitus? Could the machines be changing places every hour? Or – if Avitus was in some meadow nearby, the aviator could land with his information. He would have to sacrifice his machine, of course, but if it won him the battle Avitus would think it worthwhile. Majorian glanced to his right and saw a solitary figure on the hilltop. The fellow was not a spy, surely? Perhaps he was a curious civilian?

*   *   *

From the hilltop to the north of the road, Magnus looked down as the Roman army came into view at last. The aviators had been circling above the Roman advance guard since mid-morning. That had given him enough time to get his own troops into position.

That group of horsemen towards the rear must be Majorian and his staff.

The bulk of Avitus's army was behind Magnus, further down the reverse slope of the hill. General Edeco was sitting on the grass at Magnus's feet. The old soldier had said that as nothing was happening, he might as well get some rest.

Magnus thought that was mere posturing to reassure the troops. He admired the general's style but was too anxious to imitate him. Besides, *someone* had to act as sentry. Avitus was with the cavalry, blocking the road to Turin.

Magnus could see the enemy and his own men could see him. The men had been ordered to sit down, so they could not be seen from the valley floor. Most of the lightly armed men were lying flat. A few hardy veterans had even managed to sleep.

The Roman army was walking into his trap. They were almost there.

Rumour had it that the Roman field army was in the south and that Majorian only had his personal troops with him, less than 5000 men.

But Magnus knew how untrustworthy rumours could be. The aviators could not estimate the quality of the troops, of course. But yesterday they had been quite confident that the enemy force was less than that, perhaps no more than 3000 men. That estimate had led Avitus to risk a battle.

Magnus thought this was a mistake. "This is going to be a disaster. It can't possibly work," he muttered.

Edeco did not look up. "You've said that before, young man."

"Avitus's plan depends upon surprise, and upon closing with the enemy as quickly as possible. And we both know that's an almost impossible combination."

"It's the best chance we've got, lad."

"And even if it works, our casualties are going to be high."

"Their casualties will be far higher. They'll never dare attack us again. Besides, what alternative is there?"

Magnus glanced down at the advancing army. Yes. Almost there ... Then he hissed. "Sir! Enemy cavalry riding up the hill towards us. A scouting force. They'll be close enough to see us in three, four minutes." The enemy troopers really should have been leading their horses up that slope.

Edeco scrambled to his feet. "Only eight of them."

"But they're going to wreck Avitus's plan." Magnus turned and shouted. "Archers! To me!"

The men scrambled to their feet and came running. "Wait for my command," Edeco growled.

Majorian's scouts had not been expecting trouble and rode unsuspecting into the ambush.

"Now!" Edeco said. The archers loosed in unison and three riders went down. Another horse, scenting blood, reared and threw its rider. But the rest turned and went galloping back to their commander. Another scout fell from his saddle, but then the rest were out of range.

Magnus was dismayed. So much for Avitus's hopes for surprise. He looked down at the road below. To his surprise, Majorian's little army maintained their advance. They had reached the spot that Magnus had chosen. "There's no point in delaying any longer, sir."

"No." Edeco turned to the waiting men. "Let's go!"

*　　*　　*

Majorian thought the behaviour of Avitus's rearguard was strange. There was no panic, just a steady retreat. It was too regular – almost a dance – as if they had been practising for weeks.

He glanced again at the single figure on the hilltop. The man was now gesticulating wildly. Not a futile display of anger, but a signal. Majorian realised that his army was walking into an ambush. "Did you send any scouts up there, general?"

"Of course, sir. They haven't reported back yet, but -."

Then, with utmost clarity, Majorian knew what Avitus had done. "They're trying to trap us, general."

"Yes, probably. That's the Gaul's only hope of success. But don't worry, we still outnumber them, your majesty."

Majorian realised that Avitus had concentrated his men in exactly the right place. In this valley, most of Majorian's men would not be able to take part in the fight to come.

He glanced at the figure on the hilltop. The man, tiny at this distance, was striding purposefully down the hill. Then, as if by magic, a mass of soldiers rose from the grass, straightened into a formal line, and followed that solitary figure down the hill.

"Look!" Majorian shouted. "They've got our army trapped against the river! Avitus's men have the high ground." He tried to estimate their numbers.

Another line of enemy soldiers appeared and began striding down the hill. And then another.

He had assumed that he outnumbered them three to one. But it looked as if he had an advantage of three to two. At the most.

This was going to be a grinding fight, with only an even chance of success. That was not what he had expected at all. And the mercenaries he had hired preferred easy victories.

He glanced again at the troops striding down the hill. The enemy line was five men deep. And they were already in battle array. His own men, facing a different target, were totally unprepared. "They're going to slaughter us! General – order the retreat."

Ricimer's glare was full of contempt. "The hell I will. This is the first time Avitus has offered us battle. It's the only chance we'll get to destroy him. Yes, casualties will be high, but they'll lose ten times as many as us. When this is over, the road to Gaul will be open."

"But if we lose that many men -." The other senators only respected him because his bodyguard outnumbered theirs. If he lost that advantage in a pyrrhic victory, they would turn against him. Any talk about Gaul would be worthless.

"Run if you want, Majorian. I'm going to win this war for you."

The barbarian general turned his back on Majorian. He urged his horse forward and began shouting orders to the Roman advance guard. "Face right! Form your line there! Hold your ground. Only stand firm, and you can defeat any force that dares attack you!"

Majorian's young staff officers clustered around him. One of them was bolder than the rest. "What should we do, sir?"

Didn't these young men realise what was happening to them? "We are entrapped by superior numbers. General Ricimer has volunteered to form a rearguard so that the main part of our army can live to fight another day.

Each of you must ride to one of my subordinate commanders. Order them to face about and march back down the valley." The young men stared at him, not comprehending. He raised his voice. "Repeat those orders back to me!"

Stumbling, each man in turn did so. "Good! You have your orders! Now deliver that message to where it's needed. Go! The general's brave sacrifice will allow us to escape."

*   *   *

Claudia drove her flimsy chaise up the hill towards Tilson. She was followed by Oslaf the Dane and six men of her escort. Oslaf had a sword, but the other men carried no weapons. That would have been illegal. But that did not matter today - their main purpose was to demonstrate her status.

At least the weather was good. She could have described this as a pleasant outing if her purpose was not so serious.

They reached the top of the hill and their destination came into view. This was a village of round huts, not a grand villa. Someone had spotted their approach and the village elder and his wife stepped forward to greet them.

They made the traditional offer of refreshment. Her brother would have mocked their traditions, but she graciously accepted their gift.

She asked to inspect the hill. "What is the windward slope like?" She explained that she wanted to see whether the hill would be suitable for launching flying machines.

They were baffled, but patiently tolerated her whims. Claudia was dismayed by what she saw. The hill was too low, and the slope was too gentle. The aviators would describe this as a 'marginal' site. But it was the best she had seen so far.

She asked whether there were any other hills nearby, but they told her, proudly, that Tilton Hill was the highest for miles around.

She decided that she would write to the messenger station at Charnwood Forest. Perhaps they could make something of this site.

*   *   *

Early September

The Rhone was a fast-flowing river, but the boatmen were skilled. As the sun sank towards the horizon, the temperature dropped rapidly. Mist was forming on the water and Magnus imagined them getting lost. Looking behind him, he could see that Vienne, on the east bank, was no more than a blurred line. The man at the tiller had expected the chill and was wearing a cape with a hood.

Magnus was reassured to see that the west bank was looking more solid as they drew closer. The high riverbank hid the fine buildings beyond. The vessel barely bumped as it reached the landing stage. A flight of stone steps rose above them.

"Here we are, sir," The helmsman said. The oarsmen held the boat close against the quay and Avitus and Magnus scrambled out. The helmsman unceremoniously dumped their bags on the landing stage.

Avitus climbed up the stone steps with difficulty. "I'm getting too old for this."

"Nonsense, sir." Magnus picked up the bags and followed after him.

An official was waiting for them at the top of the steps with a ceremonial guard lined up behind him.

A week before, an aviator had arrived in Turin with the news that the Western Emperor Vindex was dying. Magnus was inclined to scoff. They had heard rumours before.

But the messenger carried a sealed dispatch from the chancellor in Vienne. Avitus had accepted that this time the rumours were true. The dispatch had contained hint that Avitus might be offered a post in the upcoming government and ended with a peremptory order that Avitus was to report to Vienne at once.

General Edeco had been suspicious, warning that it might be a trap, but Avitus had waved this aside. He had asked Magnus to accompany him to Vienne.

Magnus, eyeing the imperial guards lined up on the embankment, wondered whether the general had been right.

Avitus ignored the soldiers and pulled his cloak over his shoulders. "Good evening, Ambiorix."

The imperial chancellor bowed. "Good evening, my lord. We were told to expect you. Although you took your time getting here. If you will accompany me ..." He gestured to a servant, who scurried forward and took the bags from Magnus.

"Your letter was very vague as to why I should come here," Avitus said.

"He's dying, my friend. He's run out of time waiting for you to finish your business in Italy."

"He's been dying for the last eleven months. Every month we receive a new rumour. Can't he wait a little longer?"

Ambiorix was serious. "It's the real thing, this time. You must see him today. Tomorrow could be too late."

Avitus's lips tightened. "What does he want me for? Does he say?"

"Ah … I believe he has a post for you in the upcoming transitional government. The one you didn't want to hear about at our last meeting."

The street was made up of stone paving stones, rutted with years of use, and Avitus and Magnus had to pick their way with care.

"Have you heard any more about Majorian? Since the battle?" the chancellor asked.

"He occupied Milan, I suppose you heard about that? Then he sent his army against Turin. The numbers on both sides were large, but there was very little actual fighting. Casualties were light on both sides, thanks be to God. But Majorian was forced to withdraw and he hasn't tried again."

"You should have completed the task, but ..."

Avitus shrugged. "Yes. I don't have enough men to chase after Majorian. His army is intact and is strong enough to destroy us. Rumour has it that he's in Rome, arguing with Ricimer."

"In the end, one will murder the other," Ambiorix said.

"Possibly. But his losses were small," Avitus said. "He's claiming that the battle was a minor skirmish. I doubt if anyone will challenge him for now."

They climbed the worn marble steps to the portico. The outer wall of the building was quite blank, devoid of any decoration, giving no hint of the splendour within. It might just as well have been the wall of a warehouse. Or a prison, Magnus thought.

The chancellor sniffed at their travel-stained clothing. "I ought to make you change into your ceremonial robes. But there's no time for that ..."

"Things aren't that desperate, surely" Avitus asked.

"The emperor thinks so. Come this way ..."

They were led along a colonnade and ushered into a room half hospital, half antique display. Tall windows looked out on the formal gardens that led down to the river.

The room's principal inhabitant lay in a huge carved bed inherited from some splendour-minded predecessor.

Vindex, who bore the grand titles of emperor and acichorius, was very pale, as white as his sheets, as white as his hair. He looked as if he had spent the last year hiding underground instead of in this room.

His skin was white and wrinkled over his sunken cheeks. His eyelids were heavy and hooded over hazel eyes. His hands were white, with blue veins standing up on their backs.

Ambiorix and Avitus, and then after a beat Magnus, went down on one knee beside the bed. The emperor gestured to his attendant physician with one finger. The man bowed and left the room. They stood, Avitus rather stiffly.

"So, Lord Avitus, tell me how I look."

"Very ill, my lord."

The emperor chuckled, then coughed. "You refresh me. First honest opinion I've heard from anyone in weeks. And Ambiorix is the worst of the lot." His voice cracked, and he coughed.

He motioned Avitus closer. "I didn't call you here to chat about old times. Did my chancellor tell you my purpose?"

"Something about a post in your government. I told him then that I wasn't interested. After my disastrous adventure in Italy, your courtiers and officers would find it impossible to serve alongside me."

Vindex closed his eyes and addressed, apparently, the ceiling. "Tell me – Lord Avitus – who should be the next ruler of the Gallic Empire?"

Avitus looked as if he'd just bitten into something vile but was too polite to spit it out. "Your best general. Someone the troops can accept."

"Yes, but who is my best general? It used to be Lord Aetius. I never thought I'd outlive him. But unfortunately, he pushed Valentinian too far."

"General Edeco, then. He's guarding the Alpine frontier now."

"Use your wits, man. He's a barbarian. The Senate would never accept him." The emperor sighed. "You can quit wriggling, Avitus. You shall not wriggle out of this. No. I want to nominate you as my heir."

Ambiorix, standing next to Magnus, grinned. Avitus frowned. Magnus's heart sank.

"No, no," Avitus said. "You're not going to lay that on me. I've just achieved a complete disaster in Italy. Do you want me to ruin Gaul as well?"

"You can't blame yourself for the Vandal invasion, or for that fool Majorian," the chancellor told him. "And one failure will make you less prone to hubris."

"But I'm not a general. The troops would never accept me."

"You've just fought a battle against the best army that Rome could offer."

"I had good men. All I did was listen to the advice of my generals."

"Being able to recognize good advice when you hear it is the definition of a good general."

The emperor coughed. "A lot has happened in the last ten years. Back then, Rome was our only threat. And Rome was almost as powerful as Constantinople … Since then, Rome has lost half her territory to the Vandals. The Huns threaten us both. Vienne is more powerful than Rome."

"That won't last," Avitus said. "Rome will recover her strength."

"You may be right. But whether we're threatened by Rome or the Huns, our little empire is going to need a strong ruler."

The emperor coughed again. "I have not achieved much during my reign. But at least I can achieve a clean succession. You're respected by the senate and by the troops."

"And by King Theodoric," Ambiorix put in.

"Yes, we certainly mustn't forget him," the emperor said.

"I disapprove of most of your policies. You're too soft on the slave trade. It's vile," Avitus said.

"That's too big to tackle," the emperor said. "I have no energy to tackle lost causes. But if you want to take on the trials of Sisyphus after I'm gone, go ahead."

"Oh. You think it's a worthy cause, then?"

"You should have been a bishop, not a senator," the emperor said.

"Well, yes. Too late now." Avitus sighed. "Very well, sir, I accept the appointment."

"Good." For a moment, the emperor treasured his little victory. "Now, you had better send I that fool of a physician."

Avitus, Magnus and Ambiorix emerged from the Imperial Residence into the chilly air of evening, soft and grey with humidity from the nearby river. They were trailed by Avitus' new bodyguards. There had been a lengthy interview with Ambiorix and his subordinates. Magnus's head swam with the number and detail of subjects covered. Avitus, despite his years, had set the pace. Magnus had written copious notes. He had made a few suggestions, but most of the time he had been content to observe.

419

"His majesty said that Vienne was stronger than Rome," Avitus said. "But 'stronger' is the wrong word ..."

"Resilient?" Magnus suggested.

"Yes, that's it. All of the humiliating compromises and innovations we've made over the last hundred years seem to have given us the ability to adapt and endure. I'd like to recruit a peasant militia to defend the territory around Turin."

"That would take years. It'd only be possible if we could hang on to Turin," Ambiorix said.

Avitus sighed. "Yes. I shall have to return to Turin and face down Majorian." He turned to the chancellor. "I shall want to take some troops with me."

"Out of the question," Ambiorix said. "The emperor -."

"Using them to defend Gaul is a different matter to expending them on a second invasion of Italy. If Majorian attacks, we can abandon Turin and defend the high passes. That's always worked in the past."

"Ah. Yes, quite," Ambiorix said.

"But I shall keep Turin if I can."

"You'll have to send a message to Edeco at once," Magnus said. "Tell him to hold on until reinforcements arrive."

"Yes. Draft a note for my signature, will you?"

*

London, September

Conwyn arrived in London, on a coasting vessel, at dusk. The naval bases at the mouth of the Thames kept pirates at bay, as they had for a hundred years. The vessel sailed past the old docks and beached alongside the other vessels on the strand. Conwyn said his farewell to the skipper. He walked up the hill to his father's home, a decrepit house in the east of the city. This encounter would be uncomfortable.

Three people turned to look as he entered the main room. His mother was ecstatic at his return but, unfortunately, his brother Cynon was there too. His brother looked sour, and his father showed no expression at all. Conwyn reminded himself that still waters ran deep.

"So, the prodigal son has returned. What made you leave Italy?" father asked.

How had his father guessed? "I was accused of subversion, sir."

To his surprise, his father was amused. "That happened to me, once. How did you escape?"

"I didn't. Magnus got the charge reduced, then paid my fine. And sent me home." He rubbed the back of his hand absently.

"What's that?" Cynon asked sharply.

Damn, his brother would notice that. "As a convicted felon, I was branded. Even if I paid a fine, only members of the equestrian order can escape that."

His father was angry. "Couldn't young Magnus have prevented that?" he asked. "I thought he had powerful friends."

Conwyn flushed. "He would've had to ask Avitus to intercede. If he'd done that, he'd have created a scandal big enough to be heard in London. Magnus had an obligation to Avitus as well as to me ... it could have been worse. I could have been sent to the salt mines."

"So now you have a criminal record," his father said. "That'll make employment difficult. Will you go back to being a groom?"

"Not if I can help it," he said honestly. "I'm still fond of horses, but I'm tired of mucking out."

Cynon was indignant. "You expect us to find a job for you? A branded felon?"

"Shut up," his father said. "Someone who's been to Italy can be useful. And someone with a criminal record can be useful too."

Conwyn was intrigued. "What's that, sir?"

"I've got a new line of business. Dealing with Friesian traders. Rather dangerous. Most of them are half-pirate, so they only respect people who've been in a fight." He smiled thinly. "I've been telling them lies about the wars I've been in. If you can tell them you've fought the Huns, you'll be a great success."

He flushed. "But I was only a horse-holder."

"That's more than your lily-white brother can say."

Conwyn grinned at his brother.

Chapter 22: The future of Britain

Vienne, Late September, 456 AD

Late one afternoon, Magnus rode through the streets of the city, trying to evade the other road users. Vienne had a new emperor and the city suddenly felt full of confidence. He rode into the barracks and dismounted wearily. The ride from Turin had taken him several days. He made sure his horse would be cared for and explained his business to an orderly.

The man nodded. "You are expected, sir. The commander of the bodyguard, Gaius Ambrosius, instructed that a room should be allocated to you."

"I see. I must thank him."

"If you will come this way, sir ..." the man escorted him through the barracks.

Magnus found his room, dumped his bags on the floor and began searching through them for a fresh tunic. He wanted to get out of his travel-stained riding clothes. A visit to the bathhouse was next on his list.

He had just returned from the bath when Gaius came to see him. His friend seemed rather subdued. "Welcome back, Magnus. It's good to see you again."

"Thank you. But why the gloom?"

"The emperor wants to see you this evening, Magnus."

"Yes. I suppose he must be displeased with me."

"Well, we've received lots of complaints about your activities. All the usual tedious busybodies. I've received substantial bribes to ensure that the complaints reach the emperor." He grinned. "The local orphanage is grateful for my donations."

He managed a smile. "I see."

"I think Avitus is more angry with these busybodies who've been wasting his time. You shouldn't let it bother you." He held up a sealed packet. "I've got a letter here for you. It's from Lady Claudia. I heard you had been recalled, so I didn't send it on."

He took the packet. "Thank you."

"Well, I'll see you at dinner."

"Yes. See you then," he said absently. Suddenly, his future seemed less gloomy. He broke the seal on the letter and read through it.

The letter made it was clear that she had been very busy that summer. The governor had got a lot done, and Claudia hinted that she had somehow witnessed all of it.

She assured him that she was recovering after the death of her husband. She had duties to keep her busy. At time of writing, July, she was living in Water Newton, away from her father.

The last line, as usual, was in Claudia's own handwriting. He noticed that she had called him her dear friend. But that was just good manners. He refolded the letter.

So, she had escaped from the tyranny of her family? This changed everything. He carefully put the letter away with all the others.

Then, grimly, he dressed in his best tunic, pulled his cloak around his shoulders and went to see the emperor.

He stood stiffly to attention in front of his emperor. At the far end of the room, a pair of bodyguards and an imperial secretary waited impassively. Avitus, seated behind a heavy desk piled with documents, looked sternly at Magnus.

"Sit down, sit down. Young man, in the few short weeks on the frontier, you seem to have offended absolutely everyone."

"Yes, sir. But the people of Turin are happy, sir."

Avitus indicated a pile of letters on his desk. "Unfortunately, you seem to have offended everyone else. The landowners are outraged at your heavy-handed behaviour. The only people who are pleased with your conduct are unable to tell me so."

"I see, my lord," Magnus said woodenly.

Avitus allowed himself a slight smile. "I must admit that from a military point of view, your innovations appear to be excellent. Your successor can probably leave them untouched and concentrate on repairing the political damage you have done."

"I see, sir."

"That leaves the problem of what to do with you."

"Yes, sir." He waited.

"I have been going through Emperor Vindex's papers. A month ago, he received a plea for help from the governor in Britain," Avitus said. "The governor put a lot of effort into negotiating a frontier, but apparently that mutineer Finn cannot force his men to recognise it. Lord Gallus begs me to send an experienced general to lead his troops. Someone with experience of irregular troops, he says."

"Britain? But - you don't mean me, surely? My visit to Britain was a disaster." Magnus was reluctant. Did Avitus really think he was equal to this challenge?

"Put it down to experience. I can offer you the title of count," Avitus offered. "Commanding the new border force ... although it doesn't seem to exist yet."

"Well - a fancy title impresses the civilians and would signify that I had contacts. But reinforcements would be far more useful, my lord."

"Well … I may be able to spare you some regular cavalry for a few months," Avitus said.

Magnus was thinking of something else. Claudia, the girl he had lost, had been widowed. And - despite his unforgivable behaviour - she had bothered to write to him again. He decided to visit her when he reached Britain, if only to console her on her loss. Would her parents and the rest of the Aurelianus family consider him eligible now that he had been promoted to count? But she had cared enough to make the effort of sending a letter to him. At least he could travel hopefully.

*

London, Early October

Magnus was surprised at how green the countryside was. He had taken the short sea crossing to Dover and then rode through the woods and fields of Kent. He had become used to the Mediterranean, where the grass died with the coming of summer, the rivers shrank to nothing and dust was everywhere. He relished the richness of the British countryside.

When he reached the Thames, he took the Horse Ferry across to Ludgate, just west of the city wall. London seemed tiny compared to the cities of Italy. But it appeared to be holding its own. The docks, built to handle large ships, had been abandoned and were sliding into decay, but further upstream smaller merchant ships were beached on the shingle and were busy unloading cargo. In its small way,

London was more like Milan than Rome. The thought comforted him.

His first task was to present himself at the governor's palace. He found that very little had changed since then. Some of the faces were new, but the routine seemed unchanged. The governor's personal secretary was spare, middle-aged, and harried.

"We have been expecting you, of course, my lord. If you would come with me …" He bowed and led him to a comfortable chamber, with a brazier in the corner. "If you will wait here, Lord Cornelius Gallus will see you shortly."

"Oh. I had expected to see him at once."

The man looked shocked. "No, that would never do. Lord Cornelius Gallus insists on the proprieties." He whisked away.

A few moments later a breathless servant arrived to offer him wine and little spiced cakes. Magnus allowed the servant to pour him no more than a mouthful of wine. He had suddenly realised that he might need all his wits about him in this interview.

The secretary returned and bowed low. "Come this way, if it please you, my lord." Some of the tapestries and embroidery work decorating the walls looked new. He wondered whether the governor's lady had taken a hand. Or was Cornelius's sister still in command here?

Cornelius Gallus had been appointed by the previous emperor for political reasons. Despite that, he was a shrewd politician, and Magnus had learned to respect the man. He was tall, neat, and elegantly dressed, his hair smoothly oiled.

The governor chose to receive him formally. Despite the chill, the shutters had been pushed back to give a view of the formal garden. An elaborate mosaic covered the floor

427

and rich tapestries hung on the walls. The governor was sitting in an elaborately carved chair.

Magnus stepped forward, as ritual demanded, and favoured the governor with a half bow, equal to equal.

"Welcome to Britain, my lord count," Cornelius Gallus said.

"Thank you, sir."

"I hear that you, too, have been punished by being sent to the back of beyond." Cornelius smiled.

"Well, the emperor found it politic to remove me from the capital, yes."

"I hope you'll do me the honour of dining with me this evening, lord Magnus." The words were formal, but Cornelius's voice was warm.

"Of course, sir. Thank you."

"And what's going on in Italy?"

"Italy? How much have you heard? Majorian has made himself emperor. Ricimer defeated the Vandal fleet, so the grain supply from Sicily should get through to Rome. But, in return, he wanted Emperor Majorian to promote him to Magister Militum. Neither of them has made any move against Turin. We're raising a militia to defend Turin."

"Indeed? Well, I hope Majorian can keep the grain supply reaching Rome, but that's unlikely to affect us here in Britain. How long do you intend to remain in London?" Cornelius asked.

"Only a few days, sir. I've got a lot to do. I want to visit my father. And then I've got to visit my new command."

"Yes. The English mutineers keep overstepping their agreed boundaries. Is there any way to make them keep their promises?"

"Only by a show of force, sir."

"Yes... All this summer, they were continually raiding west. I complained to Finn, of course, asking him to keep his men in order, but he sent me one excuse after another. The raiders are confident enough to come within sight of our messenger stations. They're so sure of themselves, they mock us."

Magnus tried to appear confident. "That makes them predictable, sir. We know where to stop them."

"I hope you're right. There's a west-country faction at work, trying to persuade everyone that I ought to move the capital to Corinium. They say it's more central." He raised an eyebrow.

Magnus, unsure how to reply, stuck to the facts. "Well, Corinium's the centre of the messenger network. During the campaigning season I may base my headquarters there."

Magnus travelled to his family home, a modest farm in the upper Thames valley. Once again, he marveled at the greenness of it all. At one time, he had taken it all for granted. The farm looked unchanged, with its whitewashed walls and red-tiled roofs. Was his father unchanged too? He was a rigid moralist who had disapproved of his younger son joining the army.

The visit went better than he expected. As he rode into the farmyard his father, usually grave and dignified, strode out of the house to receive him. "Welcome home, Magnus. You must be tired from your journey. Come into my study."

"Thank you, sir." He followed his father into the house. He was surprised at how white his father's hair was.

"Take a seat, boy … You've done well for yourself, Magnus. You've risen very fast. Too fast, perhaps."

"You're probably right, sir. A few months ago, I thought I was going to fall just as fast."

"Got into trouble, did you?"

He smiled. "Not in the way you mean, sir. I helped to set up a militia to protect the frontier. Around Turin, you understand. That annoyed the local landowners."

"So, you've earned the emperor's displeasure?"

"Officially, I'm in disgrace. Privately, he's pleased with me. But the landowners and their cronies on the Senate was demanding my head on a platter, so he sent me back here."

His father seemed to be amused. "You have been busy, my boy. And what happens next?"

"I'm going up to Lincoln for a week or two, then I'll try to pull this frontier force together."

"You've been made responsible for that? But it's an impossible task." His father seemed thunderstruck.

"I know what to do. I was aide to the count at Chester, then did much the same work in Gaul."

His father waved this aside. "This new command is the third most important office in the province! Will the officers accept your authority? And some of them are English. Will these foreign mercenaries accept a Briton?"

He shrugged. "I fought the Huns. None of them can say that. Besides, I intend to stay there only long enough to select my successor."

"You don't want to keep the post?"

"I'm tired of this endless strife. I just want to settle down."

His father smiled sourly. "Nonsense. You'd get bored. And then you'd get into trouble again. The old-fashioned sort. But I don't want to preach. Your return is something to celebrate."

Dinner that evening was, indeed, something of a celebration. His mother and the cook exerted themselves, raiding the pantry for hoarded delicacies. His eldest brother, Julius, was there too, with his wife and young children.

His mother fussed over him. "All we have to drink is home-brewed beer. I'm sorry we haven't got any wine, dear."

He grinned. "I'd rather have good beer than bad wine. Besides, I've been looking forward to this, mother."

She smiled at the complement. "You ought to settle down, dear. Haven't you found a wife for yourself? I had hoped you would find an heiress in Italy."

He smiled. "I never thought of that. But the Italians don't approve of the Gallic Empire. Trying to marry a senator's daughter would have caused too many problems." He fiddled with his cup, trying to hide how nervous he was. "That reminds me, mother. Do you know where Claudia Aurelianus is now? I have a letter to deliver to her."

His father shot him a look. "You still hold a candle for her?"

He shrugged. "She wrote to me regularly, sir, asking for news from Italy."

His mother was listening with interest. "Lady Claudia is widowed now, of course. The marriage was not a happy one. But she went back to her husband's estate and stays there most of the year."

Magnus put down his cup. "Oh. That's not far from the frontier."

Julius poured himself some more beer. "How did you come to be dismissed from the emperor's court, Magnus?"

"I wasn't dismissed. I asked for a transfer because I couldn't stand the endless politicking. The court functions on corruption. Lord Avitus told me that there was nothing he could do about it and that accepting bribes was an accepted part of my duties."

Father smiled at this. "Are you turning into a moralist, boy?"

The remark amused him. "It seems so, sir."

Julius was looking surly. "Appointed as count! You'll be too proud to speak to paupers like us."

Magnus poured himself some more beer. "How's the farm going?" he asked.

"Things are getting worse. It's impossible to sell the farm's produce any more. The population of the cities is shrinking. The larger estates can sell their crops at a lower price and still make a profit."

Magnus guessed that this was an ongoing argument. Father was annoyed. "Are you suggesting that we should just give up? Become subsistence farmers?"

"If we can't sell our crops, what else is there to do, father?" Julius said.

Magnus could not stand the anxious look on his mother's face. He put down his cup and leaned forward. "Merchants from Gaul come to London. I've seen their ships. And not just from Gaul. The Frankish lands and the Friesian islands too. They say that British wool is the best they've seen. They're prepared to pay in silver for it."

Father gave him a look. "What are you suggesting, boy?"

He shrugged. "You already produce enough wool for our own needs. You could try selling the surplus in London."

"Coined silver, you say, Magnus? But they'll want our very best, I suppose."

"They can get second best at home. Why come here for more of the same?"

"Well, it's worth trying."

* * *

Claudia had visited her father's home in the Limestone Edge to escape the summer heat and the smells of London. But the visit had not been a success and she was eager to return to her husband's estate. She found that living under her mother's governance was even more galling than having to put up with her late husband's meddling.

She was helping her mother check the household accounts, in a bare whitewashed room, when her father walked in.

Her mother looked up and noticed his expression. "What's the matter, my lord?"

Claudia could tell that he was annoyed. She wondered what had ignited his wrath this time. "That young Vitalinus fellow, Magnus, has turned up. Says he came to pay his respects. He's been telling me what's going on in Italy and Vienne. Said he'd asked his friend Gaius to write to me in future. Your nephew by marriage."

Claudia gaped up at him. "Magnus is a count now, isn't he, father? Hasn't he got the task of guarding the new frontier?

He looked at her. "Do you have a fondness for him?"

She shrugged. "I don't know, father. I haven't seen him for two years. But I enjoyed his letters."

Her mother spoke up. "He's an adventurer, my dear."

"Yes, mother." She turned to her father. "Did you send him away?"

He glared. "Of course not, girl. Do you take me for a fool? He's got all the latest news. Straight from Vienne. And he's got access to the governor, so I can't afford to offend him. Invited him to spend the night. You'll see him at dinner. But I told him he wasn't to mention what he said. He promised at once, I'll say that for him."

They did not ask Claudia for her opinion, for which she was grateful. So, she would get to see him again at last. She wondered how the man himself would compare with his letters.

She took extra care when she changed for dinner, asking her maid to devote more time than usual brushing her hair. When she entered the dining room, she discovered that Magnus was seated at the place of honour, next to her father, sitting at his right hand.

She was placed to the left of her father, but further down the table. Magnus was dressed in an Italian tunic and military cloak, made from the finest cloth, but very plain, almost devoid of decoration. But the tunic was a perfect fit – it must have been especially made. His hair was carefully trimmed and sleek. Was there a hint of oil in it? His quiet restraint made her father look gaudy by comparison.

She noted that her father had put out the best silver plate to impress his guest. She was glad of her place further down the table, which allowed her to study him discreetly.

She was surprised at how much he had changed. When he had left for Gaul, he had still been a boy, immature and trying terribly hard to appear self-assured. He had suffered that defeat and had taken it very hard. Now he quietly ignored her father's bluster. But of course, he had fought another war since then. He had served on the emperor's staff and commanded men in battle. Did he think she had changed? He smiled politely when he saw her, but that was all.

Dinners in her father's household were very formal. She could only speak to the people on each side of her, which meant that she was unable to speak to Magnus. Father must have planned it that way. But she could listen to Magnus talk. He handled her father very cleverly, telling him all he needed to know.

"Count Ricimer, sir? He's achieved an important victory. And he'll try to make use of that to increase his power in Italy … but even if he does, Majorian's authority will not reach to Gaul. It's my belief that Ricimer has as much power in Italy as Majorian. And he'll try to gain more."

But father was more interested in local politics. "The governor is taking on too much power for himself," father grumbled. "This new militia will defy the landowners. We need to increase the power of the loyal patricians now that old Vitalinus is out of the way."

Magnus listened politely, but he carefully avoided committing himself to her father's policies. "In these troubled times, the governor's initiatives are useful."

"Nonsense, boy! When the Council reconvenes, in the autumn, I want to persuade the council to undo the worst of the governor's innovations."

Magnus was annoyed. "This is not an appropriate topic for the dinner table, surely."

Lady Aurelianus, ever tactful, intervened. "How long will you be staying with us, my dear Magnus?"

"My lady, I regret to say that I must leave tomorrow. I have to inspect the settlements on the Ermine Street."

Mother sighed. "I suppose you'll tell me it is your duty."

"I'm afraid so, my lady."

He was interrupted by the servants clearing away the plates. Claudia was sorry when her mother gave the signal for the ladies to leave the table.

Chapter 23: The defence of Britain

October, 456 AD

Magnus followed the servant through the corridors of the governor's palace. The servant pushed open the door to the governor's study. "Count Magnus to see you, sir."

Magnus walked into the study to find that another guest was sitting next to the governor.

The governor was an elegant man, usually quiet and complacent. Magnus thought he used rather too much hair oil.

He smiled. "Lord Magnus, may I introduce Lord Trogius, the leader of the cavalry troop from Soissons. Lord Trogius, may I introduce you to Magnus, count of our frontier defences."

The man was tall, dressed in a courtier's embroidered tunic and military cloak, worn with an aristocratic self-confidence. He was also a few years older than Magnus.

"Good morning, my lord Magnus." He spoke with a patrician accent, and there was no warmth in his greeting. Magnus assumed he resented having to take orders from a younger man.

Cornelius ignored this. "The emperor responded to my plea for help by asking the governor in Soissons to lend me some men. The governor generously responded by sending us a hundred men – regular cavalry."

Magnus told himself that a hundred men wasn't much, but it was a useful gesture of support. "That's excellent news, sir."

Trogius looked down at Magnus. "And what experience do you have, sir?"

"I campaigned with Aetius against the Huns. I commanded a troop of skirmishers."

"Which campaign was that? Gaul or Italy?"

"Both," he said shortly.

"Count Magnus is being modest," Cornelius said. "He also served on Emperor Avitus's staff for a while."

"You were at his headquarters?" The cavalry commander looked at Magnus with new interest. "Ah. I see."

Magnus realised with dismay that the man would have to be handled with a great deal of tact. The men he had brought with him would be invaluable. But he knew that the Soissons heavy cavalry would not be enough.

He smiled politely. "You may find that you have nothing to do while you are in Britain."

Trogius raised his eyebrows. "You do not intend to attack these rebels?"

"They outnumber us. I will only attack if they cross the frontier," Magnus said.

"I feel certain they will do so," Cornelius said. "They've taken up the practice of raiding across the frontier and then vanishing east again."

"Good, good. Do you want my men to remain in London?" Trogius asked.

Cornelius turned to Magnus. "What do you suggest, my lord?"

"No, we're too far from the action, here. I would suggest the Ermine Street. Cambridge in the east or Wimpole."

"Cambridge, then," the cavalry commander said.

Magnus bit back a retort. He had given the man a choice. Excellent." Cornelius smiled.

*

Magnus, carrying out his inspection of the frontier, had reached Water Newton, a minor market town on the edge of the Fens. The Ermine Street, the great military road from London to Lincoln, cut through the town. A mile to the north, the road crossed the river Nene at a bridge. The town, far from anywhere important, had been decaying for a generation. Now it was a key point on the frontier.

The town had the usual defences of an external ditch and internal stone wall. Each of the four gates was protected by a robust gatehouse. Magnus judged that the walls and the towers had been built a century before, in reaction to an earlier crisis.

Magnus climbed to the roof of the eastern gatehouse and turned to look east. At his side stood the town's magistrate and one of the sergeants of the militia. Despite the season, the sky was clear. The land was a patchwork of large fields surrounding small villages, separated by woods. This country was flat, unlike the hills he knew.

"The farmland looks peaceful, doesn't it, Maenol? You'd never guess it was threatened by a crisis."

"Yes, my lord," the magistrate said. "But the soil is rich, exactly what the rebels want."

"Yes, true enough." Two years before, the provincial chancellor had promised special privileges and concessions to any town that promised to raise a militia unit to defend a strong point on the frontier.

The citizens of Water Newton had accepted the offer with enthusiasm. Now Magnus had come to inspect the town's defences.

"I have the uneasy feeling that the raiders are watching us from those woods, Maenol." But the magistrate had nothing to say.

The sergeant helped him out. "They're feasting in their hall, my lord. They despise us. Why should they watch us?"

"Yes, they'll raid at harvest time, when there's more to steal," Maenol said.

So, the magistrate understood the problem. "I'm disappointed, you know. I had expected to see an improvement in your defences."

Maenol was a middle-aged man, plump and balding, dressed for riding. "We are determined to meet the governor's conditions, my lord."

"Are you indeed? The governor wants your militia to defend this key point."

"My lord, we've recruited six hundred volunteers here, as planned."

Magnus doubted that, but would have been grateful if the true figure were half that promised.

"We have Lady Claudia's volunteers," Sergeant Artorius said. "Two hundred strong."

The man sported a neatly trimmed salt-and-pepper beard. The beard did not hide the man's sardonic smile. He was a veteran who claimed to have served for ten years in one of the coastal forts.

Magnus realised that the militia sergeant was taller than he was and felt a moment's irritation. This peasant had probably been half starved as a child. How had he grown so tall?

Maenol ignored the sergeant's comment. "The town was dying. Then the chancellor offered us freedom from taxation. So, we jumped at the chance."

Magnus subjected him to a stare. "You haven't been given the right to defend yourselves, captain, it's an *obligation*. If you don't maintain the militia, you'll lose those rights."

The sergeant winked at Magnus. "Perhaps you disapprove of our independence, my lord."

Magnus decided the man's humour was clumsy rather than deliberately offensive. "Not at all, sergeant. I want to protect Britain from its enemies. Recruiting a frontier militia is the best way to do it."

The sergeant was suddenly all professional. "I've been telling the local people, sir, that six hundred of them isn't enough to defend the entire wall."

Magnus turned and looked along the wall. "Yes, you're right about that."

"We need a military fort, not a city wall," the sergeant said. "And there is one, just west of here."

Maenol looked sullen. Presumably, this was an ongoing argument between them. "We want to defend our homes."

Magnus judged that the low-born sergeant was more intelligent than the pompous magistrate. But the absurdities of the social system meant that the sergeant had to carry out the captain's decisions.

Magnus realised he would have to intimidate the magistrate. He had hoped to avoid that. "Captain, you don't seem to understand. I'm here to assess the ability of your militia to defend the frontier. Let's go and see this fort." Maenol flinched.

Magnus turned and made his way down the stairs to level ground. The other two men followed in silence. Magnus hated offending these people. They were enthusiastic and motivated. It was just a pity they could not admit their limitations.

440

Out in the cobbled street, the watching townsmen kept at a respectful distance. Magnus made an attempt to be conciliatory. "Maenol, the governor doesn't expect you to defeat the raiders. You won't be asked to attack them. Your task will be to slow the raiders down. But ... reinforcements may be late in coming."

The old fort did not look very promising. It was a rectangular earthen embankment and had been decaying for centuries. "This will do."

Maenol was astonished. "But …"

"Don't you understand? The raiders aren't interested in sieges. If they can't achieve a success on the first day, they'll move on. You can keep everyone squeezed up in here for that long.

"Remember, a small number of men, trying to defend the wall of a large fort would be overwhelmed."

"But we can't rebuild this place in time."

One objection after another. Magnus was irritated. But at least the man was thinking. "This year, re-dig the ditch. Use the soil to repair the earthen rampart. Next year, rebuild the gatehouses in brick or stone."

"An earthen wall? I would prefer a stone one. There's plenty of stone in these ruins."

"You said yourself you haven't time. The raiders could strike tomorrow."

Captain Maenol accepted this with a show of reluctance.

"I have to leave now," Magnus said. "I have another appointment this afternoon. Lady Claudia's villa is next on my list."

*

441

Magnus and his men rode north. The Ambrosius villa was halfway between Water Newton and Great Casterton. Its layout was sprawling, with a wide frontage.

He noted that the villa did not show any signs of damage. But, as he drew closer, he saw that one wing seemed to have been abandoned.

He ignored the grand front entrance and instead led his men to the stable yard. The staff were not expecting him.

That annoyed him. He had been careful to send a messenger. He dismounted and told a flustered house-servant that he wanted to see the owner.

Claudia appeared in the doorway and stepped into the stable yard to greet him. She was dressed in a workaday woolen gown. Her expression showed her disapproval. Her maid, following a step behind, looked equally suspicious.

She was surprised. "Magnus!"

"Weren't you expecting me, my lady?"

She indicated his troopers. "I was expecting *you*, my lord. Not your army."

"I see. I'm carrying out an inspection of the frontier. And that includes the patrician estates."

"You mean this is an official visit?"

He hid a smile. "Quite so. And, according to the rumours, this place is defended. By a private army. I would like to inspect it."

She laughed. "All we have is a few field-hands, with shields and wooden spears."

Then two broad-shouldered men hurried across the yard. To Magnus they had the look of mercenaries.

"This is Oslaf, my steward," she said, quite casually. "He's from Denmark. During the mutiny, he refused to join Finn. Something to do with a blood feud."

Magnus decided that the older man had the air of a loyal subordinate. Claudia, it seemed, trusted him. He would have liked to ask Oslaf what the relationship between them was, but he could not do that in Claudia's presence.

The two warriors glanced at Magnus's bodyguard. "You are the count? You fought the Huns? We are honoured, my lord," the older man said.

"You'd better come inside," Claudia said. Her tone was gracious, but it was clearly an order.

In the receiving room, she was at her most ladylike. Her poor relation was sitting at her side.

"Would you like some herbal tea? I have some wine, but you're on duty."

"Indeed I am. I'll accept the tea. Thank you." He sat back and explained that he was looking for useful strategic points along the frontier.

She sipped at her tea. "And you think that this villa is a useful strategic position? I don't see how."

"The Angles claim the Fens. And Water Newton marks the north-west limit of the Fens."

She nodded. "I see."

"Finn wants all the land that's more than twenty miles from a messenger station."

"Yes, the governor told me about that. He was arguing for a fifty-mile limit."

Did that mean she was in the governor's confidence? He hid his surprise. "My aviators think that there's a marginal launching site just west of here."

She was surprised. "It would be very marginal."

"You think so? Let's take a look."

Claudia had a dainty two-wheeled chaise, which she drove with skill. Oslaf saddled up and rode along behind.

On the journey, they were accompanied by one of Magnus's men. He was lean, middle-aged and did not look at all soldierly. Magnus introduced him as Enniaun Hen, one of their best aviators.

"You're from Powys?" she asked.

"Originally, my lady."

At the top of the hill, Magnus dismounted and looked out across the Fens. That was enemy territory. Then he turned and looked westwards towards the hills further inland.

"Tilton on the Hill is in that direction," Claudia said.

"Twenty-five miles away," Magnus said. He exchanged looks with Enniaun. "This is too low for a conventional launch."

"And what's an unconventional launch? she said.

The dour man spoke up. "You tether your machine to the ground with a long rope, pull the stick back, and rise up in the air like a kite. Then, you pull the release cord, push the stick forward and cut around in a spiral to gain forward airspeed before leveling off."

"It sounds scary."

Enniaun smiled. "No, it's great fun."

"You aviators are all the same. But that method wouldn't be reliable, would it? You couldn't call for help that way?"

He shook his head. "You might have to wait a month for ideal conditions."

Magnus interrupted. "But that's all that Cornelius needs."

"The ground-handlers need to be specially trained in that technique," Enniaun said.

She shook her head. "And I would have to supply them, I suppose."

He nodded.

"I always wanted to learn to fly -."

"No!" Magnus said, in a tone that made her jump.

Enniaun smiled. "Not here, my lady. You should go to one of the regular sites."

"Yes, that's what I meant."

Back down at the villa, Magnus inspected her men. He judged that they seemed to be in good spirits.

He told Oslaf that morale seemed to be good. "In Italy, I've seen enthusiastic volunteers defeat dispirited regulars. And they seem to be loyal to Lady Claudia."

Oslaf nodded. That's because she comes from an aristocratic family. They're bred to it."

"I know what you mean." He lowered his voice. "The lady is a better leader than her father. Or her brother-in-law."

Oslaf choked. "You may be right, sir. This militia - they're fighting for their homes. And so is she."

*

First of October

The Governor's secretary showed Magnus into a small, informal room. The day was warm, and the shutters had been pushed back to give a view of the formal garden. The governor was sitting behind his desk, with a pile of parchments and writing tablets in front of him.

"Take a seat, my lord Magnus."

"Thank you, my lord." He sat on an ornamental wooden chair that turned out to be very uncomfortable.

"What have you been doing over the last month?"

Magnus grimaced. "I spent most of my time along the Ermine Street, reminding everyone of the need for vigilance and encouraging the attempts to organise a frontier force."

"If you listen to the rumours, those attempts sound chaotic."

"Not at all, sir. I found a lot of people are doing their utmost. I gave a lot of encouragement and tried not to meddle." Magnus smiled. "Although I tried to ensure that everyone was facing in the right direction."

Cornelius seemed amused. "Go on." He listened attentively while Magnus made his report. "The mercenaries at Lincoln will remain loyal, do you think?"

"Unless we ask them to fight Finn, yes."

"That was what I thought. I assure you, I hadn't planned to make that mistake. Thank you for your report, my lord count. You'll have to summarise it for the benefit of the Council when they meet, of course."

Magnus sighed. "And then answer all their questions? Yes, my lord."

Cornelius smiled. "Now that's over, would you like some wine?"

"Thank you. Ah - have any of the councilors arrived in London yet?"

"One or two." Cornelius smiled sourly. "They tend to put off returning to London until the last possible moment. They say they can't stand the smell of London during the heat of summer. But they can't put it off for ever. Otherwise they can't take their places on the governor's advisory Council. Aurelianus was one of the first to arrive, though."

"Oh. I see. Thank you."

Magnus arrived at the Aurelianus household at dusk. He had dressed carefully in his best Italian tunic, of light blue wool, hose and his military white cloak.

He had originally planned to ignore any invitation he received. A meeting with Aurelianus would be unpleasant. The man would be surround with subservient clients. And, as a government official, Magnus could not be seen to be favouring one faction over another.

Then he heard that Claudia had travelled south and had joined her father in London. His priorities had changed suddenly.

The doorway was grand, with a stone arch. "I'm Magnus Vitalinus," he told the doorkeeper. "Lord Aurelianus invited me to dinner this evening."

The doorkeeper was probably a slave, but he looked Magnus over with as much distaste as his master would have done. "Very well, sir." The fellow opened the door wide.

Magnus thanked him, then walked under the archway and looked around with interest. The house was in the traditional style, built round an open courtyard, with a stone staircase leading up to the family rooms. He wondered how long the family had owned it.

The doorkeeper handed Magnus over to another servant, who led him up the staircase to the balcony and turned towards the dining room. Lord Aurelianus was already there, chatting with some balding crony. The dinner was supposed to be informal, but Aurelianus had spoiled the effect by wearing a formal, richly embroidered gown.

Aurelianus turned to greet his new guest. He hid his surprise. "Good evening, my lord count," he said with exaggerated politeness. "I am delighted that you were able to attend. I hear you visited your uncle yesterday."

"Yes, sir." he did not bother to ask how Aurelianus knew.

"That must have been an ordeal. The old man probably tried to recruit you to his cause. That's not a mistake I'll make. You serve the empire, not the factions, eh?"

He thought that was a stupid question there was only one answer that he could give. "Yes, sir."

Then Aurelianus shifted the discussion to politics. "The governor promised us a secure frontier, but his policy is unworkable. His militia are useless. These English immigrants grow more arrogant by the day."

"I always doubted the governor's judgement on this," the crony said. "What do you think, young man?"

"Have you lost one of your estates to the mutineers, perhaps?" Magnus asked.

"No, my estate's west of Corinium, thank God," the man said.

Aurelianus smiled thinly. "Magnus here has the temporary rank of Count, with all the burdens that go with it," he said. "My friends and I would be very interested in hearing your views."

"I'm sure that you will support us in the council," the crony said.

The dining room gradually filled up as more guests arrived. Everyone milled around, waiting for dinner to begin. Magnus was passed from one group to the next, each time struggling to say something tactful.

Then Claudia walked into the dining room, dressed in a sombre embroidered gown of dark green wool. She was accompanied by an older lady, dressed in blue. Magnus reminded himself that Claudia was still in mourning for her husband. And, technically, she was a member of her husband's family.

More and more guests continued to arrive. The atmosphere in this town house was less formal than Aurelianus's country villa. The guests moved about the room, joining a small group to exchange a few words and then moving on again.

"The field hands are taking advantage of these troubles," a plump man said.

"The tenants need to be kept in their place," a lady said. "If you once allow them to fall behind in their rents, they'll exploit your weakness for ever."

Magnus knew that his father would strongly disapprove of their heavy-handed methods. But, as a guest, he had to remain courteous.

"They say a fever is spreading amongst the city-dwellers," a lady said. "The bishop wants to hold a mass, asking for God's protection. But he wants us to pay for it."

"Towns are always unhealthy places," an elderly councilor said. "Perhaps we should ask the governor to bring the council session to an early close, so we could all retire to their estates."

Magnus moved from one group to another until he got the chance to speak to Claudia. She had been discreetly watching his approach.

"Welcome to London, lord Magnus," she said politely.

"Thank you, my lady," he said, equally formal.

"May I introduce my aunt, Lady Enid?" Claudia smiled. "My father and I are really only guests in her household."

Lady Enid looked doubtful. Perhaps she was wondering whether Lord Aurelianus would approve. "Have you been introduced to Lady Claudia, young man?"

"Oh, yes, years ago," he assured her.

"Lord Magnus and I have been corresponding for years," Claudia said. She smiled at him. "Thank you for the letter you sent me from Lincoln, my lord. Has the situation on the frontier changed since you wrote?"

It was all very formal, but at least he was able to speak to her at last. But why bother with questions about the frontier?

"Some of those patrician families are awkward to deal with," she said.

Was she laughing at him? "Some of the patricians are obstructive," he said. "They look down on me as an upstart. On the other hand, the officers of the new militia are mainly unpaid amateurs, but they understand how serious the situation is. Many of them are brimful of ideas. I must be careful not to dampen their enthusiasm. I've got to be very tactful."

She seemed amused by his tale. Then her smile faded. "My brother wanted to move to my father's estate in Gaul. He's worried by all these raids along the frontier. And Gaul is more wealthy than us. But Britain's too poor." she sounded anxious.

He tried to reassure her. "Well - merchants from the continent come to London. You've seen their ships. From the Frankish lands and the Friesian territory as well. They're prepared to pay in silver for British wool."

Claudia raised an eyebrow. "You think the families could sell their surplus overseas?"

Lady Enid gave him a look. "Are you suggesting that we should become merchants, young man?"

He shrugged, trying to hide his impatience. "The family would have to use an agent or middleman for that."

"Coined silver, you say, Magnus?" Claudia asked, thoughtful.

Lady Enid, full of disapproval, intervened. "My dear, I think it's time to seat ourselves at the dinner table."

Once everyone was seated round the table, Aurelianus introduced Magnus to his guests. "He has served the empire for many years and was appointed count by the new emperor in person." He seemed to assume that Magnus, as an imperial official, fully shared his reactionary views.

Magnus was seated between Claudia and her aunt Enid. Was this a deliberate choice by lord Aurelianus? Lady Enid was still suspicious of his motives. Magnus noted that the array of silverware was less flamboyant than at Aurelianus's country estate. But then, this wasn't Aurelianus's house at all.

The first course was venison, with imported spices to make it more interesting. Aurelianus boasted that the wine had been imported from the Rhone valley. Magnus was disappointed to find that it had not travelled well, but politely thanked his host.

By now, Claudia was less reserved. "My father's annoyed at the poor quality of the letters from your friend Gaius."

"In Vienne?" Lady Enid asked. For once, she did not object. Letters from the capital, sent by a relative, were unobjectionable.

Magnus was amused. "I could write and complain. Or I could go back there when my term on the frontier is up."

"I had assumed that you would be staying here in Britain." Claudia hesitated. "My mother said that marrying again would be a mistake."

He was amused rather than offended. "Well, yes, she's probably right. A widow has more independence than a married woman."

Lady Enid intervened. "Independence is an unworthy ambition."

"I'd like household of my own," Claudia said. She sounded wistful.

Their conversation was interrupted by the men at the head of the table. Most of the guests were Aurelianus's political allies, which ensured that the main topic of conversation was the forthcoming session of the Council.

"We must use the session to increase the influence of those amongst us who are loyal to the empire," Aurelianus said. "We must ensure that Lord Cornelius knows how we feel on this subject."

His cronies growled their approval. Magnus did his best to maintain a tactful silence. He knew the new militia were second rate soldiers. But they had been asked to defend the frontier, not march into the heart of rebel-held territory. Then Lady Enid gave the signal for the ladies to leave the table.

The servant impassively poured more wine into Aurelianus's glass. The patrician was red in the face. "The governor makes one mistake after another. Asking those western tribesmen to defend us is monstrous. Those savages trespass on our estates and steal our cattle! We must ask the emperor to send us troops to keep the field hands in line - yes, and to defend us against the tribes too."

Magnus knew that was impossible. "We have Majorian on our alpine frontier and the Franks on the Rhine. And the Visigoths want to grab more land."

"So, we cannot expect any reinforcements? Apart from that fool Trogius, that is."

"No, my lord. Not enough to destroy Finn's army."

"And Trogius could be withdrawn at any time ..." Aurelianus responded to this bad news by changing the subject. "Would you like some more wine, my lord? It's from the Dordogne. My best."

"Thank you, sir," Magnus said cautiously. He wondered why Aurelianus was suddenly so polite.

Aurelianus gestured impatiently. The servant poured wine for them both.

When the last course had been cleared away, Magnus told his host that it was time for him to leave.

Aurelianus was surprised. "So soon, young man?" But, playing the part of a polite host, he escorted his guest to the door.

Chapter 24: The raiding party

Mid October 456 AD

Urien was flying north and east of the messenger station of Durocobrivis. He had been chosen for this difficult task because he was a skilled aviator, but it was dull. His task was to gain as much height as he could, fly north over the flat plains as far as he could, and then turn back while he still had enough height to make it home. But there was nothing to see. Dull, dull, dull.

He had enough experience – and enough seniority – to be promoted to sergeant and put in command of one of the smaller messenger stations, but he did not care for the responsibility. Besides, it would cut down on his flying time.

News had reached the messenger station that the rebel leader, Finn, had taken over one of Councillor Aurelianus's villas as his new home. The bailiff and his family had fled, but lurid rumours spread about what had happened to the maidservants. Suddenly, everyone in Britain knew the story that Finn's wife had fled back to her kinsmen after Finn had murdered her brother.

Urien made another turn to the north. Then he saw smoke, far below, drifting across the countryside. It told him that the wind was still from the north west. So, the wind would be helping him when he turned for home. Every little extra helped. But what was causing the smoke? A longer look told him that a farmhouse was burning. It could be an accident … Then he spotted the horses. At least ten of them, little more than dots, but recognisable. That many horses on a farm was rare.

Was this the raiders? Foragers, perhaps, or a scouting party? But he was getting low. He would have to turn back. It was the most interesting thing he had seen all day. It was certainly worth reporting.

But when Urien landed back at Durocobrivis, eager to report, the captain explained he was behind with the news. "We've received a tale that a large English raiding force crossed the new frontier, south of Water Newton. A farmer put his youngest son on his strongest horse and sent him west to Tilton. That was yesterday."

"Ah." Urien was disappointed. "The boy rode through the night?"

"Yes. The messenger from Tilton reached here an hour after you took off. I didn't really believe the lad's tale, but I sent a courier to the governor, just in case."

"I see."

"The governor's in London, for the meeting of the council. I'd better sent another dispatch, to tell him what you saw."

"Of course," Urien said. "As soon as possible."

The captain was angry. "These raids are getting worse, further and further inland."

*   *   *

Braughing crossroads, two days later

Magnus pushed open the door of the large posting inn. Dusk was approaching and the large common room was already getting dark. The lamps had been lit. The place was very

455

old, dating back to the glory days of the empire. The stout wooden beams were darkened by centuries of smoke.

He looked round the crowded room. Travelers of all kinds mingled here. The two barbarian princes, each accompanied by their cronies, were sitting in opposite corners of the large room, pretending to ignore each other.

The rest of the visitors carried on their business around them, confident that the tribesmen would not break their truce.

It was unfortunate that both leaders were in Braughing at the same time, but both leaders refused to compromise. It was doubly unfortunate that Braughing had only one large posting inn.

The trooper who had accompanied Magnus gestured in what he thought was an inconspicuous manner. "That's Prince Jago, on the right, sir."

"Thank you, trooper." Prince Jago of Powys wore a neatly trimmed beard, in the style fashionable in Constantinople. Magnus glanced across the room. Prince Kai sported a bristling warrior moustache.

Magnus made his way across the room to Prince Jago and his retinue. Most of the warriors had beer jugs on the table in front of them. They were all wearing homespun tunics. The prince was distinguished by a barbaric multicoloured cloak held in place by an elaborate gold brooch. Magnus was prepared to bet that the prince's plaid cloak contained the six colours that denoted royalty.

The prince, sitting facing the door, had already noticed him. He hid his surprise. "Welcome to my table, lord Magnus. Are you too proud to speak the language of the western tribes?"

"I can only speak t' dialect of the Limestone Edge, m' lord. D'you understand it?"

456

The prince was amused by this riposte. "Well enough, my lord. Will you share my beer?"

Magnus knew that courtesy obliged him to accept. He took his place on the bench. "Thank you, m' lord."

The prince nodded to one of his cronies, who poured a generous measure of beer into a jug.

As Magnus picked up the jug, he sensed someone behind him. He turned to see Prince Kai of the Dumnonii. It seemed that the prince's curiosity had overcome his dislike for his rival. He too wore a gaudy plaid cloak. Two of his henchmen stood behind their prince.

"Are you plotting some conspiracy against me?" Kai growled.

Prince Jago's henchmen tensed. So did the trooper who had accompanied Magnus.

Magnus chose his words with care. "You're free to hear what I have to say, my lord, although it may not interest you,"

"I'll be the judge of that," Kai said.

"Will you sit at my table and share my beer?" Jago asked. His tone was mocking.

Kai's jaw clenched. He clearly resented Jago's impudence. He knew that if he accepted Jago's offer he would be bound by the laws of hospitality. Curiosity warred with his dislike. "Very well."

"So, what's your story, my lord Magnus?" Jago asked.

Magnus shrugged. "The English raiders have crossed the border. Two hundred men or more. They're heading west. The aviators brought the news to me yesterday hour ago."

"Ah!" Jago said. "A large number of men for this time of year."

"Yes." Magnus took a cautious sip at his beer. "My lord, I must ask you to lead your men against this enemy, according to your agreement."

"Of course," Jago said. "It'll be a pleasure to follow you into battle."

"And what of me?" Kai growled.

Magnus was surprised. "You and your men stood in readiness of an attack all last month. You've fulfilled the conditions of your agreement. I can't ask you to do more."

"So, I have to watch while this perfumed fop steals my glory?" Kai asked. Jago smiled behind his beard.

"I have no right to ask you to do more," Magnus said. "Your warriors are probably eager to return to their homes."

"My men are eager for battle," Kai said.

Magnus realised that the prince meant what he said. He and his warriors lived by fighting. They would not turn away from the opportunity of a battle. "You're most welcome, my lord. In this crisis I can't turn down any offer of help."

"What of that man Trogus and his troop of a hundred cavalrymen?" Jago asked. "The one sent by the emperor. He's too proud, that one."

Kai grinned. "It's unfortunate that the proud Trogus and his troop of a hundred cavalry were stationed at Cambridge ... too far away to take part in this battle."

"I've sent a message to him," Magnus said. "He'll ride to join us. As I said, I can't afford to turn away any fighting men."

"More beer?" Jago asked.

"Thank you. I've also sent a message to lord Aurelianus, asking him to send me half of his bodyguard. They'll provide our infantry."

Magnus noticed four bulky men making their way through the crowded room towards this corner. They were dressed as prosperous craftsmen in tunics and leggings, but it was obvious they were warriors. The trooper who had accompanied Magnus turned to face this new threat.

"Lord Magnus?"

The spokesman was blond, broad-shouldered, but no taller than Magnus. His three colleagues towered over him. By his accent, Magnus guessed he was German or Scandinavian. With a sense of shock, he recognised Oslaf, Lady Claudia's steward.

"Yes, I'm Count Magnus."

"My name's Oslaf. London is full of rumours that Finn's men have crossed the frontier. We want to ride north with you."

The second man, standing at Oslaf's right shoulder, interrupted. "We're from Denmark. We've a grudge against Finn."

"You're infantry?" Magnus shook his head. "I intend to ride fast."

"Yes, we fight as infantry, but we know how to ride," Oslaf said.

"How did you come by good horses?" Jago asked. His tone implied the Dane had stolen them.

Oslaf grinned. "We don't own them, of course. Lady Claudia, the widow, lent them to us. She had a grudge against Finn too, you might say."

"Lady Claudia? That's a story I'd like to hear someday," Jago said.

"Oh ... It's simply told. We were bodyguards to old Lord Ambrosius. We failed in our duty to him, so we decided to serve Lady Claudia instead."

"We couldn't join Finn, you see," the second Dane said.

"When she travelled down to London, I accompanied her," Oslaf said.

This story made no sense to Magnus. "You've been Lady Claudia's bodyguards these last few years?"

"No, sir, of course not. But I've been serving as her - steward, you might say. And I kept in touch with my friends here. So, when we learned of this raid, we asked the lady's permission to ride north."

"I doubt if I'll need infantry. But I never turn away volunteers."

"Thank you kindly, sir. I think blood feuds are evil things, they poison everyone they touch. But as you're going to fight Finn anyway, we thought it would be best if we joined in."

"Now that's a story I'd like to hear someday," Magnus said.

The Dane grinned. "The poets wrote a song about it. Got it all wrong, of course."

"Very well," Magnus said. "Gentlemen, when will you be ready to ride? Tomorrow?"

Jago looked pained. "If you want my men fit to ride tomorrow, we'll have to break up this delightful party."

The military road, the Ermine Street, led them through gently rolling woodland. The forest was kept clear for a hundred yards on each side of the military road. The leaves were turning red and brown as autumn approached. Magnus knew that the next gale would strip the trees bare but for a few days the treasure remained.

The farms they passed were small pockets of bustling activity. That work had to go on. There were wolves in the forests and now a new breed of wolf was advancing down the road towards them, but the farmers kept about their daily routine.

The weather, Magnus thought, was perfect for flying. With any luck the messengers would have been keeping an eye on the raiders.

On the afternoon of the second day Magnus reached the small unwalled town of Wimpole. This was another town that was slowly dying.

They were met by Trogius, commander of the troop of heavy cavalry.

"Good afternoon, my lord Magnus," Trogius said. His patrician accent lacked any emotion. "We arrived an hour ago. I decided to wait for your arrival because I did not want to tire my horses."

Magnus hid his annoyance. "Of course," he said.

"And what of the English raiders?" Trogius asked.

"I think they're north of here. Tomorrow we'll go looking for them."

"What other men did you bring? Do you have any infantry?" Trogius asked.

"The western princes have provided light cavalry," Magnus said. "And I've asked Lord Aurelianus to send me some infantry."

"Lord Aurelianus is a gentleman. He will keep his word."

Trogus's men went about the business of setting up a bivouac in one of the empty lots of the city.

Kai from Powys and Jago from Dumnonia ensured that their men set to work too. They seemed determined to work together despite their traditional tribal rivalries. The subordinate commanders ensured that sentries were posted, the horses were picketed, and the men were lighting cooking fires.

Trogius and the two tribal princes had taken an instant dislike of each other. Trogius looked down on the impoverished tribesmen, the princes responded by emphasising their royal lineage. Magnus realised that he was going to spend the rest of the campaign arbitrating between the two factions.

The next morning, they continued their march. Trogius was riding a showy grey gelding and his Gallic chain mail was the best that money could buy.

*　　*　　*

London

Claudia was stowing away her embroidery when she heard the heavy street door creak open. She wondered who the visitor could be, at this time of night.

She was startled when the servant announced her father. He was dressed for riding.

"Father! Have you come from your estate? What brings you here? Have you brought mother with you?"

"Your mother's outside in the carriage."

"Then I shall have to prepare a room for you -."

Don't pester me with your problems, girl." He looked angry. "It's the news that brings me here. Have you heard that the English pirates have crossed the frontier? The biggest raid in two years?"

"Yes, father. But Lord Magnus was asked by the governor to deal with it. He left for Braughing, two days ago. The cavalry are stationed there."

"Magnus Vitalinus? He'll make a mess of it, the way he did last time. I've decided to take the family to our estate on the continent." He subjected her to a glare. "All of your meddling was in vain, woman. The only thing you achieved was to embarrass your family. The pirates can't be stopped. Their raids will just get worse. Britain isn't safe any more. The only sensible option is to abandon the place."

She was angered and humiliated by this criticism. "It isn't safe to leave, at this time of year. The sailing season's over."

"I won't have any insolence from you, my girl. We'll travel down to Portchester in easy stages. We can wait there for a break in the weather."

"I'm not going with you, father. I'm staying here. Britain is my home."

He glared at her, but she refused to back down. "I belong to the Ambrosius family now."

In the end it was her father who looked away. "That can wait till the morning. For the moment, you can make your mother welcome."

She did not intend to push her luck. "Of course, father."

*   *   *

Godmanchester

The only light in the farmhouse kitchen was a single candle. "We march at first light," Magnus told the assembled officers. They were sitting round the table, sharing a jug of wine.

He grinned. "That was one of Lord Aetius's favourite orders. It's said that his Italian allies hated to hear it."

"Were you with Aetius?" Trogius asked "I don't recognise you. Were you a field commander?"

"Well – I acted as liaison between Aetius and the messenger corps. So, most of the time I was up in the hills."

Trogus's hauteur vanished. "You weren't the patrician who learned to fly?"

"Well – yes." He suddenly had the attention of everyone in the room.

"Is it as dangerous as they say?" Trogius asked.

At almost the same time, Kai asked, "Did you see any dragons? It's said they haunt the high peaks."

Magnus avoided the question by telling them about his first solo flight. It made an amusing story and diverted their attention from the fact that he was eccentric enough to learn to fly.

He was halfway through the tale when they were disturbed by shouting in the dark. The outlying pickets were demanding a call to arms.

Magnus adjusted his sword in its baldric and led the way outside. "It's at the north gate."

He looked north, but in the uncertain twilight he could make out nothing.

"Soldiers, by the sound of it," Jago said.

"Perhaps it's Aurelianus's infantry," Kai said.

"A large number of soldiers," Trogius said. "How did your vedettes allow themselves to be taken by surprise?"

"They didn't," Jago said. "Didn't you hear them shouting the alarm?"

Kai checked that his sword was loose in its scabbard. He wanted to rush towards the disturbance. Then the shouting died down.

"Perhaps we ought to wait," Magnus said. "It may have been a false alarm."

A small group of tribal cavalrymen – Jago's men - were making their way through the camp towards him. The torches they were holding up to light their way flickered in the breeze. Magnus saw they were escorting someone between them.

The tribesman ignored Trogius and addressed his prince. "Lord Jago, this man with me says he's the commander of militia infantry."

"A likely tale," Kai said.

Magnus stepped closer to see better. "No, I recognise this man. He's a sergeant of militia from Water Newton. His name's Artorius."

"Good evening, sir," Artorius said, with his usual impudence. "I've brought some of the lads to help you out."

Magnus was surprised. "Your obligation is to defend the frontier, sergeant. There's no requirement for you to perform military service so far from home."

The sergeant grinned. "Well, it's like this, sir. The bishop sent a message, asking us to help you out."

"He had no right to do that."

Artorius shrugged. "The captain thought it was a good idea. So did I. We reckoned that if the raiders won a victory down south, that'd encourage them to make another attempt further north. By helping you today, we're protecting our hands." Jago snorted, amused.

"I see, sergeant. How many men have you brought?" Magnus asked.

"A hundred, sir. May I ask, how many men did Aurelianus send you?"

"He promised fifty. So far, they haven't arrived yet. So, for the time being you're the only infantry we've got. Come on, let's inspected this company of yours."

"This way, sir." The men, drawn up in rows in the dark, carried a strange assortment of weapons. But Magnus could see that they were equipped, in a practical way, for a long campaign. They were tired from a long day's march, but Magnus judged their morale was high.

"Tell your men to make camp for the night." he said.

Trogius was outraged. "Will you let this impudent peasant defy you? He deserves to be flogged."

Magnus grinned at the sergeant's alarm. "Perhaps he does, my lord. But I need every soldier I can find. I can't afford to turn a man away."

"I expected to find Godmanchester burnt to the ground, sir," Artorius said. "But Finn must have passed it by. I think we must have passed east of the raiders, sir, on our way south. But we were travelling light, in a hurry to reach you. They were stopping to forage."

Magnus's amusement vanished. "You say the raiders are north of here?"

"North? No, I'd say more north west, sir. No more than a day's march."

"Ah. I see." That information alone was worth the militia's upkeep.

Artorius grinned impudently. "The captain wanted to come. We couldn't leave Water Newton undefended, so we rolled some dice for it."

"I see." He failed to hide his amusement.

The next day, they turned off the military road and instead made their way west along farm tracks. Artorius's infantry trailed behind the heavy cavalry.

An hour before noon, the British cavalry scouts reported back to Magnus that they had located part of the English force.

"There were ten of 'em, on horses, sir. They were foraging. When they saw us, they turned back. Probably went to report to their commander."

466

"Yes, you're probably right." So now the raiders knew where he was. "You've done well."

Magnus and his force continued on their way. Two hours after noon, they breasted a slight rise and came within sight of the main force of raiders, less than a mile away. They were driving a herd of cattle ahead of them, the profit of this raid.

In this open countryside, surprise was impossible. The English had already received warning of his approach. But, instead of fleeing from superior numbers, they reacted by withdrawing to a hilltop. They began forming a line between the imperial forces and their loot.

The force was larger than Magnus had expected. He estimated there were perhaps two or three hundred of them all told, all infantry. He remembered his last battle against the English. He outnumbered the raiders this time, but otherwise the tactical situation was similar. He could lose a lot of men.

As he rode forward, Jago at his side, he decided that he would have to try to parley.

Then the British scouts, tribesmen from Powys, reported back. "The raiders say that their commander is Finn. The Oathbreaker hisself, sir."

"Their king?" Jago asked.

"Yes, sir," the scout said.

That changed everything. The English could not pretend that this was merely a casual raid. Magnus's confidence vanished.

They stopped at the foot of the hill, just out of bow shot range.

Magnus, accompanied by his two lieutenants, Jago and Trogus, made his way up the hill. The English had formed their defensive line but were leaning on their shields, relaxed.

Finn stepped forward from the shield wall, his chain mail shining. Magnus noted that the mail was gilded. How had he paid for it?

"What is your message, little man? Is the governor offering to make me count?"

The English raiders grinned over their huge round shields. Magnus ignored them.

"No. He offers an amnesty to all of you if you abandon their loot and withdraw inside your agreed frontier."

The raiders jeered at this. Finn smiled broadly. "We will go when we have our fill of the patricians' cattle."

The negotiations had failed before they had really begun. With as much grace as they could muster, Magnus and his companions withdrew down the hill. To Magnus, this was painfully like their last battle.

The infantry had caught up with the cavalry and were forming up, facing the enemy.

"Well, there's no doubt about it," Trogius said. "There's going to be a battle in the morning."

"There's no need to wait," Magnus snapped. "We have half a day left. I want to attack them now."

"We should wait until Lord Aurelianus's men catch up with us. They're professionals."

Magnus suspected that Aurelianus's retainers were never going to arrive. "We outnumber them. Any delay gives them the chance to organise themselves. We attack now."

"Yes, my lord."

Magnus turned to Artorius. "Sergeant, I want to send in the militia infantry. I want your men to open up the English line, so the cavalry can exploit the gaps. I hope that'll force the English to run."

"We'll do what we can, sir." Artorius's usual impudence had been replaced by caution.

Magnus turned to Jago. "My lord, I want your archers to give support to the infantry."

The prince, too, was looking drawn. "Of course, sir."

The militia infantry made a brave show as they formed their square. Artorius led his men in an energetic charge up the hill at the English, but as the slope became steeper, they came within range of a hail of arrows.

The attackers lost all impetus. Their square formation changed into a wedge as the men at each end hung back. The crash of one shield wall against another was robbed of most of its effect. More and more British infantrymen added their weight to the struggle, but they could not get past that line of shields, short stabbing swords and axes.

Magnus, watching from below, tried to make sense of the desperate struggle along the English line. Several of the defenders went down. Swords rose and fell. Men reeled back, screamed, and fell.

Magnus sent forward relays of archers to keep up the pressure. The English replied with insults, catcalls, and arrows of their own, but they never once relaxed their formation. Magnus recognised that the charge had failed.

He called his men back. The infantry withdrew to extreme bowshot range. The British archers kept up their harrying tactics.

Artorius, looking haggard under the rim of his helmet, made his report. "Sorry, sir. My men just aren't disciplined enough."

"You did the best you could. How many did you lose?"

"Ten dead, twenty wounded. We're prepared to try again, sir."

Magnus felt a twinge of despair. "This is beginning to look like my last battle..."

Artorius took off his helmet. "But we're not facing their entire army this time, sir. We outnumber them. We could just ride them down."

"Yes, I know. But if they fight to the last man, they could take a lot of us down with them. Don't you see? I've got to think of the next raid. And the one after that. I've got to keep our army intact, today, so we can stop the next raid ... I'm tempted to keep them holed up until they starve."

"But if you try that, they'll slip away in the night."

"Ah, yes." The enemy would be forced to leave their loot behind, but they would be able to attack another day.

Magnus sought out Trogius, waiting with his heavy cavalry. The Gaulish commander was tall, and looked splendid in his gilded chain-mail armour. On the hilltop, the raiders had started chanting some sort of barbaric war song. Magnus tried to ignore it. "Lord Trogus, could your men break through the English defence?"

"I refuse," Trogius said bluntly. "I will not lead my men against a prepared defensive line. Sir."

"I see, commander," Magnus said.

Trogius spoke with an aristocratic self-confidence. "Cavalry cannot achieve anything against a prepared defence. You're a cavalry commander yourself. You must know that."

Magnus had to admit the man was right. They both knew that the main role of the cavalry was to pursue a retreating enemy.

"You don't have enough infantry. You should withdraw west, join up with Lord Aurelianus's men, then attack."

"No!" He had already considered that idea, and rejected it. "Very well, commander." He turned and strode away. He had to decide what to do next.

Magnus gathered his subordinates. A plan, of sorts, had come to him. He could not afford heavy casualties, but he did not want the raiders slipping away to harass another section of the frontier. He decided he had to take a risk.

In the background, the British archers were continuing their half-hearted skirmishing. The English raiders stubbornly held their line despite this irritant.

Magnus stood with his back to the enemy. Everyone in his little army was watching him. Presumably, the raiders on their hilltop were watching too. "Gentlemen, everyone assumes there will be a full-scale battle in the morning. I expect the English would assume that too."

"Of course," Trogius said.

"I want to try a night action." Everyone paid attention at that.

"Ah," Artorius said.

"At nightfall, they'll break formation and go to the stream to fill their water containers. When they do that, we charge."

Trogius was shocked. "A charge? At night? On strange ground?"

Magnus gestured at the stretch of grass to the left of the enemy on their hilltop. "There's your ground. Can you do it?"

Trogius glanced sideways, as if afraid Finn watching from the hilltop would guess his purpose. "Rabbit holes and molehills ... It could be done. But for a few water-carriers? Why bother?"

471

"Tonight, they'll build some sort of fence. Thorn bushes, perhaps. But while they're fetching water, the fence will have a gap in it."

"And you want me to force the gap? Well ... it's worth trying."

When the British archers finally stopped harassing the raiders and withdrew down the hill, the English relaxed at last. But they did not abandon their defensive position.

At dusk, the English broke their formation and began preparing their own camp.

Magnus was still keeping watch on the English. Now he told Artorius to give his men the task of preparing a camp for the night. "Build the fence high. It means a lot of work, but I don't want Finn to think it's only a pretense. Besides, he may be planning the same thing."

Artorius smiled at that. "Right, sir."

Half the horses were unsaddled and put out to pasture. Magnus and the British commanders carefully placed the sentries and vedettes.

"We'll change the vedettes frequently," he told Jago. "I want the enemy to get used to the sound of horses moving around."

The tribal commander grinned. He enjoyed this subterfuge. "Right."

The cavalry troopers tended to their horses. Magnus, with nothing to do except worry, could only fret in silence. When he saw Kai and Jago, the leaders of the tribal cavalry, approaching him together, he knew something was up.

Kai spoke first. "My lord, we ask for permission to join in this battle."

"It will be a story to tell our grandchildren," Jago said.

Magnus shook his head. "It's too risky. Powys could lose all its fighting men."

Kai was disappointed. "If the heavy guys make a gap, we can follow through and exploit it."

"No. We could lose all of you."

Kai was inclined to sulk. Jago refused to accept 'no' as an answer. "Perhaps … Half of the men from each tribal contingent could take part."

Magnus suspected that the tribal leader was determined to take part whether he was given permission or not. "Very well," he said, his reluctance evident in his tone.

Jago grinned. "Thank you, sir."

Twilight drew on towards full darkness. Magnus, on edge, carried out an inspection of the British camp. "Artorius, I want you to make sure that your militia light lots of campfires. I want Finn to think the whole army's here."

"Very well, sir."

The waiting dragged on. Magnus began to wonder whether the English planned to do without water. At last a scout appeared out of the darkness. He had taken off his weapons and armour to avoid making any noise. "They're moving, sir."

He hid his relief. "Right." He told Artorius, one more time, to guard the camp. "If the worst happens, get back to the governor with the word."

Artorius nodded, unhappy at being given this chore.

Trogius led the way back to the battlefield. Magnus and half the tribal cavalry followed, a discreet distance behind. The heavy cavalry seemed to be making a lot of noise. Spurs and bridles jingled. But there was nothing that Magnus could do about that.

Trogius was efficient enough. Under his direction, given in low growls, the heavy cavalry formed their line, as best they could in the dark. The British light cavalry were clustered in an ill-disciplined knot behind.

"The troop will advance!" Trogius shouted. His troopers urged their horses forward at a trot. More than one horse stumbled and fell, but the rest carried on. To their right, Magnus could make out the thorn bushes that guarded the enemy camp. The horses edged away from it.

Then Trogus's men came across the line of English raiders making their way to and from the stream. Magnus guessed there must be a score of them.

The English turned to face the noise, pale round faces in the dark. Then they realised they were the target of the attack. They dropped their water containers and scattered.

"At them!" Trogius shouted. His men cheered and urged their horses into a gallop. They charged after the running men. The tribal cavalry, clustered around Magnus, watched them go.

Magnus realised that his plan, weak to begin with, had just collapsed. The gate, no more than a wide gap in the crude fence, was a blank hole in the dark, wide open. But his best troops, the professional heavy cavalry, were chasing twenty unarmed men in the night. "Hell. Hell, and damnation!"

"What do we do, sir?" Jago asked. "Chase after Trogius? Bring him back?"

"Good God, no!" Magnus realised that if he wanted to salvage his plan it was up to him and his men. The despair and humiliation of the day's fighting turned into recklessness. He turned to the right, towards the enemy camp.

"Come on! Let's see what we can do." He led the way towards the gate. His men cheered and followed readily.

474

The defenders at the gate put up a brave defence. But they were greatly outnumbered and were soon cut down. Magnus could make out men inside the camp milling about in confusion, trying to find their weapons. He hesitated for a moment, then led his men through the gap. "Hurry! Hurry! Before they arm themselves!"

His men gave another cheer. He and his men cut a swathe of chaos through the English camp. Anyone who did not get out of his way in time was pushed aside by the horses. Any soldier who offered resistance was soon cut down. Fortunately, the English had no tents. There were no guy-ropes to trip over. When a barrier loomed up out of the dark, Magnus realised the cavalry had reached the fence at the far side of the camp.

"We must have killed a thousand of the devils!" Jago shouted, exuberant.

The summer dusk had faded into true dark. Magnus realised his reckless charge had trapped his men.

No! He turned his horse. "Now, let's get out of here!" Back to the gateway!"

His men cheered him again and clustered round him. They followed their path of destruction and managed to find their way back to the entrance. The defence was stronger this time but Magnus's men, together, were stronger than the haphazard clusters of raiders. The British troops came within sight of the entrance at last. They fought their way to the gateway and turned once more. Magnus felt a surge of relief. He had got his men out of that trap with only a few casualties.

"Let's do that again!" someone shouted wildly. Was that Kai? There was a roar of approval. Magnus's heart sank.

But it was too late to try again. The raiders had rallied and formed a shield wall across the gateway. Then they counter-attacked, determined to push the British away from their camp. There was a confused melee in the gateway.

Magnus realised that enemy resistance was increasing. He had inflicted a great wound on the raiders. That would be a great advantage in the battle tomorrow. His sword arm ached, and the grip was slippery with sweat. He knew that it was time to withdraw. If he delayed any longer, he and his men would be trapped. But could he do it? Would these half-trained troops follow him in time?

Then they heard shouting in the dark.

In the distance, on the far side of the enemy camp, Magnus saw a line of torches. He guessed that a British soldier had found the English perimeter fence unguarded and was cutting a way through it. One torch after another was thrown into the crude fence. He cursed Artorius for disobeying orders.

The defenders at the gate, threatened by an attack at the rear, drew back.

Magnus heard more shouting down the hill, behind him. He turned round to see a squad of British militia infantry arrive at a run, led by Artorius. Some of them were waving firebrands. They gave a ragged, breathless cheer at the sight of the British cavalry.

Artorius, panting, waved his sword excitedly. His eyes gleamed in the torchlight. "You - left some - for us, then! I sent some of my lads to create a diversion." He turned to his squad. "At them, men!"

The infantry cheered again, formed their shield wall, and charged at the English defenders. They had a score to settle. This time the raiders were disorganised and leaderless. They began to give ground.

This was too much for prince Kai. "Are we going to let townsmen do our fighting for us?" he shouted.

The light cavalry gave a cheer and followed eagerly after. Magnus cursed but had no option but to accompany them.

The defenders at the gate knew they were outnumbered. Their shield wall was pushed steadily back. Once more, the British troops forced their way into the enemy camp.

But the raiders' defence was more organised now. They all had their weapons, they had managed to form a shield wall. They were putting up a desperate resistance.

Magnus was in the second rank this time. His horse was tired, so was he, and he knew that he was supposed to be doing the thinking. This victory would be bought dear. The exuberance of the British attackers turned to grim determination.

Then, in the front rank of the enemy, he saw Finn, and turned towards him. The king had found time to put on his gilded armour.

Finn saw him at the same time. "Well met, little man!"

Kai, at Magnus's right hand, urged his horse forward. "Let me deal with this!"

Finn's sword cut down at the British infantryman in front of Magnus. The sword landed on the man's armoured shoulder but did not cut through. The blow forced the man down on one knee, but he used the opportunity to thrust up under Finn's shield. Finn parried desperately. That left his defence momentarily open.

Magnus seized the opportunity. He swung his long cavalry sword with all the energy he could muster. But the thrust was clumsy and caught Finn on the chain mail protecting his chest. The English commander was knocked off his feet. Magnus doubted that Finn suffered any more than severe bruising.

"Finn! He's down!" the Englishman at Finn's right hand shouted. The English wavered and the British surged forward. They gained six feet, then twelve. But the resistance was fierce. More than one British warrior lost his footing and never got up again.

The English warrior who had been at Finn's left stepped forward. "Magnus! You offered us terms! We retreat east of the frontier! We accept!"

The fighting slackened. The men on both sides drew apart and faces turned to Magnus. Every man retained his guard. Their eyes gleamed in the flickering torchlight. Everyone was panting too much to speak.

Could this be made to work? "Hold!" Magnus shouted. "You will return to your homes. You will abandon all of your loot. Everything."

The English warrior looked sour. "We accept."

Magnus decided to accept the offer. "Hold! A halt to the fighting!" He shouted at his men. This time his men obeyed him.

The stress of battle was replaced by exhaustion. Magnus was suddenly bone-weary. "Lay down your weapons!"

He expected the English warriors to refuse, and for the fighting to start again. "You can have them back in the morning. But tonight, you lay them down!"

That decided it. The English offered no resistance when they were separated from their weapons.

The English survivors were herded into a corner of their camp and told to get some sleep. Magnus found his own subordinates and arranged the guard detail. There was still no sign of Trogius.

He was deathly tired. "How many men did you lose in this fight, Artorius?"

"Difficult to say in this chaos. But fewer than we lost this afternoon. Mebbe three killed and ten more wounded. And we did it without Aurelianus's professionals!"

"Yes. If ever you meet any of those bodyguards, you can ask them what they were doing when you defeated Finn."

Had those bodyguards refused to march? Or had Aurelianus cravenly kept them to defend their master? But he had won his battle. Now he wanted a reward. Claudia's period of mourning was over. He could marry her at last. But that could wait. All he wanted now was sleep.

The Oslaf singled out Magnus. "Do you know about Finn, sir? Did he get away? Or is the bastard lurking in a corner somewhere?"

Magnus tried to think. "I saw him go down."

"Yes, but where? How can you be sure?"

"Can't it wait until the morning?" Magnus wanted only to sleep.

"These rebels only stopped because they thought Finn was dead. If he's still alive ..."

"Very well. Get a torch, Oslaf. Let's go and look."

He led the way to the centre of the camp, where the fighting had been heaviest. Grimly, they searched the bodies. At last, Magnus pointed to a body lying face down. "He's wearing gilded chain mail."

Oslaf turned the body over. "Yes, that's him, all right," the Dane sighed. "Trampled to death. What a way for a warrior to go."

"Be thankful," Magnus said. "If you'd killed him, one of his relatives would have to continue the feud. But death in an accident ends it."

"True, true."

Trogius and his men returned at first light. The cavalry leader haughtily ignored his faulty leadership the night before, or the fact that he had missed the battle.

479

Magnus saluted the commander. "Good morning, Lord Trogius."

"I see you fought well," Trogius said. He lowered his voice. "Finn?"

"We identified his body. He'd been killed in the fighting. Trampled underfoot." Magnus had been relieved at the discovery. It avoided the necessity of a messy execution.

Trogius nodded. "Well done, lad. His majesty will be overjoyed to hear of this success."

Magnus was bone-weary. But, prompted by Trogius, he described the battle. "A quarter of Finn's men are dead or seriously wounded. I kept Finn's surviving officers here. I plan to send the rest back across the frontier. But they're leaderless."

"Finn is dead, you say?"

He nodded. "We'll give him a warrior's funeral, along with his companions."

"Lord Aurelianus would have preferred his head on a pike."

"Perhaps. But I have to work with these English warriors afterwards," Magnus said shortly.

"Yes, of course," the commander said. "I congratulate you again on your victory. And it is a victory, young man. This will make an excellent report to Avitus. But you shouldn't have allowed the English warriors to withdraw."

"It was a close thing, sir. If they'd fought to the last, we might not have an army left."

"Ah. I see. But – do we control the east of Britain now?"

Magnus shook his head. "I can lead my men across rebel territory to the east coast; but it'll be no more than a raid. To hold the territory, I'd need a thousand infantry, for at least twelve months."

"The emperor can't provide that, Magnus."

"No, sir. But we have the advantage now. I can make these rebels respect the promises they've made. Push them off the farms they've seized outside their territory."

*   *   *

London

The governor listened patiently as Magnus made his report.

"You let the English raiders go free?"

"Only the rank and file, sir."

But what about Finn's officers? We can't let them run loose."

"I've brought them with me, sir. I wanted to find employment for them ..."

"No. Those troublemakers are a threat to society. I want these men removed. Permanently."

"Well - we could ask them to fight for the empire in Gaul. They can help defend Soissons against the Franks."

"Soissons? Very well." Cornelius smiled. "The governor needs all the help he can get. And Britain owes him a favour ..."

"May I ask – do you know where lady Claudia is, sir?"

He smiled. "Why, here in London. Staying with her brother-in-law. I think she would be glad to see you."

*

He went to the Ambrosius family's London house. He told the doorkeeper that he wanted to see the head of the family.

Ambrosius was plump, with a shrewd gaze. Magnus was surprised at his hearty welcome.

481

"I can guess why you're here. You've come about Claudia, eh?"

"Yes, sir."

"Young man, I want to explain that your marriage to my sister-by-marriage has my full support. Claudia's period of mourning has come to an end. Although I suppose we'll have to arrange the dowry."

Magnus was taken by surprise. "Yes, of course. Thank you."

Ambrosius smiled. "Of course, you'll have to stop supporting Vortigern's absurd policies."

It occurred to Magnus that he had never given any support to his uncle's policies. But he kept his peace. "It would be bad mannered on my part to defy him, sir."

"Oh, I'm not asking you to do that, young man. But you could drop your support for his notion of a mobile army. These western tribesmen."

Magnus was disconcerted. If he did not ally himself with Ambrosius, would he forbid the marriage? He escaped by going on to the attack. "I would like to speak to Lady Claudia now, sir."

"Yes, of course," Ambrosius said faintly. "Come this way."

He led the way to the formal garden, its flowers laid out in neat rows. A woman – presumably Lady Ambrosius - was sitting in the colonnade beside Claudia. Both ladies seemed impervious to the chill. Claudia looked up as they approached.

Her brother-in-law coughed. "Claudia, a moment of your attention. Lord Magnus is to marry you, my dear."

Magnus winced at the man's lack of tact. Claudia, not surprisingly, looked put out. "You haven't asked me, Magnus."

He was surprised. "Do you want a formal proposal, my lady? On bended knee? I'll do it if you want."

She blushed. "No, of course not."

"Good, that's settled," he said crisply. He turned to Ambrosius. "I expect a dowry to enable me to support my wife."

"Of course," Ambrosius said. He seemed taken aback. "Well, I have a nice little estate in the Limestone Edge."

Claudia was indignant. "But it's almost worthless, sir!" She turned to Magnus. "It's small, too far from any decent towns, you see."

Lord Ambrosius was surprised. "If you want, I can give you another estate. Perhaps another small farm in a more prosperous part of the country."

"There's the one by Water Newton," Magnus said.

"Do you want a country villa to retreat to each summer?" Claudia asked.

He smiled. "That sounds attractive."

The end

About the author

James has been writing for many years. He has written seven Steampunk novels, the Queen Victoria's Magicians', which have been published on Amazon.

He began writing the 'Empire of Gaul' sequence several years ago. Now, confined to his home by the Lockdown, he has decided to complete them.

He made several journeyed across Germany, Italy, France and Switzerland in order to research this novel.

He has visited New York and has gone snow-shoeing in Lake Placid in the Adirondacks as research for the 'Queen Victoria's Magicians' series of novels.

In the past, he has gone sailing in the Mediterranean and gained a Yachtmaster certificate. He learned to fly sailplanes and qualified to fly solo. He has sailed across the North Sea and delivered a yacht from the Spanish mainland to Menorca. More recently, he has gone hiking in the Mosel valley, the Alps and in Britain. All of these experiences have gone into his novels.

He has been reading science fiction and fantasy for many years. he is a member of the British Science Fiction Association and has attended many conventions. That experience, too, has gone into his novels.

Email: sailknot2001-2@yahoo.co.uk

Facebook: james.odell.9022662@facebook.com

Blog address: alexanderauthor.blogspot.com

Printed in Great Britain
by Amazon

69676038R00276